A Spark before the Fire

Mima

iUniverse, Inc.
Bloomington

A Spark before the Fire

iUniverse books may be ordered through booksellers or by contacting:

iUniverse
1663 Liberty Drive
Bloomington, IN 47403
www.iuniverse.com
1-800-Authors (1-800-288-4677)

ISBN: 978-1-4620-5910-2 (sc)
ISBN: 978-1-4620-5909-6 (e)
ISBN: 978-1-4620-5908-9 (dj)

Printed in the United States of America

iUniverse rev. date: 10/12/2011

Acknowledgements

I can't even begin to thank all the people who read *Fire*, especially those of you who took the time to write reviews and testimonials about my book. All the love and support I received (especially from my friends and family in Atlantic Canada) was greatly appreciated and will always be remembered. I would list all your names, but I don't want to get in trouble for forgetting anyone!

I would like to give an extra thanks to a few key people who helped me in the production of my first book, *Fire*. First, thanks to Justin Brian for taking the author photo used on the back cover. I would also like to thank Justin Hebb for helping me create my original website, being an administrator on my Facebook fan page and a number of inspiring conversations during the entire process. Thanks also to Greg Clouston for helping with technical details on my website and sharing his knowledge.

As for this book, I want to give a huge thanks to Anders Christensen (http://andersworks.com) for his help creating my cool *new* website, http://mimaonfire.com/! I also want to thank Shona Taner and Esther Murphy for their assistance in editing this book.

I would also like to thank Krista Adams and my mother, Jean Arsenault for being my 'first' readers, when I was ten!

Thank you to all my readers – you're the spark in *my* sky!

Chapter one

Jimmy Groome hoisted the heavy backpack over his shoulder yet again. The sheer weight of it made him want to just drop it on the sidewalk and leave. It probably wouldn't matter anyway, he decided. It wasn't like he was any good at school. Although his teachers had always insisted that it was because he lacked focus, Jimmy felt that the only thing he lacked was interest. Who cared about math or science? Not him. Not one little bit.

But after only a couple of months of fifth grade, things were starting to look promising. He actually kind of wanted to go to school now. Unfortunately, it wasn't because his interest in learning had taken a positive turn, it was because he had a new teacher called Mrs. Holden and she was *hot*. Not beautiful or cute. She was just simply hot. It didn't matter that she always dressed like the other teachers; Mrs. Holden's curves were obvious through her clothes and it was something all the boys in the class had noticed. In fact, the fifth grade teacher was the talk of Thorton West Elementary.

"She has nice fucking tits," Patrick Lipton had announced to the playground on Mrs. Holden's first day, earlier that month. His comment sparked an equally vulgar conversation among the fifth grade boys that noon hour. Jimmy hung back in stunned silence. Having grown up in a conservative, religious household, he definitely had never heard such comments made about women before that day. In fact, Annette Groome had recently announced to her two children that she was having doubts about them even watching *Three's Company*, due to 'an inappropriate comment' made during one particular episode. This sparked a huge screaming match between Jimmy's mother and twelve year old sister, Jillian. But that was nothing out of the ordinary.

Patrick told the other boys that his older brother had a bunch of dirty magazines. And proudly announced that, "he lets me look at them whenever I want! I just got to put 'em back when I'm done."

He had gone on to describe what the girls looked like naked, what they were doing in the pictures and who his current favorites were. "There's this really hot one named Shannon, I like her the best right now," Patrick told Jimmy and asked innocently, "Have you ever seen *Playboy?*"

Jimmy shook his head no. Although he wasn't about to admit it to Patrick, he had no idea what a naked woman looked like at all. How would he? He was barely allowed to watch television or go to movies, and certainly had no form of pornography lying around the house.

"My brother's got all the '82 issues so far," Patrick's eyes lit up as he spoke. "You've gotta come over to my house and check them out."

Jimmy did so that very same night. And what he saw fascinated him.

"How do I, umm, get these kinds of magazines?" Jimmy asked sheepishly, as Patrick pointed out all his 'favorite girls' in each issue. "Where does your brother get them?"

"He gets them at some store," Patrick replied. "I think he steals them."

"What?" Jimmy's eyes bugged out. There were at least a dozen issues of *Playboy* surrounding them on the bedroom floor. "He *steals* them?"

"Yeah, I think so. 'Cause he's only 15 and I think you got to be older to buy this stuff."

"Oh," Jimmy quietly replied. At that moment, he would've sold his soul to the devil to have his own magazine to take home. It was a whole new world to him.

The following day at school, Jimmy had seen Mrs. Holden with a new set of eyes. He wondered what *she* looked like naked. He figured the likelihood of him ever finding out was slim. But it made him at least want to go to school, so that was a step in the right direction.

Feeling some relief in sight for his aching shoulders late that fall afternoon as he finally turned the corner onto his street, Jimmy once again switched his book bag to the opposite side. Nearing his home,

Jimmy noticed someone's car parked in the driveway. It belonged to his dad's friend, Doug. But why would Doug be at their house during the day? Both Jimmy's parents were at work. No one was home. Wrinkling his nose skeptically, he picked up his pace.

Walking up the driveway, Jimmy stopped at the door and searched in his backpack for the key, which his mom always safety pinned in a secret hiding place. Before he could find it, sharp cries from inside the house caused Jimmy's blood to run cold. It was his sister and she sounded scared. Really scared.

Instinctively Jimmy reached out and turned the doorknob, finding it already unlocked. Pushing the door open and rushing inside, he started to call out Jillian's name but froze at the scene awaiting him. His heart thumping loudly in his chest, no words would come out of his open mouth. He was stunned.

In the living room, Doug was on top of his sister. Her clothes were ripped. She was crying and begging him to stop, but he was holding her down. He wouldn't let go of Jillian. He just kept grunting that she wanted it. Jimmy shuddered when Doug turned to glare at him. It was like looking in the eyes of the devil.

"Get the fuck out, kid!" His voice roared at the frightened child.

Hearing himself scream, Jimmy dropped his book bag and ran out of the house. He flew down the street, around the block and into a nearby park. Once there, he hid behind a tree.

Uncontrollably shaking, he feared that Doug would find him. The man's eyes had been filled with fury when he caught Jimmy walking into the house. What if he searched the neighborhood for him? What if he wanted to kill him? What if he told Jimmy's parents that he did something wrong? *Had* he done something wrong? Why was this man, who was supposed to be a family friend, hurting his sister? Jimmy didn't really understand what he was doing to her, but it scared him.

The November air ripped through his body as Jimmy sank to the cold ground and quietly hid behind a tree. No one else was in the park; it was too cold. It was also close to dinnertime. Most kids were home with their families. But Jimmy was scared to go home. Would he ever be able to go back again? Hot tears filled his eyes and slid down his face as he continued to shake. What if Doug killed his sister? What if he killed his entire family? He felt like a baby sobbing, but he had never been so frightened in his life.

Finally, the tears stopped and he wiped his face and nose with his sleeve. It was getting dark and he had heard that a lot of bums hung around the park at night, so he decided to leave. Carefully, slowly, he walked home, constantly glancing over his shoulder and all around. If he even suspected that Doug was nearby, he would run. But Doug was nowhere in sight. And when Jimmy finally arrived home, only his parent's car sat in the driveway.

Walking into the house, he feared that his mother was going to yell at him for missing dinner. Instead, he was met by Jillian, who grabbed Jimmy by the arm and silently pulled him upstairs and into her room. Once the door was closed, she broke into tears.

"Jimmy, please don't ever tell anyone what you saw today!" She sat on the edge of her bed and begged him with desperate eyes. Grabbing a Kleenex from a nearby box, she wiped away the tears while they both fell silent. Her alarm clock ticked loudly through the room. A blue teddy bear seemed to stare at Jimmy from the pillow on Jillian's bed. He noticed that she had a huge bruise on her arm.

His throat had dried up and he didn't know what to say anyway. It scared him to see her like this. Not knowing what else to do, he walked over and hugged Jillian. She seemed to cry even harder as she squeezed him tightly. He didn't understand what Doug had done to his sister, but he hated him.

Jillian finally let go of Jimmy and he sat down beside her. "Did he hurt you real bad?" He felt like the question was dumb, but he wasn't sure what else to say.

"Yes," Jillian grabbed another tissue and blew her nose. "He really hurt me. He raped me."

Jimmy's eyes flew open. He might've been a naive kid, but he knew that was a bad thing. "What?" His voice was small when he spoke.

"He forced me to have sex with him. You're just ten, you wouldn't understand." Jillian took a deep breath and attempted to explain things. "See, you can't tell mom and dad, 'cause it's my own fault. I let him in the house and they always told us to never let anyone in when they weren't home." Jimmy nodded, knowing that this rule was practically written in stone. At the same time, he somehow didn't think that this situation was his sister's fault.

"And I always had a crush on Doug, so I used to kind of flirt with him," Jillian admitted, her blue eyes staring into his identical set. "And Nancy said that when you flirt with guys, they usually assume that means you want to have sex with them, so it was my own fault." She referred to her friend.

Jimmy sat quietly and listened. Bravely he attempted to reassure Jillian. But he still didn't understand why this man had hurt her. After all, Doug was their parents' church friend. Weren't they supposed to be better people?

"No, you don't understand, Jimmy," she insisted dramatically. "You're too young. But when you get older, you'll see. Sometimes guys can't control themselves."

Jimmy's eyes widened. Did that mean that *he* could possibly turn into one of those guys, not able to control himself? Would he hurt someone in the same way Doug had hurt her? He didn't understand. His face was burning and the lump had formed in his throat. He could no longer speak.

"Anyway, you can't even talk about this again," Jillian firmly insisted. "You can't tell *anyone*, ever. You can't tell mom and dad. And you totally can't tell your friends. No one. *Ever.*"

Jimmy nodded as he looked down at his feet. His heart was racing and he felt sick. Not talking about this with anyone wouldn't be a problem. It wasn't like he *wanted* to rehash that moment and he certainly didn't want to get Jillian in any kind of trouble either.

"I told mom and dad that you were at Patrick's house and that's why you missed dinner. So they won't be mad," Jillian continued. "But I can get you something to eat if you want."

If *only* Jimmy had been at Patrick's house, looking at naked pictures, rather than hiding for the past few miserable hours. Biting his lip, Jimmy reluctantly nodded.

Quietly they headed to the kitchen where Jill opened a can of soup. Jimmy didn't feel very hungry, but consuming the hot liquid made him feel a little better. It was comforting. So he opened a bag of cookies, ate a few and felt even better.

The theme music for *Magnum PI* drifted up from the basement.

His parents watched it every week. Jillian sat beside him in silence, staring at the couch in the next room, the very one Doug had raped her on only hours earlier. But to look at it at that moment, you would never know of the struggle that had taken place there hours before. It was as if nothing had happened at all. When he had finished eating, Jimmy shuffled upstairs to get ready for bed.

His mom came into his room to kiss him good night just as he was climbing under the covers.

"I love my *little* boy with the *big* blue eyes!" She hugged him tightly, and a part of him wanted to blurt out the entire story, safe in her embrace. But he couldn't. As he looked into her trusting eyes, Jimmy bit his lip and quickly told her good night and that he loved her too. After she left, he felt his body explode, tears running down his cheeks, and he sobbed long into the night. He woke up the next morning from a series of nightmares. His childhood was over.

Chapter two

Doug never visited their house again. In fact, a few weeks after the rape his mother had even remarked on how unusual it was that their friend no longer dropped by. Jimmy's dad commented that he thought Doug had moved north to Toronto in order to find work, but Annette Groome was concerned.

"I hope we didn't do anything to offend him," she shook her head, frowning. Jimmy watched her calmly pour a glass of water while his sister showed no expression whatsoever. Not that he was surprised. Ever since the night of the brutal attack, Jillian had not brought up the dark topic again. When she was asked about the scar on her right arm from where Doug had pinned her down against the couch, she lied and said it was from an accident in gym class. In fact, she acted as if everything was completely normal.

Unfortunately, Jimmy wasn't so lucky. He was unable to avoid the horrible nightmares that had held him hostage since that traumatic afternoon. Sometimes they consisted of a re-enactment of that horrific scene; other times Doug would be standing over him with a knife in hand. It took away all the comforts of sleep for Jimmy. Now going to bed was torture and often left him feeling restless and miserable the next day.

If Jillian had suffered from the rape, however, it was not apparent to Jimmy. In fact, by the following year she had grown much taller and developed into a beautiful young woman. Wherever she went, Jimmy's sister had the full attention of all those around her, especially men. Guys her age were intimidated by Jillian. Other girls were jealous. As a result,

Jimmy recognized that his sister was developing a very large ego. Jillian was perfect and she knew it.

By the summer of 1983, there was a regular battle in the house about whether or not Jimmy's sister could become a model. It was almost on a daily basis that Jillian begged, screamed and threatened in order to have her shot at stardom. Glamorous and exciting, it was a world that she craved. However, John Groome seemed hesitant to allow his daughter to be put in such a vulnerable situation, while Annette simply forbade it.

"Honey, why don't you wait until you're sixteen, and then get a normal job a kid your age gets," Annette calmly suggested. "Do you really want to be involved in such a superficial world that believes that only what is on the outside matters?"

"I don't care!" Jillian would snap every time. "I don't care if it's superficial. Why don't you just let me try it to see if I like it? And if I don't, then I'll quit. But if I can get into modeling, I can make some *real* money. I could save up for college and you know how expensive that is, right?"

John nodded hesitantly. "She does have a point there, Annette. College is really expensive and you have to give her credit for showing some interest in working."

"Oh, come on," Annette wrinkled her forehead. "She's just a *child*. It's too soon for her to have a job and I don't trust that whole industry. It just seems so fake."

"So what!" Jillian countered with fury in her eyes. "I want to do it! You don't have a right to hold me back. I might just be thirteen, but I'm my own person too. You can't run my life forever!"

"I'm not trying to run your life, Jill," their mother's eyes narrowed, "but I *am* your mother and if I feel something isn't good for you, it is my duty to protect you."

"Protect me! As *if* you could! I don't *need* your protection," Jillian was beginning to yell and Jimmy felt chills run up his spine, his mind returning to that horrible day the previous fall. "I have rights too! I want to be a model."

"Don't raise your voice at me!" Annette's pupils receded to pinpoints, and Jimmy thought she was about to cry. "I didn't raise you to disrespect your family."

"You know what the problem is?" Jillian ignored her mother's last remark. "The problem is that you're so short that you'd never fucking be considered for modeling, so you want to hold me back *too*! You're just jealous 'cause I have an opportunity you've *never* had!"

With that, Jillian swung around and rushed upstairs. Jimmy jumped when the bedroom door slammed. Left alone with his parents in the kitchen, he watched as Annette Groome broke down in tears and his father tore up the stairs to Jill's room. Jimmy dropped the cookie he was eating and approached his mother to give her a hug.

"Oh Jimmy, you're such a good boy," Annette sobbed. "I never have any problems with you," she hugged him tightly before letting go. Grabbing a paper towel from the kitchen counter, he handed it to her and watched her wipe the tears away. "I just don't want to see anything happen to her; it's not that I want to hold her back. I'd never do that to either of you. I just love you both so much! I wish Jillian could see that."

Jimmy didn't reply. Instead, he once again thought back to the day of his sister's rape and how painful it would've been for his mother to find out the truth. It would kill her to know what had happened. And even though the secret weighed heavily on his heart, Jimmy saw this as yet another reason to never tell.

Eventually his parents reached a compromise with Jillian. After she turned fourteen, they would revisit the topic of modeling. If it were something she was still interested in, then they'd allow her to pursue it. Until that time, she was not allowed to bring it up again.

Meanwhile, Annette and John Groome's attention focused on Jimmy. He was surprised one evening when both his parents interrupted his homework in order to have a 'talk' with him. Jimmy expected that it would be another awkward discussion on sex, like the one his father had given him the previous year, shortly after the rape. *That* was very uncomfortable. However, they had something more unexpected on their minds.

"Jimmy," his mother looked at her son with troubled eyes as she sat beside him on his bed. John Groome sank into the battered old chair that accompanied Jimmy's desk, facing them both. "Your dad and I have to talk to you about something, and I don't want to seem insensitive because you know I love you regardless. But honey, I'm a little concerned about how you've been gaining weight in the last few months."

Jimmy looked down at the jeans he was wearing. They had once been a baggy fit but now were tight around his stomach. He was getting fat. That's what his mom was kindly trying to tell him. He just shrugged and avoided their eyes.

"Honey, I don't want to hurt your feelings," Annette continued, briefly glancing toward her husband. "You know we love you regardless of what size you are, but we're just a little worried because not only are you gaining weight, you seem a little anti-social now. You used to be busy all the time, either at your friend Patrick's house or out doing something, but now it's like you never leave your room."

Jimmy didn't want to tell them that he had never been very popular and his weight gain made him even less so. In fact, some of the girls at school often talked loudly about him behind his back, as if to make sure that he knew they found him disgusting. Meanwhile, Patrick had little time for him. Having had his fill of dirty magazines, the now twelve year old had announced to Jimmy one day that he wanted 'the real thing' rather than just a picture. He now had a girlfriend, and rarely had time for anyone but her.

But he wasn't about to tell his parents any of this, so instead he shrugged. "I don't know. I guess I don't really have anything to do."

Well, he had *one* thing to do. Since puberty hit him full force, there was only thing he *ever* wanted to do. And when Patrick went on to bigger and better things, he gave Jimmy one of the pornographic magazines.

"Maybe you should think about a hobby, Jimmy. There must be something you are interested in?" his mother asked.

"What about music?" his dad finally joined the conversation with a small grin on his face. "You're always listening to your tapes or watching videos on television. Would that be something of interest to you?"

Jimmy considered the idea for a moment. Sure, he did spend hours listening to bands like Deep Purple, Led Zeppelin and Kiss but did he necessarily want to learn how to play music? Regardless of his lack of confidence, he was intrigued.

"Maybe."

"Well, that might be an idea," his dad spoke with enthusiasm. "Maybe we can get you a guitar for Christmas or your birthday in the spring? Throw in some lessons and you'll be a rock star in no time."

Jimmy smiled at his dad and shrugged.

"The offer is there for you to think about, anyways" his father stretched and eased out of the chair.

"Or if there is anything else that interests you..." his mother rose from the bed and gently touched Jimmy's shoulder. "We just want to see you happy."

Jimmy hadn't realized just how worried his parents were over his melancholy. At first they believed it was simply the general moodiness associated with puberty. The more secluded he became however the more it concerned Annette. There was something not right with her son. She wasn't sure what, but she could sense it. And one day, the sad truth would come out.

Chapter three

Jimmy got an electric guitar when he turned twelve the following spring. Unfortunately his mom lost her job as a sales clerk a few weeks later, and his parents were unable to provide him with the lessons they had promised.

"I'm sorry, Jimmy." His father spoke gently a few nights later after dropping by his room. Although he had a good job working for the City of Thorton, a major employer in a metropolis of 300 000, his paycheck would only go so far. "We weren't expecting this to happen. But I can tell you that as soon as your mother gets another job, we'll have you signed up for your lessons. That's a promise."

"It's fine," Jimmy spoke quietly while staring at his feet. "Don't matter."

"Yes, it *does* matter." His dad insisted. "We made a promise to you and we intend on keeping it. In the meanwhile, just play around with the guitar and see what you can learn on your own."

Jimmy looked up at his dad and slowly nodded. He felt guilty when John Groome walked out of the room appearing more defeated than when arriving. It wasn't Jimmy's intention to make him feel bad.

A few days later, his father returned home with a book on how to learn guitar. The front cover boasted to making the potential reader an accomplished guitarist in 12 short weeks. His father bashfully admitted that he doubted that it's claim was true, but insisted that it couldn't hurt. "At least you can learn a bit about reading music and chords, that kind of thing." His dad insisted while flipping through the pages. "It looks interesting. Maybe I want to learn how to play guitar too!"

The father and son shared a smile. John Groome left the room and Jimmy barely looked at the book. In fact for the next week, it was rare that he even picked up the guitar at all. It spent most of the time collecting dust on the other side of the room. But eventually, curiosity got the best of Jimmy and he would inspect the guitar. His fingers touching the strings, wondering how he could go from that stage of knowing nothing, to being a pro like Eddie Van Halen. But over time, he did learn a few things. Between the book and just playing around with the instrument, Jimmy found the challenge worth the extra effort. There was something cathartic about playing and each day of the summer seemed to fly by.

And then it was back to school and junior high. Jimmy started to dread that first day back to classes long before the summer days ended. He had gained even more weight during the break and was getting an endless supply of pimples. And considering grade seven was a time when your physical appearance and social status were more relevant than anything, Jimmy already knew he'd be an outcast. He had no friends and he was ugly.

His fears were quickly confirmed in September. Although kids seemed to ignore him for the most part during the first week, that wouldn't last. Before long, he was hearing the familiar giggles behind his back. Patrick Lipton was long gone into popular land, especially since losing his virginity earlier that same year, so the two talked less and less. He was one of the few guys their age who had actually had sex, something Jimmy was starting to think he would never do. Girls hated him. They just batted their long eyelashes at him in disgust or pity. He was always nice to them though, even after hearing all the cutting remarks they made behind his back. He was always nice.

Then the day would come when Jimmy thought his luck was taking a change for the better. Suzanne Bordon, one of the prettiest girls in his classes started to talk to him. At first, he was suspicious, but quickly realized that he was just being paranoid. Why would she talk to him if she didn't like him? Sure, he would hear the snickering of her friends nearby, but maybe they were just teasing Suzanne for wanting to get to know him. After all, he wasn't exactly popular. But he really warmed up to her during their short conversations before French class everyday.

"Jimmy, what do you do for fun?"

He told her that he played guitar. Her eyes lit up slightly and she tilted her head. "Are you any good?" Her dark eye seemed to get bigger.

Jimmy shrugged and blushed. "I don't know. I'm getting lessons soon, I think." Then he politely asked her what she did for fun. She rambled on about shopping, watching television, listening to music, that kind of thing. He asked her what kind of music she listened to and Suzanne said Madonna. She returned the question and he said Led Zeppelin.

She wrinkled up her nose. "Who's that?" He attempted to explain but could hear giggling nearby and decided against in. His heart raced and he simply said, "Never mind."

Their conversations went on for weeks and quickly became the highlight of Jimmy's day. Maybe he wasn't as repulsive as he thought. Maybe pretty girls liked him too. He wasn't sure why, but then again, he didn't really understand girls at all.

By Christmas of that year, Jimmy decided to suck it up and ask Suzanne out on a date over the holidays. He watched as she blinked rapidly and a huge grin formed on her face. "No, Jimmy. Sorry." She abruptly rushed to the back of the class. The next thing he knew, several of her friends were laughing hysterically.

He wanted to die.

Jimmy's face was burning while his heart pounded wildly in anxiety. His overheated body caused the back of Jimmy's shirt to stick to him, so he sat forward in the chair while the cool classroom sent chills up his spine. They continued to laugh about what a loser Jimmy Groome was, while he felt like crawling under a rock. With the exception of the day of his sister's rape, he'd never felt worst.

He didn't hear a thing his teacher said that afternoon. Instead, Jimmy sat there and had continual self-defeating thoughts. He was fat, a loser, an idiot, and pathetic. Everyone hated him. He was a joke. And he couldn't imagine spending every day for the rest of his life being that person. He was depressed.

While everyone was happy during the holidays, Jimmy was miserable. He spent most of the time in his room, playing guitar. Sometimes, he did nothing at all but sleep – and eat.

Meanwhile, Jillian was in her glory. She was getting taller, which meant her chances of becoming a model would increase with her height. She was also very skinny, which apparently was important in the industry.

Jimmy's parents hated it and were always telling Jillian to eat more, but she always insisted she had no appetite. While he, on the other hand, seemed to eat enough for both of them during those holidays. All he wanted to do was eat, sleep and play guitar.

In January, Jillian finally got her parents blessing to try out modeling. They were paying for her photos that were to be taken by a well-known photographer in Thorton. Together they would build her portfolio and from there, she would approach agencies and look for some modeling work. She was on top of the world. Everything was going her way.

Jimmy wasn't as hopeful. He often wondered if she ever thought about the rape. But judging by her overall happiness, he was doubtful. Although his nightmares were becoming less frequent, they hadn't stopped. Jimmy still felt nervous when home alone especially at night. It wasn't as if Doug had ever come near the family again, but there was still a fear and anxiety that filled Jimmy's heart, even two years after the rape.

Since his marks were never great, Jimmy's parents decided to hold off on his guitar lessons until the following summer. That way he could focus completely on his schoolwork during the winter then guitar for his vacation. It seemed like the perfect plan in theory. However long before June arrived, Jimmy was starting to not care about guitar. After the whole incident with Suzanne before the holidays, followed by more weight gain after Christmas, he started to care less and less about his own life. It seemed hopeless and miserable. Everyday, he went to school and felt as though he was simply going through the motions. He was an outcast. Everyday, he thought about ending it all. He tried to put up a decent front for his family but behind the closed doors of his room, it was another story.

Jimmy would often think about how he'd do it. Would he hang himself? A guy in eighth grade had done that in November. All the students had gathered in a memorial for him the following week. Girls cried. Guys sat in silence. Teachers lectured about why suicide was never the answer. "Things will get better." His principal insisted. "They always do." But as the words echoed through Jimmy's head, he knew it wasn't true. That was just something adults *had* to say to kids. It was like telling them to not have sex. None of the teachers could care less if they screwed non-stop, it was just something they *had* to say in order to make parents happy. Jimmy doubted anyone would care if he died.

Other times he'd concentrate on all the reasons why he *should* do it. That was easy - his life sucked. Regardless of what his principal said during the service, maybe life didn't get any better. Maybe it'd only get worst. The only people who would miss him were his family, but maybe not Jillian. Jimmy often felt like his sister partially blamed him for the rape. After all, he hadn't stopped it. He didn't go for help. He didn't call the cops. What if he had been responsible for her getting hurt, in some tiny way? He sensed that she was different toward him after the day. After making him some soup that November evening and explaining why he could never speak of the rape again, there was a change in their relationship. She didn't talk to him. She didn't love him. That much, he was sure about.

Jimmy did feel guilty about leaving his parents behind. His mom would be devastated. His dad would quietly comfort her and eventually, they'd forget their fat son. Besides, the pain of life was just too much for him to bear. He didn't want to hurt anyone, but at the same time, Jimmy dreaded each day more than the last. He hated himself. He just wanted to close his eyes and never wake up again. Drift off into another world, where you weren't a nobody based on other people's opinions. He just wanted to be free. He wanted to die.

And so one night in June of 1985, after writing a long note explaining his decision to his family and apologizing, Jimmy found some pills in his parent's medicine cabinet and took the whole bottle. Then he put his pajamas, went to bed and closed his eyes. He may not have had the courage to save his own sister, but he *would* have the courage to die.

Chapter four

When Jimmy slowly gained consciousness, he was in a stark hospital room with his father hunched over beside him. His stomach and throat ached, and it took a few seconds for him to remember what had happened. Feelings of shame, humiliation and guilt washed over him. And something he hadn't expected; relief.

His dad looked preoccupied and at first didn't seem to realize that Jimmy was awake. John Groome's eyes were full of sorrow and anxiety; his face seemed to have aged years in only a few short hours. For a moment, it appeared that his father was praying. Their eyes met and Jimmy quickly looked away. His father asked if he was okay and Jimmy nodded mutely.

"No one is mad at you," John Groome's words were gentle and without judgment. Jimmy studied his father's face as he bit his lower lip. "In fact, we felt like there was something wrong for a long time, but we wanted to believe you were fine. That you were just going through a stage. I'm sorry it had to come to this."

Jimmy was confused. They weren't angry with him? His father was apologizing to *him*? It didn't make sense. He continued to chew on his lower lip as he thought about his dad's words.

John looked down at his hands, hesitantly. When he finally did speak, he seemed to be choosing his words carefully. "We know about your sister's rape." His serious gaze returned to Jimmy's and he gave him a comforting smile. "After we rushed you to the hospital and read your note, Jillian confessed everything."

Jimmy had almost forgotten about the note. He hadn't indicated that

Jillian was raped in it, but merely said he felt sorry for not being able to help her when she needed it. He had apologized for a lot of things in what was supposed to be the last letter he'd ever write. Now, it seemed so stupid. Was Jill mad at him? She'd been clear about never having her secret come out.

"She and your mother are talking to a psychiatrist right now. We also want the police involved, but we aren't sure yet if that will be too traumatic for Jill. We don't want to drag her through the courts and make her relive such a horrible day all over again," John Groome cleared his throat and for a second, Jimmy could see the fury cross his face. His father was never angry, so it was easy to spot. "I just wish Jillian had come to us right away. I also wish she had never made you promise not to say anything." His father reached out and gripped Jimmy's hand. "That's a big thing for a ten year old boy to walk around with every day. And it wasn't right. Nothing about this situation is right."

Jimmy could see the intense sadness in his father's eyes and swallowed hard, but was unable to stop a tear falling from his eye and sliding down the side of his face. It was the first time anyone had acknowledged the private hell he had experienced. He felt as if a weight had been removed from his shoulders. Finally, someone knew his secret.

"I--" Jimmy barely could whisper and stopped to clear his throat. His dad passed him a Styrofoam cup of water from the nightstand and Jimmy sipped from it with difficulty. "I wish I could've helped her."

"Jimmy, you were ten," John squeezed his hand again. "There's *no* way you could've physically done anything to get Doug away from your sister. The best thing you could've done was get the hell out of there,"--his dad never swore--"And get as far away as possible."

"But I should've called the police," Jimmy whispered. "I should've told someone."

"You were scared," his father insisted. "That's a pretty shocking thing to walk in on, especially for a kid. Don't beat yourself up over it. We aren't mad at you."

Jimmy still felt he should've done more that day. After a suicide attempt, it wasn't like his father was going to tell him otherwise.

Before they could discuss things further, Jimmy's mother rushed into the room. With tears streaming down her face, Annette Groome swept her son into an enveloping hug. "My poor baby! I thank God you're okay. I don't know what I would've done if He had taken you away from us."

Jimmy silently hugged his mother back, tears streaming down his face. He swallowed the huge lump in his throat and thought about how devastated she would have been had his suicide attempt been successful. He couldn't bear to allow it more than a moment's thought.

Annette finally let go of him and sat on the edge of his bed. Jimmy's father had moved back slightly, to give them some time together. "Honey, I love you so much and it breaks my heart that you felt this badly about your life!" Her tears started to flow again. "Jillian told us everything and I can't believe my two children had to live through something so horrible. I can't *believe* that Doug could do something so disgusting to our family. We trusted him."

"Jimmy thinks that he should've done something more that day," John Groome spoke to his wife, who wrinkled her forehead as she tried to comprehend. "He thinks that he should've tried to stop the attack or called the police." Annette started to shake her head, even before her husband had finished speaking.

"Jimmy, no," his mother reached for his hand, her eyes resting on his face. She had finally stopped crying. "Don't think about those things now. Jillian made you promise to not say anything and she was wrong to keep this a secret, or to make *you* keep it a secret. She put you in an awful position. Please don't blame yourself. This isn't either of your fault; you were both just children."

"Is Jill okay?" Jimmy rasped. His throat still ached.

"We have her talking to someone who specializes in working with rape victims," his mother looked away from Jimmy's face, addressing her husband now. "We both talked to her and now she wants to spend some time alone with Jillian. I hope to God she can help her."

"She will," Jimmy's father sighed. "It'll take time though."

As it turned out, Jillian wasn't the only member of the family who had to meet with a counselor. The entire family gathered the following morning to discuss the traumatic event and how it affected all of them, not just Jillian. Jimmy learned that he wasn't the only person who felt guilty for the rape. His parents felt they were partially to blame since they had introduced Doug to the family, allowing him into the house. Jillian felt responsible for Jimmy's depression and suicide attempt, while he continued to feel that he hadn't done enough to help his sister that afternoon. One man's vile actions were ripping them all apart.

Because Jimmy had tried to take his own life, he was required to meet with a psychiatrist twice a week for the entire summer, while Jillian continued to meet with her counselor. It was something he initially didn't look forward to at all. In the end, Dr Newton talked about much more than the rape. The young psychiatrist was interested in Jimmy's guitar lessons that were scheduled to start up at the end of June, and they discussed a great deal about music and television before even tackling the issue of his suicide attempt. It seemed like the psychiatrist was doing his best to make Jimmy comfortable and understand him as a person before diving into the heavier topics that required their meetings in the first place. Even when they discussed the sensitive issues, it was done in a casual manner, nothing like what Jimmy would have expected in therapy.

"So tell me," Dr Newton relaxed into his chair a few days after Jimmy was allowed home from the hospital. "If you could turn back time, what would you have done differently on the day of the rape?"

"I would've called the police."

"Okay," the counselor jotted something in a note pad, before nodding at him encouragingly to continue.

"And they would've saved my sister from Doug."

"Do you think so?" Dr Newton asked curiously. "You said the attack was already going on when you arrived in the room, is that correct?"

"Yes."

"And how long would it have taken you to locate a phone, call the police and wait for them to arrive?"

Jimmy considered the question and responded, "I don't know."

"Do you think possibly that it was too late at that point?" Dr Newton verbalized the same question that was going through Jimmy's head at that moment. It had never occurred to him that maybe calling the police or getting help might not have been as helpful as he originally thought.

"Maybe," Jimmy considered. "I guess it would've been. By the time anyone arrived to help, he would've already raped my sister."

"Do you think Doug would still be there by the time help arrived?" Dr Newton inquired softly, almost innocently but still making his point.

"No," Jimmy conceded. "He probably left right after I found them."

Dr Newton nodded. "Do you think you, yourself, could've physically removed this man from your house?"

Jimmy closed his eyes, "No."

The psychiatrist nodded.

"Maybe I couldn't have done anything, I guess," Jimmy admitted reluctantly. Dr Newton *did* have a point, but he still felt slightly responsible. It was clear however that he was supposed to arrive at the same conclusion as his doctor, so he agreed with this theory.

Their sessions together continued throughout the summer. Jimmy came to understand that he was using food as a way of stuffing his emotions back.

"Often adults will drink or pick up other bad habits as a way to escape from their problems," Dr. Newton explained. "For you, food was this source of comfort. It wasn't like you could talk to anyone about the assault on your sister, or at least you didn't feel that you could discuss it with anyone because of her insistence that you keep quiet. Food was your coping mechanism."

The doctor seemed to feel that now that Jimmy knew the source of his issues, he would stop eating so much. And to a point, he was right. But there was still loneliness in Jimmy's heart that made him unable to completely give up his vice. Sure, he had family, but it wasn't as if he had friends other than Patrick – but they rarely hung out. So, although he didn't gain more weight, he wasn't losing any either.

"Jimmy, you'll start to drop weight once you get your growth spurt," his father maintained when the issue came up in their frequent discussions. Ever since the suicide attempt, his family seemed to be always talking to him about everything and watching Jimmy like hawks. He could feel it.

"I hope so," he admitted. And he did try. Sometimes, Jimmy would attempt to do push-ups in his room, but it was so difficult for him that he usually gave up after a few. All he ever wanted to do was play guitar. Everything else was boring in comparison. "I don't want to be fat for the rest of my life."

The funny thing was that when he looked in the mirror now, he recognized an attractive face. No longer displaying a soft, round face, Jimmy could now recognize a strong jaw line beneath his fat, which was occasionally accompanied by a heartfelt smile. His sky blue eyes now danced around and were brought out even more by his black hair, which often turned up in the ends – or as his mother referred to it - a cowlick. He wasn't ugly. He was just fat.

Even his sister confirmed this fact for him. She now spoke to him again. In fact, Jill went out of her way to communicate with her brother daily, letting him know about her latest modeling offer or boyfriend. After he returned home from the hospital, Jillian had gone to his room and apologized for making Jimmy keep her secret. "I had no idea how much it was eating you up." Her eyes were full of regret as they spoke, and she admitted that the rape haunted her every day.

"You always seemed so happy," Jimmy tilted his head in interest. "I thought you had forgotten it and didn't understand why it bothered me so much."

"No, I just hid it really well," Jillian confessed, studying her long fingernails. She had decided not to go to the police, but instead focus on healing. "I was mad, and the more angry I got, the more driven I was to become a model. To show *him* that he didn't get the best of me. I thought someday I would become famous and then I'd tell everyone how he raped me and publicly humiliate him."

"Really?" Jimmy was surprised. His sister had hidden her anger as well as he had hidden her secret. "I'm sorry I didn't stop him that day."

"You couldn't have."

"I always thought you hated me for not doing anything when I saw it," Jimmy offered shyly. "I hope he dies."

Jillian gave him a small smile as a tear escaped her eye. "Jimmy, I could never hate you. The counselor I talk to say that I avoided you because we shared a secret and seeing you forced me to remember it daily. But I never hated you." Her eyes were now overflowing. "If you had died because of me and all this, I would've found Doug myself and killed him. I swear I would've."

Jimmy knew his sister was just being dramatic, but still appreciated what she was trying to say. The two shared a smile. He finally felt like things might actually get better after all.

Chapter five

When Jimmy first left the hospital, all the attention from his family was comforting. Jillian talked to him on a regular basis. His dad made sure they did stuff together, while his mother cooked him all his favorite dishes. But after a few weeks, Jimmy couldn't help but feel that maybe he was getting a little *too* much attention from his family. Somewhere along the line, it became completely smothering.

It seemed like he could barely go to the bathroom, without one of his family members checking in on him. Clearly, everyone thought he was going to hurt himself again. Otherwise, why would they monitor his every move all day, *every* day? Fortunately as time passed, both his father and sister seemed to give him some room to breathe again. Unfortunately, his mother didn't.

"Jim?" Annette Groome knocked on his door, sticking her head in without waiting for a response. It was a hot July evening and Jimmy had just barely managed to hide a copy of *Playboy* underneath his pillow in time. Irritated by his mother's constant interruptions and her lack of respect for his privacy, he found himself snapping at her.

She appeared surprised by his tone and he automatically felt guilty as she took a step back. His mother was so tiny and delicate that sometimes he felt as though the wrong words would shatter her. It was, after all *he* who had attempted suicide weeks earlier and in the process, put his family through hell. If anything, they should've been snapping at him, not the other way around. He immediately apologized.

"It's fine, Jimmy," his mother offered a hesitant smile. "It's hot tonight and we're all kind of cranky."

"Yeah."

"So, I saw something in today's paper and was wondering if you might be interested," she began earnestly. "Our church is having this social for teenagers this weekend and I thought maybe you'd like to go?"

Nope.

"It'd be a great place to meet some kids your own age," she coaxed, raising her eyebrows. "There's supposed to be music, food, games. I think it'd be fun!"

Jimmy gave a half-hearted smile. "No mom, I don't think that would be for me."

"Are you sure?"

"Yeah, thanks though," he tried to show some appreciation, but he had pretty well had enough. His mother was always attempting to get him involved in things that just didn't interest him in the least. Religion was one of those things. She often talked about how church might help to 'heal' his heart and that God would help him find the answers to all his problems. Jimmy thought it was a crock. After all, if there were a God, why was his sister raped? Why was he fat? Why did life generally suck? It didn't make sense and he wanted no part in it.

But if it hadn't been some religious event, his mother would've found another activity that they could do together. For some reason she had an obsessive need to be around him *all* the time and it was starting to become overwhelming. He loved his mother and felt awful for what he'd put her through, but Jimmy felt like she was suffocating him.

The most positive aspect of his life was the guitar lessons that he had started taking two weeks after he got home from the hospital with a guy named Sean Ryan. When they shook hands for the first time, Jimmy had no idea how much this guitar teacher would impact his life. Not only was Sean the guitarist for a popular local band Second in Line, he had also been professionally trained for a number of years. "From like age 10 to 16, I spent hours learning how to play guitar," Sean enthusiastically shared with Jimmy on that first day. "Yeah, I used to practice all the time, on top of my lessons. It was brutal but well worth it."

Indeed. Jimmy certainly didn't have to be a pro to see that Sean was extremely talented. He could play anything. Jimmy named songs that he, himself, couldn't even imagine attempting. Sean played samples of every one of them - and to perfection.

"Wow!" Jimmy's eyes widened. "I'm impressed."

"Thank you, but all it takes is work," Sean assured him. "I didn't pick up the guitar for the first time and play this stuff," shrugging, he pushed some of his long, chestnut hair from his eyes. "It's just something you learn over time. You can do it too. Maybe even better than me, someday."

Jimmy quickly shook his head. "No, I don't think so." He was slightly embarrassed at his own self-doubt.

"Sure you can; why wouldn't you?" Sean posed the question that Jimmy couldn't answer. "Jim, you can do anything you want. I know that sounds like some dumb shit they tell you in school to get you to work harder, but it's *true*. I worked my ass off and managed to learn songs I never thought I could play. I joined a band. And we're doing really well and hopefully some day we'll get signed," Sean spoke earnestly, his guitar resting on his lap. His green eyes studied Jimmy's face for a few minutes. "You know what? I'm gonna make you *that* good. That's my goal."

Jimmy smiled. Sean would quickly become the first person in his life that treated him as an equal. Unlike the kids at school, he was always respectful toward Jimmy. And unlike most adults, Sean didn't talk to him like he was some moronic child. The two often had conversations that went beyond their scheduled music lessons. Sometimes Jimmy even worried that his parents had told Sean about his suicide attempt, in hopes that Sean could tip them off if he seemed depressed again. But if he knew, Sean never gave any indication.

In the end, it was really the guitar lessons that helped Jimmy keep his head together. Sure, the counseling did help to a point, but some things never changed. He was still unpopular at school. Girls still teased or completely ignored him. Only the equally unattractive boys were his friends, which in a way made him feel like more of an outcast. He was still fat.

Suicidal thoughts still occasionally crossed his mind, but not as often as they once had. By the time Jimmy was fourteen, he generally felt like life was back to normal. Even his mother had stopped smothering him.

As the months flew by, Jimmy became a very talented guitarist and his father even began to comment on how the lessons were well worth the money. However, he was also remarking on how Jimmy mightn't need many more since he was already at such an accomplished level. "We'll keep you in lessons for this summer," Jimmy's father announced in June of 1986 - one year after the suicide attempt and his original meeting with Sean Ryan. "But we'll have to cut them off in September. And then maybe next summer, you can learn something else. How about that?"

Jimmy had no idea what else he could learn. Anxious about ending the lessons, he shared his concerns with Sean later that same week.

"Hey man, your father is right," he spoke fairly. "It has been a year and that shit gets expensive for parents. And to be honest with you, I'm not sure how much longer I'll be teaching. The boys and I think we might move to Toronto this fall and try to see if we can get noticed by some big shots at the record labels."

"Oh," Jimmy didn't mean to sound as disappointed as he did, but music was the only thing that seemed to keep him sane. The rest of his life truly sucked.

"But you know what? Why not try something else, like your dad said?" Sean suggested. "You know, why not take voice lessons? If you want to be in a band someday, chances are you'll be at least doing back up vocals. It can't hurt."

Jimmy wasn't sure if that was for him. Playing guitar in front of an audience would be scary enough. Clearly his lack of interest was displayed on his face because Sean grinned suddenly.

"I'm telling you man, you should think about it. If your parents want to put up the money for it, you may as well at least go check it out. If you don't like it, you don't like it. Case closed." He shrugged, "Besides, chicks love guys that can sing."

Jimmy smirked. He really didn't think singing was going to change anything in *that* area of his life.

"It's true," Sean remarked as he placed his guitar back in its case. "This girl I'm dating now totally loves the fact that I can sing. She could care less about the guitar thing though, but the fact that I started to sing for my band seems totally hot to her."

Jimmy faked a smile and nodded.

"You should see her - she's a knockout!" Sean assured him.

As it turned out, Jimmy would see her the following week when she dropped by the school to pick up Sean. Not realizing that their lesson wasn't yet completed, the gorgeous blonde stuck her head in the door. When she saw Jimmy, Sean's girlfriend quickly apologized and disappeared. Sean called her back.

Jimmy was awestruck. She looked like one of the girls in his magazines, but he wouldn't dare share this information with Sean. Then again, he probably already knew. The 17-year-old girl that Sean introduced as Katie Craft was perfect. She was tall with straight blond hair that fell halfway down her back. She had huge, hazel eyes that seemed to stare curiously at Jimmy, as if there was a question at the end of her dark, cherry lips. She wore a basic black t-shirt that hugged her boobs and a pair of jeans that showed off her ass. There was absolutely nothing wrong with this girl. She was perfection.

Sean introduced the two and the first thing that really captivated Jimmy was the fact that she didn't look completely disgusted by him, like the girls at school seemed to be. In fact, his eyes flew open in stunned disbelief when Katie commented to Sean that his student was 'really cute'. Jimmy felt his heart pounding a mile a minute and he managed to barely whisper a quick 'thanks' before looking away. His face burning, he quickly packed up his guitar as the couple talked about their plans for the evening. Jimmy blurted good-bye to them both before rushing out the door, where his newly licensed sister was waiting to pick him up.

All the way home, Jillian chattered about modeling stuff but Jimmy didn't hear a word. Instead he replayed Katie's words repeatedly in his head. Did she really think he was cute or had Sean's girlfriend only said that to him out of pity? He didn't know, but it still made him smile.

Chapter six

As the summer of '86 ended, Jimmy felt himself sinking back into depression. September meant returning to school. And school represented a place where his life was an irrelevant joke. To make matters worse, his guitar lessons with Sean were about to end in the last week of August. Talk about adding insult to injury.

Sensing Jimmy's disappointment, Sean started to spend more time with him at the end of each lesson, talking about music, the future, and life in general. Jimmy admitted to him during one of these conversations that he wasn't exactly well liked in school.

Sean nodded his head in understanding. "You know, my parents moved a lot when I was a kid, so I can kind of relate to you. Every time I'd go to another school, I felt like the outcast for weeks." He gave Jimmy a commiserating smile. "Kids can be real assholes, can't they?"

Jimmy nodded silently, looking at his sneakers. They were ugly, cheap shoes that his mother bought at Rothmans from the reduced bin. He hadn't bothered to protest though; an expensive brand name wasn't going to make him any more likeable to anyone. All the other kids wore expensive, fashionable clothing, while he wore baggy t-shirts and sweatpants.

"But you know what?" Sean leaned back in his chair. "It's not always going to be that way. I promise you, it *does* get better. Just ignore those losers at your school and concentrate on music. That's what I did."

Jimmy appreciated the encouragement; however, he doubted that someone like Sean Ryan could possibly relate to what he went through at school. Their situations weren't identical. Being the new kid wasn't the same as being the *fat* kid. But he was willing to take the advice about working on his music; it was something he loved.

At the end of August, Jimmy had his last guitar lesson. Sean made a few recommendations on how to improve his skill, wished him luck and shook his hand. "I've had a lot of fun working with you, Jimmy. You're by far my best student," he admitted honestly. "You're not just some dumb ass kid who saw a music video and decided that it looked cool, and took a few lessons. You're actually very serious about your music." He cocked his head, considering, as a huge grin broke across his face. "And I like that."

"Thanks!" Jimmy's face lit up. It was high praise coming from someone with such talent. Sean's band was probably the most recognized metal group in the city. Jimmy had seen Second in Line play at an all-ages show earlier that year, and they were amazing. "Good luck when you guys move to Toronto."

"Thanks man," Sean replied as they slowly prepared to leave. "I appreciate it." The two continued to talk as they left the music room and headed toward the exit. Outside, Jillian waited to pick him up while Sean glanced around the parking lot. "I guess Kate hasn't made it here yet."

"Do you need a ride?" Jimmy offered hopefully. He knew Jillian wouldn't be pleased, but at the same time, Sean was the closest thing he had to a best friend.

"Nah, she'll be along soon," Sean shrugged and smiled. "But thanks, Jim."

In the car, Jimmy sat silently, not in the mood to listen to his sister. As she rambled on about how her latest boyfriend was pissing her off, Jimmy watched in the side mirror. When Jillian slowed down at the intersection, he saw Katie pull up to the school for Sean. He knew he'd never see him again.

But as the months went by, he often thought about Sean. He wondered how his band was doing in Toronto, if they were any closer to making it in the business or if they were just one of many hopefuls in a huge city. And he thought about Sean and Katie. Were they still together? What was it like to have a beautiful girlfriend? How did it feel to wake up beside such a hot woman every morning?

Jimmy often fantasized about what it would be like to have sex with Katie. At first he felt guilty, since it *was* Sean's girlfriend. But as months went by, it didn't bother him so much. Not that he could help it, especially when his fantasies transferred into his dreams at night. They always felt so real. They were usually just quick flashes, her naked body over his while she panted in ecstasy. Other times, he'd be on top and just about to slide into her when he'd wake up. He always woke up at the worst possible time. And he *always* woke up super horny.

There was one night though, that his dream was so vivid and detailed that Jimmy awoke with his heart racing and cum on his sheets. "Oh God!" He had heard of wet dreams, but never had one before. The fact that his mother would probably see the stain was unbearably embarrassing for Jimmy. He was so fixated on the stain that Jimmy almost forgot about the dream. It had involved Katie and him having sex, but this time they finished. And it was amazing. Now Jimmy knew he *had* to have sex; he couldn't just dream about it forever. That dream turned things up a notch for him.

He realized though that the likelihood of that ever happening in real life were pretty slim, since girls ignored him. He heard some of the guys at school talking about having sex with less attractive girls that they didn't really like, just 'cause they wanted to do it. Maybe he should do that too? But even as the thought went through his mind, Jimmy knew that he couldn't do that either. Besides, he wanted it to be with someone attractive like Katie. He wanted it to be with someone he liked.

As much as he fantasized, nothing really changed for Jimmy that year. Looking around his classes, he quickly realized that his chances of getting laid in anything but a dream seemed unlikely.

The only person who appeared to be living her dream at Jimmy's house was his sister. Jillian was getting lots of modeling work. For the most part it was minor, but people in the industry seemed to really like her. They claimed it was because she was always on time, easy to work with and professional. Their parents were delighted, but they were also worried.

Since entering the profession, Jillian had lost weight. It wasn't noticeable to Jimmy--after all she was his sister and he saw her everyday--but to their parents it was a concern. "Jill, you're wasting away," his mother would often worry. To that, Jimmy's sister would shrug and insist she was fine. Other times, Annette Groome would insist that Jillian eat more. "You're too small. If you continue to lose weight, we'll have to rethink this modeling thing." This comment always led to a huge, blowout fight. Jillian refused to quit modeling and even threatened to drop out of school and move out of the house if their parents attempted to force her to stop.

"You can't run my life forever!" Jillian would scream before rushing upstairs and slamming her bedroom door.

But the day would come when the reality of the situation hit them all. It was the day that Jillian passed out at school and had to be rushed to the hospital. The doctor confirmed what their parents had already feared. Jillian was anorexic. At 5'9", she only weighed 90lbs.

Their mother cried when she heard the news. Jimmy didn't understand anorexia until his father explained it to him. His sister was starving herself or vomiting up all the food she did eat. She was doing it to stay slim, and if she didn't stop, there was a chance she could die.

Die. His sister - who was only 16 - could die. It didn't make sense to Jimmy. He was fat and everyone hated him. But his sister was starving herself and photographers loved her? Acceptance obviously came at a high cost. How could someone's weight make such a difference in social status? Even as his sister lay in the hospital, crying because she didn't want to gain weight, people sent her flowers and cards. When Jimmy was in the hospital for attempting suicide, no one sent him a thing. Then again, in all fairness, his family had probably tried to keep the whole incident low-key for his sake.

When Jimmy went to bed that night, he didn't have any erotic fantasies. He worried about Jillian.

Chapter seven

The doctor refused to release Jillian until she gained weight. She was in the hospital for almost three weeks. When she finally did get out, it was only under the conditions that she attended counseling and that her weight be regularly monitored. However in the end, even the doctors admitted that there was little they could do about Jillian's condition. It was up to her to change.

"We can try to make her eat," Jimmy's dad explained to him the night before her return from the hospital. "But we can't be assured that she isn't going to vomit the food back up again or use laxatives. Unfortunately, we can't do very much to control this situation. We can only watch her closely and hope the counseling works."

Jimmy didn't see much of a change in Jillian. She was still really skinny and clearly had issues with food. After getting home from the hospital, she turned into an overall bitch, impossible to live with at times. Especially after their parents insisted that she not model anymore. That's when Jimmy saw his sister hit the roof. Every day was a screaming match between Annette and Jillian Groome.

"The agency said that they were sensitive to my issue," Jimmy heard his sister raging at their mother. "They understand that I have this problem and said they want to work with me! They obviously care and think I've got talent."

"Jill, that is why you're in this mess in the first place," their mother complained. "You *have* to be skinny to be a model - they encourage you to be anorexic."

"The two have nothing to do with one another," Jillian would always retaliate.

One night when she thought her brother wasn't in earshot, he heard words that were like a knife in his back. "I don't want to get fat like Jimmy. Mom, he has *no* friends, *no* girlfriend. That's not normal."

"There isn't anything wrong with Jimmy," his mother was very defensive of him, much to Jimmy's relief. "He's just a little shy. It's a stage. He'll grow out of it. Besides, we're talking about *you* not him."

"Mom, he didn't try to commit suicide two years ago 'cause he's *all right*," Jillian insisted. "Why don't you just face facts?"

"Jimmy tried to commit suicide because *you* told him to hide a secret that was too much for him to handle," John Groome could suddenly be heard from the front door as he arrived home from work. His voice was strong, assertive and sent the message that he wasn't about to back down. "You're a very selfish young lady, Jillian."

"That's not fair, John," his wife jumped to her daughter's defense. "She was very scared and upset herself; she didn't do it on purpose to hurt her brother."

"No, but she has even admitted that the biggest reason for not saying anything was because she thought she led Doug on. So, in the end, Jillian was more worried about getting in trouble than anything else."

"Daddy!" Jillian began to cry and Jimmy could picture his mother comforting her.

"John, that's a horrible thing to say!" Annette Groome said in defense of their daughter. "Jillian was just a child herself. Of course she couldn't be expected to make the best decisions."

"Look Annette, I'm not at all defending Doug or what he did to Jillian," his father paused for a moment. "But she has even admitted that she invited him over that afternoon and *told* him that she wanted him to be her first. Of course, he was an adult and should've known better. However, Jill's real motive for not telling us was her fear of getting in trouble for her part in all this. She had no concerns about how this affected Jimmy before the suicide attempt."

Jimmy was stunned. Jillian had *invited* Doug over that day? She *wanted* him to be her first? Suddenly, everything he once thought he understood about the rape situation wasn't fitting together anymore.

Everyone was silent.

"Furthermore, there is nothing wrong with Jimmy," his father continued. "And Jillian, you will *not* disrespect another family member in this house."

"I was saying," Jillian voice shook from crying. "I was just saying that I watch my weight so I don't get fat like Jimmy. I said that he has no friends and no girls in his life 'cause of his weight and I don't want to be like that."

"I can't believe what a cruel person you can be sometimes," their father snapped at Jillian. "Your brother was very depressed a couple of years ago and the child psychiatrist even said that his weight gain was the result of pent up feelings; feelings that stem from what *you* asked him to hide. My biggest concern right now isn't his *social* life, it's his happiness, and playing guitar makes him happy. Not everyone wants to be the center of attention, Jillian."

More silence.

"I think maybe you should think before you speak, young lady," his father added, before starting up the stairs. Jimmy attempted to hide, but his father noticed him scurry into his room and followed him. He gently closed the door and turned toward his son.

"How much of that conversation did you hear?" His father's voice was much calmer than it had been moments earlier.

Jimmy shook his head, not meeting his father's eyes. "Not much. I just heard yelling," he sat down on the edge of his bed.

"Jimmy," his father pulled up the chair from the nearby desk and sat across from him. "Don't listen to your sister. There's nothing wrong with you. You went through a difficult phase. You're a great kid."

"Dad, is it true that she invited that guy over? I mean, Doug?" Jimmy asked with hesitance in his voice.

"Yes," his father nodded. "That's something that was brought to our attention while you were still in the hospital. I'm not saying it's her fault for the rape. I'm not saying it was right. But she should've been direct with us sooner. The reason she wasn't, was because Jillian figured we'd take her to the police to report the crime and it would come out that Doug was here because he was invited."

"And she thought she'd be in some kind of trouble," his father continued. "It just makes me angry because it was very clear that something was bothering you all along. Your mom and I had no idea what was going on or if it was just puberty. When we asked your sister if she knew what was bothering you, she always denied knowing a thing. Did she even attempt to talk to you about all this after that day?"

Jimmy shook his head no.

"I didn't think so," his father ran a hand through his black hair, sighing loudly. "That girl has a lot of growing up to do."

"Maybe," Jimmy started slowly. "What if she really didn't say anything 'cause she thought you'd be pissed at her? It makes sense."

"Yes it does," his father quietly admitted. "But we always talked openly with Jill about these things. And we talked to her about rape. We told her "no means no", even if she were on a date with some guy. Just like we told you that if a girl says no to you, you have to respect that and back off. So to be direct with you Jimmy, your sister was aware of the difference and she knew we wouldn't blame her in that case."

Jimmy thought for a moment. When his dad gave him the very embarrassing 'sex talk' a few years earlier, he'd been very clear on respecting boundaries with women. Ironically, this was before the truth about Jillian's rape came out.

"But dad, maybe I should've told you the truth?" Jimmy wasn't sure if maybe *he* had done something wrong.

His father gave him a compassionate smile. "Jimmy, you were only protecting your sister. In your eyes, Jillian was attacked by someone and was at risk of getting in trouble if anyone found out. Of course you weren't about to tell."

"Dad, she was right about one thing though," Jimmy felt his face burning. "I don't have friends and girls really are grossed out by me."

"Jimmy, when I was fifteen I didn't have friends and girls didn't give *me* the time of day," his father grinned. "And I was about 130 lbs and 5'6"." They shared a smile. His dad was now close to 6' tall. "Trust me, that's just being a teenager."

After their talk, Jimmy felt a little better. He had always thought it was his weight that turned people off knowing him, but now he realized that maybe his dad was right. Maybe being a teenager just sucked.

As 1987 progressed, Jimmy attempted push-ups a few more times, but he always failed. Then he decided instead to try to cut out junk food. He wasn't going to puke up his food like Jillian, but maybe if he didn't eat as much food? Jimmy wasn't sure. Fortunately as he got close to his 15th birthday, he started to grow taller. The bad acne that developed around the age of 13 began to disappear. He sometimes noticed girls looking at him, but still, none talked to him.

He continued to work on his guitar. Every day, he spent hours practicing; sometimes just playing around, other times trying to challenge his abilities with a new song. He even attempted to write some stuff, but refused to let anyone hear it. Not yet. And when he approached his dad about singing lessons that following summer, John Groome said he thought that was a terrific idea.

Jimmy met with his vocal coach two weeks after school ended. Her name was Cindy and like him, she was overweight, so there was immediately a level of comfort with her that he rarely had with other females. In fact, Cindy was probably the first girl close to his age that he could talk to comfortably without feeling judged. He realized that girls weren't that difficult to talk to after all, except the snotty girls, like Suzanne Bordon.

He also learned that girls really like compliments. He figured this out after telling Cindy that she had a beautiful singing voice. She blushed a little bit and said, "Thank you, Jimmy," but he could tell that the compliment had made her day. Cindy was much more relaxed and talkative with him after that. He considered that even though she was probably about 19, chances were that she hadn't had a lot of positive experiences with guys. Maybe he was on to something.

By the end of the summer, Jimmy was surprised at how well he could sing. In the beginning he was too shy to practice at home, but eventually he grew more comfortable. His mother told him regularly what a nice voice he had. So did his dad. Jillian was back into modeling and never home to comment, but that was fine. Jimmy felt like maybe things were starting to take a turn for the better.

When he started grade ten that September, Jimmy noticed right away that kids rarely teased him anymore. It still happened, but not as often. He had also grown even taller over the summer months, so his weight seemed more evenly proportioned. He wasn't skinny, but somehow he didn't look as bad.

Things were about to change a great deal in his life. Ironically it started with his horrible marks.

Chapter eight

"Jimmy, I don't understand why your marks are so bad," Annette Groome frowned as she studied her son's report card at the end of the semester. Despite the fact that he didn't mind school as much as he used to, Jimmy continued to not do well in his classes. It was almost impossible for him to concentrate on the teachers' words. Unless it had to do with music, sex or hockey, his mind drifted off. "You're such a bright young man, that's why this really surprises me. You're on the borderline with biology and math." And the rest of his marks weren't much better.

"I guess I'm not as bright as you think I am," he quipped, raising one eyebrow, causing his mother to laugh while she shook her head.

"Jimmy! You know that's not true."

"I'm just not interested in that kind of stuff, mom," Jimmy shrugged. "If two trains go in opposite directions and at different speeds, I really don't give a crap which arrives at whatever first, and biology is completely over my head."

"I understand," his mother gave him a compassionate smile. "But you need to pass these classes in order to graduate in a couple of years. What worries me is that if you're having so much trouble now, it's only going to get more difficult for you each year."

Jimmy made a serious attempt to do better. For a couple of months, his grades *did* seem to improve, but regardless of good test scores and high marks on reports, he still barely passed all his classes that June. It frustrated him and made Jimmy feel as if all his efforts were a complete waste of time. That's when his father made an announcement.

"Next year, we're getting you a tutor."

Jimmy said that was fine, but didn't really care. He was just happy that grade ten was finished. Especially since his father made him two promises for that summer. First, he was going to teach Jimmy how to drive so he could get his license. And the second thing was intimidating but necessary. His dad was going to have him work with a trainer at a local gym.

"Mind you, this will be a temporary thing," John Groome sternly insisted. "These things cost money. But considering that you've already lost weight and this is something important to you, I'll do what I can to help you out." The smile they shared told Jimmy that his dad wasn't at all concerned about the money. As it turned out, he only needed a few consultations with the trainer to get himself on track.

At the same time that Jimmy was learning how to drive, his sister was graduating high school. No longer interested in modeling, Jillian announced that she wanted to be a hygienist. Unfortunately, her marks weren't high enough so she had to upgrade during the summer before attending college in the fall. While doing so, she met a guy named Rob and they started dating. Jimmy's parents often talked about how they thought that Jillian's new boyfriend along with her quitting modeling would be just what she needed, in order to be cured of her eating disorder. Jimmy was skeptical. After all, his sister was still freakishly skinny.

The summer of 1988 was very successful for Jimmy. Not only did he get his license on the first try, he also managed to lose a little more weight and began to tone up. When he started grade 11 that fall, he wasn't in the best shape, but definitely was starting to feel better about his appearance. Suddenly, a few female classmates were checking him out. And he always noticed, even when pretended he didn't.

Probably the most surprising part of grade eleven was when Jimmy's old friend Patrick turned up in some of his classes. The two started to talk again and eventually hung out together after school. It was kind of like old times, but Jimmy couldn't help but resent the fact that his friend had all but fallen off the face of the earth for years. Pushing these feelings aside, he attempted to enjoy the fact that his friendship with Patrick was renewed.

As it turned out, the tables had turned drastically. When they were ten years old, Jimmy had been in awe of Patrick because he had access to pornographic magazines. Now at 16, Patrick was fascinated by the fact that Jimmy played guitar. In fact, after watching Jimmy play a few songs, including the opening for 'Sweet Child O Mine', his mouth fell open in shock.

"Dude, you *so* have to start your own band. You're fucking awesome!" Patrick stared at him with wide eyes. "Women *love* musicians. They'll fuck anything that's in a band. If I were you, I'd use that to your advantage."

Jimmy couldn't help but grin at Patrick's comments. It was good to see that some things never changed. His friend certainly hadn't.

However a few weeks after the two began to talk again, Patrick made a startling announcement.

"Dude, you can't tell anyone this but I think my girlfriend is pregnant," Patrick anxiously ran a hand through his dark hair and watched Jimmy with pleading eyes. "I haven't told anyone but you. I don't know what I'll do if she is. I'm 16, I don't want a kid."

"I don't blame you," Jimmy replied gently. As depressing as it was to not have a sex life, at least he didn't have to worry about *those* problems. "What are you going to do if she is?"

"Shoot my fucking self before her parents find me," Patrick rolled his eyes. "How did this happen, man? Melissa's on the pill. Isn't that supposed to be like the best form of birth control going?"

"I don't know," Jimmy answered honestly. Considering he had no sexual experience at all, it was all a mystery to him. "Maybe she forgot to take one or something?"

"I don't think so. Trust me; she doesn't want to be pregnant either."

"Maybe she's not," Jimmy tried to reassure him. "Maybe it's a false alarm."

But it wasn't. A couple of weeks later, Patrick made the official announcement to Jimmy. He was going to be a father. His fifteen-year-old girlfriend was pregnant.

"She's trying to hide it from her parents, but eventually they're gonna find out," Patrick looked genuinely depressed. It was the first time Jimmy had ever seen him so down. "I don't know what the hell I'm going to do. If her parents don't kill me, my own will."

"Is she really upset?" Jimmy tried to see the situation from every side.

"Yeah, she wants an abortion," Patrick replied. "But I think they cost a lot and plus, wouldn't she need her parents' permission or something? We have to find a way that no one finds out."

In the end, Melissa's parents somehow found out. They were pissed. Then Patrick told his own parents.

"It was a huge screaming mess," he later confided in Jimmy. "But I guess we're keeping the baby. According to both our parents, we've got to face our responsibilities. Even though neither her nor I want a kid."

"Really?" Jimmy said, feeling pity for his friend. What a mess to be in.

"Yeah man," Patrick shook his head. "It fucking sucks. And she and I fight so much; I don't want to be with her anymore. Now I'm stuck with her *and* a kid."

Jimmy felt compassion for his situation. However, he had his own problems. Just as his mother had suggested the previous year, school was getting more difficult and he was starting to fail two courses early in the semester. His father contacted the school and asked them to suggest some possible tutors. They found one named Sally Graham.

When he first met her, Jimmy thought she was really pretty. His tutor had long chestnut, wavy hair that had a hint of red that could only be seen when the light hit it the right way. Her huge eyes were brown and unlike most of the girls in his classes, Sally didn't wear makeup. Not that she really needed it. She seemed to have this natural appeal to her that outshined some of the overly done up girls. And she did have a really nice body, Jimmy noticed. Not that she was the super pretty, popular type that strutted around the school – but he was interested.

Jimmy's tutor seemed a bit standoffish when they met, tilting her head slightly and listening very attentively to him when he spoke. She would calmly nod to show understanding and only after he completely finished his question or remark, would Sally patiently explain the necessary information to him. Her goal was to become a teacher and judging by how much she helped him out, Jimmy was pretty confident that she'd succeed.

"So, you're in grade twelve?" he casually asked her after a few weeks of tutoring sessions. His voice echoed through the empty classroom, making him sound more aggressive then he really was but she didn't seem to notice. Her eyes met his and she nodded.

"Yes, then next year it's off to university," she gave him a slight smile, the most Jimmy could hope for with Sally. Patrick referred to her as the 'cold, uptight bitch' whenever Jimmy mentioned that he thought she was cute.

"Man, you've got more chance of getting in a nun's pants than hers," Patrick rolled his eyes. "That girl won't give anyone the time of day."

But Jimmy didn't care. There was something about her that he liked and since she was his tutor, it wasn't like it seemed peculiar that he'd be making conversation with her. Even though it certainly wasn't easy.

"Cool," Jimmy said with his head down. "You're really smart, so I'm sure you can do it."

He looked up and noticed her smile easing across her face. Jimmy thought of how he once had complimented his vocal coach and she practically glowed. Maybe all girls were the same with compliments. Evidently, this girl wanted to be known for her brains.

"Thank you," she replied and held eye contact with him.

"No problem," Jimmy shrugged shyly. "You'd have to be a genius to teach someone as dumb as me anything."

This time, she broke into a laugh. "You're not dumb, Jimmy," she insisted. "You're just not interested in these kinds of classes so you probably tune out when the teacher is talking. Besides you've got some kind of crappy teachers too, which doesn't help. You just learn better one on one."

He definitely wanted to go one on one with her, but remained silent and smiled.

After his compliment on her brains, he noticed that Sally seemed to warm up to him over the ensuing weeks. That's when Patrick suggested he ask her out.

"I can't," Jimmy said, shaking his head. "She's my tutor. I have to see her all the time; I'd be too embarrassed if she said no."

Plus remembering the time he asked Suzanne Bordon out and her blatant mockery of him didn't help. In the end, he didn't have to ask her out.

Just before school was about to let out for Christmas holidays, Sally asked him out.

Chapter nine

"Fuck off, man!" Patrick's green eyes became huge when he found out about Jimmy's upcoming date with Sally. The two boys were sitting in the Groome's cluttered basement on a cold December night, just a few days before Christmas. Jimmy was attempting to show his friend how to play guitar, but to no avail. Unlike Sean, he was unable to break the skill into steps. Not that it mattered. Patrick had immediately forgotten his lessons after Jimmy's news. "Are you serious? Sally Graham asked you out on a *date*? That's wicked."

"I was surprised," Jimmy quietly admitted. And nervous, he silently thought to himself. After all, it was his first date. However he wasn't about to admit that fact to Patrick. It was embarrassing enough to *know* that he was way behind everyone else his age in the dating game, without confessing it to his friend. "She's cool."

"That's putting it mildly, man," Patrick said while carefully setting Jimmy's guitar back in the case. "So, where are you taking her?"

"Don't know," Jimmy answered honestly. It was something he had given a lot of thought but still had no idea. "Maybe to a movie?"

"That's cool," Patrick agreed. "Chicks love going to movies. Make sure it's one of those girly movies, they're always into those stupid things."

But when Jimmy told his sister about the upcoming date a couple of days later, she disagreed with Patrick's opinion on the matter. In fact, Jillian insisted that Jimmy do pretty much anything *but* take Sally to the movies.

"Why not?" Jimmy asked attempting to understand why going to the movies was a horrible way to spend a first date. He had so much to learn about women.

" 'Cause you want to get to know her better," Jillian explained. The siblings were sitting in the dimly lit basement watching television when Jimmy announced the upcoming date. She automatically forgot all about the program they were viewing and focused on him. "A movie is fine later on, but when you first start dating someone it's important to just hang out and get to know them."

"But I already kind of know her," Jimmy replied. "She's my tutor. We talk all the time."

"Really?" Jillian asked, a smile lighting her tired face. "So if it doesn't work out, does that mean you'll start flunking out of school?"

Jimmy hadn't really considered the consequences if they weren't to hit it off in the dating situation. In fact, it hadn't even occurred to him that things could end poorly down the line.

"Then again, who am I to talk?" Jillian shrugged. "I met Rob in summer school. And that's working out great."

Jimmy's sister had been dating Rob since they first met in July and things were still going strong. In fact, she had even admitted to her younger brother that she thought her current boyfriend was 'the one' and the two were talking about possibly getting a place together the following year.

"So, I should take her anywhere *but* to a movie?" Jimmy anxiously repeated her advice. "So, to a restaurant or something?" He had no idea where Sally would like to go on their date. Where did kids his age go on dates? All Jimmy really knew was what he saw on television, and in TV land everyone always seemed to go out for dinner or drinks.

"Exactly," Jillian nodded thoughtfully. "I'd suggest that you check with her, but you don't have to necessarily take her to a restaurant. Let her make the suggestion."

"What if I run out of things to talk to her about?"

"Do you run out of things to talk about now?" Jillian countered with raised eyebrows.

"No, but we're doing schoolwork so we always have a lot of stuff to talk about," Jimmy considered. "We talk about other stuff, but not really a lot."

"Just ask her questions. What does she do for fun? Does she have a favorite movie? What kind of music does she like? That kind of thing," Jillian advised with a growing smile. "I think it's so cute that you have a date."

The way she said it made Jimmy feel like a loser. He was pretty sure that his sister had no ill intentions, but it was as if she were thinking of how it was cute that he *finally* had a date. He just smiled, not really knowing how to respond.

"Promise me that you won't tell mom and dad though," Jimmy insisted, his eyes begging her. "I don't want mom making a big deal out of this and acting weird."

"Oh, don't worry about that," Jillian said with a grin on her face. "You don't have to tell me what mom is like. She'd totally be all going on about how her "baby finally has a girlfriend' and stuff. Dad would probably be cool with it, but mom would be totally weird."

"Sally isn't really my girlfriend," Jimmy quickly reminded her. "It's just a date. It doesn't mean she wants to be my girlfriend."

"I bet she will," Jillian insisted, playfully punching his arm. "I bet she'll be crazy about you."

Jimmy shared a smile with his sister. Although there were times when he felt very detached from Jillian, there were many more when he sensed her unconditional love. Regardless of what the future had in store for either of them, he knew that they would always be bonded together because of the horrible afternoon in 1982 when both their innocence was ripped away.

As the days crept by without a phone call from Sally, Jimmy began to worry that she had changed her mind. It wasn't like he had any positive experiences with women to draw on, so it was very easy for him to naturally jump to a negative conclusion. He kept remembering his experience with Suzanne, when he thought she was interested in him and ended up disappointed and ridiculed by his classmates. But his fears were unfounded. She called him two days after Christmas.

During their brief conversation, Jimmy discovered that Sally had a never-ending stream of relatives visiting her home over the holidays, so she hadn't had the chance to get together with him. They made plans to meet at a popular coffee shop that evening.

When he first hung up the phone, Jimmy was excited - then nervous. She always appeared to be so calm and confident that he assumed Sally had many boyfriends in the past. Would she be able to recognize his lack of dating experience? Should he try to kiss her? He had never kissed a girl in his life - what if he messed it up? He didn't want to look like a loser. After all, she was a year older then Jimmy. Chances were good that Sally was used to dating older guys who knew how to kiss, what to talk about, and how to act when on a date. Jimmy was clueless.

They met that evening at seven. Sally was already at the coffee shop when Jimmy arrived. She looked very attractive, wearing a deep, red sweater that hugged her curves and a casual pair of jeans. Her hair somehow looked prettier than usual, but Jimmy couldn't figure out why. She also appeared to be wearing a little makeup, which she never did at school and Jimmy could smell perfume from across their table. Not knowing how else to start their conversation, he looked Sally straight in the eye and complimented her, "You look very pretty."

Sally's face turned red as she thanked him, commenting on how Jimmy looked great too. Glancing down at the black, leather jacket he'd been given for Christmas, and his casual t-shirt and jeans, Jimmy wasn't really sure how he looked any different than usual. However, he smiled and thanked her just the same.

After buying Sally a coffee and himself a diet Pepsi, Jimmy decided to take his sister's advice and ask her pretty much every question under the sun. He quickly learned that she had an older brother who was in university, a younger sister in grade ten and that her parents were much older than his own and very old-fashioned. In fact, the only reason Sally was on a date that night was because her parents thought she was hanging out with a girlfriend.

"Your parents won't let you date?" Jimmy raised his eyebrows. So much for his assumption that she had an extensive dating history.

"No," Sally replied, shaking her head. "They're really strict about that kind of thing. I think they worry that if I have a boyfriend I won't concentrate on my studies and that I'll lose sight of my goals."

"Was your brother allowed to date when he was your age?"

"Yes," Sally nodded. "But they claim that guys don't let dating make them lose sight of their goals."

Jimmy thought that was weird. After all, his sister was head over heals for this Rob guy and still managed to get good grades in college. When he shared this information with Sally, she shrugged.

"I know, but it's just easier to not argue with them. I don't exactly have guys falling at my feet anyway, so I never felt the need to really argue the point with them."

Jimmy began to feel a little more at ease as the night went on and started to talk about his music. He told Sally about the guitar and singing lessons. "Me and my friend Patrick are thinking about starting a band this summer," He grinned. "I don't know if it will go too well considering he can't play an instrument. But he seems to think he can sing, so I guess it's possible."

"That's awesome," her brown eyes widened. "Can I hear you play sometime?"

"Sure," he agreed enthusiastically. Although he wasn't sure of much, Jimmy knew that he was a talented guitarist. "Anytime."

As the evening went on, it became clear that the date was coming to an end. Once they were out in the crisp night air, Jimmy walked Sally to her car. Their conversation seemed to become awkward at that point, as he wondered whether or not to kiss her. He was absolutely frightened even thinking of the idea. His heart pounded furiously, as Jimmy stuttered through their conversation. Sally looked flustered, completely uncomfortable as she listened to him talk about something that didn't even make sense.

He wasn't sure if it was because Sally was as nervous as him, or if she simply wanted to shut him up, but suddenly she leaned in and kissed him. He could taste a sweet flavor on her lips while a gentle fragrance filled his lungs. Closing his eyes, he felt her soft lips barely against his own and he quickly followed her lead, hoping to not look like a moron. But if he did, she certainly gave him no indication. In fact, although the kiss was brief, there was something very special about it. The two of them shared a moment of vulnerability that made Jimmy suddenly see that maybe he wasn't the only person who was really nervous about that night. Perhaps she was just as worried about the kiss, her appearance and what to talk about as he had been. Maybe their fears and feelings weren't really so far apart in the end.

And as he drove home that night, Jimmy felt like he had faced a huge fear and conquered it. Maybe this thing with girls wasn't so intimidating after all.

Chapter ten

"So when do I get to meet her?" Annette Groome's eyes lit up when she learned the news that her youngest child was dating. Jimmy's original plan to hide Sally's existence quickly went down the drain when she started to call their house regularly. His mother caught on right away and he confessed the truth to her. "She sounds really nice on the phone." Annette commented.

"She's cool," Jimmy said, attempting to be nonchalant about the topic when in fact he was quite excited. He really liked Sally and she seemed to feel the same way about him. The two had been spending a great deal of time together since their original date. Of course, Sally had to lie to her parents and say she was giving Jimmy extra tutoring during their time together, since she wasn't allowed to date.

"Well, that's great!" His mother replied with a smile. Jimmy was surprised that she hadn't asked a whole slew of questions or given him some kind of advice. When Jillian started to date, their mother seemed to constantly hover over her with warnings and concerns. Maybe it was different with sons, Jimmy decided. Of course his assumption was made much too quickly. Later that same night, his dad dropped by Jimmy's room to have a discussion with him.

"Your mother wanted me to talk to you," John Groome spoke gently as he sat across from his son. Jimmy automatically dreaded the conversation, but was relieved that at least it was with his dad and not his mom. That would've been way too uncomfortable. "She told me you're dating someone?"

"Yes," Jimmy replied and quickly told him about Sally, mentioning how she was originally just his tutor. "She's really pretty and nice." Then he felt awkward and stopped. How much should his parents know about his dating life? Not that there was much to tell, so far he and Sally had only spent some time together and the most intimate thing they had done was share a few kisses. Something that Jimmy felt much more comfortable with now, than he had that first night they hung out.

"Well, that's nice, Jimmy. I'm happy for you," His father seemed sincere in his comments and the two shared a smile. Tilting his head, he added "But your mom was just concerned that you'd be careful Take things slow. There's no need to rush into anything. Just have fun together."

Jimmy nodded. He knew the underlining message here. Don't have sex. He wondered what his parents would've thought, had they known about Patrick's current predicament? His girlfriend was now four months pregnant.

"However," His father continued, "if you're ever in a situation where you think something *might* happen and you feel uncomfortable purchasing anything for protection, I want you to feel free to come talk to me."

Jimmy felt his face get hot. His father was offering to buy him condoms? Was that the underlining message? He couldn't even imagine broaching the topic with him, but then again, Jimmy also couldn't see himself going to the drugstore to buy them. And clearly if Sally wasn't allowed to date, she wasn't on birth control pills. Not that they were even close to that stage of things.

"I don't want you to be embarrassed. It's perfectly natural if something were to happen," His father ignored the fact that Jimmy was clearly very uncomfortable with their conversation and continued on. "Just don't tell your mother that we had this conversation." He then added, with a grin on his face. "She thinks I came up here to tell you *not* to do anything, but I'm a little more realistic than that."

Jimmy smiled. That sounded about right. His mother was still in denial that Jillian was having sex, although it was clear that she had been for quite some time. Not to mention the fact that she spent the night with Rob on a regular basis, now that he'd found his own apartment. Jimmy wasn't sure what the big deal was considering she had recently turned nineteen.

"Okay?" His father asked, standing up from the office chair and slowly heading toward the door. "If you ever need anything, I want you to know that you can always approach me."

Jimmy knew his father meant well, but there was simply no way he'd ever approach him about that part of his life. If he needed to talk to anyone there was always Patrick, who knew everything about sex and dating. At least that's how it seemed.

Patrick talked very openly about his sex life, with both his current and previous girlfriends. He wasn't shy about sharing details of his intimate life. Now that his girlfriend was pregnant, Patrick claimed that they had even more sex than before. "Hey, she's horny all the time and it's not like I can knock her up again," He laughed. "As my brother says, if you're stuck with a piece of crap car, you may as well drive the fuck out of it before you throw it in the dump."

Jimmy was a little stunned by Patrick's crass remark but couldn't help but laugh at the same time. His friend hardly made it a secret that he had no intention of staying with Melissa after she had the baby. In fact he even told Jimmy that since the she was pregnant anyway, that her parents saw no issue with the baby's father spending the night with their daughter now. Something he took complete advantage of for his own pleasure.

With Christmas vacation coming to an end, Jimmy was a little disappointed that he couldn't spend New Year's Eve with Sally. Although it would've meant her meeting his parents, he had been willing to overlook that uncomfortable detail in order to hang out with her that evening. Unfortunately she didn't think it was a good idea.

"My parents aren't suspicious that I'm supposedly giving you extra help with your schoolwork during the holidays," Sally said during one of their late evening phone conversations. "But I think they'd be a little suspicious of me giving you tutoring lessons on New Year's Eve. Even *I'm* not that big of a nerd."

Jimmy smiled on the other end of the line and with disappointment, agreed that she was right. The last thing they wanted to do was to make her parents suspect that anything was going on between them. They already kept her on a strict schedule and if they learned of her dishonesty with them, he'd probably never have the chance to spend time with her.

So instead, he spent New Year's Eve with his parents in the family's drafty basement, watching a live show airing from Toronto. It wasn't so bad. His mom ordered in pizza, they talked and laughed while viewing various bands playing live on television. For the most part, the family wasn't really paying attention to the entertainment portion of the Toronto celebration until one specific band came on. It was Second in Line.

"That's Sean's band!" Jimmy felt his eyes widen in surprise. Turning up the volume, he moved closer to the television while his parents contributed positive remarks in the background. Not that he was listening. Jimmy's attention was glued to the set.

Although Jimmy had heard that Second in Line was building in popularity, he had no idea that they were at the level of success that allowed them to play amongst some famous celebrity bands. He was impressed and proud. Jimmy wished he had stayed in contact with his former guitar teacher, so he could congratulate him. Unfortunately he hadn't. But Jimmy knew one thing was for sure, he'd have to find a way to see Sean's band play live.

Jimmy wondered what it would've felt like to play in front of thousands in an outdoor show. It must've been beyond exciting. He had only been in the audience for a couple of big shows in his life – and that included a Kiss concert with his dad a couple years earlier. And even then, he could feel an intoxicating energy in the room. It was the most amazing experience of his life. It was overwhelming and energizing at the same time.

When the cameras occasionally jumped to members of the audience singing along to Second in Line songs, it was clear that the band had a huge following. Jimmy imagined himself on stage with all those fans watching him play guitar. His heart raced as he continued to stare at the television, transfixed by what he saw. *This is living.*

But there was something very different about Sean. Jimmy couldn't pin point it, but it was almost as if his zest for life had been drained from him as he played before the audience. Jimmy just assumed he was nervous. After all, how could you feel anything but excitement when playing in front of such a massive audience?

The next day, Jimmy had a whole new lease on life. He was going to lose more weight, learn to perfect his guitar skills and, if possible at all, Jimmy wanted to start a band. Just like Sean, he wanted to play in front of cheering audiences. He wanted it more than anything. And when

Patrick stopped by later that same day, Jimmy told him about watching Sean's band on television.

"That's fucking cool!" Patrick admitted, while flipping through the television channels. "The same guy who was teaching you guitar is in a famous band now? Wow, no wonder you're such an awesome guitar player."

"I don't think I'm as good as him," Jimmy admitted, "but I plan to get better." And he would. Although he spent a great deal of time practicing, he now intended to work even harder to become the best.

Patrick seemed to stop what he was doing and turn his full attention to Jimmy. He slowly nodded, one eyebrow lifted slightly as he listened.

"I want to do that, man." Jimmy spoke honestly and hoped that Patrick wouldn't make fun of him. He paused for a moment. "I want to start a band. I want to do what Sean is doing. I can't imagine doing anything else."

Patrick started to nod while a grin crossed his face. "Sounds like a plan. I can sing, if you play guitar."

"Cool." Jimmy replied. He knew he was onto something. It felt right. He wanted to start a band and become famous. He wanted to be a rock star.

Chapter eleven

Jimmy Groome's life started to take a turn for the better. No longer the fat kid, he was toned and in better shape than most of the other kids in school. He had a pretty girlfriend in Sally and a best friend in Patrick. He was about to start a band. Everything seemed to be falling into place. He felt excited and hopeful about life. Then things changed. And it started with a phone call in early March of '89.

Jimmy woke up on a Saturday morning to the sound of knocking on his door. Groaning, he turned to glance at his clock. It wasn't even 9 am yet. His parents usually let him sleep in on the weekend. "Yeah?" His voice croaked. "What is it?"

Jimmy's bedroom door slowly opened and his mother stuck her head in the room. Her forehead was wrinkled in worry, automatically alerting him that something was wrong. "Honey, can you get the phone?" She hesitated. "It's Sally and she sounds very upset."

Wearing only his boxers, he wasted no time jumping out of bed, grabbing his sweatshirt and running to the nearest phone in Jillian's room. She was at Rob's so he would have some privacy. Nervously, he picked up the receiver and heard his mother hang up the downstairs phone.

"Jimmy, they found out!" Sally was crying and barely audible. "One of my mom's friends saw us out last night and told my mother."

Still groggy, Jimmy thought back to the previous night. He had taken Sally out for coffee, which was the only thing he could afford until finding a job. It seemed pretty innocent. People who were just friends did that kind of thing; it didn't indicate that they were necessarily dating.

"But we could've been meeting to talk about school stuff, couldn't we?" Jimmy stretched, glancing at the Billy Idol posters on his sister's walls. "It doesn't mean they know anything."

"No, I'm not talking about when we went for coffee," Sally corrected him. "I'm talking about later on, when we were in the car kissing."

Although the couple usually attempted to keep their affections limited to his house when Jimmy's parents weren't around, there were times when they *did* kiss in public, but usually when no one else was around to see. The last thing they wanted to do was risk her parents finding out that they were dating. Apparently, their efforts had not been enough.

"Oh," Jimmy replied and bit his lower lip. "So, what did you tell them?"

"The truth," Sally spoke honestly and began to cry again. "I told them that we were dating and they said we had to break up. I tried to explain to them that we've been together for two months and it hasn't affected my grades, but they wouldn't listen. They said it was too close to graduation and there was too much at stake right now to mess it up with raging hormones."

Jimmy wondered if that's why his marks were so bad in school. He definitely had raging hormones, but his own parents certainly hadn't forbidden him to date. In fact, they seemed to encourage it. Sally's parents weren't being fair.

"I don't understand," Jimmy confessed. "You're almost eighteen. They can't run your life forever." Suddenly he envisioned his own sister yelling the same thing out to their parents only a couple of years earlier. Was it just a girl thing? Did parents not want their daughters to grow up? "Don't they trust you?"

"They say it's not me that they don't trust. It's you." Sally sniffed and Jimmy felt his heart sink. "I told them that they could meet you, but they said that it didn't matter. I am not to date until I graduate."

Sally's graduation wasn't until June. Three months. Grief filled his heart when he began to realize that there wasn't a solution to this problem. Her parents had already made up their minds and they weren't about to listen to reason. They were being stubborn and unfair.

"Why don't you just fight it," Jimmy felt slightly annoyed with Sally's passiveness. "You have a right to say something. You don't have to sit back and just take it, tell them how you feel. Tell them you aren't doing anything wrong; that *we* aren't doing anything wrong."

"You don't understand," Sally began to whine. "My parents won't listen. Jimmy, I can't just tell them that I won't follow their rules. It's not that simple."

Thinking back to how his sister reacted in previous years, Jimmy had to disagree. Jillian certainly had a stronger will to fight for what she believed in even at the age of 14 or 15, so why couldn't Sally? He didn't understand.

"Whatever," Jimmy finally replied, suddenly full of resentment. "Do what you got to do," and he hung up on her.

Staring at the phone, he was a little stunned. Jimmy had never hung up on anyone in his life. But it simply pissed him off that when it came right down to it, Sally couldn't even take a stand for their relationship. It was almost like she used her parents as an excuse to get rid of him.

The phone rang again almost immediately and he ignored it. As he left his sister's room, his mother met him in the hallway with a curious expression on her face. "Sally is on the phone again. Do you want to get the phone downstairs?"

"Nope," Jimmy grabbed a towel in the hallway closet and headed for the bathroom. "I'm taking a shower." Entering the bathroom, he slammed the door shut. He didn't need this shit. What was Sally's problem? Pushing the thoughts from his head, Jimmy turned on the shower and removed his clothes before ducking underneath the hot flow of water. He really cared about her and she had just dropped him like nothing. And because her *parents* said she couldn't date? Even his mother, a super religious woman, allowed her kids to date. Sally's story was a crock of shit.

After finishing his shower, Jimmy pulled on his robe and headed downstairs. His dad sat at the kitchen table, sipping a coffee and reading the newspaper. He glanced up when Jimmy entered the room.

"Good morning," he set down his coffee cup. "It's early for you."

"Yeah, I had a rather shitty wake up call this morning," Jimmy poured himself a cup of coffee. Since dating Sally, he had developed a taste for the brew that once seemed bitter and revolting to him. Sitting across from his dad, he bit his lower lip.

"Your mom said that Sally called and she was crying. That definitely wouldn't be a pleasant way to wake up," his father said and closed his newspaper.

"It wasn't," Jimmy confirmed, adding extra sugar to his coffee. "Apparently, her parents found out we were dating and told her we had to break up."

"That seems kind of harsh. Am I missing some details, Jimmy?"

"Nope," Jimmy reassured his father, seeing the suspicious look in his eyes. "We didn't do anything wrong. It's just that she was never allowed to date in the first place and apparently we broke the rule."

"So, she's been keeping it a secret that the two of you were together?" John Groome appeared curious. "Did you know that she wasn't allowed to date?"

"Well, yeah," Jimmy confessed, realizing that he probably didn't look any better for being part of the lie. "I just figured it wasn't a big deal anyway. She's almost 18, Dad. She's going to university next year. It seems kind of stupid."

"I have to admit, I don't agree with her parents' rules," his father admitted. "But they are *their* rules and it isn't really my place to get involved. Is there a reason why they have such an issue with her dating?"

"No, they just think that if she's dating she'll lose her interest in school work or her marks will fall, some shit like that." Jimmy said while rolling his eyes. "Please, until Sally I never dated at all and my marks sucked ass, so I don't get their logic at all."

His dad let out a quick laugh. "Well, you definitely could build a case there, Jimmy," John Groome sat back in his chair. "Your marks actually improved a great deal."

"Yeah, well I can't make a case to them when they don't even want to meet me," Jimmy said, sinking farther down in his chair. Suddenly, he felt depressed.

"It's certainly not a fair situation," his father agreed. "Maybe you should call her back. She called a few minutes ago and I think your mom took a message from Sally earlier too."

"What did she say?"

"Nothing to me," his father stood up and poured another cup of coffee. "Just asked that you call her back. She may have said more to your mother, I'm not sure. You can ask her when she gets back from the grocery store."

Jimmy sighed loudly and tried to decide whether or not to call Sally. He didn't.

Patrick dropped by after lunch and Jimmy told him about the fight.

"That sucks man," Patrick shook his head. Since Jimmy's parents weren't at home, the boys were planning to practice guitar. "But why didn't she just say something? Fuck, if I can face *my* parents after knocking up a girl, then what's her problem? You were just dating, not having S&M parties and doing drugs for fuck's sake. Sally needs to grow a backbone."

"That's kinda what I thought," Jimmy confessed. Even his mother thought the whole situation was strange. In fact, Annette Groome was a little insulted that Sally's parents assumed the worst of Jimmy without even meeting him.

"Oh so get this," Patrick shook his head in disgust, while rolling his green eyes. "Now, my parents want me to get a job. Which is fine, I don't mind. But I have to give like all my paycheck to my ex since she's pregnant. As if I even know that she's spending the money on the kid."

"Your ex? I thought you and Melissa were still together?" Jimmy wrinkled his forehead. "Thought you were like doing her every night?"

Patrick laughed. "Yeah, that didn't last long. So we started fighting all the time and we broke up."

"Well, you wanted to end it with her anyway, didn't you?"

"Yup," Patrick nodded with a grin on his face. "Done."

"I gotta find a job too," Jimmy sighed. "I keep applying everywhere, but when you don't have experience, no one wants you."

"Tell me 'bout it," Patrick agreed. "Mind you, I'm not looking too hard since I can't even keep all the money anyway."

"They can't make you give your entire pay check over," Jimmy insisted. "They don't got a right to do that, baby or not."

"Everyone seems to be in agreement on it," Patrick complained. "Just like having the baby, everyone seemed to think it was a good idea except me, but once again I'm out voted and have no say in my own fucking life. Lovely."

Jimmy didn't envy Patrick's situation at all.

Patrick once again attempted to play guitar. He wasn't very good even though he got his own for Christmas and claimed to be practicing.

Then Jimmy played and Patrick sang. There was no denying that his cocky friend had a pretty good voice. Unfortunately, once they both started working, Jimmy was concerned neither would have the time for a band, especially with school factored in. When he raised his concerns to Patrick, his friend wasn't worried.

"We'll find the time," Patrick insisted. "Fuck that, I have to have something for myself. If I can't work a job and keep the money and I've got to go to school, I want to have something I want to do."

The boys continued to practice until the doorbell interrupted them. Both ran upstairs and Jimmy answered. Sally was waiting outside. Patrick rolled his eyes, grabbing a muffin from the kitchen counter to eat, while Jimmy and Sally shared an awkward moment.

"Hi," Jimmy finally said.

"Hi, I just dropped by 'cause you weren't answering the phone and I needed to talk to you," Sally said nervously, as she walked in the door. "I thought you were avoiding me."

"You *dumped* him," Patrick abruptly replied to Sally's comment, earning him a glare. "What do you expect him to fucking do? Run to the phone every time you call. Not likely."

Jimmy wanted to laugh but didn't. Sally continued to glare at Patrick who seemed unconcerned with her reaction.

"Anyway man," Patrick said, looking past Sally as he finished his muffin. "I gotta jet. Apparently, if you knock up someone, even if *they* dump you, you're still supposed to go to some kind of birthing classes with them." Grabbing his jacket, he turned toward Jimmy just as he reached the door. "Don't you wish you had my life?" He rolled his eyes as he walked out.

"Why are you friends with him?" Sally asked, glaring toward the closed door.

"Cause I like him," Jimmy replied hastily. Why did Sally think she had a say on who his friends were? "So you stopped by because you wanted to talk to me?"

"Yes," Sally replied, meeting his eyes. "I'm sorry about everything, I really am. My parents are being unreasonable and I can't get them to listen to my side."

"Whatever."

"Jimmy, please," Sally said with tears in her eyes. "I don't want to break up. I care about you."

"Well, what are we supposed to do?" Jimmy quietly asked. "I mean, your parents won't let you out of the house if they think you'll be with me."

"They said I can still tutor you," she asserted. "But just at school, not at your house anymore."

"You're here now, aren't you?" Jimmy was becoming slightly irritated with the whole situation. It was getting way too complicated.

"I'm not supposed to be," Sally admitted. "I snuck out. But I had to see you."

Without saying another word, she moved closer to Jimmy and began to kiss him. As much as he wanted to tell her to stop, he couldn't. The kiss was very explosive and he felt her hands traveling down his body. He heard himself moaning as her fingers worked on the zipper of his pants, while his own hands moved up her sweater. He felt his breathing becoming increasingly heavier until a bright light from outside ripped him out of his lustful stupor. His parents were home.

Chapter Twelve

Things really heated up between Jimmy and Sally after they 'broke up'. Suddenly, the relationship that had once been limited to kissing and holding hands became something completely different. With the exception of their tutoring sessions that were held at school, every time they met was in secret. And every meeting they had was intense.

"So, you guys seriously haven't had sex yet?" Patrick's green eyes lit up as he asked one night during one of their 'jam' sessions, which still only consisted of the two of them in Jimmy's basement. Both were actively looking for a couple more guys to form a band with them, but hadn't been successful yet. The only people they had found were either terrible or assholes. "Wow, I would've thought that she'd want her cherry popped by now. Jesus, didn't you say that since that shit with her parents that Sally's been all over you?"

"Yes," Jimmy reluctantly admitted. That was an understatement. At first, he felt like her main goal was just to get him hard and then leave him to suffer. Not knowing how to remedy that situation, he had confessed his circumstance to Patrick. Of course, his friend knew exactly what to do. He told Jimmy to make Sally want him as much as *he* wanted her. Jimmy had done just that and it worked. "I mean, we're doing everything *but* having sex."

"Seriously?" Patrick's eyes widened. "You got that Miss Uptight to go down on you? For real, man?"

Jimmy nodded. Of course she had no idea what she was doing when she got there, but he felt it wasn't necessary to share that information.

All he knew was that every time they fooled around, he wanted to go all the way. But she was scared and that's what Jimmy reported back to Patrick.

"Yeah," he said after giving it a moment's thought. "Girls are like that. They're all into love and shit. Guys just wanna get laid. It's totally messed up."

"But we plan to do it soon," Jimmy said, fingering a difficult chord sequence. "She said between now and when I turn seventeen; and that's only about a month away."

"Yeah man, your birthday is in May, isn't it?" Patrick said, reaching into his pocket. Pulling out his wallet, he threw three condoms at Jimmy. "You may as well have 'em cause I don't need them."

Patrick was back on with his pregnant girlfriend, although Jimmy was skeptical of how long that would last. After the baby was born, the girl's parents insisted that she go back on the pill, so Patrick automatically assumed he was home free. Jimmy was surprised at his friend's casual attitude, but gladly took the condoms.

"Thanks, man," Jimmy slid them into his pocket and wondered if he'd have a chance to use them in the immediate future. He didn't want to wait another month.

"And if you can't figure out how to use them," Patrick said with a grin, "You don't deserve to get fucked."

After that night, Jimmy wouldn't see much of Patrick for the next couple of weeks. His daughter Hope was born three days later. Jimmy was surprised when his friend called to tell him the news with excitement in his voice. Then within a week, Patrick found a job. It was just at a fast food restaurant, but it was still employment. And three days after that, he called Jimmy with a proposition.

"I hate the job. It sucks," Patrick confessed to Jimmy over the phone. "But, they're hiring and I told them about you. So, if you want a job, come in and talk to my boss."

"I thought you said it sucked," Jimmy replied hesitantly.

"It does," Patrick boasted. "But if you're there with me, it'll be more fun. Especially when I'm spitting on the food for the asshole customers. Plus, we can cover for each other when we steal the food."

"You steal food?" Jimmy laughed, not surprised by his friend's antics. "Seriously?"

"Like *every* fucking day, man." Patrick's voice was full of humor.

"Wow, is it that easy?" Jimmy asked. Not that he really wanted to eat a lot of greasy burgers, especially after dropping all his weight. He was now down to a 'normal' size and even his sister regularly commented on how she had a 'hot kid brother'. And Sally certainly didn't mind his body, especially now that he lifted weights in the basement every night.

"Man, with the two of us there, it'll be a blast," Patrick coaxed, attempting to sell the job. It wasn't much, but it was better than nothing.

Jimmy agreed to drop by to talk to the manager of "Top Dog Burger" later that day. He was immediately hired for the popular fast food chain and started working that same week. Within his first shift, Jimmy quickly saw why his friend hated it. Customers were rude and didn't care that employees were new to the job. Children ran through the dining room, laughing and screaming, often dropping their food on the floor. Kids they went to school with regularly went out of their way to give Jimmy and Patrick a hard time. Overall, the experience was horrendous, and the pay wasn't much better.

"I go home every night and stink like a fucking burger," Patrick complained to Jimmy, who sympathized. Of course, it did give the two some spending money. Although Patrick had to hand some of the pay over to his girlfriend for the baby, the percentage of his money taken away seemed reasonable to Jimmy. What was left of Patrick's pay was what he referred to as his 'fun' money.

"If I'm going to get fucked up the ass by customers all day," Patrick obnoxiously reported to Jimmy one day, "then you better believe that I'm having fun with the money that's mine at the end of the week."

That's when the two boys started to drink. It was, of course, something Patrick had done before, unlike Jimmy, whose only experience with drinking was limited to wine at Christmas or during special occasions. Although Jimmy didn't like the bitter taste of alcohol in the beginning, he quickly realized that getting drunk was the best escape from real life. It relaxed his mind from all the thoughts that mockingly danced around, intruding on his peaceful existence. And it was something they started to do every weekend. Neither of their parents knew and Sally didn't like it.

"Where do you drink if your parents are so strict about that stuff?" she asked curiously, her eyebrows knotted up in frustration.

"At Patrick's house," Jimmy reluctantly confessed, looking into her disapproving eyes. "His parents are never home on the weekends."

"You shouldn't be doing that," she insisted, apprehension crossing her face. "I had a cousin die of alcohol poisoning. That's why I don't drink."

Jimmy didn't say a word. After all, this was the girl he wanted to have sex with, so he wasn't about to argue with her about anything. Best not to push his luck.

"Yeah, you're probably right," he smiled sweetly, something Jimmy had noticed that she liked. "I probably won't do it again."

But he did. Every weekend. He usually threw up, sobered up and got home before his midnight curfew. Patrick said that they just had to start drinking early in the night and then everything would be cool before either had to face their parents.

"Thank my brother," Patrick shrugged when Jimmy remarked on the smart idea. "He's done all this shit before and always got away with it. He knows the drill."

They drank whatever they could get their hands on. It didn't matter if it was beer or bourbon. They didn't care. As long as it gave them a buzz, Patrick said they could always find something to mix with it to kill the taste. It took them away from the stresses of school, work and in Patrick's case, fatherhood. Neither thought it was a big deal.

Jimmy was impressed that his friend actually stepped up to the plate when it came to the baby. Patrick paid child support, and tried to help Melissa with Hope, although he admitted to not knowing much about babies. "She's cute," Patrick referred to his baby girl while the two were at work one night, "But a lot of work and no matter what I do, I always seem to be doing it wrong. I can't change a diaper right. I never know what to do when the baby cries. I'm trying though."

Although Patrick was not as bitter about his role as a father once the baby was born, he very quickly developed a wandering eye again. Jimmy knew that it was just a matter of time before his relationship with Melissa went belly up for good.

As April of '89 slowly came to an end, Jimmy's hope of losing his virginity seemed to be fading. He was starting to wonder if Sally ever had any intention at all of having sex with him. They still fooled around regularly, but he wanted the real deal. He was growing tired of waiting. But every time he brought it up, Sally always had the same excuses.

"Jimmy, I'm taking enough of a chance sneaking out to see you now," Sally reminded him. They usually got together at his house when Jimmy's parents were out. They assumed Sally was just his tutor again; so they had no idea that she was often in their house, or about their regular make out sessions in his room. They thought he spent all his time with Patrick or playing guitar in the basement.

"I don't see why that would matter," Jimmy said suspiciously. "Sneaking out is sneaking out."

"But if we actually do it, especially for the first time," Sally explained, looking at the floor as her face grew red. "I don't want to just jump out of bed and go home like nothing important happened. Maybe it's not a big deal to you, but it is to me."

Jimmy felt his heart sink. Of course it was a big deal to her. All along, he was treating it like a challenge, but to her, it was special. Not that it wasn't to him, but ever since their short break up earlier that year, he felt himself sometimes holding back on an emotional level. Clearly, she wasn't doing the same.

"Jimmy, I really care about you," her eyes watered slightly as she spoke and she quickly wiped away a stray tear. "I don't want to just hook up with you and be casual about it. I want us to be together."

"We will, once you graduate," Jimmy assured her. "I don't plan to go anywhere."

"But what about when I go to university this fall?" she asked, her brown eyes studying him intently. "What are we going to do then? I might end up living in another province."

"It'll only be for a year," Jimmy gently reminded her. "Then I'll go wherever you are. I don't care what I have to do." He said the words that she wanted to hear. It wasn't that he didn't mean them so much as Jimmy wasn't sure if he meant them *yet*. But as he'd soon learn, sex changes everything.

Chapter thirteen

"I'm engaged!" Jillian screamed excitedly only seconds after arriving home from her weekend at Rob's apartment. Waving her hand through the air to indicate she was wearing a shiny, new ring, Jillian's face was glowing. Jimmy had never seen her so happy. Not to mention their mother, who quickly ran over to hug her daughter. Jimmy couldn't help but notice that Rob wasn't with her and thought that was kind of weird. Wasn't that something they should be announcing together? It didn't seem like they were dating very long – or were they?

"Congratulations!" John Groome was entering the kitchen at the same time as Jillian's announcement and quickly rushed over to hug his daughter. Reluctantly, Jimmy rose from the kitchen table where he was doing homework to join the family in their huddle at the kitchen door, while his parents inspected Jillian's diamond. Both parents commented on how beautiful the piece of jewelry was, while Jimmy smiled and agreed even though he really had no idea about that kind of thing.

A stray tear escaped his sister's eyes as she pulled Jimmy into a hug. A strong vanilla scent that he assumed was perfume, filled his lungs, causing his stomach to turn. Quickly excusing himself, he rushed upstairs to the bathroom where he threw up. Leaning over the toilet, he heard his mother calling his name outside the door.

"Honey, were you sick again?" Her voice was full of concern. "Maybe I should take you to the hospital in case it *is* food poisoning. Did Patrick's mom take him?"

"No, she didn't and I'm fine," Jimmy calmly insisted over the bitter taste of vomit lingering in his mouth.

Of course, neither of them had food poisoning. It was simply an excuse he had come up with in the early hours of the morning when his mom found him puking in the bathroom. The real reason he was sick had more to do with the bottle of tequila that he and Patrick had shared the night before, to celebrate Jimmy's seventeenth birthday. Just to make his story sound more valid, he called Patrick earlier that day and they collaborated on their story. "I'm feeling better. It's just Jill's perfume that set me off this time."

"Okay, Jim," his mother spoke gently and he started to feel guilty for lying to her. "I should call that pizza place on Monday and give them a piece of my mind. Food poisoning is very dangerous."

"I know, mom."

Jimmy flushed the toilet and splashed cold water on his face. After rinsing with some mouthwash he found under the sink, he studied himself in the mirror. His black hair was starting to get longer, hanging over his ears and a cowlick curled close to his neck. A deathly pallor shadowed his face, betraying his few sessions of vomiting since the previous night. He had really toned up in the previous month and he'd noticed Sally often glaring at other admiring girls. And yet, some things still remained the same – he was seventeen and *still* a virgin; things were starting to look hopeless.

He'd had a drunken discussion with Patrick about that very issue the previous night. His friend made a few suggestions, but even thinking about it was depressing. Sally's excuses just never seemed to end.

He finally made his way back downstairs and into the living room, where his sister was the center of attention, discussing her proposal and the plans she and Rob were making together. He stood in the doorway for a few minutes, before finally deciding that it wasn't necessary to participate in their conversation. Grabbing his schoolbooks, he headed upstairs. The phone rang just as he reached the top and he rushed to his sister's room to answer it.

"Hi," Sally's voice was on the other end of the line. Music from *Hysteria* was in the background and Jimmy sat down on Jillian's bed. "Did you and Patrick have fun last night?"

"Yeah," Jimmy replied. A sense of rebellion rose inside him and he told her that the two of them had been drinking. He knew that bothered her and in a way, that's what he wanted to do. Even though Jimmy knew he had no right to expect sex from her, he felt as though she were holding it over his head. Promising that the day would come, but it never did. "I just threw up again."

"Why do you want to drink if it makes you so sick?" she asked with some judgment in her voice. "It doesn't make sense."

"'Cause it feels good at the time," Jimmy insisted and then added, "Haven't you ever done something that just felt good at the time?" He already knew the answer.

She sighed loudly over the phone. Obviously his remark was more cutting then he realized. At one time he would've apologized for it, but not now. He was tired of the games. If she didn't want to be with him then Jimmy just wanted to know the truth. She could remain a virgin for the rest of her life, but he wasn't going to.

"Actually, the reason I'm calling is because my parents and sister aren't home," Sally sounded nervous as she spoke. "They drove to Toronto to see some kind of musical or something...." her words seemed to drift off. "I was going to ask you to come over. I think it's time."

Jimmy suddenly became very alert. "I'll be there in a few minutes."

After hanging up the phone, he flew into his room and changed. Inspecting his appearance in the mirror, he decided that all he needed was the condoms that Patrick had given him. Grabbing the packages hidden in his nightstand, Jimmy shoved them in his pocket and headed downstairs. "Can I borrow the car?" he called out in his father's direction. John Groome nodded his approval and Jimmy grabbed the car keys, waving at the women without interrupting their conversation.

He seemed to get stuck at every red light between his house and Sally's, but he finally made it there. Noting that her parent's van still wasn't in the driveway, he pulled in. Jumping out of the car, he headed towards the door. Sally was waiting for him.

"You probably shouldn't have brought the car here. What if one of my parents' friends see it here and tell them?" Her face was full of worry as he walked through the door.

"Then you tell them that I dropped by for some notes. I don't know, let's just not worry about that right now," Jimmy snapped, not meaning to and automatically wondering if that attitude was going to shut down his chances for *yet* another day. He was beyond horny at that point and didn't really care if the whole neighborhood saw his car there. "I'm sorry," he apologized. "I'm just tired of sneaking around like this. It's just getting to me, I guess."

"I know, me too," Sally sadly admitted. She closed the door and locked it. "But it's only for another month."

"I know."

"Then my parents promised they would let me date."

"I know."

Jimmy glanced around the modern-style home that he had only managed to visit a handful of times. Nothing was ever out of place here – no dust was on the furniture, and no stains on the carpet – unlike his own comfortable home.

She gave him a small, nervous smile and bit her lip. "Do you want to go upstairs?" At that point, Jimmy would've done it anywhere - on the floor, in front of the door, it wouldn't have mattered - but he didn't say that. Instead he gave her a small smile and reached for her hand.

"Sure." his voice was gentle and sweet, something that didn't go unnoticed by Sally, who gave his hand a squeeze and pulled him upstairs.

Entering her room together, she pushed the door closed before they sat on the edge of her twin bed. Def Leppard songs could still be heard from the CD player, on her white dresser. They'd been in there before, when her parents were obviously not home and messed around a few times. He wasn't really sure why taking things to the next level was so difficult for her; after all, it wasn't like they'd never been intimate.

She seemed scared. Until that moment, Jimmy had never realized how frightened she really was to lose her virginity. She started to cry.

"I'm sorry," she quickly wiped away her tears. Jimmy automatically reached out to touch her hand and was surprised to find her body shaking slightly. "I don't mean to be such a baby about having sex. I know that's not normal. All the girls in my class talk about it like it's no big deal, so I'm not sure why it is to me."

"It's okay," Jimmy whispered and moved closer to her. "You don't have anything to be scared of, it's just me. It's not like *I've* done it before either. And I won't tell anyone."

"I know," she smiled and squeezed his hand. "Are you scared too?"

Jimmy almost laughed at the thought. But then he realized that he probably was a bit nervous. Just not enough to hesitate doing it. "A little.

But if I didn't do all the things that made me nervous, where would I be?"

He wasn't really sure if that statement made sense, but Sally appeared to accept it, leaning forward to kiss him. Jimmy slid his hands around her back and pulled her closer until she was on top of him. Quickly realizing that this position might actually make things happen a little faster than he intended, he moved on top of her and away from her, experiencing a momentary sense of trepidation. What if he was terrible?

Jimmy and Sally weren't shy to remove their clothes in front of one another, having crossed that bridge many times before in their exploration. But he continued to sense her fear as things progressed and he was starting to wonder if she was going to change her mind at the last minute. He also wondered if he was going to be able to last that long. Patrick had warned him about that and advised him to think about something else, other than the fact that he was about to get laid. That was a little easier said than done, but somehow he was managing.

It seemed to take forever before Sally allowed him to reach for a condom on her nightstand. Jimmy's fear that he wouldn't be able to put it on right quickly came to light when he broke the first one. "Fuck!" He rubbed his forehead. This seriously couldn't be happening. What the hell had he done wrong? He sighed, reaching for another one, as Sally quietly watched. This time, he managed to get one on. It was tighter than he expected for some reason.

Moving back toward Sally, he began to kiss her again hoping she didn't change her mind. From the way she responded, she seemed to want him even more than before. Jimmy took a deep breath and tried to think about anything but how he was slowly sliding in between her legs. It was hard, especially when he started to feel undeniable sensations he had never experienced before that night. It definitely was *much* better than the other stuff they did. Sally whispered that he was hurting her, but insisted he not stop. Not that it lasted very long. Jimmy felt like he had died and gone to heaven.

He pulled out and found blood on both the condom and the sheets. "Are you okay?" Jimmy asked as he attempted to calm his breathing. His heart pounded wildly in his chest and he felt slightly guilty for enjoying something that Sally clearly hadn't. "I'm sorry, I didn't mean to hurt you."

"It's fine," She reassured him. "I knew it would hurt. That's why I said not to stop. I just wanted it to be over with."

Jimmy nodded and removed the condom. Grabbing a Kleenex on her nightstand, he quickly wrapped it up and put it in the garbage beside the bed.

Finally, he wasn't a virgin.

Chapter fourteen

June of 1989 was a busy month. Not only was Jillian moving out of the Groome residence to live with her fiancé Rob, she was also making wedding plans with their mother. Jimmy wasn't sure why, as they hadn't even set a date yet. The couple both claimed they wanted to finish college and 'get settled' before they jumped ahead to the wedding, but for some reason the engagement ring seemed to automatically give Jillian a reason to pore over issues of bridal magazine. Fortunately, his mother was so busy discussing the upcoming wedding with Jillian that she rarely paid attention to what Jimmy was doing. That was probably a good thing; especially considering the things he *was* up to.

To begin with, finally having sex with Sally seemed to open a gateway to the couple doing it all the time. After that first night together, Jimmy had assumed that his girlfriend wasn't remotely interested in trying it again, but he was wrong. In fact, it quickly became the only thing they *ever* did. Sally had even purchased issues of *Cosmopolitan* and other magazines because she insisted there were a lot of sex tips in each issue. And she was anxious to try every one of them.

The next surprising thing about losing his virginity was how much their encounters seemed to increase Jimmy's interest in Sally. He grew much more attached than he ever expected and actually felt like he was in love with her. But it wasn't like the kind of love he was used to seeing on television. He suddenly felt like he was constantly walking on unstable ground. He worried that she'd break up with him and wondered regularly what would happen when she went to university in the fall. It was looking like she was moving to the east coast for school, which was like a knife in his heart. He always thought love was supposed to be wonderful and fulfilling. If that was the case, then why did he feel so restless and stressed?

Now Sally was the one who took risks. She still had Jimmy over when her parents were out, but now she didn't seem to care if her younger sister Robyn knew about their secret encounters.

"Aren't you scared that she'll tell your parents?" Jimmy asked Sally the obvious question as she led him upstairs to her room one afternoon. With less than an hour to 'hook up', she just shrugged, as if she didn't really want to waste time explaining things to him. However, when he repeated his concerns later, Sally went on to explain that the two had an agreement.

"I don't tell our parents when she has boys over," Sally explained as the two of them quickly put on their clothes, "And she doesn't tell on me."

"Are your parents as strict with her?" Jimmy wondered out loud and Sally just rolled her eyes and said yes. Sally's reference to 'the boys' that her sister had over indicated to him that she probably wasn't as nervous about sex as Sally; and he felt guilty over the fact that this intrigued him. In fact, judging by the way Robyn was checking him out upon his arrival to the house, she was far from shy. Her eyes automatically dropped from his face to his crotch, then back up to Jimmy's eyes again. The younger of the sisters didn't appear to be embarrassed by her actions.

When he later ran down the stairs alone, he caught Robyn watching him again. Sally was still upstairs, so he nervously waved at her before heading toward the door.

"Your face is awfully flushed for a study date," Robyn called out behind him and he turned to see a mischievous grin on her face. He just smiled back and left.

Ironically, Sally did still help Jimmy with his schoolwork, and when he finished grade eleven a few weeks later, Jimmy insisted that he wouldn't have passed if it hadn't been for her. Meanwhile, she was graduating and was allowed to date. Her parents had no issues with her seeing Jimmy at that point.

"The funny thing is that they insisted that I did great this semester because I stayed single," Sally laughed when Jimmy picked her up for their first 'official' date a few days later. They were supposed to be going to see a movie. They were actually going to his house to 'watch movies'. His parents were going to be home, but hopefully in bed early so they could have some privacy in the basement. "I told them they were right because I don't want Robyn to get off easier than I did!"

"Really? I'd think that after what we went through, you'd want her to have an easier time than you"

"Please!" Sally said with a huge grin on her face. "My sister is a complete tramp. The last thing she needs is to have anything easier than it already is for her."

Once school was finished, it meant more work for Jimmy. While Sally went off to a government work program for the summer, he was stuck flipping burgers for eight-hour days. At least Patrick was at his side. His friend was currently single again, once again not able to get along with Melissa, now that the realities of parenthood were setting in. Looking after a baby was much more difficult and stressful than he had originally thought, especially now that he was expected to baby-sit on occasion.

"I just can't do it," Patrick confessed one day while they worked side-by-side in the kitchen at work. "I just have no clue what to do with Hope or why she's crying. I feel like I'm in over my head."

Jimmy had no doubt about Patrick's discomfort with the situation. Jimmy wouldn't be any better off. That's why Sally was on the pill (and apparently had been for at least six months before meeting him) and he continued to use condoms. At first, he felt awkward purchasing them, but eventually he just didn't care. The last thing he wanted was to become a father, like Patrick had. He was in love with Sally, but he certainly didn't want a kid at seventeen.

"Maybe it'll get easier," Jimmy commented uncertainly. "It's still pretty new, man."

"I know, but it'd help if Melissa and I weren't fighting all the time," Patrick complained, wrapping someone's burger and pushing it down the chute. "And this place doesn't pay shit. I don't know if I should get another job or what the fuck to do." Jimmy nodded, noting the smell of grease that filled the air – all in all, it was a pretty repulsive job.

Of course, any ideas Patrick had about leaving Top Dog Burger were quickly eliminated a few days later when a new girl was hired. Her name was Candace and she was Patrick's type. She was a tiny brunette with big brown eyes and, although she appeared to be only fifteen, apparently she was almost eighteen. Patrick wasted no time and asked the new girl out on a date. They were an item by the following week.

"We can't tell anyone else who works here other than you," Patrick confided in Jimmy as they sat in his car during a break, sharing a joint. The two had tried pot previously, but only recently had decided that it would help take the edge off working such a shitty job. "If the boss knew, he'd start scheduling us apart. At least, that's what Candace thinks."

Jimmy thought she was probably right. Their boss tended to try to separate him and Patrick when he could, since he was aware of their friendship. However, the shortage of staff during the busy summer season often forced him to schedule the two together. "Don't worry, I won't say anything, Pat."

"I know you won't."

Jimmy smiled, inhaling the last of the joint that was burning his fingers. "We so need a roach clip."

"I've got one at home," Patrick seemed to be lost in thought. "Listen man, what do you think of Candace? She's cool, right?"

"Yeah, for sure," Jimmy insisted, quickly looking away. What he didn't want Patrick to know was how much Candace flirted with *him*, when his friend wasn't around. She was cute, so it was difficult not to flirt back, especially when she accidentally touched him. Not that Candace did so in any sexual way, but she would touch his arm or back, her fingers often lingering a little longer than necessary. Jimmy had to wonder what kind of girl flirted with him then went on to have sex with his friend a few hours later.

"Yeah, that's what I thought," Patrick replied, seeming relieved. "I just keep thinking she's seeing someone else too. I hope not, I really like her."

"I'm sure she's not," Jimmy said what he thought Patrick wanted to hear, not wanting to admit why he doubted her loyalty to his best friend. "Just be careful."

He and Patrick managed to gather two other guys together that summer and officially start a band they called Charm, featuring Patrick as the singer. The new guys, Ben on drums and Stan on bass, were pretty good. Together the four worked on songs. They mostly focused on stuff by other artists like Guns N' Roses and Skid Row. During the summer, they had two gigs that were both pretty irrelevant, but nevertheless provided some experience on a stage. If Jimmy hadn't been assured of his feelings about being a professional musician before those shows, he was certain afterwards. There was no greater feeling than being on stage, he'd later admit to Patrick. "Other than having sex, this is fucking it!"

Patrick loved being on stage, but the appeal for him seemed to rest more with the women in the audience. He liked their attention much more than he enjoyed the feeling of being on stage; it didn't seem to fill him up in the same way it did for Jimmy.

Although he had always dabbled in writing his own songs, it was after their band started that Jimmy really concentrated his efforts to create his own music. He wasn't sure if Charm was ready to be presented with his ideas, so Jimmy held back and just worked on new songs on his own. It wasn't necessary to bring them forward yet.

For the majority of the summer, neither of his parents seemed to notice any change in Jimmy. They didn't notice when he was stoned, came home late after a night of drinking with Patrick, or that he was having sex regularly. He was actually surprised that they weren't alert to anything he was doing. In fact, the only thing his mother complained about all summer was the fact that he was growing his hair.

"Jimmy, honey you need to get a haircut," his mother remarked one afternoon, when he arrived home from work. The ironic part was that he was baked at the time, but she hadn't even noticed. "It's starting to get long and messy looking." She pushed a strand of black hair from his eyes.

"Well, that is sort of the idea," Jimmy gave her his most charming grin. "I'm in a band and it's pretty normal to have longer hair when you're in a band."

"I wish you'd cut it," she replied. "You have such a handsome face and beautiful blue eyes. All that hair is hiding them."

"I'll think about it, mom."

"Thank you, honey."

Jimmy actually thought his hair was pretty tame compared to that of most guys in bands during the late eighties. His hair was shaggy more than anything, but he thought it was funny that his mom commented on it.

His dad, however, seemed aware that something was different with his son. Jimmy could tell by how he studied his face from time to time. One day he dropped by Jimmy's room and asked him how things were. "With the band? Sally? Your job?" His dad seemed to be leading up to something, but he wasn't sure what. "You've got a lot going on."

"Yeah, I do," Jimmy agreed. "Everything's cool."

"Okay," his dad seemed hesitant. "Well, if you ever need anything or need to talk, let me know."

He got up to leave and stopped. "Oh, I saw your guitar teacher on the news tonight."

"Sean?"

"Yeah, they were saying that he's up for a lot of awards or something," he shrugged, a grin spreading across his face. "He's pretty popular, isn't he?"

"Oh, for sure!" Jimmy replied. Second in Line was always on the radio, not to mention the music channel on television. Jimmy felt proud whenever he heard of their on-going successes. "Sean's the best! He's going to go really far."

"I believe you're right." his father smiled as he left the room.

Chapter fifteen

Jimmy's summer flew by. The combination of work, Sally and his band seemed to occupy most of his time. Before he knew it, the end of August was approaching and reality set in. He dreaded the fact that Sally was soon leaving for university.

"So, what are you going to do when she goes?" Patrick asked, passing the joint back to Jimmy as the two sat in his car during their afternoon work break. It was a busy day at work and Jimmy was already depressed enough without thinking about his girlfriend moving to another province. "Are you guys going to do the long distance thing?"

"I hope so," Jimmy admitted reluctantly, staring at his dirty uniform pants. Secretly, he was a little worried. Although they had been having a very active sex life all summer, in recent days he noticed Sally backing off from him a little at a time, canceling dates or claiming the onset of her period. He thought they were just excuses, because something didn't feel right.

"What's she saying?" Patrick asked, pausing to inhale deeply and then closing his eyes as he slowly blew out the smoke. "Do you think she's pulling some bullshit with you?"

"Don't know," Jimmy answered honestly. "Maybe. I try to not think about it."

But he did think about it. Every day. And on Sally's last night in Thorton, as he sat beside her on the back step of his house, Jimmy secretly wondered if it was the last time they'd be together. As the evening grew dark, it became difficult to see her face and read her eyes, but the awkward silence between them was undeniable. He felt nauseous and confused.

It didn't matter that Sally was saying all the right things; something just wasn't connecting for him. She told him that they wouldn't break up, insisting that they'd spend every long weekend and vacation together, and he was always welcome to visit her in Nova Scotia. They'd talk on the phone regularly and everything would work out fine. Maybe he could even apply to the same university. Whatever happened, they would make it work.

Jimmy wondered how she could be so disconnected from him. Was this the same girl, who once blushed every time he complimented her? Wasn't she the girl who wanted her first time to be with him? When did they move away from that place? Was it all a lie? How could he make her see how strongly he felt about her? Desperately, Jimmy found himself blurting out the words that he had held back for so long

"Sally," he pleaded, trying to see through the darkness into her eyes. "I'm scared that you're going to move away and forget about me." He hesitated and took a deep breath. Everyone always told him to be honest about how he felt and maybe they were right. "And I don't know what I'd do because I love you."

The words seemed to send a jolt of shock through Sally and for a moment, he thought he saw regret in her eyes. He didn't know what else to do at this point. He could only tell her the truth; maybe it would make a difference

"Jimmy," she was slow to respond. "I care about you very much. I mean, after all, you were my first." Sally gave him a gentle smile, "But I don't love you."

Her words were like a punch in the face. Feeling a mixture of humiliation and anger, Jimmy looked away. His heart raced and his throat grew dry. Suddenly he was back in junior high reliving the embarrassment with Suzanne Bordon. In silence, he bit his lip.

"Jimmy, I'm sorry," she touched his arm, but he refused to meet her eyes. "I *do* care about you. And I think maybe you're just confused because we lost our virginity together. I think that we'll always have a special place in each other's hearts because of that, but love takes a lot more time."

"So, I don't know what I feel?" Jimmy countered; anger was slowly building up in his heart. She was being condescending and dismissive.

"No, I'm not saying that," Sally quickly denied. "I just meant that you probably feel like you're in love with me, but when you look back at this down the line you'll see that it wasn't love."

Those words stung Jimmy and he suddenly didn't want to talk to her anymore. He felt it was very insulting to imply that he didn't even know his own feelings. She was talking to him like he was twelve. Was Sally suggesting that it wasn't possible for a seventeen year old to be in love?

Standing up, he gazed down at her sitting on the step for a moment before shaking his head and turning for the house. He suddenly felt nothing for her, nothing at all.

"Aren't you going to say something?" Jimmy could hear the panic in her voice as she abruptly stood and reached for him. You're just going to walk in the house and leave me here?"

"Yeah, have a nice life," Jimmy glared at Sally and closed the door behind him, leaving her on the step. Alone.

Walking up the stairs to his room, his body felt like its weight had doubled in the last 5 minutes. He felt exhausted and his sense of loneliness that was even more intense than back in his fat days. He closed his door & silently slumped on the edge of his bed.

Their entire conversation filled his head and he swallowed the lump in his throat. He was honest with his feelings and where did that get him? Sally had basically implied that he was too stupid to know how he really felt about her - as if he were a child. What was the point of putting himself on the line for some chick that was just like all the rest? Sally was just another version of Suzanne Bordon, only interested in making him look stupid.

Maybe women were all heartless and cold. After all, hadn't he seen that side of his sister? She had manipulated him to hide her secret when he was ten years old, even though it was fucking him up. What about all the girls who laughed at him when he was fat? Many of them now checked him out as he walked through the hallways, their eyes lingering on his body as he passed them. What about Candace? She was dating Patrick, but constantly making suggestive comments to him. Did women not have a conscience? This situation with Sally was just the latest reality check.

His theory seemed valid when Patrick called him the next day to announce that he was done with Candace. Apparently, he had caught her 'hanging off' another guy at a party. He didn't really get into the details, other than to say that her hands were 'all over' someone else. Enough said. Jimmy got the picture.

"Of course, I can't work with that skank anymore," Patrick angrily insisted. "So, I dumped her last night then quit my job today."

"Really?" Jimmy was surprised. He would miss their times together at Top Dog. As much as he hated the job, being able to hang out with a friend all day was cool. "It's gonna suck not having you there, man. Everyone else that works there is so fucking lame."

"I know, but I can't deal with her every day," Patrick spoke honestly. "Plus, I got a lead on a job at a grocery store. I figure it can't be as bad as the burger joint."

Jimmy had to agree. There was definitely no glamorous side to working with greasy food all day. He figured his job would be pretty boring from that point on, since Patrick was gone, but he was in for a surprise.

When his shift began at four the next afternoon, Candace was already at work, looking gloomy and depressed. Jimmy smiled at her upon arriving at work, carefully hiding his own feelings of contempt. In his mind, she was no different than Sally, just another girl who thought she could play a guy for a fool. Yet, if the same thing were to happen to her, she would be the first one to cry about what assholes men were. For some reason, women seemed to believe that they deserved respect even when they didn't earn it.

However, Jimmy treated Candace the same as always at work. He didn't mention her break up with Patrick. He also avoided the obvious elephant in the room; the fact that her former boyfriend no longer worked with them. It was just another day at the office.

As the night moved forward and staff covering the late afternoon rush went home, Jimmy and Candace were left alone to clean up. She took care of the dining room and served customers while Jimmy washed dishes and finished everything in the kitchen. Candace took that opportunity to open up to him after the restaurant closed.

"I guess you know what happened with Patrick?" Her eyes studied Jimmy's face anxiously. "I mean, I'm not sure what he told you, but it was a big misunderstanding."

Had he had more faith in women, Jimmy probably would've believed her. But he didn't.

"Yeah well, I try to not get involved," Jimmy said, avoiding eye contact with her. "It's none of my business."

"I just know we have to continue working together and I don't want you to think I'm some big slut. At least, that's what Patrick seemed to think of me last night," Candace began to sniff.

Great! Here come the fake tears.

"But he won't listen. It's like he already had his mind made up ahead of time," Candace said, and big tears rolled down her face. "I can't believe he just quit this place because of me. I mean, what does that tell you? He is so cold."

Jimmy looked into her face and suddenly felt guilty for judging her so harshly. He didn't like seeing girls cry, regardless of the situation. As he moved closer to Candace, he began to wonder why Sally hadn't cried when they broke up. They had been together much longer than Candace and Patrick and yet she didn't seem to think he was worth her tears. In a way, it softened his opinion of the girl standing in front of him.

"I'm sorry Candace," he comforted her; setting down the sponge he was using to clean the prep table. "I really don't know what to say. I wasn't there so I don't like to pass judgment."

His heart went out to her. In a way, she was expressing what he wasn't able to with Sally. His own feelings were stuck somewhere, lodged in his chest and refused to come out. He gently placed his hand on her arm to show compassion. But rather than feeling comfort from his action, she seemed to cry even harder. Jimmy felt really uncomfortable and empathetic toward Candace and carefully pulled her into a hug. He was surprised when she held onto him tightly, leaning her body into his. He was even more surprised that he started to feel aroused as she held onto him and his breathing became labored.

Candace started to let go and slowly looked up into Jimmy's eyes. She wasn't crying anymore. His heart raced as he watched her fingers slowly move up the side of his face, softly massaging the skin beneath them. Her mouth moved up to meet with his, her lips softly touching his while her other hand boldly traveled down and into the front of his pants. Things heated up quickly.

Jimmy found himself pushing her against the wall and pressing his body tightly against her. Their kisses became much more intense. Fingers were moving everywhere, exploring. He was hard and she was moaning as he slipped his hand into her pants. She wasn't wearing underwear.

"Do you have a condom?" she whispered, "Please tell me you have a condom."

He did, in their staff room, where there was a table. A table he could fuck her on.

"Yup," he led her into the tiny room. Opening his locker, he pulled out his backpack and ripped through it until he found a condom. The next thing he knew, he was screwing her on the same table their staff ate on daily. She was moaning loudly, making much more noise than Sally had ever made, her legs wrapped tightly around him as he leaned over her. Candace was not shy about what she wanted him to do and how she wanted it done. When they were finished, Jimmy's leg felt shaky as he removed the condom, wrapping it in a paper towel and threw it in the garbage. They quickly dressed.

"We can't tell Patrick about this," Jimmy said right off the bat. "I hope you didn't do this as some kind of revenge thing on him."

"No," Candace insisted as she buttoned her uniform shirt. "I've always been attracted to you. It just happened. I didn't plan it."

"Good," Jimmy studied her face and hoped she was telling the truth. It was possible he may have found another reason to go to work everyday.

Chapter Sixteen

Candace kept her promise to Jimmy, and Patrick never found out that his best friend and former girlfriend were hooking up every chance they got. They tended to have quickies at places like Top Dog Burger after closing. Their options were limited, since Jimmy's mother had quit her job and was always at home. When he suggested going to Candace's place when her mom wasn't home, she insisted it was impossible. Apparently she had a younger sister that liked to blab.

"What if you were to bribe her or something?" Jimmy whispered to Candace one night, his heart still racing after the frantic sex they had just had. They were actually in his bed. His parents were out, but he wasn't sure for how long. "There must be something that will make your sister keep a secret?"

"No, trust me, she won't keep her mouth shut." Candace sighed.

The two had agreed that their relationship was only physical and temporary. Especially since Candace had a new boyfriend. Unlike with Jimmy, she was holding off on having sex with him in order to 'build a relationship'. In the meantime, she continued to hook up with Jimmy. Although he went along with it, Jimmy had zero respect for Candace.

"Doesn't she have her boyfriends over once in awhile?" Jimmy referred to the girl he hadn't actually met. All he knew was that her sister was slightly younger than Candace, and if looks ran in the family, there had to be lots of guys wanting to drop by for a visit.

"No," Candace laughed. "Hardly. Guys don't like my sister. She's fat."

Jimmy felt every muscle in his body tighten as the words rang through his head. "Really?" He casually asked. "Is that a fact?"

"Yeah she's like, gross." Candace replied with a short laugh. "There's no way in hell any guy would give her the time of day. She'll have crushes on guys, but they basically ignore her. She spends every weekend just sitting in her room and eating cookies or other junk. That's why she hates the idea of me having a guy over 'cause she knows no one wants a fat girl!"

And you wouldn't even be here tonight if I was still fat.

Jimmy cleared his throat and didn't reply. He didn't want to hear anymore, but that didn't stop Candace from talking.

"There was one time when she had a huge crush on this guy," Candace paused for a moment. "I think it was in seventh grade. Anyway, he found out and totally embarrassed her in front of their entire class. Called her a cow. She came home crying."

You don't sound too fucking sympathetic.

Jimmy cleared his throat again. "Really?"

"Yeah," Candace said with a hint of laughter in her voice. "I felt bad at first, but I figure it's her own fault she's fat. No one makes her eat all that food and never exercise. If I ate like her, I'd be the same size. Do you know what I mean?"

Jimmy finally shifted to meet her eyes. She seemed unaware that anything she had said was out of line. Anger ran through his veins as he returned her innocent gaze with an icy cold stare. "You know what?" He drawled, "I called you over here tonight 'cause I wanted to fuck you, *not* 'cause I wanted to hear your sister's life story."

His remark ended the night quite abruptly.

Candace never spoke to him again other than when it was necessary at work, and Jimmy was just as happy that she didn't. Although she was very open sexually and he had certainly gained a lot of knowledge from their encounters, he was repulsed by her attitude toward fat people. Nothing in the world would ever make him forget how painful it was to walk into a room full of people, only to witness looks of disgust. And it was always the pretty, popular girls who put him under the microscope. Girls like Candace. From that day on, he despised her.

But she *was* also Patrick's ex. And even though Jimmy's best friend was once again in a relationship with Melissa, he still felt guilty for messing around with Candace. Chances were good that Patrick would just laugh if he told him the entire story, but he wasn't about to take the chance just the same. Nevertheless, it was much easier to forget the entire experience, especially when Candace quit a few weeks later to take another job.

As the year slowly came to a close, Jimmy and Patrick learned that a winter festival was to take place at their school in early January. One of the events being planned was a variety show that would allow students to showcase their talents. The posters all over the school encouraged everyone to sign up for the event and when the night was over, a winner would be declared. Already a few of the girls who Patrick referred to as the school's 'virgin princesses' had signed up to do such things as play the flute, perform ballet and read poetry.

"Reading poetry?" Patrick studied the sign up sheet and rolled his eyes. "How fucking stupid is that? And flute?" He shook his head. "Man, a rock band is *so* going to stand out beside all of that. I mean we will blow those poor fuckers out of the water."

"That's what I was kind of thinking too," Jimmy agreed as the two walked away from the sign up sheet. Patrick had already put Charm down to take part, and so far, they were the only band to do so. Although a part of him worried that they were probably barking up the wrong tree, another side of him kind of liked the fact that they were going to play in front of the school. He tried not to think about it because it made him nervous.

"Who's the ballerina?" Patrick asked with a smirk on his face. "I always wanted to nail a ballerina. They're so dainty and small."

"I have no clue," Jimmy replied and wondered if that meant that things weren't going so well with Melissa. He didn't bother to ask though.

"So get this," Patrick completely changed the subject as they walked down the hallway toward the one class they shared together. It was math and they were both failing. "I found out that my brother's friend is doing tattoos really cheap. I'm thinking about getting one done this weekend. Want to come?"

"Sure," Jimmy was intrigued with the idea. "Is he any good?"

"Yeah man, he did one for my brother last week and it fucking rocked," Patrick went on to give a detailed description of the artwork that was now displayed on his sibling's back. "As soon as I saw it, I *knew* I had to get one too."

"What are you getting?" Jimmy asked as they walked into their classroom and sat side by side.

"I don't know for sure yet," Patrick confessed. "But the guy's got a ton of magazines and stuff that you can look through, or you can just bring in a picture. You know, something for him to work with. I'm thinking of getting something tribal. I'll decide when I get there."

Jimmy accompanied Patrick to his appointment that weekend. Excepting a tattooed, surly looking man who lived in a dirty apartment, Jimmy was surprised when the tattoo artist ended up being a skinny little guy who lived in a suburban house. In fact, Joe was twenty-three years old and was renting out his parent's basement as both his home and an unofficial work space.

"Tattoos are just something I do on the side," Joe explained to both the boys as they walked down the steps to his apartment. It was simply furnished but clean and well lit. He lead both Patrick and Jimmy into a separate room that had huge posters of various tattoo designs on one wall, while another carried actual photos of his finished work. Jimmy studied them and was impressed. This guy really did have talent.

"I went to art school for two years and now I can't find a job in my field," Joe went on to explain, while pointing at the various posters. "A friend of mine got me into doing tattoos and I've been doing them for about a year or two."

"What did you want to be doing after college?" Jimmy asked curiously.

"Well my dream was to design comic books or CD covers, but it's so difficult to get into that kind of thing," Joe confessed while sitting down in a chair. Jimmy and Patrick did the same. "When you're in college, you know, they always make it sound like the sky's the limit. Like you can do anything and when you get out, all these opportunities will be sitting on your doorstep," he slowly shook his head. "Not quite true. I take photos for a local newspaper. I could've done that without studying for two years."

Jimmy nodded in understanding. Teachers always talked like college was the solution to every problem and a guarantee of future success, but realistically not everyone could have their dream job. Joe's story only proved his theory. It made him wonder why he was even bothering to complete high school at all.

Joe brought out a pile of magazines that featured tattoo designs. With much consideration, Patrick chose a tribal piece called 'Mad Face' to be put on his back. Joe nodded and quickly rattled off the price, told him how long it would take to finish the tattoo and asked when he wanted it done.

"Can you do it now?" Patrick asked sheepishly.

"Absolutely, as long as you have the time," Joe agreed.

Twenty minutes later, Jimmy sat beside his best friend as Joe carefully drew the outline of the tribal tattoo on Patrick's back. It was fascinating. Grabbing one of the magazines, Jimmy glanced through it at the various designs. Some were really detailed while others were simple.

"Hey Jim, are you getting one too?" Patrick's green eyes glanced from the magazine to Jimmy's face. A grin slowly crossed his face. "If for no other reason, get one to give your mother a heart attack."

Jimmy couldn't help but laugh. His mother definitely *wouldn't* like the idea of him getting a tattoo. He thought back to the day that Jillian came home with an extra piercing at the top of her ear. Their mother had been furious. "Nah, I wouldn't tell her," Jimmy insisted although he did admit that he planned to get one too. Joe said he had time for something simple that night, so it was a go. "I'll get it on my arm. Since it's winter, I'll be wearing long-sleeved shirts all the time. She won't even see it till spring." After all, he was having sex, smoking weed and drinking and his mother seemed oblivious. She'd never notice a tattoo.

But Jimmy had greatly underestimated the situation. He'd barely removed his jacket that evening, when Annette Groome rushed over to his side. "Jimmy, your arm is bleeding through your sleeve. Did you get hurt at work today?" Although there were only a few drops, there was no denying it. He had to tell her the truth. And he did so, while carefully raising his sleeve to show her the finished product. He started to explain that it was a Celtic symbol called the Triquetra, which represented different things to various people. To him at that specific time, it represented the past, present and future. Little did he know that later in life, it would symbolize 'the power of three', another meaning believed to be associated with that particular symbol.

His mother wasn't impressed. All the color drained from her face.

"Jimmy, I can't believe you got a tattoo!" Tears formed in her eyes while John Groome crossed the room to study the work. He didn't appear to be as alarmed as Jimmy's mom. "How could you do that? How could you do that to your body? I'm so disappointed in you."

Jimmy felt the smile fall from his face. How could he explain to her that there was something about having a needle in his skin that made him feel alive? That watching the image being formed on his arm was symbolic to him because it represented a new phase in his life? It wasn't so much that he wanted a tattoo, as he *needed* it. But she wouldn't understand. In her mind, it was horrible and dirty.

"Jimmy, where did you get this done?" His mother shook her head in disbelief. He noted that she actually looked physically ill as she spoke to him. "You don't even know if this person uses clean needles? What if he used it on a dozen people and one of them had AIDS?"

"No mom," Jimmy shook his head and held back his amusement of her overreaction. "He opened a new needle for both me and Patrick and broke them after he was done. He never reuses needles."

"Patrick?" His mother rolled her eyes and looked at Jimmy's dad, who still didn't appear to be upset over the tattoo. "Figures! This was his idea, wasn't it?"

"No," Jimmy lied. The last thing he needed was for his mother to hold another grudge against his best friend. "It was actually mine."

"I just can't believe it. I don't even know my own son anymore!" His mother stormed out of the room, leaving Jimmy behind with his father. Feeling that she was purposely attempting to make him feel bad, Jimmy automatically shook his head in frustration.

"Don't worry," His dad gently commented. "She'll calm down. I personally like it." Both father and son shared a smile.

But the tattoo controversy would quickly be forgotten later that night when the family received news that Jillian was in the hospital. Rob had recently discovered a secret stash of laxatives hidden in the couple's closet and she admitted to trying to lose weight. At first he had attempted to help solve the problem, but when Jillian passed out earlier that day, it was painfully obvious that her eating disorder had returned and she needed professional help. Suddenly, Jimmy's tattoo didn't seem like such a horrible affliction to his body.

Chapter seventeen

"So, how is the anorexic princess?" Patrick casually referred to Jimmy's sister while the two sat amongst the Groome's Christmas paraphernalia in the basement. Various gifts were scattered across the floor, crowding both in their own sections of the room. Jimmy wasn't sure why, but all the clutter made him more anxious than usual.

Charm had been getting together regularly in order to prepare for the winter festival that was to take place at school the following month, but on this particular afternoon, it was just Jimmy and Patrick playing around with their guitars and shooting the shit. "Is she still puking her guts out every chance she gets?"

"I dunno," Jimmy admitted, showing little emotion. However on the night that his sister was rushed to the hospital, it had been another story. Like the rest of his family, Jimmy worried that Jillian would never find her way back to normal eating patterns. Then there was the shock he felt after seeing his sister lying in the hospital. "She's really fucking skinny, man. It's kind of scary."

Patrick looked up from his guitar, concern evident in his eyes. "I don't get it, Jim. Why does she starve herself? I thought she was done with that modeling shit?"

"To be honest, I don't get it either," Jimmy shrugged and looked away. "But she like, started crying during Christmas dinner last week. It was this big emotional fucking mess."

"Fuck off! Right during Christmas dinner she decides to have some kind of breakdown?" Patrick raised his eyebrows. "No offence man, but your sister is a drama queen. I realize she's got problems and all, but at the same time, she *kind* of seems to make things worse than they have to be."

Jimmy considered his words, but didn't reply. He felt torn on the subject. While a part of him agreed with his friend, he couldn't help but feel that Patrick was being much too harsh. Her doctor had explained to the family that it was a psychological problem that Jillian was dealing with rather than something she brought on herself. Either way he knew it was scaring the shit out of his family, especially their mom.

"So like, how do they treat this anorexia shit?" Patrick set down his guitar as he yawned and stretched. "Like seriously, you can't force someone to eat."

Jimmy shrugged. He was starting to wonder himself. "There isn't much you can do other than try monitoring her eating habits. She's going to counseling, but we've all been down this road with her already and I still don't know the answer." He continued to pick at his guitar while thinking carefully about what he wanted to share with Patrick. Obviously, he couldn't tell him what had started the entire mess. He couldn't tell Patrick about his sister's rape.

"Only a woman would get a fucked up disease like anorexia," Patrick commented, shaking his head. Although his words sounded insensitive, Jimmy realized that his friend's eyes told a different story. "Oh and speaking of fucked up women," he managed to lighten the mood with his words, "I saw Sally the other day."

Jimmy looked up at his friend and frowned. "Oh yeah, I suppose she's home for the holidays?"

"Yeah man," Patrick seemed to be easing into the topic. "I saw her at work." He referred to the grocery store where he was a cashier. "She was like…ah, she was with some guy." His green eyes flitted around the room uncomfortably, before landing on Jimmy's face. "Ah, I think he might've been her boyfriend."

"Probably," Jimmy said with a forced carelessness, looking at the floor. The truth was that he'd been thinking about Sally a lot throughout the holidays. His mind traveled back to the previous Christmas when he was excited about their first date. Somewhat bitter, he wondered if it had been worth it all, in the end.

"I just thought you should know," Patrick said apologetically while finishing his coffee. "I mean especially if you ran into them or something."

"Thanks," Jimmy replied, knowing that his friend meant well by his gesture. As it turns out, he didn't run into Sally during the holiday season, but he did see her sister on New Year's Eve when she dropped by Top Dog Burger.

"Jimmy, is that you?" Her familiar voice came from behind while he wiped a table. He turned to look into Robyn's eyes. At least he attempted to, but the fitted tank top that she wore under her jacket was very distracting. "You work here?"

"Yeah," He shrugged, giving her an embarrassed smile. "Not much of a job, but its work."

"Hey, at least *you* have a job," Robyn's cheeks turned pink and she looked away from him. Jimmy was surprised by her reaction. Sally's younger sister always struck him as bold and flirtatious, not someone who would be shy around a guy. In fact, Jimmy's ex was often infuriated with her sister's bold words and actions toward him when they were still dating. It suddenly occurred to him that perhaps Robyn did these things on purpose to upset Sally. And suddenly, he had an idea of his own.

"You don't work?" Jimmy asked casually, giving her his biggest smile. "Oh that's right, your parents probably won't let you."

"Oh my God, I'm surprised I'm allowed to *breathe*," Robyn dramatically rolled her eyes. "I'm not allowed to work, have a boyfriend or stay out past eleven. It's like living in a prison."

"I remember your parents being like that when I was dating Sally," Jimmy sympathized. "That must really suck."

"It does."

"I mean Sally was kind of more of a school person but you seem more…. social than her," Jimmy spoke thoughtfully, gazing into Robyn's eyes. She really was a pretty girl with long, dirty blonde hair and a beautiful smile. Like Sally, she had big brown eyes, but they seemed to be warmer in comparison. In fact, there was something more approachable about the youngest of the Graham sisters.

"I am," Robyn admitted. "I've thought about running away, but I have no money 'cause I'm not allowed to work." she frowned. "It's like I'm trapped."

"It sounds that way." Jimmy replied gently, wondering why girls were always so dramatic? He suspected that she managed to escape more often than she implied. Unlike Sally, she probably put up more of a fight when it came to her freedom.

"So, I take it that you aren't doing anything tonight," he guessed as he glanced towards the counter, but none of his coworkers seemed to notice that Jimmy was socializing rather than doing any work.

"I can't go anywhere, 'cause Sally and her new boyfriend are staying home to make sure I don't leave the house while my parents are out," Robyn appeared frustrated. "I hate her new boyfriend; he's a boring loser like her." Her face softened into a smile. "He's not cool or cute like you."

Jimmy smiled gratefully. "Thank you, I think I needed to hear that right about now." It was nice to know that Sally's new man wasn't anything to write home about.

"It's true," Robyn insisted. "You know what? You should come over tonight and hang out with me."

Jimmy grinned. Bingo.

"I don't know, Robyn. It might be kind of weird with Sally and her boyfriend there," Jimmy attempted to sound hesitant. "We didn't exactly end things on great terms."

"Well, here's the thing," Robyn moved closer to him and spoke in a low voice. "Sally and I already made an agreement. I can have someone over for the evening while our parents are out. As long as I don't tell them that her and this guy are doing it in her bedroom when they aren't around, then she won't tell on anything I do."

Some things never changed. Still it stung a little bit knowing that Sally was with another guy. Not that he had a right to have an opinion on the matter, but it was still weird hearing about it. In a way, it pissed him off more.

"So, what time?" Jimmy barely spoke over a whisper as he stared into her heavily made up eyes. "Tell me and I'll be there."

Later that same night, after a quick shower and change, Jimmy headed to Robyn's house. It felt weird pulling into her driveway, walking up those familiar steps and knocking on the door. Unlike all the other times, Robyn answered the door and his ex wasn't in sight. As they climbed the steps to her room together, he noted that Sally's door was shut and he could hear quiet voices inside. Were they having sex? He bit his lip.

Reaching for his hand, Robyn led him inside her room and closed the door. Once again her whole persona changed. Unlike the sweet girl from the restaurant earlier that day, he was now seeing a completely different side of her. Robyn quickly removed her clothes until she was standing before him only wearing a matching pink, lacy bra and panty set. Suddenly, whatever was or wasn't going on in the next room didn't matter. Her body was perfect and he couldn't stop staring.

"You don't waste any time," Jimmy murmured as she approached him and ran her hand under his t-shirt and up over his chest. She teased him, letting her hand wander toward his jeans in her exploration then stopping again.

"I'm not my sister," Robyn breathed, covering his mouth with her own and reaching for his zipper. Within minutes, Jimmy found himself naked and lying on her bed as she rode him. He couldn't believe how fast things were happening. He always thought that girls generally like *some* foreplay. There was no doubt in his mind that Robyn was really into the sex. Like, *really* into sex. Unless she was out to win an Academy award, she was definitely enjoying his moves. He lost himself in the intensity of the encounter and found himself involuntarily making more noise than he had meant to. At a certain point he didn't care anymore because the sex was way too explosive. The absolute stillness in the house when it was over made him realize just what he had done.

After regaining his composure and agreeing with Robyn that they'd have to 'hang out' again soon, a promise he fully intended on keeping, Jimmy put on his clothes and got ready to leave. When he reached the bottom of the stairs, reality hit him hard. Sally was waiting for him, a frown on her face and her arms crossed over her chest. He stiffened his shoulders and looked at her gravely.

"So, this is how you get back at me?" she snapped, her face turning red. "You *use* my sister."

"Judging from what just happened up there," Jimmy gesturing toward the ceiling, "I think *she* used *me*."

He didn't see it coming but he felt the sharp sting on his cheek as Sally slapped him across the face. After a shocked silence, he started to laugh. He felt like all the anger and sadness from their break-up was suddenly lifted off his shoulders and disappeared out of the room. Without saying another word, he continued to laugh helplessly as he walked out the door and into the cold air of the night. Getting into his parent's car, he drove home and crashed in front of the television set for the rest of the night.

The next morning he awoke to the shocking news: Sean Ryan was dead.

Chapter Eighteen

"Oh man that's fucked up," Patrick replied as he slouched on Jimmy's couch on New Year's Eve day. He'd dropped by late afternoon and announced that his parents were fighting and he was too hung over to listen to them bicker all day. When Jimmy curiously inquired as to why he hadn't dropped by Melissa's house, Patrick just rolled his eyes and said 'Don't ask'. Enough said.

"I know, I couldn't believe it either," Jimmy mournfully referred to Sean Ryan's death. The ironic thing was that he'd had a dream about his former guitar teacher just prior to waking that morning. He'd been in the audience watching his idol play when suddenly Sean stopped, turned toward Jimmy and signaled for him to join him on stage. That's when he woke up to learn the horrific news. "I fell asleep with the TV on and woke up and there it was, right in front of me." Although he was careful to show no emotion outwardly, his heart was beating a little faster and his face grew warm as he told the story. What Jimmy *wasn't* about to tell Patrick was that when he opened his eyes that morning, he swore that for just a split second, he saw Sean on the other side of the room. A chill ran up his spine just thinking about it.

"Wow," Patrick pulled his baseball cap down over his eyes in response to the light that suddenly shone through the small basement window. It was the sun setting. "Fuck that's bright today!" He groaned, and Jimmy silently observed his friend from a chair on the other side of the room. "It sucks, man, 'cause Sean was really fucking cool. I still can't believe he used to teach you guitar!" Patrick peered through the sunlight toward

Jimmy, but the intensity was too bright, and he finally gave up, rubbing his head while leaning back into the couch.

"Yup, he *was* the best," Jimmy quietly affirmed, slouching down in the recliner. "I can't believe he's gone."

"And he was only like 22, right?" Patrick asked, and then shook his head after seeing Jimmy's nod. "Was *he* drinking and driving or was it someone else?"

"Nah, it wasn't him," Jimmy quickly denied. He felt an obligation to make that point as clear as possible to protect Sean's memory. "It was his band's drummer that was drunk and he was driving."

"And he lived?" Patrick frowned. "That fucking sucks man. But you know what? That guy is gonna have to live with this the rest of his life. So he's gonna wish he were dead too."

Jimmy agreed. The band's drummer had walked away with only a few minor injuries, while Sean had died immediately. It was a tragic situation, but it didn't seem to matter who was to blame or what happened, because in the end, it didn't change anything.

Later that same day, when Jimmy was playing his guitar alone, he remembered his dream and started to really think about it. Had he really seen Sean that morning, and was Sean trying to tell him something? He wasn't sure if dreams even really meant anything. Was there such a thing as ghosts? Feeling completely overwhelmed, Jimmy decided that he had to get out of his house. He had to go somewhere. He had to do *something* or he was going to lose his mind.

So he went outside into the frigid, January night and walked. With no particular direction in mind, he wandered the streets until he finally found himself in the park - the same park he had run to when he was ten years old and had discovered his sister being raped. No one was there, and for a long moment, he stood and just looked around, enjoying being alone in the stillness of the night

He found a park bench and promptly sat down. Digging into his jacket pocket, he found the joint he'd brought and quickly lit it up. As he inhaled the smoke, his mind drifted away into another place, a place where he felt safe and separated from the rest of the world. He thought about everything that had taken place since that horrible day of his sister's attack. His mind lingered on one memory: the time when Sean had reassured Jimmy that he could accomplish anything he wanted in life. Of all the times he had heard that remark, how come that was the first time that Jimmy really believed it? Was Sean right, *could* he really do it? Could *he* be a rock star?

Then he thought about Katie, Sean's girlfriend. Where was she now? Had the two stayed together? Sean had always been so close—mouthed about his personal life in the media that no one really knew his status. Fortunately, she wasn't in the car at the time of the accident. Only two people were, and one of them was dead.

Jimmy found his mind wandering between conversations that he had with Sean years before, and the accident scene shown on the news that morning. He felt his eyes burning when he remembered the last guitar lesson they'd had together. Sean was always someone he could talk to about things. Jimmy recalled telling him about how kids treated him in school - how they teased and tormented him all the time. Sean had insisted that it would get better. He promised. He had been right in a way, but in another way, it wasn't getting any easier at all.

Finishing the joint, he tossed the roach away from the bench. He had never felt as alone in his life as he did at that moment. He rose from the bench and headed home, deciding to call it a day and go to bed.

He didn't have any dreams that night.

A few days later, Jimmy felt much more self-assured as he walked through the hallways of his high school. At least he attempted to convince himself of that as he listened to Patrick make plans for the upcoming Winter Festival that was taking place the following week. The band was only allowed to play one song. There were so many other candidates 'displaying their talents' that night, that it cut the original amount of performance time.

"Fuck man, I thought we'd at least get to play two songs," Patrick complained as he simultaneously checked out a girl's ass while talking to Jimmy. "That's what I was told, but apparently our band has to cut down so there's more time for everyone else or some shit like that."

"Not totally unreasonable," Jimmy attempted to placate him. As the festival was to take place in front of both students and parents, he wasn't exactly crazy about doing more than one song anyway. Even though he already had some experience on stage, it was pretty nerve wracking. "It's all good. We'll do our song and blow the rest of the performers out of the water."

"Fucking right!" Patrick insisted.

The boys carried that same enthusiasm right up until the day of their show. It was on a Friday night after a weeklong celebration of winter activities. Some were as ridiculous as building miniature snowmen on the school's property while others were as simple as having special meals served in the cafeteria. It wasn't exciting as far as Jimmy was concerned; pretty lame, in fact, but the night of the Winter Festival Variety Show would prove more interesting.

That night, Jimmy and Patrick found themselves sitting through everything from a bad stand-up comedian, some horrible poetry, various students playing instruments borrowed from the music department and a couple of dancers. Patrick's fantasy ballerina ended up being quite a bit less attractive than he had hoped. Overall, the night was pretty boring and the boys just assumed that Charm was automatically going to win the contest. Patrick laughingly remarked that considering the lack of real talent that night, Charm could win on their reputation alone, without even performing. Jimmy couldn't help but laugh at Patrick's cocky attitude because, although their band wasn't perfect, it was much more memorable than anything they had viewed that night.

There was a brief intermission that allowed the band time to set up before their performance at the end of the night. Although a few people had left the audience after their friends or relatives had their turn performing, many stayed. Jimmy guessed that between 200-300 people would see them perform that night. It was scary, but he was determined to do it. He knew Sean would tell him to do it, even though his fears were astronomical.

After much consideration, the band had chosen the song 'Talk Dirty to Me' by Poison, because it was a fun song and one that seemed pretty popular amongst their peers. Especially the girls, as Patrick pointed out. "Plus, it's suggestive, but at the same time, we can't get in shit 'cause it doesn't say anything too bad."

Their performance went off without a hitch. The audience truly seemed impressed with the band's ability to play the popular song almost to perfection. Especially Jimmy, who was oblivious to the fact that many people in the audience were viewing him with a new set of eyes that night. He was no longer the fat, shy kid who avoided other students. Jimmy Groome was now very hot and extremely talented. He stood out in the band. Many who once wouldn't have given him the time of day, suddenly found him acceptable. But he didn't see any of this as he played, only occasionally looking out into the audience. He was too pre-occupied with getting the song right and staying in the moment. It had to be perfect.

During the applause that followed, Jimmy thought about his former guitar teacher. He wondered what Sean Ryan would've thought if he had seen Jimmy's band perform that night. As the spotlight shone down on him, gently touching his face, something told him that maybe Sean wasn't so far away after all.

Chapter nineteen

*P*atrick was wrong. Not only did their band *not* win the variety show, the members of *Charm* were all hauled into the principal's office the following Monday morning. Apparently, they had greatly underestimated the sensitivities of their audience. Had it just been the students, Jimmy was certain there wouldn't have been a problem, but since the parents were also viewing their performance, it was a different matter.

"Come on!" Patrick attempted to plead their case. Jimmy, Ben and Stan remained quiet. Jimmy silently wished that his friend wouldn't somehow manage to get them in even *more* trouble. "There's no swearing in the song. I mean it's played on the radio all the time, so it's obviously not *that* bad. It's not our fault if someone gets offended. Any song could offend *someone*, couldn't it?"

"You bring up a good point," Mr. Atkins leaned back in his chair and watched the four boys carefully. He was an older man with almost no hair left and a huge stomach. He looked like he was about to give birth, Jimmy thought to himself. "However, this is public education and therefore we have to take the public's complaints into consideration. And I received several complaints that the song was sexually suggestive and parents felt that it was in bad taste to sing it at a school event."

"So why can't we just get detention or something?" Patrick argued. "Why are we being kicked out of school?"

"Detention is for minor occurrences such as showing up late for class," Mr. Atkins raised his eyebrows. "As you probably already know, Mr. Lipton."

"Isn't this a minor occurrence?" Patrick asked innocently, conveniently ignoring his remark. "We didn't have a clue we were offending anyone."

"You performed a song called 'Talk Dirty to Me' in front of other students and parents and it never occurred to you that someone might be offended?" Mr. Atkins asked with a small grin on his face. "Come *on* Patrick, let's be honest here."

Patrick answered with a shrug.

"Hey I understand what you're saying," the principal seemed to be talking just to Patrick at this point, as he leaned forward in his chair. "I really do. And personally, the song didn't offend me at all. Unfortunately, I can't listen to this many complaints from angry parents and simply give you detention. If most of these complainants had their way, you'd all be suspended for the week. But I said one day is sufficient."

"But you are the principal. You can do what you want." Patrick made a last attempt to change his mind.

"And the public pays my bills every week, so I unfortunately have to take their concerns into consideration," Mr. Atkins scanned the others boys' faces. "I personally think you are all very talented and I encourage you to continue with your music. However I will have to suspend you for today."

The other two members of Charm didn't seem to care and shrugged off the whole incident. In fact, they both had been kicked out of school previously and merely saw it as a day off to hang out at the mall. Patrick was more concerned with the fact that Charm hadn't won the variety show. Jimmy had his mother's car and offered to drive Patrick home.

"My mom is going to hit the roof," Jimmy remarked as soon as they headed out onto the road. "I wish I could fake her signature on this fucking slip that we have to get signed 'cause I'm gonna hear about it all day."

Patrick began to laugh. "Don't worry about it man, just tell your mom it was *my* idea and she'll forget all about it. She blames me for all your bad behavior." He laughed even harder. "At least the behavior she *knows* about. Speaking of which, have you hooked up with Sally's sister since New Year's Eve?"

Jimmy had told him the whole story on New Year's Day. Not surprisingly, his best friend loved it.

"No, actually," Jimmy said as a grin crossed his face. "Wonder what *she's* doing today?"

"Probably at school," Patrick said as he played with the car radio. "Maybe you can catch her between classes for a quickie. Ask her if she has a friend. Better yet, she's pretty hot, ask her if she has time for *me* after she's done banging the shit out of you."

Jimmy couldn't help laughing. "I really have to look her up. Sally should have gone back to university by now, so the coast is probably clear."

"Man, I still can't believe you fucked your ex's sister. And with Sally in the next room!" Patrick said as he slouched back in his seat while a Guns N' Roses song filled the car. "Wow, you keep doing shit like that and I'll have to make you my idol."

"I should be your idol anyway, asshole," Jimmy joked as they drove up to Patrick's house. His mom was shoveling snow from the front step and looked at the car suspiciously. "Is your mom going to lose it when she hears about the suspension thing?", Jimmy asked.

"Nah," Patrick said, leaning forward to grab his book bag from the floor. "Funny thing is, Jim, after you've knocked up a girl in high school, for some reason everything else you do wrong seems to pale in comparison." He smiled and started to open the car door. "Now your mother, on the other hand, is going to fucking freak." With that, Patrick jumped out of the car, smirking as he slammed shut the door.

Jimmy drove home, already dreading his mother's reaction. Patrick was right. Annette Groome freaked when she found out that her son was kicked out of school.

"Mom, it's just for a day," Jimmy attempted to explain himself. "The principal even said he didn't think the song was that bad, but he had to listen to complaining parents. *You* were there, did you think it was that bad?" he challenged her. "Cause if you did, you didn't say anything about it all weekend."

"Jimmy, you know that's not true. I did question whether or not it was appropriate for a school event," his mother reminded him. She was wearing a pink sweatshirt and pants, while a Kathy Smith exercise video continued to play in the next room. "You said it was fine, and now look."

Jimmy merely shrugged. He didn't think one day was a big deal.

"It's that Patrick Lipton that you keep hanging around," she insisted. "He was always a bad kid and he's not any better than when you first met him. Getting a girl pregnant in high school, getting tattoos, what else is this boy doing that I *don't* know about?" her eyes challenged Jimmy's. He certainly wasn't about to tell her anything to add to her case.

"He's cool, mom," Jimmy insisted. "He's my friend and I like him."

"Jimmy, I'm going to have to talk to your father about this," she shook her head, walking away. "I'm very disappointed in you."

Fortunately, Jimmy was still allowed to go to work that evening. He was relieved to get out of the house and away from his parents. Not that his dad had said anything about the incident. He was sent up to Jimmy's room after work to 'talk some sense' into him, but in the end, John Groome basically agreed with the principal on the matter and didn't feel that his son had done anything too outrageous. Both parents signed the slip that was to be returned to Mr. Atkins the following morning and that was pretty much it.

Monday nights were rarely busy at Top Dog Burger. Jimmy was a little frustrated to be stuck with two new guys who seemed incapable of figuring out anything on their own. Their incompetence just encouraged him to smoke a joint on his break. He recognized the fact that there was clearly something wrong when he had to get high in order to get through a short shift at work. But just as he walked back to the restaurant at the end of his break, another car pulled up beside him. He was surprised to see who was waving at him: Suzanne Borden.

Jimmy hated the fact that he still had a crush on the girl who once went out of her way to humiliate him. Looking around he quickly realized that she was alone and therefore she had no audience to impress, so maybe he had the upper hand? Well, then again, maybe not. As soon as she smiled at him, Jimmy felt his heart begin to anxiously race.

"Hi," she rushed toward Jimmy, who stood awkwardly and waited. Suzanne's dark eyes sparkled as she smiled at him. She briefly looked away then back into his face. Jimmy was bewildered. She hadn't spoken to him since he was twelve years old. It was the same day she had humiliated him in front of classmates when he asked her on a date - one of the worst days of his life. And now she was approaching *him* as if they had been buddies for a lifetime. As much as he hated her, he still wanted her.

"Hi," he finally replied, but didn't offer anything else. Not a smile or any encouragement to continue their conversation. He wasn't sure what to think of all this yet.

"I saw your band play on Friday night," she casually began, shoving both hands in her jacket pockets. As she looked up at him, batting her long eyelashes, he could only stare at her perfect face. Why did girls who were complete bitches always have to be hot? Patrick had always insisted it was because they *could* be and men still wanted them. Jimmy suspected that Suzanne knew this all too well.

"Oh yeah?" Jimmy drawled, sounding bored.

"Yeah, and you guys were *amazing*," Suzanne smiled at him with such sincerity that it was difficult to hold old grudges against her. Maybe she had changed. "I thought you looked great on that stage. You looked like a real rock star. All the girls were checking you out."

"Really?" Jimmy asked skeptically. She was full of shit. "Well I gotta get back to work." He pointed toward the building behind him.

"Oh I was just going in," Suzanne followed him. "My parents both work late so I'm usually in charge of getting my own dinner. I thought I'd get something really *bad* tonight."

"I see," Jimmy nodded and continued to walk. Like he gave a fuck.

"So, I was hoping to see you too. I mean, I wanted to tell you how good the show was on Friday," she rambled, and Jimmy only half listened. But then she said something that really grabbed his attention. "I was actually wondering if maybe you'd like to hang out sometime?"

Jimmy stopped in his tracks. They had just entered the restaurant and both the newbie's were staring at him and Suzanne with interest. He gave them each a dirty look and they attempted to look busy again.

"Ah, what?" he finally asked.

"I thought maybe we could hang out sometime," Suzanne's face turned red when forced to repeat her original question. "Maybe like, go to a movie or something?"

"I guess," Jimmy replied skeptically while a voice in the back of his head asked him what he was doing. This was the same girl who once made him feel like a piece of shit when the tables had been turned, and he had asked *her* out. "A movie?"

"Or you know," she shrugged. "We could just hang out at my place and watch a movie. My parents aren't usually around, so we'd have the house to ourselves."

Bingo.

"Sure," Jimmy smirked, and wondered what Patrick would say when he heard this story. "That sounds great."

Chapter twenty

"Are you fucking shitting me?" Patrick asked abrasively while stretching out on the Groome's couch. Jimmy had just told him the Suzanne story. He wore a mischievous smile on his face while shaking his head in disgust. "So basically, when you were fat and not socially acceptable, she was a cunt. But now that you're in a band and all that shit, suddenly she wants to jump on your dick? Am I getting this right?"

Jimmy laughed. "I don't know if I would put it *quite* that way, but yeah, she laughed at me when *I* asked *her* out a few years ago. Now she's inviting me over to her house and saying how her parents won't be home."

"And she wants to jump your dick," Patrick repeated his crass remark and yawned. "Yup! Got it." Jimmy couldn't help but to laugh. It was starting to feel like Jimmy's best friend was taking up permanent residence in the Groome household. Since the year had begun, there were few days when Patrick *couldn't* be found in Jimmy's basement after school. The only exception seemed to be when either was working.

"Kind of looks that way."

"So if you want my advice, and I seriously don't know *why* you would," Patrick raised one eyebrow as he watched Jimmy drink a coffee on the other side of the room. "I'd fuck her and dump her. Never call her again. Avoid her calls. Just is a total prick to her."

"I don't know if I could do that," Jimmy almost choked on a mouthful of coffee. Maybe it was time to just let go of what happened in the past and move forward. Maybe Suzanne was a nice person now. *Maybe* it was time to take a girl seriously again.

"Why not?" Patrick's eyelids were drooping, as if he were about to fall asleep. "You said she hasn't even talked to you since that time you asked her out. Not until she saw our band play last week." Patrick hesitated for a moment. "Plus she's hot, so you don't want to pass up the opportunity to nail her." He shrugged. "But like I said, I'm probably not the best person to take advice from either."

Jimmy considered his words for that night as well as the rest of the week. Their date was scheduled for the coming Friday night at her house and as much as he wanted to hold a permanent grudge against the girl who once looked down her nose at him, he couldn't help but look forward to their date. He was actually a little nervous. In fact, he was a lot nervous.

Things sure had changed with time. The same girl who used to ignore him in the school hallways, now went out of her way to acknowledge Jimmy as often as possible. It didn't matter who was around, Suzanne always gave him a big smile, batting her eyelashes as he walked by. For the remainder of the week, Jimmy also noticed that she was always wearing short skirts or strategically ripped jeans to school. It was a bit surreal to him.

"Fuck, she's on a mission," Patrick commented on one of the days that Suzanne was wearing a super short skirt. His eyes were following her as she walked away from them both. "Man, if you don't want to fuck her, *I* will," a mischievous grin crossed his face.

Jimmy smiled, but didn't reply to his comment. Instead he inquired about Patrick's current status. "So I take it that Melissa is out of the picture?" He noticed that his friend wasn't saying much about his on again, off again girlfriend lately. Not since New Year's Eve.

"Oh fuck man," the smile automatically fell from Patrick's face as his eyes looked downward toward his shoes. "Don't ask."

"Okay."

"Let's just say this much," Patrick's eyes met with Jimmy's and were suddenly filled with a seriousness that he rarely revealed. "Never have a kid with someone unless you *know* you plan to stay with them. 'Cause otherwise things get way too complicated."

Jimmy didn't inquire any further. He knew that Patrick's

relationship with Melissa was difficult even before the baby arrived, but had deteriorated over time. It was once revealed during a drunken conversation that Patrick could barely tolerate his ex, but did so in order to stay a part of his baby's life. Although technically he had every right to spend time with his daughter regardless of whether or not he was with Melissa, it was clear that she wasn't going to make it easy for him to do so. Considering how much he had once loathed the idea of becoming a father, it amazed Jimmy to see how much Patrick now loved his daughter, Hope.

"Well either way, I'll let her know you're available," Jimmy returned to the original topic to lighten the mood. The last thing he wanted to do was to upset his friend.

"*Now* you're talking," a gleam returned to Patrick's green eyes.

The week slipped by and the next thing Jimmy knew, it was Friday night and he was getting ready for his date with Suzanne. After a quick shower, he pulled on his jeans and a t-shirt he got at a *Kiss* show. Stuffing some condoms in his pocket, he headed out the door.

Arriving at Suzanne's house, Jimmy took a deep breath and slowly walked up her steps. It felt strange. Momentarily he wondered if he was once again the center of some kind of joke, like ringing the doorbell only to discover that she had given him someone else's address - or walking into a house full of people who were mocking him. He wasn't the seventeen-year-old Jimmy Groome walking up the steps to Suzanne Bordon's house that night. Instead, he was the fat, twelve year old kid who had no experience with girls. But he knew it was a dragon he had to slay and therefore pushed his fears aside and rang her doorbell. Hearing footsteps on the other side, a part of him was surprised when it was Suzanne who answered the door. There was no one else in the house and she genuinely looked pleased to see him.

"Hi," she smiled shyly before moving aside to let him in. "Come in."

"Thanks," Jimmy murmured as he followed her into the house.

He noticed right away that her family was poor. There was no doubt about it. Even though the house looked average on the outside, inside it was nothing like he expected. The kitchen was dirty and cluttered, with dishes lined up on the counters. The smell of stale popcorn permeated the room. Glancing into the living room, Jimmy noted that the chairs were old and stained while the carpets were faded and threadbare. His place looked pretty fancy in comparison. It never would've occurred to him that the same girl, who acted like she was better than other students, lived in this dump. But he remained silent. In a way, it made him feel bad for her.

"Sorry about the mess," she seemed to notice him inspecting the room. "My parents aren't home much to clean."

Jimmy merely smiled. "Don't worry about it."

"Come in," she led him into the next room. She was wearing loose jeans and a sweater that zipped up the front. His first thought was 'easy access' and he wondered if Suzanne had been thinking the same thing. "I got us something to drink," she pointed toward a bottle of rum, sitting on the coffee table. It looked like it had been fished out of a dumpster. Beside the liquor sat a bottle of cola and two empty glasses.

"Cool," Jimmy replied, shrugging out of his jacket and throwing it on the back of the couch. There was something about seeing her home that caused Jimmy's nerves to dissolve. Nevertheless, he definitely wasn't going to turn down a drink. "You can be the bartender."

He watched her mix the drinks noting that she wasn't shy while adding the alcohol. What surprised him even more was how fast Suzanne knocked back her drink. He was barely half finished his first drink when she was well into her second. By the time she was on her third drink, the bottle of rum was getting very close to empty and Suzanne was definitely drunk. Jimmy watched her stagger to the bathroom and listened as she began to slur her words. He was beginning to feel a little embarrassed and turned off by her intoxication. However, that quickly changed when she invited him to her bedroom. Clearly he wasn't as fucked up as her, but he was feeling pretty good and was definitely up for anything.

She grabbed his hand and stumbled toward a room at the end of a short hallway. It was slightly cleaner than the rest of the house, but not much. Clothes, makeup and textbooks were scattered all over the floor. They navigated through the mess to her bed. He was about to kiss her when she started to talk.

"Ya know, you know what?" She lurched through her words, leaning slightly away from Jimmy – he could still smell the rum and Coke fumes on her breath. "I was like so scared to ask you out. I didn't think you liked me very much and I...I just had to, sort of like, do it anyway without even thinking." she rambled, and Jimmy bit his lip as he listened to her speak. They had spent most of the night discussing safe topics, like television and music. Now Suzanne picked the most inappropriate time to discuss her feelings; he was buzzed and horny and didn't care about her hesitation to ask him out.

"And like, I thought you hated me," she confided and he noted that she leaned farther back; her sweater lifted slightly revealing her flat stomach. "After that time in grade seven or whatever." Suzanne appeared confused and was waiting for Jimmy to reply. When he didn't, she carried on, "I think you thought I was interested in you back then, do you remember?"

Hurt and resentment swelled up inside of him as he nodded.

"And I was like, I can't go out with this guy, so I tried to break it to you gently, 'cause I didn't want to hurt your feelings. But you looked like you were going to like, cry or something when I said I wouldn't go on a date with you." Suzanne began to giggle, as if they were joyfully reminiscing over their younger days. As if no one had been damaged by her thoughtless behavior.

She tried to break it to me gently? I looked like I was going to cry? And now she's laughing? This is funny to her. I was humiliated that day and wanted to die right there, in the middle of class and she's treating it all as a joke???

Jimmy was not amused. He felt an intense anger rise inside of him. If Suzanne had even admitted to being cruel to him on that horrible day years earlier, it wouldn't have been so bad. An apology would have gone a long way, but her twisted take on that day was insulting and infuriating. Maybe he was wrong to not let it go, but it was difficult to forget when someone was purposely hurtful in order to look 'cool' to friends.

"And anyway, I thought for sure you wouldn't go out with me, so I-

Jimmy was sick of listening to her. At that point, he decided to do exactly what Patrick had suggested: fuck her and dump the bitch. Jimmy broke off her endless stream of conversation by kissing her feverishly, sliding his hand into her pants and between her legs as she moved against him. She was moaning as he quickly unzipped her sweater to reveal her black, lacy bra. Removing both the sweater and bra, he moved on to her jeans. Within seconds all her clothes were on the floor beside the bed and Jimmy was undoing his pants. He had no intentions of removing his own clothes; all he needed to do was get his dick out.

Jimmy made sure that Suzanne was satisfied – extremely satisfied. It was the best revenge: make her want him even more before dumping her. Then she'd understand what it felt like to be disrespected.

When it was over and her breathing had returned to normal, Jimmy threw the used condom on the floor, despite the fact that there was a trash can right beside the bed. Standing, he pulled up his boxers and zipped his jeans. She watched him curiously as he started toward the door.

"Where are you going?" she demanded, and he could hear the emotion in her voice. "You're just going to leave? Just like *that?*"

Jimmy slowly turned around and licked his lips. His eyes gave her a quick once over before he casually nodded. "Yup, pretty much."

"So, what? Did you just come here tonight to get in my pants?" Suzanne asked with tears in her eyes as she sat up and started to quickly get dressed.

"See, you and I see things different," Jimmy suddenly felt very confident and cocky. "When we were kids, I was the nice kid asking you out and you humiliated me in front of the entire class. But *you* seem to think that you let me down easy. And *now*, you seem to think that I only came over here to fuck you. But in reality, *you* only invited me here in order to get drunk and fucked." Jimmy paused as he saw anger mix with tears in her eyes. "See what I mean? We tend to see the same situations in very different ways. But that's fine, probably just a girl/guy thing, right?"

With that, he turned once again to leave.

"You're a fucking asshole," she yelled behind him.

"Yeah, but I'm an *asshole* that just *fucked* your brains out and you liked it," Jimmy heard anger creep into his voice just as he reached her bedroom's exit, and turned to add, "And considering it was like throwing a hot dog down a hallway, I think I did pretty good."

He left.

Chapter twenty-one

Suzanne avoided him after that night. On the off change that Jimmy saw her as he walked through the hallways of their school, their eyes rarely met for more than a second before Suzanne looked away. At first, Jimmy felt guilty. Maybe *he* had been out of line. Maybe his words and actions had been much too harsh. That never lasted once he recalled her cruel words from when they were twelve, not to mention Suzanne's inaccurate account of the situation. There were times when Jimmy would wonder if his *own* recollection of that incident from years earlier was incorrect, but he knew it wasn't. There were just some things that could never be forgotten.

If Suzanne avoided Jimmy's eyes, her friends certainly didn't. Oddly enough, they actually looked at him with intrigue rather than hatred. And to Jimmy, that didn't make sense. Chances were good that Suzanne had given them the entire account of their night together, possibly making it sound even worse than it actually was, and yet her two best friends, Tammy and Paula, looked at him with curious eyes. He didn't know much about either of them, but the fact that they were friends with Suzanne didn't make him want to get to know them.

A few weeks following his encounter with Suzanne, the first of her two friends approached him. Jimmy was on his way to math class when Tammy stopped him in the hallway. She was pretty in a sort of child-like way, with shoulder-length curly hair and pale blue eyes. She had a tiny body and delicate features, making her resemble a twelve year old. Not exactly a turn on, however her blunt directness caught his attention.

Within two minutes of their conversation, Tammy told Jimmy that she wanted him to be her first.

"What?" He was stunned by her candor.

"You heard me," she pouted, briefly looking away from his eyes. "I want you to be my first. I don't want to be a virgin anymore. It's embarrassing and I want my first time to be with you."

Jimmy studied her face. "Don't you want it to be with a boyfriend?" He hoped that she didn't think that *he* was going to start dating her.

"No," she sighed. "Guys don't like me." He could see some sadness in her eyes and automatically decided to say no. This just wasn't right. But then, Tammy said something that hit closer to home. " Even if I do wait, chances are it's probably going to be with someone who just dumps me afterward. Plus, I don't want to be a virgin anymore, I feel like I'm the only girl in school who is one."

Jimmy briefly thought about what she was saying. Tammy *was* right. He knew first hand how it felt to not want to be a virgin and he also understood how it felt to be dumped. Even hearing other kids talking at school made it clear that first times were never very special. That was just a myth parents told their kids to make *themselves* feel better.

"Why me?" Jimmy quietly asked. "Is it because of Suzanne?"

"No," Tammy shook her head. "She hates you. I just feel like you'd be cool with doing it and cause I think you wouldn't tell everyone. I mean you didn't tell everyone about Suzanne."

She was right. He had only told Patrick.

Jimmy agreed and they got together that weekend. It was a little awkward, but unlike Sally, she wasn't scared and didn't insist that he 'get it over with'. So Jimmy was surprised when Tammy started crying after they had sex. She attempted to wipe the tears away before he noticed, but wasn't successful.

"Did I hurt you?" Jimmy automatically started to rethink his decision to take her virginity. Maybe he had made a mistake. It hadn't been the most exciting sexual experience of his life, but it wasn't like each time could be.

"No," she appeared embarrassed and tried to recompose herself. Tammy's voice was very soft and gentle, unlike the bold girl who had approached him a few days earlier. "I was just thinking that maybe no boy would ever want to do this with me again. I don't exactly have the hot body every guy looks for."

Jimmy understood what she meant. Tammy was very undeveloped compared to other girls their age and almost looked as if she hadn't hit puberty at all. He felt bad for her simply because he'd had his own share of body image issues in recent years.

"It'll get better," Jimmy insisted. "I promise."

After that day, Tammy would shyly smile at him in the hallway at school, but she never attempted to hook up with him again. By graduation, she had a boyfriend.

Of the three girls, Paula was the most hesitant to approach him. She wasn't bold and direct like either Suzanne or Tammy. But one night when at Jimmy and Patrick were at a party, Jimmy was left alone with his bottle of tequila while his friend took off with some random girl. The next thing he knew, Paula was drinking it with him. And somewhere in a drunken haze, the two of them ended up having sex in the park close to his house. Unlike both Tammy and Suzanne, Paula did *not* leave him alone. She wanted to be his next girlfriend.

"You do realize that your friend Suzanne hates me," Jimmy reminded her during one of many phone calls she made to his house since their drunken mistake.

"So?" Her voice was slightly abrupt over the phone and he could sense her annoyance. He knew the drill; when girls didn't get what they wanted, it wasn't too long before their fangs came out, ready for attack.

"So? You would take the chance of losing a friend over a guy?" He asked, but in all honesty, Jimmy didn't really care about that issue at all. He just wasn't that interested in Paula. He certainly didn't want to proclaim her as his girlfriend. In fact, the more women he hooked up with, the *less* he wanted a relationship. It just seemed girls always had issues. They played games, lied, cheated and generally were clingy. Who needed that shit?

"I like you Jimmy," She whined. "I'm starting to have feelings for you."

Jimmy firmly told her that he didn't feel the same and he didn't want to hurt her. Although she said she understood, she continued to pursue him. If Paula wasn't calling his house, she was attempting to talk to him at school. Suzanne started to notice at some point and began talking to Jimmy again too. She even apologized for the stuff that happened when they were kids, and then she completely stunned him by suggesting that they hook up again. He said no to both girls and meant it. But during another party a few weeks later, Jimmy got drunk and somehow ended up hooking up with both of them at different times during the same night. He was wasted and went home just before eleven. The next day, Patrick called him with the news.

"Man, you're my fucking idol!" He raved excitedly.

"What?" Even though it was one in the afternoon, Jimmy was half asleep.

"Not only do you have these two psycho bitches wanting to jump your dick, now you've got them *fighting* over it," he began to laugh. "What the fuck do you do to get them to *fight* over you?"

"What are you talking about?" Jimmy muttered, rubbing his eyes.

"Suzanne and Paula got in a fight after you left the party last night," Patrick sounded astonished. "Over *you*, you fucktard."

"What?" Jimmy was suddenly wide-awake. Obviously, Patrick was teasing him. "You aren't serious?"

"Serious, I *am*." Patrick insisted. "They were pulling hair and punching, slapping and crying. Over you!"

"I doubt it was over me," Jimmy started to laugh at the possibility.

"Fuck off man, it was over *you*." Patrick persisted, humor in his voice. "*I* was there and *I* heard them saying it. Have fun with that situation!"

"That situation is officially done. I don't care how drunk I get," Jimmy vowed. "They are both fucking crazy."

"Hope you used a condom with those dirty bitches," Patrick commented through his laughter. "I think Suzanne fucked some other guy after the fight."

"Yup, I always use a condom."

"Good, I don't want to go to your funeral 'cause you get AIDS, you dirty fucker," Patrick continued to take jabs at him.

Jimmy not only used condoms religiously, he bought them regularly at the same drugstore. He originally chose it because it was small and quiet. The entire world didn't need to know that he was buying condoms on a very regular basis. It was a necessary evil. However, because the store was so small, Jimmy always seemed to get the same cashier ringing in his purchase. She was young and really cute. Her dark eyes would study him curiously and he could tell what she was thinking. One day he answered the question that was in her eyes every time he dropped by the store.

"Yeah, I have a *lot* of sex," he gave her the same smile that other girls called charming and she blushed. On a whim, Jimmy asked her out and was surprised when she accepted. Later that same night, the cashier discovered firsthand why he bought so many condoms.

"Fuck, now I'll have to change drugstores," he joked with Patrick about it later that week. "I really *liked* that store too."

"I can't believe you fucked the girl at the drugstore. Man, you are fucking *dirty*." Patrick shook his head while laughing, as the two had their lunch in the school cafeteria. "You haven't been having sex for a year yet and already, there's been how many? Like seriously man. This is like a hobby for you now."

"I don't know if it's a hobby," Jimmy attempted to explain himself. Although Patrick was praising him, Jimmy couldn't help but feel some sense of embarrassment over his promiscuous behavior. "It just sort of just happens. I guess I'm just curious."

"You're preaching to the choir, man," Patrick laughed. "But you're getting a rep as a dog around here. I've heard girls talking and shit. They'll like talk about you in disgust and then like two minutes later they'll say something like (Patrick broke into falsetto with a fork full of soggy fries in the air) "But he's so hot." He rolled his eyes and Jimmy broke into laughter.

"Am I still your idol?" Jimmy asked innocently, attempting to eat his soup while still laughing at his friend's over-the-top antics.

"Yup and very soon, I think I'm going to start a scoreboard for you in your basement."

"How are you gonna explain *that* to my mom?" Jimmy joked with him.

"I'll tell her I'm tracking your marks or something."

But Jimmy knew his mother was painfully aware that his marks were horrible.

"Yeah man, that won't work. I'm flunking out of at least two classes," Jimmy decided to allow their conversation to calm down before attempting to eat more of his lunch. "She'll know it's not about school."

"Whatever man, I'm still tracking it. Maybe we should have a competition."

"That's sick," Jimmy paused to consider. While he was a little revolted by his recent behavior with women, he did enjoy the attention that his misadventures brought with them. "But I like it."

Chapter Twenty-two

He knew it was wrong, but he couldn't bring himself to care. After seeing the true colors of girls like Suzanne, Candace and Sally, it was difficult for Jimmy to feel guilty about his little competition with Patrick. So what if he didn't take the opposite sex seriously? Until recently, they certainly hadn't taken *him* seriously either. He realized it was partly his bitterness from when he was the fat kid that was to blame for his lack of compassion.

For the month of February 1990, the two boys would see who could have sex with the most girls. They had to be honest with each other. Neither could make up stories of girls they had 'hooked up' with if in fact, nothing intimate had occurred at all. It didn't have to be actual intercourse either. Patrick insisted that a girl had to physically get either of them off in some way, to count as one of their 'hook-up' girls; it didn't matter *how* they did it.

Since their high school was overcrowded with teenage girls, it didn't take long to get the ball rolling. Patrick was very forward and blunt, which often worked in his favor. He had no problem walking up to a girl and telling her that she was hot. His sheer boldness stood out in comparison with many teenaged boys who were shy to approach a girl. Patrick didn't care; if he decided to get together with a girl, he was usually successful. And his successes gave him extra points in their competition.

"I'm surprised that you haven't tried to hook up with any teachers yet," Jimmy joked one afternoon as they walked out of the warm, stuffy school into the crisp winter air.

"Hey, remember that hot teacher from fifth grade, wasn't it?" Patrick began to laugh.

"Yeah, you mean Mrs. Holden?" Jimmy grinned. "She was pretty cute."

"Yeah," Patrick said with relish and a wicked look in his eye. "Wonder what *she's* up to these days?"

"You're a dirty dog, man." Jimmy began to laugh. "A *really* dirty dog."

While Patrick seemed to prefer the more direct approach, Jimmy thought that charm was key. He would make eye contact with the girl he wanted to get with, smile at her and eventually ease into a conversation. It was his friendly, easy-going nature that seemed to win girls over in the beginning, but once he'd found his comfort level, Jimmy would compliment the girl in question. He knew that women loved to be flattered; he could see it in their eyes. It just seemed like every remark that suggested that she was pretty or unique would lower a girl's walls. Maybe they didn't always believe his words, but they *wanted* to believe them. And for the most part, Jimmy was being sincere when he told a girl that she had beautiful eyes or that he loved her hair. The only problem was that he didn't necessarily like the *girl* as much as her attributes.

As February came to a close, both boys were neck and neck in their competition and in the end; they agreed it was pretty much a draw. Although Patrick had a lot of various sexual activities to add up his numbers, Jimmy had more actual intercourse during the month of February. His numbers were growing rapidly as the one-year anniversary of losing his virginity slowly began to creep up; it was something he never would've expected, especially a year earlier.

With the month of March came the realization that both Patrick and Jimmy may have been popular on the dating scene, but they'd have to really pull up their socks in order to graduate that year. Jimmy was failing Math and Biology while Patrick was pretty much in the same boat, with the addition of English. Neither of them wanted to spend another semester in school, but it wasn't looking promising at all. In a way, Jimmy didn't care. Although he was working part-time, he wasn't ready to jump into the real world just yet. Patrick was anxious however, saying that he wanted to go to college eventually, once he figured out what he wanted to do with his life.

Jimmy already knew what *he* wanted to do with his life. Music was the only thing he truly cared about. Unfortunately, Charm hadn't played together since their show in January and the band seemed to have parted ways, but he continued to practice daily. It was discouraging to Jimmy, but at the same time, he felt like he needed to get together with a group of people who were more serious. When it came to his first band, it was clear that he was the only one who wanted to make a career in the music industry. Because of Sean Ryan, he felt confident that this goal was within his reach as well.

Patrick was very supportive. Jimmy liked the fact that his friend didn't ridicule him for wanting to someday be a rock star and appreciated his encouragement.

"Unlike the rest of our so-called band, you actually have a chance of going out there and doing it," Patrick told him when it became apparent that Charm was a thing of the past. "I'm telling you, you've got a fucking load of talent. If you want to be in a big rock band, then that's what you gotta do."

"I hope you're right," Jimmy replied uneasily.

"I *am* right," Patrick insisted. "Fuck man, you had Sean Ryan for a teacher. If that doesn't assure you a place in the world of stardom, I don't know what does."

"I'm sure he had other students too," Jimmy said. "We can't all be stars."

"So, you were probably the only fucking good one of the bunch," Patrick persisted loyally. "You even said that he always gave you extra time in your lessons and really seemed to want to make you a better player. So, take that as a sign that music could be your future."

It wasn't Patrick's future, however. He admitted that being part of a band was something he enjoyed, but it wasn't for him. Not that Jimmy's friend had any clue what he wanted to do with his life. It seemed that being a father somehow made Patrick feel limited. He obviously couldn't afford to spend years in university. Jimmy didn't think that it was fair, but had to admit that the responsibility of a child did weigh heavily on his friend.

As the month of March slowly drew to a close, Jimmy spent most of his spare time at work. Because of a staff shortage, he was working around 30 hours a week on top of school. Although his mother felt strongly that it was time for him to quit his job in order to focus on school, he managed to convince her that it didn't matter at that point. He had already failed a few tests and his marks were continuing to sink. In the end, Jimmy felt that September would be a fresh start for him and he promised her that he'd make every effort to graduate the next time around. Although she didn't seem completely satisfied with his answer, she did accept it.

Things on the dating front were a little slow too. Since Patrick and Jimmy's competition in February, word had gotten around school that they were both 'dogs' and weren't at all interested in dating anyone in a serious way. Needless to say, when either made an effort to capture a girl's attention, it was often met with either glares or skepticism.

"The worst part man," Patrick complained one morning before classes began, "Is that most of these girls want it as bad as either of us, but they just don't want their stupid friends to think they're sluts or whatever. It's like you somehow save their reputation if you call them your girlfriend. It's just so fucked up."

"Well those girls actually might want relationships too," Jimmy calmly suggested, but his friend was insistent that it wasn't the case.

"Please, these are the same girls who get drunk, fuck a guy, then try to say *he* took advantage of *her* while she was drinking. And you know that most of the time, it's just an excuse, 'cause she wants the guy too."

Jimmy just grinned. His friend had an interesting perspective on everything. He didn't always agree with him, but at the same time, he understood where the guy was coming from regarding women. Dating and relationships were simply not like they appeared on television and were often a lot more complicated in the real world than the innocent view that the mainstream media portrayed. Teenagers were curious and wanted to experiment as they slowly pushed themselves through to the adult world.

A few weeks later, Patrick approached him with an idea. Apparently another high school in Thorton was having a 'pre-exam' teen dance in late April. "I think we should crash it."

"You want to crash another school's dance?" Jimmy raised his eyebrows. "Won't they know that we aren't students there?"

"Nah, we'll get around it." He insisted. "Plus, all the girls there have no fucking clue who we are, so we'll have a better chance of hooking up."

Jimmy reluctantly agreed. He didn't really think they had a hope in hell of getting through the doors, but shrugged and said he'd go along with the plan. Much to his surprise on the night of the dance, the door people didn't hesitate to allow them access to 'The Spring Fever Event'.

"The girls here are fucking hot!" Patrick murmured as they walked into the dimly lit gymnasium.

Jimmy wasn't as enthused. To him, it was just another school dance. No one really captured his attention. So, as the night wore on and Patrick eventually took off with some girl, Jimmy decided to go home. As he wandered the hallways of the school attempting to find a bathroom on his way out, he came across a couple having a very heated argument in a quiet corner of the school. A quick glance confirmed no one else was around, and although he simply wanted to take a piss and leave, doing so would require him to walk past the arguing couple. That was something he didn't really want to do with the sheer tension that filled the hallway.

"Why did you do this to me!" The girl sounded devastated and Jimmy held his breath and hid behind a door at the end of the hallway. He could see a tall guy with short, dark hair hovering over a very small girl. The guy's sheer size made it impossible to even *see* what the girl looked like. Jimmy assumed he was some jock.

"What the fuck? I never told you that we were going to have a relationship." The guy's deep voice filled the hallway and Jimmy shrank back slightly. The last thing he wanted was this huge fucker catching him listening in on their conversation. Especially since he was only attempting to find a washroom in the first place. "We hooked up and that's it."

Jimmy rolled his eyes. He just wanted the argument to be over with and for them to move on. So far, it seemed pretty lame. Some girl was ragging at a guy who didn't want a relationship – why did women always try to manipulate men into getting tied down? Why couldn't they just have fun and move on? Was that so terrible?

"But I thought you really liked me." Jimmy could sense strong emotions coming from her voice and began to feel guilty for his negative assumptions regarding her intentions.

A loud, frustrated sigh came from the guy. "I do – just not in that kinda way." His voice became somewhat gentle, then within mere seconds, abrupt and sharp once again. "You're hot, but not someone I can see myself with – it's not you, it's just me who's fucked up."

Jimmy could hear her crying and bit his lip. He felt his heart grow heavy as the agonizing sobs filled the hallway. Ever since the day of his sister's rape, the sound of a woman experiencing intense and authentic emotional pain was almost too much for him to bear. And this stranger's sobs were a tremendous mix of honesty and misery that enveloped him. He realized that he was much the same as this guy. In the same situation, Jimmy was often overwhelmed with such an urge to escape the uncomfortable moment that he simply said whatever he could to flee. He never thought about the girl who was being disappointed and hurt, but only of himself and *his* own discomfort. It was the first time he experienced this situation from the outside, and he didn't like the view.

Chapter twenty-three

Jimmy wished he hadn't overheard that conversation because it caused his conscience to alert him to a whole series of questions; did the girls he had sex with and dumped feel this way? Had he ever made a girl cry? It was something that had never occurred to him before that night. When he thought back to all the times he could've made girls feel like less of a person, guilt began to trickle in. It was the first time he realized that his actions and words had consequences.

After the couple concluded their argument that night, the guy stomped off, leaving behind a crying girl. Jimmy considered coming out of his hiding place and approaching the stranger, but decided against it. That would be just weird. However, another part of him felt like he owed her something – although, clearly not personally; in a strange way she represented *all* the girls he had been so cruel to in the previous months. But then again, he wondered if he had any right to judge the situation. Maybe there was much more to it than he was witnessing. Perhaps the girl was clingy? A stalker? Manipulative? But even as he went through the possibilities in his mind, nothing really seemed to ring true. Maybe it was time to change.

Not that Jimmy Groome wanted a relationship either. It just wasn't something he saw in his immediate future. Maybe never. But he did love sex and wasn't about to slow things down in that area. Unlike Patrick, he wasn't about to lie to the girls he met. Jimmy wanted to be honest and straightforward about his intentions. And his intentions were to get laid and nothing more. There was a part of him that thought it would be impossible to ever commit to any girl. He didn't believe that anyone could ever captivate him in that way.

Jimmy even considered that maybe he wasn't normal. All around him, his classmates were involved in relationships. Since breaking up with Sally, he had no interest in having a relationship himself. It didn't matter if a girl was really pretty, cool, fun – it was irrelevant. It was almost as if he was closed to any emotions. There was a side of his emotions that was dead and maybe it would forever be that way. But while drinking with his best friend one evening, Jimmy told him the story about the arguing couple and how it had affected his perception of himself.

"Wow, that's pretty fucked up," Patrick poured himself another drink as he contemplated the situation. "Do you really think you're that bad? That *we're* that bad?"

Jimmy shrugged with the shadow of a grin on his face. "Yeah man, I kind of think we are *that* bad. I'm starting to feel like a complete dick."

"You know, you never promised anything to any of these girls," Patrick confidently pointed out. "So, I wouldn't sweat it. I mean, just be straight with them from now on about your intentions. And maybe stop sleeping with girls that you actually *hate* like Suzanne or girls like Sally's sister who was more about revenge."

Jimmy considered his point and eventually, his concern began to fade from his mind.

By the time Jimmy's eighteenth birthday rolled around in May, he was sure of one thing; he wasn't going to graduate that year.

Previously there had been a slight hope of finally finishing school, but that was long gone. Although he was slightly disappointed, it allowed him more time before officially becoming an adult. He wasn't ready to move out of the house, stress over money and be miserable in a crappy job. At least while he was still in high school, he could put off the realities and responsibilities of life. He had a plan.

During the summer months, he would start a new band and practice even more than usual. Also, Jimmy would work as much as he could in order to buy a car. That fall he would return to school for half days, while continuing to work as much as possible. By the time he had completed his last two courses in January, Jimmy hoped to have enough money to move out on his own. If not, he would at least have his own set of wheels.

Patrick was also returning to school that fall. Then he planned to go to college. Jimmy had no such plans, but he wasn't about to share this information with either of his parents. They just naturally assumed that his education wasn't going to end with high school, especially now that his sister was about to graduate from her program. He didn't have the heart to tell them the truth just yet. He knew that they'd never support his dream to be in a rock band.

On his eighteenth birthday, Jimmy couldn't help thinking of Sally. He remembered the day that they'd lost their virginity together and how scared she'd been. So much had changed in the past year. There were rumors that Sally was now engaged to some guy she met at school. Some super smart university man. Jimmy assumed it was the same one who was with her during the holidays a few months earlier. Meanwhile, one year after losing his virginity, Jimmy had slept with almost thirty girls.

Turning eighteen seemed to change how women looked at him. Suddenly he was considered an adult, which greatly increased his prospects. Patrick had finally obtained fake IDs for both of them, so the two boys began to frequent bars. Unfortunately, that put a huge dent in Jimmy's plans to save money for a car, but it was worth it. The women they met at bars were often ready, willing and able to do just about anything – and unlike high school girls, *they* weren't expecting relationships. It was rare that Jimmy went out and didn't pick up before the night was over. And since he was officially eighteen, he no longer had a curfew.

At first his parents didn't question why he didn't return home until almost 4 am every Saturday and Sunday morning. Sometimes Jimmy didn't return home at all if he had to work early the next day. Since he had an extra uniform at work, it wasn't unusual for him to crawl into Top Dog Burger with red eyes, hair still damp from the shower and overpowering mints that hid the hint of alcohol on his breath. Fortunately, his boss didn't care as long as he showed up. Although Jimmy had many flaws, no one could ever say he didn't arrive in time for work. That was never an issue.

When his parents decided to question him on why he suddenly kept such late hours, he lied and said he was at Patrick's or another friend's house for the night. However, one Sunday morning when Jimmy wandered through the kitchen door at 6 a.m. he was surprised to find his father at the kitchen table. Drinking a cup of coffee, John Groome looked up from his weekend paper and observed his son's disheveled appearance.

"Late night?" His father raised both eyebrows and tilted his head. "Jimmy, you look like you've been through hell and back." He studied his son – the red eyes, dirty clothes and uncombed hair. "Why are you just getting in now?"

Jimmy wasn't about to tell him the truth. After a night of partying at an after hours bar, he had left with a hot twenty-five year old and the two ended up going at it until the sun rose in the Sunday morning skies. That had been his sign that it was time to go home. Fortunately, the girl was passed out, so he managed to get out the door without waking her.

"I crashed at Patrick's house for a bit," Jimmy ran his hand through his hair and decided that perhaps it would be a good time to go to his room and away from his dad. The smell of liquor, mixed with pot and some of his hook-up buddy's perfume emanated from his clothing. He just wanted to go upstairs and sleep for the rest of the morning and possibly some of the afternoon.

"C'mere and sit down for a sec," his father pointed at the chair beside him. Jimmy reluctantly did as he was asked. "Jimmy, what's really going on here? I don't believe for a second that you were just hanging around Patrick's last night. Your mother might believe it and fortunately for you, she's still sleeping."

Jimmy shrugged. "We were just out, hanging out and stuff with some friends. Nothing serious."

"Jimmy, I know that it's your life and I respect your privacy," his dad took another sip of his coffee. "I trust you, but I'm a little worried. It's not like this is the first time you've walked in the door at an ungodly hour. I know I'm not always sitting in the kitchen, but I still hear you. Sometimes you don't even come home. Is there anything I should know? Do you have a girlfriend or are you involved in something you shouldn't be?"

Jimmy gave his dad a small smile and shook his head. "No, dad. I'm fine and I don't have a girlfriend. I just like going out and hanging with some friends, that's it."

John Groome gave him a long, penetrating look before finally nodding. "I know your mom is worried about you, but I keep trying to assure her that you're fine. I just hope I'm telling her the truth."

"I *am* fine," Jimmy slowly stood up from the table in hopes of ending their conversation. His body was so exhausted that he actually felt weak. "I just like going out with my friends and that's it. We're not doing anything wrong. Everything's good. I'm fine."

Jimmy could barely keep his eyes open at that point and was relieved when his father finally seemed content with his answers, so he could head upstairs to his room. There, he sank into bed and fell asleep. And he had a dream about the crying stranger from the high school dance.

Chapter twenty-four

Jimmy didn't graduate in 1990. Despite the fact that he had given his mother plenty of advance notice that he would be returning to high school in the fall, she still didn't take it well. Fortunately, he was able to avoid her for most of the two days following the bombshell. Jimmy thought she'd get over the news before their family's weekly Sunday dinner with Jillian and Rob. He thought wrong.

"I just don't think there is any *good* reason for not graduating this year," Annette Groome announced over the evening meal, which consisted of roast turkey and vegetables. Normally, he would've salivated at the delicious aromas, but not that day. "I really think you were working too much. You spent too much time socializing with Patrick Lipton. You should have put more focus on your studies."

"Kinda late now, mom," Jimmy muttered between bites of his food. He was hung over and wasn't in the mood for a lecture. He had staggered home around 3 a.m. that morning and once again, his father had been waiting for him. John Groome was close enough to smell the alcohol on his breath and see the two hickies on his neck. The fact that his mother noticed too probably contributed to her unpleasant mood. Busted.

"She *does* have a point," his father took over. "It's not the end of the world that you're returning to school in the fall, but it *was* preventable."

"I thought you were doing better in school," Jillian piped up. Jimmy noticed that she was pushing food around her plate more than eating, while Rob's eyes continually scanned her actions. Evidently, she wasn't eating again.

"That's when he had a tutor," his mother reminded Jillian. "That nice girl, Sally. Jimmy, why did you ever break up with her? She was such a sweet girl."

"Phew!" Jimmy dramatically rolled his eyes, attempting to ignore the irritation in his mother's eyes. "Yeah, whatever." He grew uncomfortable and began to eat faster.

"Jimmy, you don't have to give me attitude just because I asked you a question," his mother pointedly glanced at the larger of his two hickies, while he self-consciously shrank in his chair. "I just said she was a really nice girl."

Everyone at the table stared at him. He shrugged. "'Cause she dumped me."

"I saw her at the mall last week," Jillian quietly remarked, while setting down her fork. Rob's eyes darted toward the fork and he frowned. "She was asking about you."

"I bet," Jimmy quipped, thinking about the last time he'd seen his ex-girlfriend. It was New Year's Eve after he had sex with her sister.

"Is she back in Thorton?" His mother directed the question toward Jillian who nodded.

"Just for the summer."

"Jimmy," his mother turned her attention back to him, "Maybe you should call her. If she was asking about you, maybe she misses you. I think it would be good if you had a *steady* girlfriend again, so you'll calm down a bit." He knew she was referring to the screaming match they'd had earlier that day. It was the first time Jimmy had ever yelled at his mother, and it was over the fact that she finally realized that her son was no longer a sweet, naive boy who did nothing wrong. Reality had hit her like a ton of bricks and she made it clear to Jimmy that she did *not* approve of his behavior. "She was always really good for you."

Jimmy shrugged.

"It can't hurt to just call and say 'hello'." Jillian looked at him with concern in her eyes while her fiancé grinned. Jimmy had a feeling that his sister's boyfriend was probably the only person at the table who understood him at all.

"I'm not calling Sally," Jimmy insisted and finished his food. "I promise you that she doesn't want to talk to me."

"You don't know that," his mother pushed the topic a little further, adding to the tension around the dinner table. "If she was asking about you, maybe she misses you."

"No mom," he persisted with frustration, wishing she would just drop the topic. "She doesn't want to talk to me."

"Why not?" She refused to let up.

Sighing loudly, Jimmy turned toward his mother. "Do you *really* want to know the answer to that question?"

"Jimmy, I'm sure it's not as bad as you think," she challenged him while everyone else seemed to hold their breath as an uncomfortable silence filled the room.

"Cause… I *screwed* her sister, that's why." He watched the shocked expression on each of their faces before he abruptly rose from the table, dropping his fork on the plate and stomped toward the stairs. *Why couldn't she just leave it alone?*

The darkness of his bedroom seemed to welcome Jimmy as he closed the door behind him and didn't bother to turn on a light. His blinds were still down, so the room was dark and cool on the warm, spring day. He had barely walked across the room and sat on his unmade bed when someone knocked at his door. It was Jillian.

"What?" he sighed, as she gently opened the door, her eyes peering through the dark. "Did they send you up here to 'set me straight' or something."

"No," Jillian spoke softly and shook her head. "Can I come in?"

He nodded and switched on the lamp next to his bed. Jillian gently closed the door and crossed the room. She pulled the chair out from behind his desk and sat down, facing her brother. "Jimmy, I'm sorry I said anything. I didn't know any of this stuff. I hope I didn't upset you. Are you okay?"

"Yeah just hung over," he casually stretched, attempting to hide his frustrations. After all, it wasn't Jillian's fault that he had become the black sheep within the family unit. "I'm fine."

"No, I don't mean that," Jillian's eyes were full of sadness as she spoke and she seemed to quickly tune into his overall mood. "I mean in general. You've really changed a lot in the last year."

"I just, I don't know," Jimmy's voice was low, almost a whisper. "I just like going out and partying with Patrick, it's no big deal. All the kids my age do that. It's hardly like I'm out of control, but mom and dad don't think that's normal. I don't get why 'cause I never miss work and it's not like I quit school. It'll all be fine, Jill."

"What about that comment you just made about Sally's sister? Is that true?" Jillian asked, nervously twisting her engagement ring. "Did you really have sex with her sister?"

"Yes, while Sally was in the next room" he shared and began to laugh, than realized that he was a little ashamed to admit this to his sister.

"Oh, God! Jimmy!" She sadly shook her head. "Why would you do that?"

"Honestly?" Jimmy shrugged and felt a wave of depression hit him. He would never be accepted in his family. "Cause the night before Sally moved for university, I told her how I really felt about her, and she blew me off."

"Really?" Jillian asked, understanding dawning on her face. "That must've really hurt."

"Yeah, well, whatever."

"It obviously really hurt *you*, Jimmy. What did she say?"

"She told me that basically it was all in my head," Jimmy quietly replied and avoided her eyes, choosing instead to look at the floor. "Like I was some fucking moron who didn't know my real feelings. It was just a joke to her."

"Yeah, that's pretty cold," his sister gently agreed. "I wouldn't have appreciated that either, if I were in your shoes."

"Yeah, it was like really cold. So I told her to go to hell and we broke up."

"And her sister?"

"She always flirted with me," Jimmy sighed and looked back into Jillian's eyes. "And then she invited me to her house on New Year's Eve. Things happened, and Sally just happened to be there."

"Jimmy," a grin escaped her lips as she finally stopped fighting it. "That's so bad. I can't believe you did that!"

"I didn't care. I guess I wanted to hurt her for what she did to me."

"That's understandable." his sister sympathized. "But you just seem to have gone from being super loyal to Sally to really casually hooking up with her sister. That's what I mean about how you've changed. The Jimmy I used to know wouldn't have done that. You can't let one girl affect the kind of person you are, 'cause you're only hurting yourself."

"I know."

"And the hickies?" She raised an eyebrow questioningly.

"Just some girl I met last night."

"Is she nice? Do you really like her?"

Jimmy couldn't even remember the girl's name, but he wasn't about to tell this to his sister. "Nah."

"Jimmy, don't become one of *those* guys."

"What guys?"

"The ones who get hurt by one girl and then never let anyone close to them again," his sister gently replied. "Don't do that."

"I won't," he promised her. But the truth was that Jimmy had no interest in being serious about any girl. It just wasn't in his heart to be faithful to anyone any more. All he cared about at this point in his life was his music and partying. His summer was going to be about starting a new band, casual hook-ups and making enough money to buy a car. Nothing else.

His mother barely spoke to him for the next few days. About the time that she started to come around, Jimmy went out and got another tattoo. This one was a Gemini symbol on his right arm. His mom didn't make a huge deal about it like the last time, but merely shook her head in frustration. Jimmy was getting used to this reaction and he had a feeling it was only going to get worse.

Fortunately, his family didn't see him all that often during the summer of 1990 because Jimmy spent most of it at his job. He continued to work in the greasy fast food restaurant, but vowed that it was just a matter of time before he quit. The entire atmosphere at his work was getting him down. Plus, it wasn't paying enough. He wanted to save as much money as possible in order to have a car before September. By mid-July, he felt pretty confident that his goal would be met.

As diligently as he saved his money, Jimmy always made sure that he had enough left over for the bars, where he continued to get by on a fake ID and a charming smile. There was a constant flow of girls in his life. This only seemed to increase at the end of summer, when many new girls moved to the area for college. Much to his disappointment, however, he still did not have a band.

Chapter twenty-five

Much to his surprise, Jimmy didn't mind returning to school that fall. He actually felt superior to the other students because he was slightly older, was getting into bars every weekend and he had just bought a car. Although the Toyota Corolla was only a few years old, it had already seen its' first accident by the previous owner and in turn, some major repairs and a lot of mileage. Jimmy didn't care; he was so excited to actually own a car, that those details seemed irrelevant.

"Fuck man," Patrick quipped the second time he climbed into the Corolla, which just happened to be the first day back to school. "This car isn't old and it already has a ton of mileage on it. Guess your car and your dick have a lot in common." Patrick pulled on a pair of sunglasses and flipped on the radio. "So, where are we off to?"

"School, dumbass," Jimmy reminded him as he took his foot off the brake and eased back onto the street. "I don't know about you, but I don't get up this early to do much else."

"But it's just orientation and all that shit, can't we skip today?" Patrick frowned defiantly. "Do something fun?"

"Nah, we better go and make sure we've got the courses we need sorted out," Jimmy insisted, slightly paranoid that he wouldn't be able to get the two classes he needed in order to graduate. The last thing he felt like doing was returning to high school *again* the following semester. He wanted to get it over with. "We'll skip out early though."

"I don't know man," Patrick sounded frustrated. "I feel like I'm fucked regardless of what I do. Even if I graduate, I'm fucking limited because

Melissa is always reminding me that I have responsibilities with Hope. I understand that she's my kid and all, but I don't want to work at a fucking grocery store forever. I really want to go to college, but I can't afford to do that *and* pay child support. I don't know what I'm going to do."

"Doesn't she get that you can help more in the long run if you have a solid career?" Jimmy really didn't understand the situation. Did having a child while still young mean you were trapped forever? His friend had always done everything he could to help out with his daughter or to give Melissa money, but nothing ever seemed to be enough. Sometimes it felt like Patrick's ex held their daughter over his head more than necessary. He was hardly a neglectful father and there were lots of teenage moms in their school who had absolutely no support from the fathers of their babies.

"She doesn't care," Patrick revealed. "In her mind, I ruined her life, so now she's going to ruin mine."

Jimmy didn't think it was appropriate to refer to their kid as something that 'ruined' their lives, but certainly he understood Patrick's logic. It was simply bad timing and Jimmy was glad to not have that problem. He always insisted on using condoms, even if the girl he was with attempted to sway him by saying that she was on the pill. It wasn't worth the possible risk.

"What do your parents think?" Jimmy asked.

"They want me to go to college too. But Melissa wants me to get a factory job so I can make more money and be locked into slave labor all my life. I can't seem to win no matter what."

Jimmy's dilemma was somewhat the opposite of Patrick's. His parents wanted him to go to college and he had absolutely nothing holding him back, other than the fact that he wanted to be a musician and school didn't interest him in the least. Whenever Jimmy tried to explain his dream of being a rock star to them, they ended up arguing. He found it really strange that his parents, who got him into music in the first place by paying for both his vocal and guitar lessons, were now discouraging him from making a career of it.

He and his mother had grown further and further apart as time went on. He was no longer her beautiful little boy. She often pointed out that she didn't even know him anymore. Jimmy would never admit it to anyone, but remarks like that were pretty difficult to hear. He got the impression that now that he was no longer looking and acting according to her expectations, he was no longer acceptable to her. When he had short hair, no tattoos, was a virgin, passed everything in school, had a steady girlfriend and was fat, Jimmy was a delight to his mother. Now that he didn't look and live as she expected, he felt like he was nothing to her.

So adding on the factor of his rock star dreams didn't help. Anytime the topic came up, his mother would sigh in exasperation and tell Jimmy it was time to grow up. "You're a very talented musician, but realistically most people just don't make it in the music industry. It's time you calm down and set realistic goals."

His dad was a little more tactful in his comments, encouraging him to continue with his music, but suggesting that it was better to have something 'more sustainable' to fall back on. "I know you're very talented Jimmy and I'd never suggest otherwise," he calmly explained. "I just don't want you to get your hopes up too high. There are a lot of kids out there with the same dream and there are only so many people who are actually able to achieve them. I'm not saying it won't be you, but I am saying that sometimes talent isn't the biggest factor. There's a lot of music out there from people who have limited talent and there are a lot of musicians like you, who have trained for years that never make it. Sometimes in life, it's the luck of the draw."

Jimmy thought they were full of shit. Sure, if you *believed* that your chances of making it were limited, you probably wouldn't succeed. What about Sean Ryan's accomplishments? Jimmy was sure that his former guitar teacher was discouraged many times but he didn't let anyone get him down. And in the end, his talent prevailed.

It wasn't only that Sean Ryan had talent. The former member of Second in Line always had a great attitude. He had been positive, upbeat and excited about life. Jimmy purposely attempted to adopt these characteristics. There were actual times when he would stand back from a situation and wonder how Sean would've dealt with the same predicament. It wasn't all the time. But really, what better way of becoming successful than to emulate someone you idolized. It didn't matter if he was dead; he was still Jimmy's idol.

Fortunately, he had much more luck forming a new band in September than he had all summer. Together with three other guys at his school,

Jimmy started a band called Zero to One. It was definitely a step up from Charm, but as the months moved forward, it was clear that this wasn't the band that would bring Jimmy to the top of the charts. For the time being, it gave him more experience performing in front of audiences. Not that Zero to One did a lot of shows, but their lead singer's tireless efforts at finding places for the band to play occasionally paid off. Most of the band being under legal drinking age greatly limited their possibilities, as it was almost impossible to play at any bars. There was a coffee house that was happy to have them perform after 9 pm, and they occasionally played at parties and youth dance clubs. Jimmy kept telling himself that it was just for experience at that point. Something told him that if his former guitar teacher were still alive, he'd tell Jimmy exactly that same thing.

In school Jimmy made an extra effort to do better this time around. He concentrated in his two classes and was determined to pass them both.

It was only a few days into his new schedule that he noticed how hot his math teacher was. She was very pale, with long dark hair and an amazing body. New to the school, Miss Black probably wasn't much older than her students and her discomfort with teaching kids who were practically her peers showed. In fact she appeared so nervous on the first day of class that Jimmy felt bad for her. He certainly wouldn't want *her* job.

But as time went on, the young teacher seemed to grow more comfortable. Jimmy watched her intently and eventually he noticed that while speaking, she looked in his direction quite often. It was just quick glances, attempts to appear casual, but eventually it seemed more and more obvious that she was checking him out as much as he was checking her out. So on one Friday morning, Jimmy had an idea. When class had concluded, he approached Miss Black at her desk and asked her for some extra help.

"I didn't graduate last year because I was an idiot and didn't get extra help," he grinned and looked away shyly. "So, this year I want to make sure I understand what I'm doing right away so I don't get too far behind."

"That's very smart of you, Jimmy." Miss Black's green eyes searched his face while she slowly pushed a strand of her dark hair behind her ear.

"I'd be more than happy to help you, but I have classes booked right to the end of the day. Maybe after school?"

"Ah, that's fine, I don't have to work today so I can stop by later," he smiled as he returned her gaze. The truth was that he *did* have to work, but it would be the first time he ever called in sick, so why not? "If that's okay?"

"Sure," she gave him a reassuring smile. "I'll meet you here at three."

They did meet at three, and Miss Black helped him with the math homework he'd had trouble understanding. But as they sat alone in the empty classroom, the halls of the school now silent, it was pretty clear that the attraction that Jimmy felt for the teacher was mutual. What started off as a math lesson, eventually turned into a conversation about how Miss Black was new at the job and very nervous. She told him about her recent break-up with her boyfriend, followed by a move to a new city and finally all the issues she was having with her roommate. Jimmy listened to every word. He didn't care, but he listened.

The two had been moving closer and closer to one another, until Jimmy looked into her eyes and sensed that he could kiss her and she'd have no objection. Much to even his surprise, their kiss quickly turned very heated and the next thing he knew, they were in her small office at the back of the classroom. After quickly locking the door, Jimmy and Miss Black got creative on her desk, and that's when he felt confident that he would pass math that semester.

Chapter twenty-six

Everything seemed to be where Jimmy wanted it to be in the fall of 1990. School was only half days. He was a shift supervisor at work, guaranteeing him decent hours and a higher pay rate. Zero to One did a few shows, but not enough to take up too much of Jimmy's time. He preferred it that way since he didn't foresee the band going anywhere and also because it allowed him time to write his own songs to be used in the future. He continued to have an active social life on the weekends and women were still a big part of his life. These women included Miss Black. But Jimmy now knew her as Beth.

Their affair that had started in the teacher's office in September had progressed to her apartment. They met often and both had the understanding that there were no strings attached. It was about sex and nothing more. Then one day, something changed.

In the early hours of a Saturday morning in December, Jimmy stumbled into her apartment after leaving the bar, as she had requested. Her advances didn't get far before he passed out. A few hours later, he woke with the worst hangover of his life, and regardless of how much Beth attempted to seduce him, it was a wasted effort.

Clearly frustrated, she left him alone to sleep until almost 11 a.m. Then she woke him.

"We have to talk," she came straight to the point, sitting beside him on the bed. Even though Beth was no longer in the mood to fool around, Jimmy had noticed the outline of her naked body beneath the sheer white nightdress and started to get hard. Suddenly, he wanted to fuck her more than anything and while Jimmy's mind raced ahead to what he planned to do to her, he continued to make eye contact and nod as if he were listening. But he wasn't. At least not until he heard the word 'pregnant', then suddenly she had his full attention.

"WHAT?" He hadn't meant to yell, but the words seemed to erupt from his throat. "You're pregnant?" Jimmy was no longer aroused.

"I didn't say I was pregnant," Beth wrinkled her forehead and she pushed a strand of dark hair over her ear. "I said I was late. It's probably nothing, but it got me thinking. What if I *were* pregnant?"

"Ah, you shouldn't be," Jimmy quickly reminded her. "You're on the pill, right?"

But even as he said the words, Jimmy cursed himself. Beth and Sally were the only girls that he'd ever had sex with, without using a condom. Sally dumped him and now Beth could be knocked up. *Fuck!*

"I am, but there's always a chance that it won't work," she pointed out, wrinkling the material of her nightshirt between her fingers. She was avoiding eye contact with Jimmy and that made him nervous. "Things can go wrong, right?"

"Did you take a test?" Jimmy was abrupt and to the point. If she was pregnant, he wanted to know and as soon as possible.

"No," she admitted sheepishly. "Not yet."

"Then let's go get one," Jimmy started to jump out of bed, causing his head to ache. It was going to be a long day.

"No, just wait a second," Beth gently touched his arm and he sat back down, covering his eyes with his hand. The throbbing in his head was quickly becoming worse. "We need to talk about a few things."

No good conversation started with 'we need to talk', this was something Jimmy knew for a fact. No parent or chick ever started a conversation he wanted to have with those words.

"What's up?" Jimmy attempted to sound casual.

"Jimmy, I don't know how to say this," Beth hesitated before looking into his eyes, "But when I realized that my period was late and I could be pregnant, I kind of realized that maybe I *wanted* that to happen. That I wanted to have a baby with you."

Jimmy's first instinct was to run. However, he had to handle this situation in the most delicate way possible. After all, this woman was also his teacher and he had to continue dealing with her for the remainder of the semester. "I thought um,' Jimmy chose his words carefully as pain continued to shoot through his temples. "I thought we decided to keep this casual. I mean, you were pretty clear that you didn't want a relationship when this all started."

Her exact words had been, "I just want you as a fuck buddy, nothing more." So much for that, Jimmy thought. Why did women say things they didn't really mean? Had that been for his benefit or had she just recently developed these stronger feelings for him?

"I know," she agreed. Her face seemed to open up and she turned slightly, so that she was looking in his eyes. "I swear, I didn't intend to develop feelings for you. In fact, I wanted to keep things as casual as possible. It wasn't until I thought that I could be pregnant that I realized how much you mean to me."

Jimmy didn't know what to say. However, he was growing tired of hearing the word 'pregnant' thrown around so casually. He wanted to know whether or not she was and couldn't think beyond that burning question. He certainly wasn't ready to push the possibility of a baby aside in order to discuss feelings. Especially considering that he didn't have any for her.

"I think we need to step back here for a sec," Jimmy spoke evenly, but felt guilty for his lack of feelings. "First we need to know whether or not you are pregnant. And second, outside of the bedroom, we barely know each other. It's not like we're dating. We get together and have sex. We don't talk about shit or get involved in each other's lives, so how could you develop feelings for me?"

Her gaze dropped down to her hands, and Beth's green eyes began to tear up. "Jimmy, you can't have sex with someone that much and not develop feelings for them. It's unnatural."

Jimmy didn't agree. He'd had sex with her many times and he didn't have feelings for her. It wasn't like he didn't care at all, but he didn't care in the same way as she did for him.

"I understand Beth. I really do," Jimmy spoke softly. "But, I don't want a relationship right now. I don't think I'm capable of having a relationship, possibly ever again. I just…can't."

"Why not?" she asked as tears ran down her cheek.

He pretended to not notice and spoke honestly, as he shrugged. "I don't know. I just can't for some reason. I've been like this since I broke up with my first girlfriend. I can't explain it; I just don't have it in me to have a relationship. I'm sorry if that hurts you. I think you're a sweet person and really, you deserve better than this." Jimmy waved his hand over the bed to indicate their affair. "If you want more than just some casual sex, then I'm not the guy you should be with at all. I can't give you what you want."

Tears continued to stream down her cheeks as he battled his guilt. Why *was* he that way? Why couldn't he commit to anyone? He didn't want her to hate him.

"I'm sorry," he whispered. "I can leave now if you want?" She didn't reply but just cried. Jimmy thought he should hug her, but had a feeling that any touching would lead to something more so he held back. "I'm *really* sorry. Do you want me to get a test for you at the drugstore?"

She shook her head no. "I have one, I just was scared to find out. Now I'm even more scared," she gasped through her words and Jimmy felt compassion for her. What if she were pregnant? Where did that put them both? What a fucked up situation.

After crying for twenty minutes – 'cause Jimmy was *definitely* watching the clock – she finally calmed down enough to take the test. It was negative. Jimmy practically skipped on his way home. Not quite; he still had a massive headache, but suddenly, it didn't seem so bad.

Math class became incredibly uncomfortable for Jimmy after that day. Fortunately, Christmas holidays weren't far off; after New Years, there were a limited amount of classes before the final exam, then he'd be done. Hopefully. He was a bit worried that Miss Black would hold him back because of the unpleasant end to their affair, but she didn't. It would've been difficult for her to do so, since his marks in math were pretty decent. Not great, but decent.

In January, both Jimmy and Patrick were officially finished school. While Jimmy started to look around for a better job, Patrick began to fill out trade school applications. A mechanics course was starting in June, and he wanted in.

"Then I can fix your piece of shit car when it breaks down," Patrick said with a grin on his face. Jimmy's friend was always the first person to diagnose anyone else's car troubles. It was just something he had always done. It had never occurred to Jimmy that Patrick would want to make a career as a mechanic, but he did, and after poring over the application form and worrying that his attempts would be in vain, he was accepted.

Meanwhile Jimmy was doing everything possible to *avoid* applying for college. Once he had graduated high school, his parents felt that nothing was standing in his way of going to college. Jimmy didn't agree and knew they'd never accept the fact that he didn't want to go.

"I just finished going to school for practically my entire life," Jimmy argued his point. "I need some time to figure out what I want to do," he was lying. Of course, Jimmy knew exactly what he wanted to do, but he also knew there was no way his parents would accept his real dreams. So, he would just have to stall them for the time being, until he could afford to move out of their house and concentrate on his music.

Although they both accepted his decision, his mother was always dropping little hints about going to school. Sometimes she left pamphlets in his room, just to let him know about a course she had heard about that might be of interest. None of them were of interest to Jimmy.

And if it wasn't school, his mother was hinting around about his single status. She felt it was time for him to settle down and find a real girlfriend. Jimmy didn't know how to explain to her that he simply didn't have it in him to do so. He didn't think he ever would. So, rather than attempting to explain his feelings on this issue, he also put it on the back burner and told his mom he was taking his time, waiting for the 'right' girl. Of course that made his mom ecstatic that he was finally taking girls seriously. Little did she know, Jimmy was sometimes sleeping with up to three different women a week. And if he could've slept with three different women a night, he certainly would've made the effort. After the messy situation with Beth, he decided that all relationships had to be kept very casual. Only have sex with the girls once and always use a condom. He wasn't going to make *that* mistake again.

As for Beth, he only saw her one more time after leaving school. He just happened to walk into a video store one night in time to see her holding hands with some guy, the two of them laughing while checking out movies. Jimmy smiled and left the store.

After finishing school, Jimmy's band drifted apart. His new goal was to find a *good* band to join; a group of musicians who were as serious about music as *he* was, and he wouldn't settle for anything less. It was time to take his life seriously and start working on his dream to become a rock star.

Chapter twenty-seven

Jimmy friendship with Patrick began to fade after they left high
school. It was almost as if their journey together was finished
and they were now on separate paths. Patrick was going to school
in June and Jimmy was staggering on what appeared to be, a road to
nowhere.

Not to say that Jimmy had lost faith in his dreams. That wasn't the
case. But there was definitely something more concrete about going
to school and learning a trade. People took it much more seriously. It
didn't matter if you worked just as hard to succeed in a creative pursuit;
it simply wasn't respected in the same way as working toward a diploma.
And even though Jimmy had no problem standing behind his goals,
there were times when he felt that defending them was becoming a
draining exercise. Almost to the point that he felt it would be simpler to
just not tell anyone his goals. Since most people didn't personally know
anyone who had succeeded in the arts, they didn't believe it actually
happened. Unfortunately, Jimmy saw people's lack of faith as a reflection
on *him* and his abilities, rather than a reflection on their own personal
disappointments and jaded points of view.

"When are you going to college?" Jillian sprang the question on
him after Easter dinner at the end of March. Fortunately, their parents
weren't around to jump into the conversation. Both were relaxing in the
living room while their adult children cleaned up after the family meal.

His sister wrapped up the remaining food to put in the fridge, while
Jimmy loaded the dishwasher. "Dunno. When I decide what I want to
do with my life." He noted that Jillian's dinner plate was almost as full as

it had been at the beginning of their meal, an hour earlier. He wondered if the rest of the family had also made that observation.

"You have to start thinking about these things, Jimmy." She lectured while leaning against the kitchen counter. "You can't live with mom and dad forever. You need to get a real job." Her eyes searched his face. "Mom's worried that you'll just keep wanting to do that whole band thing and waste your life away."

So this was what it was about. His mother had put Jillian up to talking to him. Great.

"I like doing the *band* thing." he insisted. He was about to meet some new guys who were looking for a guitarist later that week. They were all a little older than him but were pretty active in the local music scene. Jimmy was excited when he learned of their interest in adding him to their line up, but of course, he had no one to share his news with since no one else shared his excitement for music. Even Patrick seemed to be lost in his own little world after high school, especially since getting back together with Melissa yet *again*. "I'm only 18 Jill, I'm hardly wasting my entire life on anything yet."

"I know," she nodded. "But the longer you leave college, the less likely you'll do it."

"Says who?" Jimmy sat at the kitchen table and his sister crossed the room and joined him. Her eyes quickly jumped to his latest tattoo, the Chinese symbol for strength on his lower right arm, which he had come home with only a few days earlier. His mother hadn't even commented on this one, but just shook her head in frustration. "Maybe I just need some time to figure things out."

"I understand," Jillian sympathized, examining her own hands. Her eyes suddenly jumped back to his face. "I just worry about you sometimes." She seemed to choose her words carefully. Although his sister didn't say *why* she worried about him, Jimmy knew it was because of the rape. The two of them had never been the same since that day and sometimes, Jimmy wondered if they ever would be normal again. "I just worry that your future will be messed up."

"Why would my future be messed up?" Jimmy was growing frustrated with this conversation, but hid it well. He wasn't angry with his sister. She'd been through enough. However, he didn't understand why his going to college was somehow going to put everyone's mind at ease. Did they seriously think he was some kind of loser who would live with his parents forever? Work a dead end job for the rest of his life? Did everyone think he was pathetic? Did he really seem that hopeless?

"Jimmy, come on," her eyes pleaded as she shook her head. "You have no future goals, you work in fast food, you live at home and you can't have a serious relationship with a girl. I want you to be happy. I want you to have a full life. I want more for you than this Jimmy, we all do."

"Who says I won't have more?" Jimmy pushed a strand of dark hair behind his ear. The length of his hair was just another thing that irritated Jimmy's mother. She was constantly telling him to get it cut because no decent employer would ever hire him 'looking like that.' "Why do you assume that I don't want more out of life, Jill? Just 'cause I didn't get engaged and go to college right after high school doesn't mean that I'm some kind of bum."

"I don't think you're a bum, Jimmy." his sister carefully insisted. "I just worry. You party a lot and you're not even 19 yet."

"I will be soon," Jimmy reminded her.

"I know," she quietly replied. "But it's not just the partying. It's the girl thing. I'm still in touch with a lot of my old friends and I hear stuff about you, Jimmy." she hesitated. "A *lot* of stuff."

"So?"

"So?" Jillian's voice rose slightly. "So, I have friends telling me how you're like this dog at the bars. You have a reputation for picking up a *lot* of women. I don't even know *what* to say when people tell me these things, Jimmy. What am I supposed to say when friends tell me that they know women who've taken you home?"

"Who cares, Jill?" He shrugged. "Its just sex and it's not like I lie to them and say it's something more. They know what they're getting into."

"Yeah, but I don't like the fact that *my* brother has become one of *those* guys." Her comment hit him like a ton of bricks. "You're better than that, Jimmy. Don't you want more than to just screw whomever and go on to the next girl? Not to mention the fact that you could catch something? What if you get some girl pregnant? I mean, do you even think about these things? Do you even *care* about these things?"

"Of course I think of these things. I'm not stupid!" Jimmy sighed in frustration. He didn't want to have this conversation with anyone, let alone his sister. "I don't want to have a relationship. I know that would make *you* more comfortable, but I don't want to be tied down with any girl. That's just the way it is. I don't care if you or mom and dad don't like it, it's just how it is."

"But don't you want more? What if you're overlooking a great girl because you didn't get to know her?"

"Great girls don't pick up strangers in a bar." Jimmy retorted with a grin on his face.

"What?" His sister's face turned red and her voice rose. "What a double standard! So it's okay if *you* pick them up at the bar, but because they let you, they're the sluts? Is that the way you think, Jimmy?"

"Nah, I didn't say that."

"You implied it."

"I just *meant* that girls that go to bars and take random guys home don't want a relationship or they wouldn't do that," Jimmy hesitated, realizing that his earlier comment probably came out wrong. "I'm not saying I'm better than them, in fact I'm probably worse. I'm not a great guy either and if a nice girl walks up to me at a bar and seems sincerely interested in me, I tell her that too. I don't fucking pretend to be into her to get in her pants, I tell her like it is. I'm a dog, I like to fuck and I don't want a relationship. If a girl follows me around after that, chances are she's no better than me."

Jillian frowned.

"So to answer your question Jill, *no* I don't think I'm overlooking a nice girl." Jimmy rose from the chair. "I don't want to be with anyone and I kind of doubt I ever will. In fact, I have no desire at all to wake up every morning and look at the same girl. So can we *please* just drop this subject?"

Then he left the kitchen and went to his room. But for the rest of the night, he thought about what his sister had said to him. Maybe there was something wrong with him. Even Patrick seemed to settle into relationships with little trouble, while Jimmy had slept with more women in the last two years than most men did in a lifetime. It just felt good. Women intrigued him. They fascinated him. He would look at their lips and wonder what it would be like to kiss them. He wondered what their bodies would look like naked, how they'd taste, if their skin was soft and what kind of noises they made in bed. There were *so* many things that crossed his mind when he looked at an attractive woman and curiosity often got the best of him.

Later that week, Jimmy met the band that was considering him to replace their guitarist. He was pretty excited about the prospect; Planet One was well known in Thorton and considered to be on the road to success. It was through word of mouth that the band's lead singer, Scott, had heard of Jimmy and it was clear only a few minutes into their initial conversation that they were on the same page about many things. Both wanted to be rock stars and neither was interested in doing anything else with their lives.

"Yeah, my family wants me to go to college," Jimmy confided during their first meeting at Scott's place. Apparently he was living in the basement apartment of his parent's house. The place was very cold and smelled funny, but Jimmy didn't care. Scott seemed like a cool guy and at twenty, admitted that he had been singing since the age of ten. Like Jimmy, his parents had encouraged him and even paid for some extra lessons. Now they didn't understand why he wanted to do it professionally.

"It's crazy shit man," Scott shook his head while setting a Fender guitar, one of many in his collection, on a really cheap-looking stand. It looked like something you could purchase at Rothman's department store in a reduced bin. "My parents were just like yours. They paid for all these fucking lessons, then told me to quit music and get a real job." He shook his head and Jimmy could barely see his face through his massive amounts of hair. "Who knows?"

"Trust me, I know all too well." Jimmy gave a fake smile and wondered if Scott was high. He certainly seemed out of it. But at the same time, what difference did it make? Half the famous bands were probably on drugs and it didn't affect their success, so why should Jimmy care if this guy was fucked up? As long as the band worked, it didn't matter.

"So like, you gotta meet the rest of the boys," Scott's glazed eyes stared at Jimmy. "We totally got a fucking awesome band. Everyone has the same goal and wants to make it in the industry. And you can play guitar, so come over this weekend and meet the boys."

Jimmy ignored the bad feeling he had in the pit of his stomach and went with it. After all, he wanted to be in a success-driven band and it sounded like these were the guys who would help take him to the next level. What could possibly go wrong?

Chapter twenty-eight

Jimmy met the remainder of Planet One that weekend and he was genuinely impressed. It was clear that he was stepping into something big.

First there was Jeremy, the band's lead guitarist. He was more of a musical nerd than anything. He seemed to know the dates and facts on any influential artist since Elvis and was the brains behind the band. With black, curly hair and black-framed glasses, he definitely didn't strike Jimmy as a musician, but the boy could play. There was no doubt that he was very talented and serious about his music.

Nick was the drummer and was probably the oldest member of Planet One. He was definitely in his late twenties and was a big, burly guy who appeared slightly unpleasant in the beginning, but actually was really friendly, proving that looks were often deceiving. He was the talker of the band and spoke with a great deal of confidence, choosing his words very carefully.

The bassist Ron seemed like a nice guy as well, but just like the singer Scott, it was pretty clear that he rarely said no to drugs. The two seemed a little messed up, but since both eased through their practice, Jimmy didn't think it was an issue. Obviously, whatever they were involved in was something they could keep under control, but Jimmy had been around enough to know that these guys weren't just smoking a little pot.

Their first practice together went great. Jimmy seemed to fit into the band perfectly and it was apparent that the other four members were happy with his abilities. Jeremy compared him to a couple of legendary guitarists and gave him a few tips that were actually quite helpful, while Nick talked endlessly about previous bands he'd been in and how Planet One was a huge improvement. All in all, Jimmy felt he was on the right track.

The band had some shows lined up, which Jimmy looked forward to, since he hadn't been on stage in what felt like ages. They agreed to get together and practice as much as possible and continue on what they believed to be their road to stardom. Everything was back on track and Jimmy left the practice that day feeling better about his life than he had in months. Maybe things were finally coming together. Maybe this band would be what brought him to the rock star status that he craved.

The next thing he had to do was get another job. He was at the end of his rope with Top Dog Burger and felt it was time to move on to a job that suited him better. He wanted to work at a bar. Although he applied at various drinking establishments in Thorton, his first choice was The Purple Dragon, which was also his favorite watering hole. So when the manager called him a few days after dropping off a resume, Jimmy was over the moon. They set up an interview for the next morning.

Mark Whitman's office was located in the downtown area of Thorton. Jimmy was surprised to find an older man in a business suit waiting for him behind a desk. Somehow he had thought a bar's manager would be much more casual and Jimmy began to second-guess his own attire of jeans and a t-shirt. However, the clothing didn't seem to be the factor that interested Mark Whitman. After asking Jimmy about his current job, the band he had recently joined, and his future aspirations, he inquired why Jimmy wanted to work at The Purple Dragon.

"I guess because it's my favorite place to go," Jimmy spoke earnestly. "I love the vibe. There are a lot of cool people there. I just think it would be a fun place to work."

"I understand, but I'm going to be honest with you," Mark Whitman leaned back in his chair and studied Jimmy. The middle-aged man was balding and had a weathered appearance but he was still a pretty cool guy. "I don't see you at The Purple Dragon."

Jimmy felt his heart sink. Feeling rejected, he simply said a quiet, "Oh."

"Now don't get discouraged," Mark continued while moving forward in his chair. "I *do* see you working at a bar, just not *that* particular bar."

Jimmy raised his eyebrows. So, there was still hope.

"I work for a company called Steele-Stuart Entertainment. I think you might be confused and think that I actually *own* The Purple Dragon, but I merely run it and three other local bars. I'm in charge of staff, supplies, that kind of thing. I have to decide where someone like you would best be suited within this company. My feeling is that you would be better suited for another bar called DanceX. I'm not sure if you've heard of it?"

Jimmy wrinkled his nose. It was a dance club. Not really his scene. He and Patrick had gone there a few times when they wanted to be guaranteed on picking up. It was the meat market of Thorton bars.

"I know what you're probably thinking," Mark began to laugh after watching Jimmy's reaction. "But hear me out. DanceX is more popular with young women and of course, young men who want to meet women." He paused for a moment. "For that kind of establishment, we need attractive and charming young employees who represent the bar. And right now, we need a couple of young men to serve the customers either at the bar or as a busboy."

Jimmy suddenly realized what Mark Whitman was looking for in a bartender. He wanted the male version of the young woman who smiled at you sweetly, while leaning forward and showing you her embellished cleavage. Jimmy would be expected to flirt with his customers, suggest expensive drinks and charm his way into all the tips possible. It was a role he could easily play.

"I understand," Jimmy replied.

"I would have to start you off as a busboy," he glanced over Jimmy's application and squinted. "Jimmy it says here that you aren't quite 19."

Fuck! Jimmy was so used to going to bars at this point, that he often forgot that he wasn't exactly legal drinking age yet.

"Didn't you mention that The Purple Dragon was your favorite bar?"

"Yes," Jimmy replied and quickly thought up an explanation. As it turned out, there was no need.

Mark grinned. "That's fine, Jim. I don't need you to elaborate," he pushed the resume aside. "What we'll do is start you off as a busboy and then in a few weeks, we'll put you on the bar with a trainer on the slower nights. That way you can learn all the drinks and procedures, and eventually you'll be moved into the busy nights. Does that sound good to you?"

"Sounds great!" Jimmy smiled. "When do I start?"

"Is next week too soon?"

Jimmy gave his notice at the restaurant later that day. His boss wasn't exactly happy that he didn't give two weeks, but Jimmy didn't care. He was just so relieved to have this job, that he didn't give a crap about Top Dog Burger. His parents however, were not as enthused about either his band or his new job.

"Jimmy, shouldn't you be focusing on other things," Annette Groome nagged while his father silently listened to their conversation. "Why are you wasting time on a band and why would you want to work at a bar? Places like that are so dirty and at least at the restaurant, you were a manager."

"It was fast food mom, hardly what I'd consider a restaurant," Jimmy commented with humor in his voice. "And on top of that, they'll let anyone be a shift supervisor there. Especially for nights, 'cause no one else wants to do it. It's not much of a job, plus I can make tips at the bar. I haven't got a raise at Top Dog in ages."

"But why not go somewhere else with that supervisor experience and try to build on it?" Annette seemed completely baffled by his decision. Jimmy was frustrated by her attitude. He silently decided that his next change would be to move out and get as far away from his family as possible. He didn't need this shit.

"'Cause I want to work in a bar," Jimmy insisted. "It'll be fun."

His mother once again appeared frustrated and ended the conversation. This was the norm now; she complained, refusing to even consider his side of things, and when she had nothing more to fight back with, she grew annoyed and ended the conversation. Every day he felt less and less accepted by his family. He could see their disgust for his lifestyle every time they looked at him. He was the black sheep.

By Jimmy's birthday, the band was getting pretty regular gigs at various places around town and he was a couple of weeks into his new job at Dance X. As it turned out, it wasn't so bad after all. Pretty girls surrounded him all the time and being sober, he had a great advantage when it came to picking up women. Unlike the drunk slobs who were desperately trying to impress the hot, drunk and often horny women at the end of the night, Jimmy could pick out the one girl who most caught his eye and ease into a conversation. His easy-going nature and charming personality automatically gave him an advantage over the drunks who were often acting like fucking idiots. He was cute and girls liked him.

And so, Jimmy went home with more girls than ever before. He even had a couple of incidents in the bathroom *while* he was working, that were notable. Needless to say, he thoroughly enjoyed going to work. His immediate supervisor was well aware of his popularity with female customers and quickly had him trained on the bar. Before long, Jimmy had pissed off a lot of long-term employees of DanceX because he was often given the busiest shifts to tend. Not only was he fast, but he also had a way of selling girls doubles, when they wanted singles, and elaborate and expensive drinks when they were indecisive. One employee who had worked at the bar for a number of years quit a few months later saying that Jimmy was being shown favoritism.

"Jimmy, don't listen to that," Mark commented in early July, just after the employee in question quit. The bar's manager often frequented the establishment to make sure things were running smoothly and made it known that Jimmy was his top bartender. "You're awesome and you're making these other kids look lazy in comparison. You've made the standards for this place higher and that's something that overall makes you stand out as an employee. Good on you!"

Mark raised his beer to Jimmy and then took a long drink. "Plus the women swarm to you. What more can you want from a job?"

Jimmy grinned. The women swarmed to him all right. Unfortunately, unlike the days when he just went to a bar, he couldn't escape or avoid the ones he'd casually hooked up with in the past. And for some reason, they assumed that past encounters with Jimmy, also meant future encounters as well. They often didn't.

Overall, Jimmy loved working at the bar. He was making amazing tips, and having a lot of sex and free drinks at the end of the night. What more could he want?

Chapter twenty-nine

The summer of 1991 went quickly for Jimmy Groome. He spent it doing things he wanted. Between the band, the bar and girls, each day flew by. His average day consisted of sleeping until around two in the afternoon, then either practicing with Planet One, playing a show or working. Realistically, he never really had a night off, but Jimmy didn't care. He was enjoying his life. So it made sense that his family was *not* happy, and they made this known on a regular basis. It was probably for this reason that Jimmy began to do things that he knew would piss them off. It wasn't that he was *consciously* trying to irritate them more, but for some reason it seemed to happen.

It would be something as simple as making too much noise when he got home from work or having members of the band calling him too late at night. Then there was his appearance; Jimmy's hair was long and hung in his face and he knew Annette Groome *hated* it. And then there were the tattoos. They became an addiction to Jimmy. He seemed to crave a new one every other week and soon his arms had a small collection of various symbols that were meaningful to him. He wore ripped jeans and t-shirts that his mother would often sneak into the garbage when he wasn't around, but Jimmy always found them just in time.

"Wow, how did *this* get in *here*!" Jimmy rummaged through a garbage bag one afternoon after spotting his favorite Ramones t-shirt tossed on the top of the clear bag. "Must've just accidentally fallen in the garbage when I wasn't looking."

Jimmy's mother ignored his sarcasm. In fact, she often ignored *him*. But the final straw followed one of his 'adventures' after work one night that included a girl and a *lot* of shooters. Jimmy awoke on the floor just inside the doorway of his home. John Groome was standing over him, an angry expression on his face. Feeling a slight draft on his back, Jimmy realized that the front door was still wide open and the night air was moving up his ripped t-shirt. He suddenly remembered the scratches covering his back and there were bloodstains on his shirt.

He slowly rose from the floor. Feeling stiff from sleeping face down, Jimmy moaned slightly in pain. "What's going on?" He muttered in confusion, feeling a throbbing explode through his head as he slowly sat up. "What time is it?"

"It's almost five a.m. and I just found you passed out on the floor!" John Groome snapped while closing the door. It wasn't like Jimmy's dad to raise his voice, so clearly shit was about to hit the fan. "You just passed out in the doorway and judging by what I see in the front yard, that was after vomiting. You somehow made it into the house, but you left the door open for just anyone to walk in-

"Please dad, I was lying right here," Jimmy attempted to joke. "I would've woken up if someone had walked on me."

"Jimmy, this isn't funny," his father stared at him with cold eyes. "Be glad your mother is still sleeping and wasn't awake to see this and furthermore, you're bleeding through your shirt. Just what the hell do you do when you're out till all hours of the night?"

"Fight off wild animals," Jimmy said and laughed uncomfortably at his own joke, running a hand through his hair. "I don't know what to tell you dad. This is just my life."

Shaking his head his dad quickly dismissed him. "Go to your room please; we'll talk about this more after you've slept it off."

Jimmy gladly obliged. He woke at 1:30 the following afternoon. All the memories from the previous night came floating through his head and he knew he was about to become homeless. His mother was going to fucking lose it when she heard what happened. Throwing on a sweatshirt over his bloody shirt from the night before, Jimmy slowly made his way downstairs to face the music.

His parents were sitting at the kitchen table waiting for him. As soon as Jimmy sat down, his mother wrinkled up her nose in disgust.

"You smell like alcohol and vomit, Jimmy. Couldn't you at least take

a shower before coming downstairs?" Her eyes were filled with disgust. "What is *wrong* with you?"

"Annette, please," his father gave her an intense look then turned his attention to Jimmy. "We have a big problem here and we all have to sort it out together as a family."

Jimmy nodded and pushed some hair out of his face.

"We're worried about you, to be honest. You drink all the time, you have no plans for the future and from what Jill tells us, you're pretty casual with women," his father paused as if he were waiting for Jimmy to protest, which he didn't. "My concern is that you're going down a really bad path. You know your uncle Norm is an alcoholic and sometimes we worry that you could be in trouble too."

"I'm not an alcoholic," Jimmy quietly protested. He was feeling particularly depressed and alone in that moment. "Alcoholics wake up in the morning and drink, I don't do that. They can't live without drinking, I can. I'm just having fun."

"Jimmy," his mother's eyes filled with tears and he had to look away. He didn't want to make his mother cry. "Are you sure it's not an escape? I'm scared that it has something to do with that incident when you and your sister were kids..."

"You mean the rape?" Jimmy cut her off. He knew his mother hated using that word, but that's what it was – his sister had been *raped*. Brutally raped. Jillian still had a scar on her right arm from where her attacker had pinned her to the couch. She still had an eating disorder and an obsessive need to make everything perfect. Jimmy still occasionally had nightmares about the day and it was almost ten years later. It was hardly just an 'incident' – in fact, it had become the topic that no one talked about.

"Jimmy, please!" His mother's tears were now running wildly down her face.

"What?" Jimmy felt anger grow inside of him. "She was *raped*, mom. It wasn't just some random incident. Last night, me passing out in front of the door, now *that* was a random incident. My sister having some asshole force her to have sex because he got off on being with a kid is rape! Her losing her virginity because some dirty old fucker, that was a friend from *church*, forced himself on her is *rape*! Don't try to make this something minor, 'cause it's not."

"Jimmy!" His father raised his voice while Annette Groome was becoming visibly more upset by the second. "Please don't talk like that in this house! That's your sister you're talking about."

"I know!" Jimmy snapped. "But you guys seem to forget it's your *daughter* who has to live with this everyday. You don't think there's a day that she doesn't think about being raped? 'Cause there isn't a day that I don't remember seeing it."

Everyone fell silent. Jimmy could feel his heart pounding wildly and he just wanted to run away and never look back. He didn't want to think about it anymore. He *couldn't* think about it anymore.

"You're right," his father finally spoke up. "I don't think there's a day that we *all* don't think about it. Annette and I have to live with the fact that we brought this man into our house."

"And that we trusted him," his mother whispered, wiping away her tears. "We trusted that man; we thought he was a good person. And then we learn that he hurt our daughter like this, that he hurt our *family* like this." She shook her head sadly. "And look at you, Jimmy. Do you really think you'd be living this kind of lifestyle if you hadn't seen what you saw that day?"

Jimmy stared into his mother's eyes and slowly shook his head no. She was right. He knew that everything he did was a reaction to the rape, - being fat and his current lifestyle were a reaction to this childhood trauma – it was no coincidence. The problem was he didn't know how to live any differently.

"Jimmy," his father's voice broke their eye contact and he turned back to John Groome. "We think that maybe you need to move out of the house for now. We think it's best for everyone. Your sister agreed to take you in, provided you respect her space and rules. You're welcome to come back in the future, but right now, I think we all need a break from one another."

What his father meant to say was that they needed a break from *him*. Jimmy moved out the next day.

It wasn't until Jimmy moved in with his sister on the first of September, that he realized how neurotic she could be. Everything had its place and she didn't want anything moved. Dishes had to be in the sink, the toothpaste always had to be capped, and lights always had to be turned off after leaving a room. She checked to make sure the stove was turned off repeatedly before leaving the apartment; all windows also had to be shut if they weren't home, in case it rained. Any appointment or sudden change in plans upset her day. Jillian wanted everything to always be in order. Jimmy wasn't sure how Rob put up with the bullshit 'cause *he* certainly wouldn't have if other living arrangements were possible.

As much as her behavior drove him crazy, Jimmy couldn't help but feel pity for his sister. She was living in her own prison. But then again, so was he. Jillian had a few rules for her brother while he lived at her place. There weren't many, but he respected them. She insisted that he not make noise when he got in late, always locked the door behind him and never brought friends to her place.

"Especially girls," she stressed and he grinned. "And keep *away* from my friends! I *can't* stress that enough Jimmy, don't try to seduce my friends."

He laughed, but wasn't exactly attracted to most of Jill's friends. They were mostly a mixture of gay guys and high maintenance bitches from her modeling days. The girls from her work were either much older, or not attractive. Not that he would've purposely created a tense situation by fucking one of Jillian's friends.

Jimmy was also warned to keep away from Rob's sister, who occasionally dropped by the apartment. Her name was Darla and although she was cute, Jimmy wasn't interested enough to be kicked out of his current home. Yet he always noticed her watching him carefully, and although in the beginning, it was sort of flattering, eventually it grew annoying. Her eyes would observe him while she talked to Jillian and he walked through the room. What was her deal?

It was on a Sunday afternoon after working at the bar all night, that Jimmy stumbled into the kitchen to find Darla and Jillian having a conversation that quickly halted as soon as he entered the room. Jimmy gave them both a small grin, grabbed a bottle of juice and started back to his room. He wasn't in the mood for this shit so early in the day.

"Jimmy, come here for a sec," Jillian called out. "Darla wants to talk to you."

Rolling his eyes, Jimmy slowly turned around and faked a smile. "Yeah?"

The two girls exchanged looks and it made him nervous. "Jimmy, I don't think I've told you this before, but Darla is a psychic," his sister began, and although Jimmy smiled and nodded, his mind was going in the opposite direction. This was the *last* thing he cared about in that moment. "And she's getting all these messages about you."

"It's true, Jimmy," Darla spoke up and a smile crossed her lips. "Your sister says you don't believe in this kind of thing; however every time I see you I can just feel the spirits all around me. They have so much to say about you."

Jimmy couldn't help it at that point. He burst into laughter.

"I know you aren't a believer," Darla said, without appearing to be insulted. His sister looked slightly embarrassed, however. "But I really think you would benefit from at least hearing me out. You can take whatever I say and do as you wish with it, but I really think you need to hear some things."

She continued to smile and Jimmy just shrugged. Opening the bottle of juice, he stared at the orange liquid and his stomach felt squeamish. "Sure, whatever."

"I'll go to the living room," his sister stood up and quietly left the room. Jimmy started to feel nervous. What the fuck was up with this chick? He had no doubt that his sister believed all this psychic bullshit, but he didn't.

"Sit down," She invited, pointing at the chair Jillian had just left. As he sat, Darla dug through her hippie purse and pulled out a deck of tarot cards. Jimmy found the cards intriguing because of how ancient and weathered they were. He watched as Darla shuffled them, closing her eyes in deep concentration. As she opened her eyes, she spread the cards across the table, instructing Jimmy to pick some out randomly. He didn't really pay attention to the absurd paintings on each or the pattern Darla put them in. He wasn't even really listening to her predictions; that was until he heard something about his band.

"I see music all around you." she studied the cards carefully. "You'll always be surrounded by music. It's as much a part of you as the blood running through your veins. And not many people really understand that about you, Jimmy. They don't see it, but don't be discouraged - they will."

Jimmy nodded and remained quiet.

"You're like a spark in the sky," her eyes met with his and then returned to the cards. "You have this glowing energy all around you and your future successes will be great. But you have to always walk toward them; you can't wait for them to find you. You always have to make the world know what you want or you'll never get it." Jimmy considered her words, and decided she was right.

"I see a lot of charm in you." she grinned. "And that takes you down many different roads and will help you out someday with things that really matter, such as your future career in the arts. And your future love, of course."

Jimmy had been taking a drink of juice when he heard Darla's last words and began to choke in laughter. "Future love? Give me a *break*! You had me *till* you said that."

"There is a future love, Jimmy!" She persisted, giving him a slow smile. "A great love, at that. I knew you wouldn't believe me when I said it, but it's true. You will be at a low point before you meet her and she'll reawaken your hope. But it won't be an easy journey - but it is a journey you'll want to take."

There was something very haunting about her words and Jimmy somehow found himself believing her. "But, I-

"But you don't believe me," Darla murmured. "But you're happy the way you are? That won't last. Jimmy, these cards just tell me that you're running as fast as you can from what haunts you. But anyone who runs too long grows tired."

"Who is she?"

"You haven't met her yet," Darla confirmed. "But you will. Sooner than you might realize, but not as fast as you'd like and besides, it's not time yet."

"Can you tell me anything about her?" Jimmy's face grew warm. He couldn't believe he was actually asking this question.

"I can tell you that she's someone you'll meet through a mutual friend. I see someone between you, so I assume that's how you'll meet." Darla continued to study the cards, despite her obvious exhaustion. "You'll be very protective of her for some reason, but I can't see why. But you are *extremely* protective of her, pretty much from day one."

That surprised Jimmy. The only woman he had ever been protective of was his sister. He even heard himself saying that out loud.

"But this one, you will be."

"You can't tell me more?"

"No, I'm sorry Jimmy." Darla's lids were drooping slightly. "But I see you married within five years."

Jimmy almost fell off his chair.

Chapter thirty

"*there's a future love, Jimmy…A great love, at that….*"

He hated the fact that Darla's words intrigued him. And even
♦ ♦ ♦ more than that, Jimmy hated the fact that he believed them.
They hit just a little *too* close to home to not be true. She was right,
he was running from everything that haunted him and he did so with
every drink he took and every woman he screwed. It was a race from his
life, and he just wasn't winning. But to be married within five years was
another thing. Jimmy just couldn't picture it and so, therefore it must not
be true. At least, that's what he tried to tell himself. His sister wasn't as
convinced.

"Jimmy, she's right about a lot of things," Jillian claimed later that day,
as they sat together at the kitchen table. Rob was watching television in
the next room while the siblings quietly drank coffee. His sister's eyes
were full of worry. "Including some really bad shit. So, if Darla predicted
something awful, I want to know what it is."

"She predicted that I was going to be married within five years."

Jillian's eyes sprang open in shock. "Oh my God, Jimmy! You had me
so scared. From the way you were talking, I thought Darla had predicted
your death or something! But marriage, wow!" A huge smile crossed her
face. "I guess a leopard really *can* change his spots."

"Hey now, let's not get ahead of ourselves," Jimmy genuinely enjoyed
watching his sister laugh; it was something he didn't see enough of
anymore. "I haven't met anyone that inspired me to even date seriously let
alone marry, so I wouldn't count on this prediction being true."

"Jimmy, she's usually right," Jillian gently replied as she sipped her coffee. "She doesn't just make this stuff up and hope it comes true. She's really got a gift. I'm telling you, Darla is the real thing."

"But me, married?" Jimmy laughed at the possibility, but secretly he did entertain the thought briefly. Could he really see himself in a relationship? Would someone ever amaze him enough to make him want to settle down? He wasn't sure why the idea was so interesting to him, but Jimmy wasn't about to admit it to his sister.

"Hey, you never know," she gave him an affectionate smile and playfully hit him on the arm. "Maybe Jimmy Groome will decide to grow up someday."

"Not likely," he smiled, avoiding her eyes. "No time soon."

But he did think about it — and often.

Darla's talk of his future successes also intrigued him. It was one thing to aim toward a goal, to dream a dream, but quite another to have some kind of affirmation that it would come true. Sure, psychics probably weren't the most reliable sources, but at the same time it gave Jimmy a sense of hope that he greatly needed. Although the next time he met up with the rest of Planet One, he wasn't so certain. How was this band supposed to make it to the top when two of its members were heavily involved in drugs?

In the beginning, Jimmy hadn't seen the drug use as an issue. He thought it had no effect on the band one way or another. If Scott and Ron wanted to do coke or whatever on their own time, so what? As long as it didn't affect how the band performed, who cared? However, Jimmy was starting to see some cracks in his original theory. They started when Scott didn't show up for a Planet One show. Fifteen minutes before they were expected to be on stage, their singer was still missing in action.

"Ah man, he'll show," Ron insisted through his own drug-fuelled state, which was something that concerned Jimmy on its own, let alone their more pressing problem of being singer-less. "Don't stress man, he'll show. Scott always shows."

Jeremy didn't look so convinced. His huge, brown eyes were full of worry as he exchanged glances with Jimmy. He clearly didn't seem so sure of Scott's dedication to the band. In fact, Jeremy looked as if he was going to have an anxiety attack, causing Jimmy to feel his own heart suddenly racing with fury. Where the fuck was Scott?

"Jim," Nick spoke gently while hesitantly turning toward the band's newest member. "Listen man, I know this is a lot to ask, but would you be able to fill in for Scott? You sing backup and, to be honest, you might be our only hope."

Jimmy was stunned. His heart pounded furiously and he felt his throat become dry. While he was probably the only other person in Planet One who could sing, he wasn't at all prepared. Jimmy had never sung lead in front of an audience before and the prospect was frightening.

"He'll show," Ron maintained, but as the clock continued to click nearby, everyone's hope of Scott making an appearance faded.

"Jimmy, if we have to cancel at the last minute it's gonna look like shit for the band," Nick reasoned with him. "I don't want to push you out there, but at the same time man, you're our only hope. You've actually had lessons. Fuck, you'll probably do better than fucking Scott." Nick's eyes suddenly became dark as he shook his head. "The fucking asshole, I can't believe he's doing this to us again."

"*Again?*" Jimmy asked.

"Yeah, Jim, but that's a long story," Nick sighed. "I almost punched the fucker in the head last time he pulled this shit on us and he insisted he wouldn't do it again." He shook his own head, glanced at the clock and back at Jimmy's face. "You can sing man, the rest of us suck and if we cancel out, it's gonna fuck us over."

Jimmy took a deep breath and agreed to do the show. Of course, he was absolutely petrified over the prospect, but at the same time he knew that sometimes you just had to suck it up. This was one of those times. He couldn't see the rest of the band get fucked over by Scott's instability. Plus, if Jimmy *didn't* sing, he was sure the entire band would be equally as pissed at him as they were at Scott. Even if he fucked up, at least they'd be happy at his attempt to save them in a bad situation.

Luckily the show started soon afterwards, giving Jimmy little time to contemplate his fears. Nick quickly reviewed the list of songs they were doing that night with Jimmy and attempted to reassure him, but when the four boys went on stage a few minutes later, Jimmy knew he wasn't ready.

The audience seemed surprised and intrigued when Jimmy took over the role as singer that night, along with playing guitar. He felt as though he was being accepted with open arms. The girls who sat at a nearby table in the smoky bar appeared as interested in checking him out as they were with his voice, while Jimmy pushed through his nervousness and sang each song almost to perfection. There were a few times when he had fucked up the words a bit, but it wasn't a big deal. After all, Scott did that on a regular basis and he was much more used to singing before an audience.

There was something very different about being on stage singing as opposed to just playing guitar. People looked at him differently. Not just the girls at the nearby table, but everyone. There was a distinct respect in their eyes as they watched Jimmy, possibly even admiration. He wondered if perhaps it was because most people would've been afraid to walk on stage and sing? It certainly took more guts to do than simply play guitar. All the focus was on him, and Jimmy was surprised to find he was actually enjoying it. It wasn't as bad as he had anticipated.

The show finally came to an end and Jimmy practically flew to the bar. Nick met him there.

"Thanks Jimmy," he nodded, with a smile on his face. "You saved our asses and you did pretty fucking good for having no warning at all."

"I was scared shitless, but it's fine. I knew it wouldn't be so bad once I got going." Jimmy tried to make light of the entire situation. "I didn't want the band to be fucked over 'cause of Scott."

"The fucking asshole," Nick shook his head and ordered them both a beer. "He is going to hear it from me tomorrow, I can promise you that much."

"Are you sure he didn't get the dates mixed up or something?" Jimmy attempted to show some fairness. After all, he was still relatively new to the band and didn't want to get caught up in any old battles.

"Nah, he knew," Nick assured him. "He knew. He's just all fucked up on some shit and probably forgot the day or just didn't care. He's a bum."

"Yeah, I suppose you can get pretty messed up on coke."

"Let's hope its just coke," Nick rolled his eyes. "You never know with that guy. He's already been to rehab twice and we keep giving him chances, but this might be his last one if I have anything to say about it."

Jimmy had a feeling that Nick's opinion held a lot of weight with the band.

As it turned out, Scott was allowed one more chance. He had some excuse about a dying relative. Jimmy wasn't sure of the details, but didn't ask questions. It wasn't his concern. Nick let it go, but was pretty firm with Scott that it wasn't to happen again.

Jimmy remained the back up plan. If Scott didn't show, Jimmy was to sing. It was the unspoken rule.

As the year came to a close, Jimmy continued to stay with his sister and Rob. There were times when he could've cut the tension with a knife in their apartment, especially when Jillian wasn't eating, but overall things were good. He respected their rules and they didn't give him grief about his lifestyle.

One night shortly after Christmas, Jimmy came home from work to find a CD sitting on his bed with a note from his sister. Apparently a girl from her work had received it as a gift, didn't like it, and since Jimmy was in a band, thought Jillian's brother might want it.

Picking it up, he studied the cover: a photo of a baby in water swimming toward a dollar bill. The band was called Nirvana.

Chapter thirty-one

He was obsessed. There was something about the *Nevermind* CD that immediately captivated Jimmy. It was a new sound that stood out and inspired him to grab his own guitar and learn each riff. The lyrics ranged from raw and honest to poetic and beautiful. It was music he connected with and which captivated him. Soon everyone began to discover the band called Nirvana as they exploded into mainstream music. The heavy metal phase was fading away while the grunge generation took over. And Jimmy Groome was the first person in line to join.

It seemed to happen overnight. Suddenly, everyone in his age group shopped at the Salvation Army and wore either Doc Martens or actual combat boots purchased at a military surplus store. Girls paired large, clunky footwear with cute skirts and clothing that typically shouldn't have worked together. But it did. It was a different generation and many people who weren't part of it, didn't understand it.

It was all about the music. It was rare to step foot inside a bar where a band was playing and *not* hear at least one grunge song in their set. Planet One was no exception; their musical style was evolving ahead of the mainstream. Jimmy firmly believed that was what made their level of popularity rise in early 1992, while other bands faded away.

Some problems continued to plague Planet One; specifically the difficulties they had with Scott. Although Scott had been managing to show up to their gigs, the issue was his behavior and overall lack of professionalism. He would often screw up lyrics, zone out in the middle of songs or just talk gibberish to the audience. Most of the time, the band managed to cover it up, but they all knew that Scott's days were numbered. Like a bad relationship that was slowly coming to an end, the amount of time Scott had left with Planet One was limited. At the end of January, when he started to laugh in the middle of a performance and curse at the audience, Jimmy and Nick exchanged looks and knew what they had to do.

Jimmy grabbed the mike and in an effort to salvage the show, announced to the audience that they were taking a 'short break', but it was clear that people were already pissed off. They were ready to turn on the entire band for the disrespectful and crude remarks made by the singer. From the audience's perspective, Planet One was a unit, and the fact that the band members were individuals didn't matter; they believed that Scott's words represented how the whole band felt.

Nick suddenly erupted from behind the drum set, grabbed Scott by the neck of his t-shirt and dragged him off stage. Jimmy quickly followed, in case he needed help, although it didn't appear he did. Nick punched Scott in the face so hard that Jimmy actually thought he heard the singer's head crack as it was abruptly twisted to one side. Distorted, Scott jumped away from Nick and flew toward Jimmy. Before he even knew what was happening, Jimmy felt Scott's fist connect with his face. He'd never been punched before. As he was reeling from the blow, he heard the singer comment on how he knew Jimmy was trying to push him out of the band. For a split second, Jimmy was stunned by both Scott's remark and his attack, but that quickly turned to anger. Infuriated, Jimmy jumped forward and punched Scott in the stomach, knocking the wind out of the singer.

By this time, a crowd was gathered around the three members of Planet One. Nick's face was bright red, and he didn't seem fazed by the fact that Scott was gasping for air as he dragged him toward the exit and pushed him outside. The bitterly cold January night didn't discourage the bar's patrons from following the three band members outside, where Nick didn't hold his anger. First he verbally attacked Scott and punched him again with such strength, that the frail singer fell back into the snow bank. The bar's bouncers finally made an appearance and ushered everyone back into the club. Everyone, that is, but Jimmy and Nick.

"You guys can't be starting fights like that," the bouncer, who was smaller than Planet One's drummer, cautiously warned the two of them.

Judging by his weak attempt at authority with Jimmy and Nick, they knew nothing would happen to either of them. They were allowed back in the club, the proviso being that they find a way to get rid of Scott. No one was particularly concerned about his well-being, but the bar owners wanted the coked-out singer off their property. Nick pushed Scott into a cab and handed the driver some money. He then pointed toward the bar's door and gave Jimmy a long look.

"Got quite a shiner going on there, Jim." Nick smiled and seemed to relax as he reached for the door. "You're not going to be too pretty for the ladies tonight."

"Never stopped me before," Jimmy quipped as they walked through the entrance and saw the remaining two members of Planet One sitting on the edge of the stage and waiting. Jeremy looked especially stunned by Jimmy's black eye.

"What happened to Scott?" Jeremy seemed hesitant to ask as they climbed back on stage, while Ron simply looked like he didn't care. "He's okay, right?" The band's guitarist muttered the last few words, almost as if it were a secret that would remain between the four of them.

"Yup, in a cab and on the way home." Nick said with finality as he gestured for the rest of the band to take their places on stage. "Let's finish the show, Jim's singing."

"But, should we continue now?" Jeremy asked uncertainly as he stood up, while Ron did the same and the others jumped on stage. "I mean, just start again?"

"Yup." Nick grabbed the microphone, apologizing for their 'former' lead singer's behavior and insisting that the band was not going to let that setback stop their show. The audience seemed enthused and excited after the announcement, a complete turnaround from the restless and frustrated feeling in the room only a few minutes earlier. By thinking on his feet, Nick had saved their band from getting a bad reputation.

Jimmy was a little out of sorts when he first stepped up to the microphone, having just been in his first fight and witnessing their lead singer being abruptly kicked out of the band. However, he jokingly apologized to the audience for it being such a 'dull' night and then took over the vocals for the band - permanently.

While things with his band seemed to improve, Jimmy saw a decline in his own family relationship. Since moving in with his sister, neither of his parents had been in regular contact with him. Jimmy would be the first to admit that he was a fuck up, but found it hurtful that his own family would choose to essentially ignore him. Jillian had regular phone conversations with their mom and although she didn't admit it, Jimmy was pretty sure that she and Rob still went for Sunday family dinners at their parents' place. It sent a very strong message to him that he was no longer a part of the family.

The staff at the bar must have recognized his orphaned state because they all became his new family. Jimmy had a strict rule about not hooking up with any of the girls from his work, which wasn't a problem since most of them knew his player reputation, but they all loved him just the same. The girls his age came to him for boyfriend advice, knowing he'd be honest and direct with them. A couple of older women mothered him, always giving him hugs and telling him to take better care of himself. One of the women even brought him Tupperware containers of food after large family meals, insisting that they were just going to throw it out anyway. But Jimmy knew better. There seemed to be an invisible plate always set for him, despite the fact he wasn't at any of the actual meals. It was one of the few times in his life that Jimmy felt genuine respect and gratitude toward women. He was impressed by how their mothering instincts naturally recognized a loner that needed unconditional love.

The guys he worked with were cool too. Most were impressed that he was in a popular Thorton band and encouraged him to follow his dreams and avoid being stuck working at a bar forever, as some of them had. "It's not any kind of life for a young person like you," one of the older employees remarked to Jimmy one day. "Me, I have a family to consider, but you're young and talented, so go for what you want in life."

Based on these types of comments, Jimmy couldn't help but feel that a family and mortgage tied you down in a way that was disastrous. It made him further doubt the predictions that Darla had made months earlier. The last thing he needed was anything or *anyone* tying him down and taking him away from his dreams. No thanks.

Mark Whitman was one of his biggest supporters and encouraged Jimmy to hang posters up to advertise his band's upcoming shows, claiming he didn't care if the shows were played in one of his bars or not; he just wanted to help out Jimmy, a good and loyal employee. A somewhat skeptical Jimmy realized that having someone from a popular band working in his bar wasn't bad for business either. It didn't exactly keep the girls away.

All and all, things were going well early in 1992. The band was successful. Jimmy loved his job. Life was simple. Until a familiar face on the other side of the bar started a downward spiral.

Chapter thirty-two

He had to look twice before deciding that it was her. The same beautiful eyes, blonde hair and flawless figure as she had years before, when Jimmy was merely a kid. How many times had he thought about her, dreamed of the first girl who ever gave him a sincere compliment? Katie Craft was standing across the bar from him.

At first, he didn't think she recognized him. After all, it had been a few years and pounds since she had seen him last. And even then, it wasn't like his former guitar teacher's girlfriend had met him more than a couple of times. It would've never occurred to him that she would remember his face, but she did. Once again, her words knocked down walls inside of him that no one else ever could.

"You still have the same beautiful smile that you did when I first met you." She leaned over the bar and gently touched his face with the tips of her fingers. Although it was only for a split second, Jimmy felt energy reverberate from every place that she touched. Katie tilted her head and watched him with interest. "Do you remember me?"

"Y-yes," Jimmy stuttered and instantly felt like the same awkward kid that he had been when they met the first time. There was something unsettling about knowing that she remembered him back then. It was rare for people who once knew the 'fat Jimmy' to now associate with him, so the whole idea of someone knowing that part of his past made him feel vulnerable. He didn't like it. "I'm surprised you remember me. I'm nothing like the kid I used to be."

"Well you have grown up." She studied him intently from the other side of the bar. "But you still have the same face and beautiful blue eyes as you had back then. It's Jimmy, right?"

"Yeah," he grinned sheepishly, glancing around the bar.

"I'm Katie."

"I remember," Jimmy flashed her a seductive smile before quickly looking away. "I'm really sorry about Sean. I was upset when I heard about what happened to him." For some reason he couldn't find it in himself to say the word *dead* even though they were both very aware of Sean's death.

Her smile faltered and Jimmy immediately regretted bringing up the topic. It was probably insensitive, but it was hard to avoid the elephant in the room. "It was a shock," she responded evenly, nodding her head. "It was devastating to everyone in his life."

Her words sounded more like a rehearsed answer than anything from the heart. Not that he thought Katie should start pouring out all her emotions at his bar, but at the same time, it almost seemed insincere and it made him question how Sean's death had really affected her. Hadn't they been engaged at the time? Was there more to the story that he didn't know about? Jimmy was afraid to ask. Fortunately the awkwardness between them was interrupted when the bar started to fill up as customers arrived looking for a drink. Katie disappeared. She returned for a few brief moments here and there throughout the night, but never for very long. Jimmy noticed that each time she dropped by, she was becoming increasingly intoxicated. When Katie stopped by his bar at closing time, she was smashed.

"Are you going to be okay?" Jimmy was genuinely concerned for Katie. He wondered what Sean Ryan would think if he saw this haggard version of his fiancée. Not that it was the first time he had seen women who started off the night looking perfect and beautiful, stumbling around dead drunk at closing time, makeup smeared and hair completely disheveled. At least her skirt wasn't buttoned crooked and her clothes didn't smell of vomit like some of the girls he saw wandering around at the end of the night. It was pathetic.

"Yeah," she drawled, leaning against a wall close to his bar. She teetered back and forth a bit, indicating that she was probably ready to pass out on the floor. Feeling a sense of compassion combined with obligation toward Sean, even though he was dead, Jimmy offered to drive her home. She seemed disorientated, but accepted with a mumbled "Thanks."

All the way to her apartment, he worried that Katie would either pass out or vomit all over the inside of his car. If she passed out, what would he do with her? He couldn't exactly take her back to Jillian's place and he had no idea which apartment was Katie's when he *did* arrive at her building. He didn't exactly want to clean vomit out of his car either, but he knew driving her home was the right thing to do.

Arriving at her apartment, Jimmy parked the car and helped her out of the passenger side. She stumbled and almost fell over, but they managed to get into the building and up to her place. Katie's hands were shaky, so he unlocked her door and helped her inside. Once there, he noted that her place was pretty small and plain. No decorations or girly things like flowery curtains and crap like that. In fact the entire apartment was sparingly furnished which surprised him, but then he wondered if maybe she'd just moved? Jimmy wasn't sure.

Falling back on her couch, she invited Jimmy to sit with her. He hesitated to do so and wasn't sure why. He was still very attracted to Katie, but for some reason it felt wrong to initiate anything with her. It was clear by how she was looking and talking to him that she wanted sex. Jimmy had been around enough to read the signs. Women were never as subtle as they thought; it was usually pretty obvious when they intended to hook up. It was in their body language, the way they looked and spoke, and it was something he knew well.

Jimmy sat beside her and within minutes they were making out. He was immediately aroused and started to remove her clothes. Despite how horny he was and how hot she was, Katie was much too drunk to participate. She just lay on her back, occasionally moaning or moving slightly, and consequently the sex was horrible. But she wanted him to stay, and even though it went against his better judgment, Jimmy agreed. He automatically regretted it.

First there was the vomiting. They had barely gotten into her bed when Jimmy watched her grab a nearby garbage can and puke up what appeared to be spaghetti she had eaten earlier that day. He was almost sick himself. Fortunately, she cleaned up her mess and opened a window. The cool, mid-March air filled the tiny bedroom and caused Katie to be cold and automatically curl up to Jimmy. He was relieved that she had brushed her teeth after puking, as she got closer and began to kiss him again. Watching her get sick, however, had really turned him off, and for the first time in his life he couldn't get it up. He didn't even *want* to; it didn't matter how sexy her body was, it just wasn't happening. He slipped out of her apartment early the next morning while she was still sleeping.

Katie started to show up at his bar every night. Every night, she got drunk. And *every* night, Jimmy would drive her home. However, after that first night, he avoided having sex with her. Usually he just dropped her off and left, often going elsewhere to party or 'hang out' with another girl. But one night, she became emotional as he drove her home and started to cry. He hated it when drunken girls went all manic after getting loaded. What the fuck was with that anyway? But he felt bad for Katie, so when they got to her apartment, he went inside and asked her what was wrong. It was then that the truth came out; the whole truth.

In tears, Katie admitted that she never had gotten over Sean's death. She blamed herself because they'd had a fight that night and he'd left with a drunken friend on a whim, getting into the car that would drive him to his death. Jimmy tried to tell her that it wasn't her fault, but she wouldn't listen.

"It *was* my fault," she whimpered, make-up running down her face. Katie began to shiver and cry harder. "I knew the guy he left with was fucked up, but I was so mad at him at the time, that I didn't care. I didn't *care*." Her desperate eyes stared steadily into Jimmy's and he sensed her anguish. "Now he's dead."

"You have to let it go." Even as he said the words, Jimmy knew it was easier said than done. Had he let go of his own regrets of not helping Jillian on that horrific day he found her being raped in their family's living room? Yet, he knew his words were correct.

Noting that she was still shivering, Jimmy offered to get her a blanket or sweater. Katie nodded and said there was a black sweater at the end of her bed. What he found in her room was something else.

Unlike the last time he'd been in her room, it looked like a bomb had gone off. Makeup, clothing and garbage were scattered throughout the room. He was half expecting to see a rat run out from under the bed. Liquor bottles were all over the place; scattered on her bed, nightstand, on the floor and nearby dresser. Most of the bottles had contained vodka and all were empty. On her dresser were various pill bottles. Some he recognized as anti-depressants and others seemed to be strong pain medication. Jimmy slowly reached for the sweater on Katie's bed and noticed something fall out of the pocket; a small bag of white powder fell on the floor. Jimmy reached over to pick it up. Was it....

"It's cocaine," he jumped when he heard her voice behind him. Although Jimmy hadn't done anything wrong, he felt as though his eyes were witnessing something he wasn't supposed to see, so he was blunt with her.

"You do all this?" He gestured around the room at the liquor bottles, the pills and the coke. In a soft voice, he asked, "Katie, what are you doing with your life?"

"Hopefully, sooner or later I'll be ending it." She sounded so child-like in her reply that he felt powerless and depressed.

The room was suddenly very silent. This wasn't the Katie he remembered, the beautiful blonde with friendly eyes and a warm smile, the one Sean Ryan was so much in love with years before. When he was still alive. Apparently his death had taken away a part of Katie too because she was only a fraction of the person she used to be. He understood, because he also felt as though there was part of him that was dead.

"Do you really feel that way?" Jimmy felt obligated to ask, even though he wasn't prepared to hear the answer. "Do you really want to die?"

"It's not that I want to die," she explained as she moved closer to him. Her angelic eyes looked into his through the dried up makeup smeared around them. There was a stillness in the room that sent a chill up his spine. "On so many levels I'm already dead. I'm just going through the motions now. I haven't been here in years, not since Sean died." She began to cry again, however this time; it wasn't from the overwhelming affects of alcohol, but from sincere and heart-wrenching pain. Jimmy moved forward and hugged her, as he listened to the most anguish-filled sobs he'd ever witnessed. He felt the same sense of panic and helplessness as on the day his sister told him about the rape. In the distance, he could hear an ambulance roaring through the streets while his heart raced in fear. What could he do to make this better? What could he say? How could you save someone from drowning if you couldn't even swim yourself?

"You have to find yourself again," he whispered while gently running his hands up and down her back. "You have to move forward." But he already knew his words were wasted. She'd never be the same again. It would be idealistic to think that something, anything would bring her back. He knew better; there was a deadness in her eyes that was only recognizable to someone who had known her once before, when she was another person all together.

Eventually she stopped crying. Letting go of Jimmy, she reached for the bag of white powder he'd dropped on the floor and opened it.

"Have you ever done coke before?" She asked and Jimmy shook his head no. "Do you want to?"

He wasn't sure what made him say yes, maybe an inner misery that was brought out by her confessions or maybe because he just wanted to try a new kind of poison. They both sat on the edge of her bed and Katie grabbed a nearby mirror then went to work. It was just like on television. She used a blade to separate the lines, located a small straw and inhaled the white power. Jimmy did the same and automatically felt a high like he had never experienced in his life. He quickly understood why people became addicted to it as he fell back on the bed and felt Katie climb on top of his body. Unlike the first time, the sex that night was amazing. It lasted most of the night, and the next morning he awoke with bites all over him, most of which he barely remembered. Seeing that she was still asleep, her naked body lying beside him, Jimmy got out of bed. He quickly dressed and left. A part of him felt enormous shame over the night he'd just experienced.

He never saw Katie Craft again. She died of an overdose three weeks later.

Chapter thirty-three

Jimmy heard the reports of Katie's death on the radio. Local DJs were discussing how the fiancée of the late Sean Ryan had passed away 'suddenly' in her home. Even in death, she was still associated with Jimmy's former guitar teacher and idol. He wondered if that was part of the reason she never got over Sean's death. How could she ever separate from him in her mind when no one else did? She didn't have her own identity.

Katie's death hit him much harder than Jimmy would've expected. He thought about her all the time, even finding himself at her funeral a few days later. Not many other people showed up. Those who were there watched him curiously, but no one talked to him. When the funeral was over, he slipped out the back door before anyone else and walked to the nearest bar; there was no other way to escape all the thoughts that haunted him.

What if he died that very day? Who would even care? His parents would probably be sad, but not surprised in the event of his death. They'd assume that his lifestyle was the reason for his sudden demise. In their eyes it would be his fault, for being irresponsible and living recklessly. Maybe they'd be right.

Jillian would miss him. Even though Jimmy and his sister were very different people, there was no denying that they loved each other. There was a very special bond between the siblings. Jimmy certainly didn't know what he'd do if anything were to ever happen to Jill. There were times that he feared having to face this very real possibility, especially in view of her eating disorder. There was always a chance she could take a turn for the worse and possibly die. The body could only take so much abuse. Ironically, where his sister deprived her body of food to punish herself, Jimmy polluted his own with alcohol. Maybe in their own ways, they each wanted to hurt themselves. At least that's what Jimmy thought.

After a few drinks that afternoon, he stumbled home and told his sister that very theory. Jillian had made them both some strong coffee and they were sitting alone in the living room. His words were met by a long silence, and at first Jimmy thought he should've kept his opinions to himself.

"You're probably right," she finally admitted. There was sadness in her soft voice and Jimmy felt like he might have hit a nerve. "It's no different than when we were kids. I still don't eat very well and you just exchanged food for drinking. I mean, look at you Jimmy, it's not even dinner time and you're loaded."

"It was a rough day," he stared into his cup of black coffee for a few moments, then met her eyes and quietly told her about Katie and her death. He left out the parts about having sex with her and the coke, but told her the rest. "I just sat at her funeral today and thought to myself, 'What if that were me up there?' Jill, she hardly had anyone at her funeral. I kind of think it would be the same if I died. I don't think a lot of people really give a crap about me and it bothers me more than I thought it would. Although, I guess that'd be the least of my problems if I died." He was joking, but his sister failed to see the humor in his comment.

"Jimmy, don't talk like that," Jillian's forehead wrinkled and she seemed on the verge of tears. "I don't know what I'd do if anything ever happened to you. And when you say stuff like that, it worries me a lot. Especially with what happened when we were kids."

She was talking about his suicide attempt. Jillian was clearly concerned that he'd try to hurt himself again. So was he.

"Jill, I'm not going to do anything if that's what you're worried about," Jimmy insisted, as much for her sake as for his. He saw from her face that she was reassured, but not much.

Jimmy was silent for a few minutes while he finished his coffee. "You know, she never got over Sean dying. It's been how long? A couple of years?"

"Well you don't just forget someone 'cause they die," Jillian spoke gently. "I know you haven't had a lot of experience with relationships

Jimmy, but when you love someone – *really* love someone, it doesn't just go away. Death is the absolute worst possible way to lose someone under any circumstance, especially one as tragic and sudden as Sean's. I can't even-

Her voice trailed off, but Jimmy knew what she was thinking. Jillian couldn't imagine losing her own fiancé in the same way that Katie lost Sean.

For the next few weeks, whether Jimmy was at work with a smile on his face or on stage singing, Sean Ryan and his fiancé were often in his thoughts. He mulled over questions that he hadn't explored with his sister. One of them was a fear that he would someday die without first experiencing love. Ever since hearing Katie's tearful confession on the last night they were together, Jimmy wondered what it would be like to have someone love him *that* much. To have a woman feel like a part of *her* died if his life suddenly ended. Although he was usually the first person to deny ever wanting a relationship, there was something about *never* having a girl love him that much that really was unsettling. Granted, he wasn't quite twenty and therefore still young, but then again, Sean and Katie had been too, and now they were both gone.

His depression only increased in the following weeks. Not only had the band learned that their former singer Scott had been arrested for possession, now their bassist was causing them difficulties. It was clear that Ron's brain was too polluted with drugs to focus on the task at hand. He made too many mistakes and he didn't have the same level of motivation as the rest of the band. They'd have to find another bassist. They managed to stay positive, until early May when Jeremy broke his hand while playing basketball. Someone had been pushed into the band's guitarist, and the weight and impact resulted in a visit to the emergency ward. Everyone was completely discouraged.

"We'll have to put everything on hold for now," Nick said resolutely after Jeremy's accident. "There's nothing else we can do."

But Jimmy already knew that the band was pretty much finished. Incidents with Scott, and then more issues because of Ron, had given Planet One a bad reputation on the bar scene and fewer promoters were calling them to do shows. It was probably better to cut their losses. Although no one had said as much, it was understood.

His job was also proving to be frustrating for Jimmy. Working in a bar had seemed fun in the beginning, but dealing with drunks on a regular basis was starting to wear on Jimmy's nerves. It was just the same shit every night. It was such a game. People came out to the bar, got loaded and used alcohol as an excuse for everything: getting into fights, or just being complete idiots. It was disgusting and it made Jimmy see that there was absolutely *no* way he could work in this kind of environment for the rest of his life. It would eat away at his soul if he did.

In the first week of June, Patrick surprised him with a call. The two hadn't talked in months. He phoned to tell Jimmy that he was excelling in college and about to do on-the-job training at a local car dealership. And there was more.

"So you're not going to fucking believe this man, but I'm getting married," Patrick's news sent waves of shock through Jimmy. Patrick was engaged? He was surprised at the twinge of disappointment he felt. Was everyone around him changing and leaving him behind? First Katie's death, then his band broke up, he was starting to hate his job and now his best friend was history. Since Melissa didn't like Patrick hanging out with Jimmy when they were just in a relationship, there was no way he'd ever see his best friend again once he was married.

"You're fucking with me, right?" Jimmy teased, covering his own feelings of loss. His best friend was gone now too.

"Nope, things have been going really well since I went to college and I grew up and we decided to take the plunge and just get married," Patrick explained enthusiastically. He didn't even *talk* like the Patrick that Jimmy once knew. It was weird. "Plus we have to think about Hope too. Can you believe she's three already?"

"No man, I guess time goes fast," Jimmy said and congratulated him. They talked for a few more minutes before hanging up. Then Jimmy went to the nearest bar and drank until he threw up.

Chapter thirty-four

Jimmy's depression continued to simmer for months. With no band or close friends in his life, he had more time to do less productive things. He partied regularly, slept with women he barely knew, and on a couple of occasions got into fights. Just as with drinking, playing music, hooking up with new women and experimenting with drugs, getting into barroom brawls seemed to give him a high. As with everything else, the momentary adrenaline rushes were never enough and sent him crashing even further. Even though he wanted to stop this destructive behavior, there was a part of Jimmy that needed it in the most intense way. It was the only thing that reminded him that he was still alive and wanted to keep it that way. But there were days when he doubted this and toward the end of summer 1992, those moments were becoming more and more frequent.

Possibly the worst part of it all was how happy everyone else in his life was.

His sister was starting to make wedding plans for sometime in 1994. Jimmy wasn't even sure of the date. It wasn't that Jillian didn't share the information, but rather that he often chose not to hear it. As much as he wanted to see his sister happy, conversations about wedding days were of no interest to him. At that point in his life, Jimmy thought love wasn't anything more than a joke. A myth. Something that Hollywood used to make movies out of and a fairytale that adults liked to tell themselves, even though they knew it wasn't true. People got together because they didn't want to be alone or couldn't handle life on their own. That was the truth about love, as far as Jimmy Groome was concerned.

Needless to say, he didn't particularly want to hear Patrick talk about his upcoming marriage either. It wasn't planned for a couple of years, but that would still be too soon for Jimmy. He had already changed. It wasn't that Jimmy was jealous, but the whole idea of being the only person in his inner circle who didn't have a significant other, was suddenly very obvious to him. His sister had someone, so did his best friend. Jimmy still kept in contact with Jeremy and Nick from the band, and both had girlfriends. Everyone at the bar was either married or in some stage of a relationship. And then there was him. Alone. The worst part of it all was that his lack of belief in love made Jimmy confused about why he even cared at all.

"I have to find a new band." Jimmy announced to Patrick during one of their few conversations in the autumn of '92. In a way, it was meant to interrupt his friend's talk of future plans; the career, the marriage, more kids, buying a house, all of it. Jimmy couldn't listen to any more, so he felt the need to add his own personal goals. There was really only one at that point; get in a band that had potential and get it signed. That's it; all he wanted, all he had.

"You'll find one," Patrick encouraged as the two sat in a seedy coffee shop close to where Jimmy worked. "Jesus man, you're like the best fucking guitarist around. I'm surprised that people aren't actually seeking *you* out."

Jimmy rolled his eyes. "Fuck, really? I can think of two reasons. The two coke heads that were in my last band." he let out a sigh of frustration. "If those two fuckers ruined *my* chances because we were all in the same band, I don't know what I'm going to do."

"I doubt it, but if they did, there's always possibilities," Patrick insisted and once again Jimmy felt like he was talking to a stranger. *Who the hell is this guy?* "If you really had to, you could always move and start fresh in somewhere like Toronto."

"I know but I don't have any contacts there at all," Jimmy sighed and wondered if he could even afford the move. After all, his plan since finishing high school was to move out on his own, and yet he was still living with his sister. There were many days he felt stuck in every way. Maybe he had no options.

"There's always a way, you'll figure it out," Patrick persisted. "Look at my life. I mean I got a girl pregnant in high school! I drank and I partied right along with you, but things came together for me."

Jimmy didn't say anything, but wondered if his friend was *really* happy. How many times had he and Melissa broken up over the years? It was difficult to imagine that things were suddenly blissful. Jimmy suspected that much of Patrick's loyalty toward Melissa sprang from the fact that they had a kid together. He also wondered if his friend really wanted to be a mechanic. Had Patrick found what he was looking for and how could Jimmy do the same?

Even his parents were happy. During one of the few occasions when they invited Jimmy to their house for a family meal, they spoke excitedly about a cruise they were planning for the coming year. No decisions had been made yet, but they were investigating a few options and checking out vacation packages. While they talked about that and his sister discussed her wedding plans, Jimmy sat quietly at the end of the table and felt like the outsider. No one asked what he was doing. They *knew* what he was doing and didn't particularly care. So he sat in silence and wondered how the entire scene would look if he wasn't in the room. Then he thought about how the scene would look if he weren't in the world at all. He decided that it wouldn't be much different and that thought made him want to leave. Instead he quietly sat and listened to the loud ticking of a nearby clock.

Every day in late September and early October he would sit in rooms and wonder what they would look like without him there. Would anyone even care? It crossed his mind at work. His eyes carefully watched the regular barflies as he wondered if they would even notice if he wasn't there anymore. What about his coworkers? They'd get used to it, he decided. Life went on. Well, not his obviously, but most people's did.

October seemed to drag him down even further and he wasn't sure why. He was just mindlessly walking through each day, not really paying attention to details but covering his basic needs. He ate when he was hungry, worked when he was scheduled, fucked when he was horny and slept when he was tired. And played his guitar every chance he got. Occasionally he would drink, but it didn't affect him in the same way it once had. It didn't make him laugh and have fun, it filled him with melancholy. He would sit alone and think. And when people were around, he wouldn't listen to them, but simply smile and nod. Occasionally he'd listen to enough of the conversation to reply to questions, but then he stopped listening again. Not that it mattered; he quickly realized that most people were so consumed with talking about themselves that they didn't even notice he wasn't listening. People were self-absorbed; they truly believed they were the center of attention. It was a real eye opener.

The only joy Jimmy found in life was music. He listened to Nirvana over and over again. Jillian would joke that she knew every Nirvana song by heart because it played *non-stop* in her apartment. He knew she didn't really care though. Jill would make remarks like that and smile, while her eyes searched his face as she tried to hide the fact that she was carefully studying his mood. She probably wondered if her brother was still in there, somewhere.

He wasn't. There were times that he would think about a comment that Katie had made to him months earlier. He was already dead; it was just not official yet.

Early in November, Jimmy received a call that sprung him back into life. It was Patrick.

"Man, there's this new guy at work who's looking for another guitarist for his band," Patrick sounded more excited than Jimmy felt at that moment. "He's pretty fucking serious about making it in the industry. I told him about you. About how you were trained by Sean Ryan, everything and he said he wants to talk to you."

"I don't know man, I'm just not into it anymore-

"Jimmy, snap the fuck out of it!" Patrick's words were harsh and were like a punch in the face to him. He opened his mouth to reply but couldn't speak. "Jesus fucking Christ man, I don't know what you're taking or what's going on with you lately, but you've got to get your fucking shit together again."

"Now there's a really fucking cool guy who wants another guitarist for his band and I told him about you," Patrick began to repeat the facts in a sterner tone this time. "And he wants you to call him. *You're* the one who keeps saying that you want to be in a rock band that makes it and this could be the one!"

Jimmy opened his mouth to protest, to remind Patrick that he'd thought that last time and things hadn't worked out. However he didn't get a chance.

"It's this guy William, his brother, some kid on drums and a girl is singing."

"A girl?" Jimmy was intrigued. "Really?"

"A girl you *shouldn't* fuck, Jimmy." Patrick sounded very serious, but started to laugh. "Please, if you join this band, *don't fuck the singer.* Okay, got it?"

"I can't promise that," Jimmy said and heard laughter in his own voice. "But I'll try. So, what's this guy's name again? William?"

Chapter thirty-five

Jimmy decided that Patrick was right. He had to snap out of it. Unfortunately, it was easier said than done. Jimmy had sunk so far down into misery that coming back up again wasn't going to be easy, but he had to try. His first step to getting back on track was to call William Stacy about this band thing. Jimmy knew that music was the only thing that would make him feel alive again. He thought this guy from Patrick's work sounded cool on the phone, and the two agreed to meet the following evening.

But even as he drove to William Stacy's house the next night, Jimmy just wasn't into it, and at least not in the way he should've been. At one time the possibility of getting into a new band and starting fresh would've been exciting, but not now. His climb out of this depression wasn't going to be an easy task. It took him weeks to get to this low point so he guessed it would take just as long to get back. Assuming he got back at all.

After working in a bar for so long, Jimmy prided himself on summing people up quickly. William Stacy was no exception. As soon as he answered the door, Jimmy could see that he was a very serious person who was probably wound a little too tight. He shook Jimmy's hand and politely invited him in – a little formal, but clearly William was a nice guy. He quickly launched into what he was looking for in a guitarist and his goals for this band he was forming. Jimmy almost laughed at how seriously this guy took himself, but after being in a band with a couple of crackheads, it was a nice change of pace.

He noticed that although William had long hair, wore ripped jeans and had a few days worth of facial hair; he still had the pretty boy look that appealed to girls. That was definitely an advantage as far as Jimmy was concerned, because he didn't think he was going to get far on his looks. Charm and a cute smile, yes – but not on his appearance. Every band needed the 'hot' guy to capture female fans; it was just a fact.

After a short discussion on their musical influences, most of which were very similar, Jimmy and William headed to the basement and both grabbed a guitar. After about twenty minutes of demonstrating their abilities, it became unclear who was auditioning for whom. It was fun though. Whether it was William playing something by Steve Vai or Jimmy doing a particularly difficult Jimi Hendrix song, both seemed equally impressed with the other.

"Wow, you're fucking good William," Jimmy announced when they took a brief break. "How long have you been playing, man?" His eyes roamed the crowded basement and he quickly jumped into another question. "By the way, this is a good place to practice. Is it your house?"

"No, it belongs to a friend of mine who's away for a year," William shrugged. "He needed someone to keep an eye on it and I needed a place to stay, plus the band can practice in the basement. Provided that we don't rehearse late, obviously." He cleared his throat. "As for music, I've been playing since I was about twelve. Not to say I was great at first, but eventually my dad broke down and paid for some lessons."

"Yeah, mine too," Jimmy nodded and looked at the ground. "I had an awesome teacher."

"Patrick said that Sean Ryan was your instructor, was he serious?" William asked, appearing skeptical.

"Yeah, he taught me everything I know," Jimmy sighed as his mind flashed momentarily to the last time he saw his idol face to face. Then he thought about the last time he saw Katie. "Umm, he used to teach part time before he moved to Toronto and things really started to happen with his band. I was just a kid at the time."

"Wow, that's really cool. I bet that's why you're so good now, you had an excellent teacher." William spoke earnestly and Jimmy simply smiled and changed the topic.

"So you work with Pat?"

"Yeah, I just started working there not long ago. He's a nice guy." William smiled and Jimmy thought about how much his friend had changed. At one time, he doubted that William would be saying that about Patrick. "So where do you work, Jimmy?"

"At DanceX, I'm a bartender."

"I just moved here, but isn't that a really skanky dance bar?" William raised his eyebrow and a smile crept across his lips.

"Yeah, I know, everyone says it doesn't seem like somewhere I'd be working." Jimmy gave a short laugh. "It wasn't really my idea, I wanted to work at another place, but they plunked me there. At least I make great tips and there's lots of drunk and horny girls to hook up with."

William gave him a skeptical look. It was time to change topics once again.

"So, tell me about the other people in the band." Jimmy jumped in.

"Well there's me and my brother Michael," William set down his guitar. "He plays bass. Our drummer Eddie is living in Springdale, where Mike and I are from, but he plans to move to Thorton when he graduates this spring."

"Graduates?"

"Yeah, he's still in high school," William replied and rushed to add, "But he's excellent. Eddie was actually in my last band, him and Mike. We kind of ditched the singer and moved on." He didn't bother explaining things any further and Jimmy didn't ask.

"So, tell me about the singer. It's a girl, right?" Jimmy asked enthusiastically, quickly jumping ahead. "Is she hot?"

William studied Jimmy's face. It was only for a split second, but there was definitely some hesitation to answer. "Yeah, Tarah's pretty."

"Cool." Jimmy smiled, wondering if something was up with William and this chick. He decided that it was once again time to change the subject. Jimmy started to talk about some of the music his previous bands played and before he knew it, he and William were playing 'Smells like Teen Spirit' by Nirvana. It was fun. It was cool. And from there, they just continued to jump into various songs without any discussion just going with the flow. Then William suddenly stopped.

"Did you hear something?"

A doorbell abruptly rang twice.

"Oh shit! I forgot Tarah was coming over tonight," William put down his guitar and ran upstairs. Jimmy sat on a nearby chair, resting his guitar on his lap and idly gazing at the empty staircase. He could hear a girl's laughter and voice as she spoke excitedly, however Jimmy couldn't make out her words. He was anxious to meet the band's singer. The fact that it was a woman was intriguing to him. Considering how high William's standards seemed to be, clearly this Tarah girl had to be good to be even considered – really good!

Jimmy watched as they came down the stairs, laughing and talking together. He gently placed the guitar on the floor without looking away for even a second. He didn't even blink.

Tarah was tiny – he didn't guess her to be much over 5 feet tall and she had an almost childlike figure. Not that she was *too* skinny because he definitely *did* notice the subtle curves underneath her clothes. Tarah's long, blond hair flowed down her back almost reaching her waist, while her makeup was modestly applied. She spoke in a soft and sweet voice that was neither presumptuous or weak, but very alluring and seductive. Although she glanced at him on the way down the stairs, it wasn't until she and William reached the bottom step that Jimmy noticed her blue eyes sparkle as she observed him from where she stood. For a moment, he wished that they were alone in the room.

"So this is Jimmy Groome, the guy I was telling you about," William seemed hesitant to make the introduction, but Tarah confidently walked toward Jimmy. He stood up and reached out to shake her hand, while staring into her face. It took him a minute to realize that he was probably standing a little too close to her, as he looked down into her curious eyes. "And this is Tarah Kiersey."

"Hi Jimmy," she tilted her head slightly. He noticed that her fingers were small and delicate, as she gently shook his hand and smiled. Jimmy felt his heart begin to race and his face become warm. She was beautiful. Tarah slowly let go of his hand. "I've heard a lot of great things about you."

"You too."

"Jimmy and I were just playing around with a few songs. Sorry again about not hearing the doorbell sooner," William seemed to speak a bit harsher than earlier and Jimmy sensed that there was *definitely* something going on with these two. Clearly he felt threatened by Jimmy in some way; otherwise he wouldn't have been so abrupt. "If you want to join in, Tarah?"

"Nah, I have a bad sore throat tonight," she moved away from Jimmy, but he noted that she sat in a chair closer to him than William. "I think I probably overdid it this week."

"You might not be singing properly," Jimmy suggested and then automatically regretted it. They were both looking at him funny and he felt like a dick. "I mean if you sing more from your throat, you can strain your voice. I didn't mean it as an insult." He spoke apologetically and felt himself blush. His heart was about five seconds away from jumping right out of his chest. He hadn't felt this nervous around a girl since his first date with Sally years earlier.

"No, that's fine," she shyly smiled and glanced toward William. "He actually told me that last night. It's just funny you mentioned it too."

Jimmy was relieved when he and William began to play again because it gave him a chance to refocus. When they took another break, they discussed more of their musical influences. Tarah occasionally jumped in with some comments, but mostly sat back to listen. She didn't seem to miss a thing, even glancing over the collection of tattoos on his arms. Jimmy was very conscious of how many times he looked in her direction because he knew that left to his own devices he would be staring at her all night, so he went out of his way *not* to do that. Instead he timed his glances so that they didn't seem suspicious. Jimmy wanted to see if she was checking him out the way that other girls did when they were into him, but he couldn't tell. Then again, he reasoned, he didn't care much about most girls, so he had nothing riding on it. There was something he really liked about Tarah and for some reason, it *did* matter what she thought of him.

Jimmy finally reluctantly announced that he had to take off and go to work, Tarah inquired about his job. She seemed surprised when he told her it was at DanceX, but didn't say anything.

William nodded as the three of them stood up and officially asked him to join the band. "It's yours if you want it."

Jimmy nodded, glancing toward Tarah before he realized what he was doing. "I'm in." Feeling like he was in a daze, he still managed to keep up his end of the conversation as the three of them walked upstairs toward the door. The entire evening felt surreal to him and he didn't understand why. It was like being high, but he wasn't.

After shaking hands with William, Jimmy opened the door and

headed outside. But not before saying good night to Tarah, then winking at her. They shared a smile and he left.

In his car, Jimmy sat silently for a minute. His heart continued to race. What was he doing? He couldn't join this band. How was he supposed to work with this girl? It was one thing to be in a band with a cokehead, an asshole or someone with no talent. But it was quite another thing to work with a hot chick that intimidated him. The ironic thing was that she seemed completely harmless and sweet. So why did Tarah Kiersey scare the hell out of him?

Chapter thirty-six

Jimmy couldn't sleep that night. His mind was running a mile a minute. Although a part of him was excited about the prospect of joining a new band with obvious potential, another side of him was reluctant; and it was because of Tarah.

It really didn't make sense. How could a girl he didn't even know affect him so much? *No* girl ever had before that day. Sure, at one time Sally could've asked him to walk out into the middle of traffic and he would've obediently done so with no questions asked. But he was just a kid back then, a horny teenager desperate to lose his virginity. Nah, that wasn't completely true; he *really* did think he loved her and was very hurt when she rejected him.

Katie Craft also had an affect on him, but that was a little more complicated. He didn't love her. Jimmy wasn't even sure he *liked* her. But she had been Sean Ryan's ex and it was hard to watch her self-destruct in front of his eyes. Sometimes he wondered if he was supposed to witness the disastrous end of her life. Was someone, somewhere trying to send him a message? A warning? Was his own life going in the same direction as Katie Craft's? Would Jimmy also burn out while he was still young? Would he die alone and with no one around who cared? He thought of the almost empty room on the day of her funeral. He finally decided that someone was trying to send him a message. It was time to get his shit together. He was tired of running on empty - and even more tired of just running. At twenty, it was time for Jimmy to get his life together.

And something told him that joining this band was a perfect start to a new life.

But then, there was *that* girl.

As he finally drifted to sleep that night, Jimmy decided that it was probably nothing. Chances were that the next time the band hung out, she'd do or say something that would put her in the same category as most other women he met. Either that or his original interest would dissolve for some other reason. He was worrying about nothing. His inability to care for a woman wasn't about to change suddenly.

However, he didn't sleep well that night. Fragments of dreams were floating through Jimmy's mind when he woke up the next afternoon. Having a comfortable stretch, he felt the bright sun hitting his face through the broken blinds causing him to close his eyes. Lightning - a sudden thought flashed through Jimmy's head and his eyes flew wide open. He thought back to the school dance that he and Patrick crashed years earlier. He remembered the couple that was having a passionate argument in the school hallway and the girl involved that haunted his thoughts for days afterward - Was Tarah *that* same girl?

The resemblance was uncanny. But what were the chances? Could it be? Would it be? Maybe Jimmy was over-thinking the entire matter. After all, what were the odds? A nagging feeling encouraged him to investigate.

So when Tarah answered the door to William's house the following Saturday afternoon, Jimmy didn't waste any time as he walked into the house. "What high school did you go to?" Thinking quickly, he rushed to add a lie. "You look like a girl who was in my math class."

He put down his guitar and amp then quickly glanced at her. She was wearing a burgundy smock and ugly uniform. She still looked cute though. Apparently a little taken aback by his question, Tarah's eyes widened and became large and she opened her mouth.

"You work at Rothman's?" Jimmy hurriedly asked her another question before she had a chance to answer the first one. Feeling awkward and his face burning, he began to stutter. "S-sorry, I guess I'm all over the place, as usual." He smiled self-consciously and looked at his feet. *Fuck! Really smooth Jimmy!*

He slowly looked back up and noted that she was giving him a warm smile. Music could be heard floating up from the basement, where the boys were apparently already practicing without them. Jimmy met her eyes, attempting to hide his embarrassment.

"Don't worry about it," Tarah gently replied and then went on to name her high school - which *wasn't* the 'school dance' school, making him wonder why she seemed so familiar to him? Why did he feel as though they had met before? It was a bit surreal. The more he stared into her eyes, the more he was *certain* they had met before; there couldn't be any other logical explanation.

He was so preoccupied, he almost missed Tarah explaining how she had just left work, and was about to change when Jimmy rang the doorbell. "I knew the guys probably wouldn't hear you in the basement, so I rushed back to let you in." Her soft voice was slightly hypnotic to Jimmy's ears. He could've stood just inside William's front door and listened to her all day.

"Thanks," he smiled awkwardly. Reminding himself of the golden rule that girls liked being complimented, Jimmy was about to say something flattering to her when William came running up from the basement. *Shit.*

"Hey, Jimmy. I thought I heard you up here," William's eyes seemed to jump between Jimmy and Tarah, as if he were studying the situation. "Um, the rest of the band is downstairs if you want to meet everyone."

"Sure." Jimmy spoke cheerfully, as Tarah reached for a black, leather bag on the floor. Grabbing it, she scurried down the hallway and he momentarily considered following her. Instead, he grabbed his gear and trailed behind William to the basement where the other guys were waiting. Jimmy automatically knew which was which. The miserable looking fucker must be William's brother, since it wasn't unusual for siblings to be polar opposites. And the quiet, nervous one was younger, and therefore the drummer. As it turned out, Jimmy was right.

Michael Stacy barely managed a civil 'hello' to Jimmy. Judging by the look of disdain on his face, it was clear that William's brother had already made up his mind about the band's new guitarist. Not that Jimmy gave a fuck.

Eddie Thompson was much more pleasant in comparison. He seemed like a nice guy, friendly but reserved. Overall, the band was going to be made up of a strange mix of people. They all couldn't be more different. It was an interesting dynamic.

Michael automatically launched into questioning Jimmy. What bands had he been with before and what kind of music had they played.

Jimmy answered both questions and was met with laugher. His eyes glanced toward a perplexed William while Eddie seemed to shy away from the entire conversation.

"Don't tell me you're into that grunge shit?" Michael said derisively, shaking his head. "I should've known *that* right away." He gestured rudely at Jimmy, who was wearing the typical attire – ripped jeans and blue flannel shirt over a worn t-shirt. "The whole Kurt Cobain thing and all his followers."

"What the fuck is that supposed to mean?" Jimmy snapped and had the sudden urge to punch this asshole in the face. The only thing that kept him from going over the edge was hearing Tarah coming down the stairs. Wearing a grey sweater, fitted jeans and Doc Martens, she seemed to be taking in the argument. Clearly, Jimmy wasn't going to give in. "Grunge is taking over and any *real* musician would know that."

Tarah started to giggle behind him. He turned and saw a look of approval on her face. Eddie saw Tarah's reaction and his face lit up in a smile. William looked stunned.

"Oh, so I'm not a *real* musician?" Michael rolled his eyes. "Nice! Where did you find this guy, William?"

"Okay, enough of this shit guys," William seemed to discredit his brother's remarks. "And Michael, we all have different influences and music preferences. That's what's going to make this band better, *that's* what I want." He glared toward his brother who seemed to shrink under William's eyes. Jimmy made eye contact with Tarah, which was cut short when William announced that they should get right into practicing.

It was awkward at first. Jimmy just kind of went with the flow and played along with whatever song the others played around with. At first, Tarah didn't jump in. Probably because the band was all over the place with no real direction, until William suggested a song he had recently heard Tarah sing.

Glancing around the room, he asked if everyone knew 'Barracuda' by Heart.

Jimmy felt confident and quickly replied, "I sure do."

Michael did too, but Eddie wasn't sure if he had heard of it.

"Come on man, you gotta know this song," Jimmy encouraged and started to play it. Eddie nodded and eventually joined in. He didn't have it perfectly, but he got into the rhythm, and William and Michael joined in. They were warming up, until William suggested they start from the top. That's when Tarah began to sing.

Jimmy felt his eyes widen and his head abruptly turn in her direction as he continued to play. He was expecting a gentler version of the song. In fact, judging Tarah on her size alone, he hadn't anticipated such a strong singing voice. She pretty well matched Ann Wilson's vocals in the original song. There was no arguing that this girl was incredibly talented. So it irritated him when Michael attempted to get her out of the band later that afternoon.

Tarah had run upstairs to get a drink of water when William's asshole brother started to insist that they needed another singer. He referred to Tarah as a 'dumb bitch' and suggested that they actively start looking for a male to replace her. In his eyes, having a girl in a band was just 'not cool'. Worried that she would overhear Michael's insensitive comments and think that they were all on the same page on the issue, Jimmy once again flew into him.

"She's hot and she can sing. What the fuck more do you want?" Jimmy snapped. Hearing her shoes at the top of the stairs, he knew she could hear them talking about her. "Get the fuck over it."

William then jumped in to both calm down and convince his brother that Tarah was the perfect choice for the band. Jimmy shook his head in frustration while the two discussed the topic and crossed the room to where Eddie sat behind the drums. He suggested that the two of them jam together and mentioned a few songs that they in turn played around with. 'Light my Fire' by the Doors turned out to be a favorite of both his and Eddie's.

"Hey man, can you play it faster?" Jimmy asked while he noticed Tarah returning to the basement with a glass of water in hand. Her face was pink and he suspected she was upset over the conversation led by Michael earlier on. He wanted nothing more than to go over and reassure her that William's brother was a douche and his opinion didn't matter, but held back.

What the hell was he doing? He had to keep his head together.

"Sure can," Eddie's eyes sparkled. Clearly music took this kid out of his shell. The two began to play a much faster version of the original song and Jimmy sang. At least, he kind of sang. It was more like screaming by the end of it and just as Jimmy felt the energy in the room rise, they both stopped and started to laugh. He noted that Tarah was doing the same. He liked seeing her smile. The two made eye contact, that's when Jimmy noticed William watching this interaction, and he looked away.

"We should call the band Fire because of that song. I think that would be a cool name," Eddie quietly suggested. "What do you guys think?"

Everyone exchanged glances and began to agree. Michael shrugged in disinterest. Both William and Tarah gave an enthusiastic 'yes' and Jimmy grinned as he thought about how appropriate the name suited the combination of tension and chemistry in the room. His eyes met with Tarah's once again. "Sounds perfect to me."

Chapter thirty-seven

"I know this band is different," Jimmy was relaxing on his sister's couch one Saturday afternoon a couple of weeks after his first meeting with William. Between the band, his job and his social life, his energy level was wearing pretty thin. Jimmy knew he wasn't eating or living right, which didn't help matters. "Everyone is so professional and talented. It's amazing."

"Wow, that's great." Jillian encouraged softly as she entered the room with a cup of tea in hand. She was wearing her workout clothes and Jimmy was surprised that they actually made her look a little healthier compared to everything else she wore. He had noticed that she was eating better recently, so maybe there was hope yet. "I'm happy that *you're* happier."

"I am." Jimmy watched his sister sit on the edge of her chair on the other side of the room. It was rare for her to just relax and chill out. There was always something she had to do, or *thought* she had to do. She never seemed to just enjoy life.

"I shouldn't say the entire band is professional and talented," He grimaced, thinking of Michael. William's brother was the only person that really dragged the band down. His attitude was draining to everyone else and it seemed like he went out of his way to take jabs at both Jimmy and Tarah on a regular basis. He told his sister about it. She frowned.

"Why is he still in the band?" Jillian asked while shaking her head. "Is he really talented?"

"Not really," Jimmy shrugged. "But he's Will's brother, so we *all* have to suffer 'cause of family loyalty or whatever the fuck that's about."

"No, family loyalty is having your brother living with you when your parents kick him out," Jillian joked. "Not being in a band together."

"Oh, you're *too* funny." Jimmy grabbed a pillow and pretended that he was going to throw it at his sister. "Please! I'm a good tenant. I clean up after myself, always pay my rent on time and I follow your rules. I've never once fucked a girl under your roof." He gave his sister a mischievous grin and she almost choked on her tea.

"Thank you, Jimmy. I appreciate you not bringing girls back here. And yes, you are a good tenant." She added. "But maybe this Michael guy isn't normally like that? Maybe he just doesn't like you and the singer?"

"Nah," Jimmy shook his head. "Sure, I could've offended him. It wouldn't be the first time I had that effect on someone I just met. But Tarah's different. She's really sweet, I don't know why anyone would have an issue with her."

"Sweet?" Jillian's eyes seemed to double in size. "Did I seriously hear my brother, the *dog*, refer to a girl as being *sweet*? I've never, in my life, heard you say a girl was sweet. Did you finally turn a corner and stop hating women?"

"I never hated women. Are you serious?" Jimmy began to laugh. "Guys who hate women don't date as many as I have."

"Dating women doesn't mean you *like* them." His sister sat back in her chair and crossed her legs. This meant she was settling in for a serious conversation, otherwise Jillian would've already been off and running again. "Jimmy, we both know that there's a reason why you go from girl to girl and never settle down. And it's not because you're just some jerk. You genuinely have some issues with women."

Jimmy just shrugged. He knew she meant well, but he wasn't interested in being analyzed by his sister. "I dunno, Jill."

"So, what's the deal with this singer?" Jillian raised her eyebrows and gave a bright smile. "What makes this Michael guy hate her and you call her 'sweet'?"

"I'm starting to wish I didn't use that word," Jimmy groaned and momentarily closed his eyes. "I don't know. She's really talented and nice, you know, just an overall cool chick. Michael doesn't like her 'cause he doesn't want a girl singing for the band."

"Oh." Jillian looked annoyed and rolled her eyes. "What an ass."

"He *really* is," Jimmy agreed. "Him and I got in an argument on the first fucking day. He's an asshole."

"And you don't foresee him being kicked out of the band."

"Nope."

"And the girl?"

"Oh no." Jimmy was adamant. "She *definitely* won't be kicked out of the band."

"No, that's not what I mean." Jillian finished her tea and set the cup on a nearby table. "What's the deal? Do you have some kind of crush on her?"

"Why would you say that?"

"Because your face turned red when you were talking about her," Jillian informed him, leaning forward in her chair. "So, what gives?"

"Well, yeah I guess." Jimmy decided that he might as well be honest. "But it don't matter. I think her and William might have a thing going. And he's like a fucking saint beside me, so, you know."

"No one is a saint, Jimmy."

"He is," Jimmy insisted. "You know, he doesn't drink or smoke, do drugs, anything like that. He definitely doesn't have the reputation with women that I do. I mean, who would you choose – William looks good on paper. I don't. End of story."

Jillian gave him a sad smile and he noticed she didn't reply. But she didn't have to because the answer was clear. So, why even bother?

But when he was in Tarah's presence, it was another matter entirely. He didn't *want* to be interested in her. In fact, considering that they were in the same band, it was the *last* thing he needed. There was something that made him want to be around her all the time but his self-doubts prevented him from pursuing anything further. It was just a phase. Eventually it would pass. It wasn't like any girl ever grabbed his attention for long, so why would this one?

Nonetheless, keeping her out of his thoughts was easier said then done. Especially considering the amount of time they spent together practicing. Not that the entire band was able to get together more than a couple of times a week. Eddie was still in school and living in Springdale, which was about an hour away, so he was limited to weekends and holidays. Michael worked most evenings at a restaurant, and William had most evenings and weekends off. Tarah's schedule was all over the place, but she also had a lot of nights and weekends off. Jimmy worked most nights at the bar. So getting together as a group wasn't always easy. William, Tarah and Jimmy usually managed to get together the most to practice. It was generally a relief not having Michael around, and Eddie practiced a lot on his own, so he was always in good shape.

A couple of weeks before Christmas of 1992, William announced that Fire was scheduled to play their first show in January at Jerry's.

"It's not the best bar ever, but it's all right." Jimmy nodded in approval. He glanced around at the other four band members. "You gotta start somewhere."

"Yeah, but we're the first band out of five bands playing," Michael was quick to point out the negative. "So basically we're just background noise while people are showing up or waiting for the band that they *really* want to see."

"Well Mike, we're new," William curtly reminded him. "No one even knows us yet. We should be happy for the opportunity to get some exposure. I think it's great."

"Yeah *Mike*," Jimmy jumped in. "It's not a popularity contest, it's about having a chance to play in front of a group of people. We have to start somewhere."

William's brother just rolled his eyes and didn't respond to either of them. Eddie smiled and quietly added that he was looking forward to their first show. Tarah nodded in agreement with a smile that appeared to be forced. Jimmy noticed that she wasn't herself during the rest of the rehearsal, but decided not to get involved. It was none of his business. It was best that he just try to keep away from her.

Christmas came and went. It was awkward spending time with his family, especially when his mom tried to convince Jimmy to go to church with them during the holidays.

"Jimmy, you haven't come to church in years." Annette Groome needled him. "Can't you at least come this one time for me?"

Thinking of how his parents had all but abandoned him since September, he shook his head. "Nope, not interested in anything involving church."

When she didn't get the response that she wanted, Jimmy's mother's true colors appeared. She turned a cold shoulder to him and barely spoke to him for the remainder of the holidays. In turn, Jimmy left early on Christmas day and went to a bar. He got loaded, picked up some random girl and took her to his sister's apartment. Quickly recalling his agreement with Jillian, he told her she had to leave.

"What the fuck?" the girl snapped as she quickly dressed. "You were so nice at the bar and now you're an asshole. Sister? Yeah right, you have a girlfriend on the way home don't you?"

"Nope, I don't have or want no girlfriend and I *did* tell you that at the bar," he replied, putting on his clothes. "And yeah, maybe you're right. Maybe I was nicer at the bar, but I was horny and drunk. So were you. And you were nicer then too."

She slapped him across the face and left. He just laughed. Fuck them all, Jimmy decided. Women were all the same. It didn't matter if it was your mother or some skank from the bar. As long as everything was going *their* way, everything was fine. But if they didn't get their way, all hell broke loose. He didn't need that shit in his life.

The January show rolled around quickly and Fire was more than ready. Their practices went smoothly and Jimmy felt they were very strong as a band. And it showed. Fire's first official performance went without a hitch. It was perfection. Tarah captivated the audience. Her vocals were amazing. She could hit notes that were difficult and Jimmy was genuinely impressed. There was something sexy about how she glided across the stage. Not that it mattered, he decided. It was merely an observation.

After the show, the boys decided to take their equipment back to William and Michael's borrowed house, and then return to Jerry's for the evening. Eddie wasn't allowed to stick around the bar since he was underage, so he was going to crash at the house for the night. While they were taking the gear down to the basement, William privately confided to Jimmy that Tarah had been petrified to sing that night.

"Seriously?" Jimmy asked, setting down an amp. "'Cause fuck, she looked like she was in the zone. I wouldn't have guessed that she was at all nervous."

"Yeah, she never played a whole show before tonight." William spoke quietly since Michael was just upstairs and this was information Fire's bassist didn't have to know. "She just did a song here and there on stage. This is her first band."

Jimmy nodded, and although logically he knew he should just leave well enough alone, he had an impulse to know everything about her.

"So, like, what's her deal anyway?"

"Tarah's deal?" William looked at him curiously. "What do you mean?"

"I don't know, where did you find her?" Jimmy wasn't sure how to ask if she was single or if William was pursuing her, so he hoped it came up somehow in conversation. "If she wasn't in a band before, where did she come from?"

"Oh, through a friend of hers," William answered casually. " We used to date ages ago."

"You used to date Tarah ages ago?" Jimmy decided to play dumb, even though he knew that William was actually referring to this 'friend'. "Yeah, I kind of sensed like a weird, you know, chemistry thing between you."

"Between me and Tarah?" William grinned and went on to explain. "Nah, I dated Tarah's friend, Wendy. She was actually at the show tonight. That's who Tarah is hanging out with now at the bar."

That didn't really answer his question at all. "Oh, I see. You dated her *friend*."

"Yeah, a long time ago." William didn't elaborate on that situation. "I just met Tarah maybe a month before you. Wendy told me she sang and things just sort of came together from there."

Before Jimmy had a chance to dig for any more information, Michael returned to the basement and asked if they were ready to head back to the bar. Jimmy was ready. He planned to get Tarah drunk and see what she said. William might be tight-lipped, but he doubted she would be after a few shots of tequila.

Chapter thirty-eight

When they returned to the bar, the first thing Jimmy noticed was that there was a bottle of water in Tarah's hand – so much for his plan to get her drunk enough to talk. Was her avoidance of alcohol related to the fact that William didn't drink? The evidence was adding up.

Jimmy would have preferred to continue being blissfully ignorant to any of the obvious clues. Instead, he wasted no time in inviting Tarah to the bar and buying her a shot of Tequila. Then they both bought a Tequila Sunrise and returned to the table, where the four remaining members of Fire sat with this Wendy chick that William apparently used to date. She was friendly, but Jimmy recognized a desperate need for attention when he saw it. He sold drinks to numerous girls like her at his bar. Wendy's boyfriend was clearly a fucking dirtbag. Jimmy wasn't sure if he was just out of prison or simply hoping to give that impression, but he was a guaranteed loser.

Not that it really mattered. Jimmy's focus was Tarah. He noted that William didn't pay much attention to her throughout the night. No more attention than he gave anyone else. Maybe *she* had a thing for *him* and not the other way around? It was still kind of sketchy.

Then Michael made a cutting remark to Tarah after someone complimented her voice. The band's bassist made it blatantly obvious that he felt Tarah didn't have the talent that others admired. It was an unnecessary remark, even if it had been true - which it wasn't. Jimmy watched as Tarah sank a little in her chair and avoided everyone's eyes. Her cheeks turned pink and she remained silent. No one said anything for a split second, probably because everyone expected William to jump to Tarah's defense. After all, the asshole was *his* brother. But he didn't, Wendy did. She told Michael to fuck off. Jimmy jumped in right after her to attack Michael.

Despite their passionate defense, Tarah appeared defeated and slightly depressed for the remainder of the night. Her drinks started disappearing faster. Eventually Jimmy did get to have some short drunken conversations with her, but only one stood out. It started when William left for a few minutes to go to the washroom, to talk to someone, whatever – Jimmy didn't really give a fuck, he was just happy that he was gone *somewhere* out of earshot.

By then, Wendy and her man were gone, and Michael had vanished at some point as well. Jimmy and Tarah were alone. It was one of the few times since they met, that he actually had a few minutes to talk to her without William around.

"So, you're pretty fucked up. I guess that whole drinking water thing from earlier tonight didn't work so well," Jimmy teased her. Leaning closer to Tarah, he noticed that she smelled good. Delicious even. So, he told her.

Tarah laughed delightfully. "Delicious? I've never been told I smelled delicious before." He noticed that she was slurring her words. She looked slightly tired and her eyes were red.

"Bet you taste it too," he regretted the stupid remark as soon as it left his mouth. But it was just that time of night; Jimmy was drunk and horny. He proceeded to tell her that too, while she continued to giggle.

"I heard you were like *that*." Tarah leaned in close to him, and he caught himself trying to sneak a quick look down her top. "You know, like a player or whatever." She stumbled over her words, but the message was still clear: Tarah thought he was a dog. No, Tarah *knew* he was a dog. But how could he let her know that his feelings for her were not just about lust? Not to say that lust wasn't dictating that particular conversation, he admitted to himself wryly.

"You don't have to be a player to be horny as hell," Jimmy attempted to redeem himself. As an afterthought he realized that it probably didn't work. "I just admit that shit more than someone like say, William would. But I guess I don't have to tell *you* that."

"Huh?" Tarah asked and the smile seemed to fall from her face. "What do you mean?"

"I mean it's kind of obvious that there's something going on with the two of you," Jimmy decided to stretch the truth slightly and see what came out of it. He quickly wished he hadn't said a word.

"Really?" Tarah seemed very pensive as she spoke. "Is it really *that* obvious?"

Jimmy had his answer. He could almost hear the little voice in the back of his head saying, "See, did you really have to ask?" He didn't like the answer. He *really* didn't like the answer. Suddenly, he felt sober. He felt like he had a knot in his stomach and his heart started racing. He wondered if his feelings were obvious, because Tarah seemed to be carefully studying his face. And just when it appeared that she might say something, William returned. *Fucking figures.*

"Hey, what's going on?" William asked casually, but Jimmy could see him taking in the entire situation. After all, he had the advantage of being sober and seeing everything much more clearly. Tarah remained tight-lipped, merely shrugging with a smile. Jimmy yawned and acted completely uninterested before making an excuse to leave the table. Telling a lie that he would return, he walked out of the bar and into the frosty January night. If Tarah's comments hadn't awakened him, then the frigid night air certainly did. It took him almost an hour to hike back to his sister's apartment, but he didn't care; it gave him time to think.

The next time he saw Tarah at a practice, she acted completely normal around him. He figured she probably didn't remember the conversation they'd had on the night of Fire's first show. She had been so drunk at that point in the evening that it was unlikely that she remembered much. She did mention how hung over she had been the next day, but that was about it.

From visits to strip bars to drunken nights with girls who didn't matter to him, Jimmy did the best he could to get Tarah off his mind. He didn't have time to himself anyway, between the bar and Fire. Ironically, it was he, William and Tarah that put the most effort into promoting the band and booking shows. It worked; Fire was quickly gaining in popularity, and promoters were contacting them on a regular basis to do various shows around Thorton. It was encouraging and Jimmy believed they were on the path to success. He could feel it.

All the extra work was exhausting to Jimmy. Partying 'til dawn, then sleeping a few hours before getting out of bed to either put up band posters or make some calls, usually followed by long nights at the bar. There was always something. When it got to the point that he could barely stay awake at work, Jimmy got someone at the bar to find him some speed. That seemed to do the trick. There were days when Jimmy could feel his heart racing so much that he thought he was going to die. There were days he really didn't care if he did. Life was like a tornado and he somehow got caught in the middle and wasn't sure where he'd land. Maybe nowhere.

Although there were subtle hints that William and Tarah were involved in a relationship, nothing was confirmed to the band until March. When William told Jimmy the news, he faked a big smile and said 'That's great'. He didn't mean it. Maybe he was being two-faced, but what else could he do? It was like Jimmy had once told his sister, William simply looked better on paper. He was the saint and Jimmy was the sinner. They couldn't have been more different.

Jillian regularly inquired about the band and had even caught a couple of shows. She often asked if there were any 'new developments' with Tarah. Jimmy would shrug. "She's still dating William. What more can I tell you?" He hated when Jill would ask, because it was always followed by a look of pity. It was the 'my pathetic little brother' look and he hated it. It was about to get worse: at the end of March, Jillian announced that she and Rob were about to buy a house.

"That's cool," Jimmy said, playing dumb. He already knew that she was going to ask him to *not* join them when they moved. Not because he had done anything wrong, but because it was just time. He could feel it.

Jillian explained that there would be some time they'd be in limbo, between when they left their apartment and bought a house. They were planning to stay with Rob's parents. In other words, Jimmy was out that summer.

"But mom and dad said you could stay with them again, until you get back on your feet," Jillian added anxiously. "You must have some money saved up though, so you shouldn't have to stay too long."

Jimmy had very little saved up. Although he didn't admit it to his sister, after rent, most of his spare money went toward car repairs and insurance. Not to mention alcohol, pot and speed. Then there were the condoms and the occasional late-night subs. And he didn't make all that much money. Tips were good, but Jimmy was still technically a minimum wage worker. Most of the money the band made went toward posters, equipment and other expenses.

Seeing the concern on her face, Jimmy gave her a gentle smile. "It's okay, Jill. You don't have to look after me forever, I'll be fine."

"I know," she nodded but her eyes still looked sad. "I just know how your relationship is with Mom and Dad."

"It'll be fine," he reassured her. "They won't be as cool to live with as you, though."

Jillian smiled and did something no one else in his family ever did - she hugged him.

Chapter thirty-nine

"Jimmy, you can't be serious! You're too sick to do a show!" Jillian chastised her brother on a Saturday afternoon in April as she stood over his bed. The two had spent the better part of the previous night sitting in a hospital waiting room after Jillian had discovered her brother on the couch, wrapped in blankets and shivering. As soon as she touched his forehead, she insisted that he see a doctor. Although Jimmy usually would've refused, he was too sick and weak to put up a fight. "Your temperature was through the roof last night and the doctor said to stay in bed for a couple of days. You can't get on stage. You need to take care of yourself."

"I can't miss the show, Jill." Jimmy sat up in bed. Although his sister did admit that he looked slightly better, he clearly wasn't out of the woods yet. "I felt like shit for the last few days and except for last night, I still managed to get my ass to work and practices. I can do this show too. I'll just come home right afterward instead of partying the rest of the night."

"Jimmy, I really wish you wouldn't do this," Jillian spoke very gently to him now. "I feel like you push yourself too much. I think that's why you got sick in the first place."

Jimmy knew why he got sick in the first place. Since discovering the wonderful world of speed, he had been burning the candle at both ends. It had finally caught up to him. He didn't tell Jillian that; she was worried enough already.

Later that night, Jimmy met with the band at William's for a short meeting before the show. Tarah's eyes popped open when she let him in.

"Jimmy, you're as white as a ghost!" She hesitated for a moment while he shrugged and avoided making eye contact. He looked like shit and knew it. "Are you okay?"

"Not really, but it's fine," Jimmy assured her, meeting her eyes for a moment. He could see that she was sincerely concerned and quickly looked away. Sometimes he wished that she'd just be a bitch to him. It would be so much easier. Whenever she showed any kind of caring or compassion, it made him want her more. "Thanks though." He quickly brushed past her and headed toward the basement to meet up with the rest of the band.

And the show went on. Jimmy felt like his body was dead weight as he stood on stage, but he played like a pro. It was that kind of dedication to performance that propelled the band in gaining recognition and growing in popularity.

But they also attracted some less pleasant attention. It started with some audience members heckling them a couple of weeks later. It wasn't the first time, but it was the worst, and things quickly spiraled out of control.

They were playing a dingy biker bar in the 'bad' end of town. At first Jimmy hadn't noticed anything out of the ordinary, just a bunch of rowdy young guys sitting near the stage. When Tarah abruptly stopped singing, he realized that some of them were yelling at her.

"Hey you dirty whore, why don't you take off your clothes and really entertain us?" one of the inebriated guys in the audience called out, and the entire table began to laugh.

"Do you have a problem, asshole?" Tarah yelled back at him. She appeared strong and composed, but Jimmy was close enough to see that she was almost in tears. He quickly glanced in William's direction to see his reaction. Although he looked genuinely concerned, it was clear that he wasn't about to defend Tarah. And *that* really pissed off Jimmy. It was his fucking *girlfriend* and he couldn't even jump to her defense when she needed him.

Fuck him.

"Yeah, fuckhead," Jimmy roared back, taking off his guitar. He felt the blood rushing to his face and he was ready to attack. The entire table of guys were now hurling insults and attempting to instigate things further, when suddenly a beer bottle flew past Jimmy's head, barely missing him.

Furious, he flew off the stage and attacked the first guy who got in his face. It wouldn't have been much of a fight, considering that the asshole was so drunk that he could barely stand up, however, his table full of friends were quick to rush to this guy's defense. Fortunately, all the boys from the band were now right behind him and ready to help. Much to Jimmy's surprise, it was Michael who was the first to jump full force into the middle of it. William's brother might have been an asshole, but he certainly didn't back down from a fight.

Out of the corner of his eye, Jimmy saw a group of bikers crossing the room towards him and felt his stomach turn. Would he be on the shit list for starting a fight? He could feel his heart pounding in intense fear.

Great! We're fucking dead.

But he was wrong. The bikers began to attack the hecklers from the audience. And it wasn't pretty. Jimmy saw one of the kids with a knife held up to his face. After being told to get his 'pussy ass' out of the bar, the guy in question ran like a bitch right out the doors. Jimmy didn't see what happened with two of the others, but they quickly followed the first guy, one of them running so fast that he tripped on his own feet. One by one, they left. The burly bikers looked slightly amused by the remainder of the drunken kids who stupidly shot their mouths off at them. Jimmy forgot to breathe when one of the bikers reached into his pocket and pulled out a gun. Everyone jumped back.

"Look here, you fucking pussies. This is *our* bar and you don't come in and disrespect us," he remarked calmly, as if he were just having a casual conversation with an annoying kid. It was obvious that no one in that room would ever admit to seeing anything out of the ordinary that night. The implications were obvious. One of the guys started to cry and begged to have his life spared through his tears. Jimmy almost felt sorry for him. Almost.

The guy holding the gun started to laugh, while the other bikers around him joined in. Shaking his head, he stashed his gun. The bikers herded the last two hecklers toward the door, then with one quick swoop, grabbed each of them and threw them out of the bar, like sacks of potatoes, laughing hysterically. Jimmy and Michael joined in, while Eddie scurried past them and out the door. William looked anxious as he walked toward the exit as well. Jimmy and Michael joined the bikers, chatting like old buddies. It was kind of strange but the entire fight was a huge rush for Jimmy. He loved it.

"Hey man, did you see where our singer went?" Jimmy tried to sound casual but noticed Michael giving him a strange look.

"The hot-assed blonde?" one of the biggest bikers asked. "Yeah, saw her going outside with Lila, so she's in good hands."

Jimmy and Michael talked with them for a couple more minutes before they all headed outside. The bikers proceeded to light up, while Jimmy glanced around for the band. He quickly spotted Tarah and the others on the opposite side of the entrance. She was with an overweight brunette who looked like one of the biker chicks who has been hanging out at the bar. He and Michael headed in their direction.

"Thanks for jumping in to help," Jimmy reluctantly showed his appreciation before they met up with the others. "You saved my ass."

"Bands are family, man," Michael surprised Jimmy with this stern comment. "We might fight with one another, but no one fucks with my boys- and, ah girl." He seemed slightly reluctant to add the final word, however something in Michael's voice suggested that he was accepting Tarah as part of the band.

Jimmy could definitely understand how he considered the five of them like a family. Although there was a great deal of dysfunction within the band, it was comforting to know that they were solid as a group, especially when faced with difficult fans and critics – and their days of dealing with both were just beginning.

As Fire's popularity grew, so did their female fan base. Jimmy had his share of attention, but it was nothing compared to William's. Jimmy knew it was the boy-next-door image that made all the chicks hot for William, and even though he didn't give a fuck about most of the girls anyway, the fact that Tarah was so gaga over him as well was a major irritant.

By autumn, change was definitely in the air. The band had just finished playing a show at Devil's Eight, and Jimmy was heading to the bar rather than back home to his parent's, where he was now living. Reaching for his wallet, he was alarmed not to find it in his jeans. He flew outside to check his car and was relieved to find it between the seats. As he turned to go back inside, he encountered something he never expected to see.

In a dark corner on the side of the bar, he watched William kissing a tall brunette. And not the accidental, drunken kiss either. This was definitely what Jimmy would refer to as a 'let's fuck later' kiss. There was a big difference. He was stunned and quickly rushed away before either of them noticed him watching.

A part of him wanted to tell Tarah everything, but the thought of hurting her was unbearable. Finally he decided that it was better to not get involved. He suspected that it would just end up blowing up in his face.

Instead he headed to the bar and ordered some tequila shots. Sitting with his back to the world, he was surprised when he turned around to see Tarah sliding onto the stool beside him. She looked upset. For a moment, he wondered if she had caught William, until she spoke.

"I was just in the bathroom and there was this girl in there crying. It was so sad." Tarah's blue eyes were huge and Jimmy looked away with an effort. Then she said something that grabbed his attention.

"She's overweight, and I guess some guy made some crude comments to her about her size, some really *mean* remarks. She was devastated. Her friends were in there trying to comfort her but it wasn't working." Jimmy looked back into her eyes and for the first time in months, he didn't look away. He just stared. He could feel how sincere Tarah was in her concern. "She was saying stuff like she'd be better off dead, and I just felt so bad." Lines of worry were showing on Tarah's face, and there was a world of compassion in her eyes. This story hit a little too close to home for Jimmy.

So while William was outside making out with another girl, Tarah was in the bathroom feeling heartbroken for a girl who she didn't even know – a fat girl, who felt worthless after being humiliated. It took Jimmy back to seventh grade all over again and the cruel remarks from Suzanne Bordon. Biting his lip, Jimmy searched her face as he concentrated on what she was saying.

"Anyway," Tarah finally broke eye contact and laughed self-consciously. "You probably think I'm nuts for worrying about someone I don't even know."

"Not at all," Jimmy replied gently and then he hesitantly continued. "I actually think it says a lot about you, Tarah. It says that you're probably one of the most amazing people I know."

She looked very surprised by his remark and a smile slowly lit up her face. But before she could say anything, a young couple approached them.

"There you are, Tarah! You're a hard woman to find."

Tarah swung around. "Bobby! Sorry, I was just here and there." She laughed then quickly introduced Jimmy to her brother and his girlfriend. After watching the three of them walk away, he continued to drink. His feelings for Tarah were just too strong and he had to drown them any way possible. Tequila always worked.

Knocking back the last of his shots, he decided to go home. His eyes automatically searched the room for Tarah. He had just located her and was about to go over and say goodnight when he suddenly saw her swing her head around. Following her gaze, Jimmy saw William standing across the room with the same girl he'd been kissing outside. Just as Tarah turned around, the brunette reached out and grabbed William by the goods. *Oh fuck!*

Everything happened quickly. Jimmy felt his mouth fall open in shock as Tarah flew across the room and attacked the brunette. William grabbed Tarah and pulled her away, but she managed to loosen his grip and start back at the brunette. That's when the bouncers came along and threatened to toss them both out. Tarah's brother appeared to be in the middle of everything, verbally attacking William. Tarah's eyes filled with tears and she ran outside. Jimmy's first instinct was to follow, but when he saw her brother rush out behind her, it was clear she was in safe hands. William headed out after them. They'd kiss and make up - he could already predict *that* outcome, Jimmy thought bitterly.

The brunette in question, who was supposed to have been kicked out, now joined Jimmy at the bar. Despite his attempts to avoid her, she started up a conversation.

"What the fuck is with that girl?" She snapped after ordering a beer.

"You mean, his girlfriend?"

The brunette turned and gave Jimmy a wide-eyed look. "He has a girlfriend?"

Chapter forty

Shortly after moving back to his parent's house, Jimmy started suffering from insomnia. Lying awake at night, his brain ran full force into dark places that he conveniently managed to avoid during daylight. In the stillness of the night - it was harder to escape the truth.

First, he was living at his *parent's* house again. These were the very people who had kicked him out a year earlier; it wasn't just that they had kicked him out of their house, they had done all they could to kick him out of their *lives* too. Oh sure, he was always welcome to return to his family's embrace, but there were always conditions. In order to be accepted he had to quit drinking, go to college and take life more seriously. And there was one more thing; his mom wanted Jimmy to go to church too.

"Are you serious?" he laughed the first time she asked him. It was only about a week after Jimmy's return home and he was having a cup of coffee with his mother. Until the topic of religion was brought up, the two of them were actually having a civilized conversation. "I'm not going to church."

"Jimmy, can't you do this one thing for me?" she asked, letting out a long, frustrated sigh. "It would mean so much."

"Why?" Jimmy was genuinely curious. "Church is *your* thing, mom. It's not mine. Why should I go and pretend I want to be there, when I don't."

"But if you go and just listen, you might get something out of it," she insisted. "I really think it might give you some direction."

"I don't need direction."

"Well that's where we disagree," Giving him a sad smile, she looked down into her coffee cup. "Jimmy, you're 21 and its time to start settling down a bit. Time to grow up and become responsible."

Jimmy didn't understand why he *wasn't* being responsible. After all, he rarely missed work or anything related to his band, he hadn't gotten any girls pregnant, and he wasn't in debt. But when he attempted to explain this to his mother, it was clear that they had different definitions of responsibility. She wanted him to 'settle down'.

"What do you mean by that?" Jimmy shot back.

"Get a better job, go to college," she paused as she considered. "Have a *steady* relationship."

Jimmy didn't respond. His mother was hitting a nerve and had no clue.

"I just wish you'd meet a nice girl," she gave him a warm smile, "Someone who will fill the void in your heart."

"Mom, I-

"Jimmy, *please*." The gentleness in her voice and sadness in her eyes as she spoke breached all his defenses. "I know there's something missing for you. That's why you do all these crazy things like drink. And it worries me a lot. I don't know how many times I fear that the phone will ring in the middle of the night with someone telling me that you're in the hospital or worse."

Her words hit him hard. Rather than argue back, Jimmy remained silent.

"I just thought that maybe religion or love could help give you what you need," she tried to explain, her eyes flickering around uncomfortably, and for a moment, Jimmy feared she was going to cry. "I don't care what you do or how you act, I *know* there's a loving person still in there. And I just wish you could meet someone who could fill your heart in a way that your family was never able to."

"We tried," she continued, running her fingers nervously over the brim of her cup, "But you were given a real challenge at a very early age and maybe we didn't handle it right. Maybe if we had done something differently, you'd be happier now. I don't know, Jimmy. I just wish that someday you would meet someone who can bring that happiness into your life."

That conversation haunted him. It was one of the reasons for his insomnia. Late at night, he contemplated her words. He wondered if she was right, if he did have a void in his heart, and if that was the reason he drank. It had never occurred to him that his parents actually worried about him getting hurt or dying, and if that affected their sleep. He knew he didn't live the cleanest lifestyle, but he had never considered the possibility that his actions might hurt anyone else. The thought that his parents might care about him or worry about his well-being was foreign to him.

The other thing that kept him awake at night was Tarah.

When his mother spoke of someone filling his heart, Tarah's face was all he could think of. But it was impossible; Tarah was in love with William. It didn't matter how many times they argued, what he did behind her back, or how much Jimmy cared about her, because she would never feel the same way about him. Even though Tarah didn't know about Jimmy's feelings for her, in a way he still felt as though he had been in direct competition with William – and lost. It didn't make sense, but Jimmy felt like the person who was rejected even though he really hadn't been, except in his mind.

The night Tarah spoke so compassionately about the overweight girl crying in the bathroom, he knew something had changed. As Jimmy looked into Tarah's eyes and heard her speak so candidly about her concern for someone she didn't even know, a girl who was being tormented over her weight, he knew he was falling for her. It was heartbreaking: He was falling for a girl who would never feel the same way about him. Even if William suddenly disappeared from the picture, Tarah would never want to be with someone like Jimmy: she'd never even consider it.

It made him livid. How many times had *he* defended Tarah while William stood by in silence? It wasn't because he was the non-confrontational type of guy -- William would often defend his brother, but he would never do the same for his own girlfriend - it didn't make sense to Jimmy.

Why was he kissing another girl on the night of their Devil's Eight show? How many other girls had he kissed since being with Tarah? Had he had sex with any of these skanks who hung around the bars, trying their best to get his attention? Was there a *reason* why Tarah was so jealous of these girls? Had she sensed something? It was almost unthinkable to Jimmy that William had done something to cause her to be so insecure.

It really pissed Jimmy off. It didn't matter what happened, William would always be the 'good' guy, and Jimmy would always be the 'bad' one. Once you had either label, it took a lot to convince anyone that you were a different kind of person.

The ironic thing was that Jimmy really *did* like William. Excluding the Tarah situation, he respected him. He was talented, smart and ambitious, an overall good guy. Jimmy couldn't dispute that point, and knew that these were probably all the reasons Tarah fell in love with him. In late October, the couple announced that they were moving in together. Since the friend that William was housesitting for was scheduled to return in December, he and Tarah were planning to find an apartment for December first. Although Michael seemed insistent that he was moving in with them, it became clear in November that William had actually stood up to his brother for the first time ever. He said Michael would have to find his own place.

"Why don't we get a place together?" Eddie suggested towards the end of November 1993, while the three remaining band members sat together in a coffee shop. They were hanging out after practice while William and Tarah had some alone time. Jimmy didn't want to think about their 'alone' time. He half-heartedly shrugged at the suggestion, while Michael actually reacted positively.

"We gotta find another house so the band has somewhere to practice." Michael said while tapping his fingers on a coffee mug. "I think between the three of us, we can swing it. Maybe get another roommate too?"

Eddie enthusiastically agreed. Jimmy nodded. He didn't really care. Maybe a new home was what he needed to sleep again. He didn't suspect how much his life was about to change.

Chapter forty-one

Fire's popularity was rapidly expanding, and Jimmy only anticipated better things in the new year. They had gone from being virtually unknown to one of the most popular bands in Thorton. Patrick was convinced his childhood friend would become a star. Nick and Jeremy from his former band had been impressed by the performances they'd seen. Jimmy's family had even seen a few shows, and had to admit that he had been right to follow his dreams.

Overall, Jimmy was encouraged about the path Fire was taking. They were now playing outside of Thorton and had a consistent following with fans. Their original music was catching on at shows and that was an indication that they were headed in the right direction. It was one thing to capture attention with cover songs, quite another to do so with originals. Tarah, William, and he wrote their music. However, Jimmy did his best work alone. He wrote about personal subjects like his own discontent and frustrations in life.

He certainly had a lot more to write about, knowing that Tarah and William were nearby, living their 'happily ever after'. Which didn't really make sense to him, since they had been in a relationship for about a year already, so why would their living arrangement matter to him? But for some reason, that step made it more real. His way of dealing with it was to avoid the band unless he was working with them. And to fuck every girl he could get his hands on. Unfortunately, his new roommates didn't appreciate it.

"Do you have to bang the shit out of every skank in Thorton in *this* house?" Michael complained one afternoon just after Jimmy crawled out of bed and wandered downstairs. "For fuck sakes man, I'm at the other end of the hallway, and I get woken up at like 3:30 every morning."

"Jealous?" Jimmy gave a half-hearted grin as he walked away. "I pay my rent man, I'll do whatever I want. Just be happy I'm not gay and you're not hearing high pitched moans coming out of a guy every night."

"Other than you?" Michael sneered.

"Yeah, but mine aren't so high pitched," Jimmy calmly retorted as he grabbed his jacket and stepped outside. Going for coffee was his way of escaping Michael.

The worst part was that he didn't even care about having sex with so many random girls anymore. Sometimes he did it for the sole purpose of pissing off Michael. He was thinking of taking it easy with women though, after an experience with a girl who he later learned had Hep C. Even though he always used condoms, it was a little too close for comfort. He made a doctor's appointment and got tested for everything. Fortunately, it all came back clear.

He didn't anticipate a relationship, but maybe he could find a more permanent fuck buddy with no commitments. After his disappointment with the Tarah situation, Jimmy would've been quite content to lead a long, happy life never caring about another girl again. Even thinking about her with William was painful, no matter how much time passed. Relationships were meant for a different kind of guy. Guys like William and Patrick were the ones who lived the happier ever after script. They might even deserve it more than him.

But things are often not what they seem. He found that out when Patrick called him at the end of January and asked to meet at a nearby bar for a drink. The seriousness in his voice alarmed Jimmy, and he accepted the offer. When they met later that night, Patrick revealed his shocking news. He had just found out that Hope was not his daughter.

"*What?*" Jimmy was stunned. "You can't be serious!"

"Unfortunately, I am," Patrick miserably twisted his untouched beer in front of him. "Melissa and I had a really bad break-up a couple of months ago and when I told her I wanted shared custody, that's when the truth came out."

"What? I don't get it," Jimmy felt like he was in the middle of a nighttime soap opera plot. "I didn't even know you two broke up, let alone this."

"I didn't say anything. I just wasn't ready to talk about it. I was pretty fucking miserable, especially over the holidays," Patrick confided, his eyes darting around the room. He wasn't the same person Jimmy had grown up with. He was broken. Even his voice was that of a stranger. "My parents paid to have the tests done to make sure that she was telling the truth. She was."

Jimmy just shook his head. "Fuck man, I don't even know what to tell you. That's horrible." He joined Patrick in silence for a few minutes. He felt sincere compassion for his best friend. "When I think of everything you've done over the years to make things work with Melissa and everything you did for Hope. Only to find out she wasn't yours? I-I can't even imagine!"

"I know," Patrick sighed, finally taking a sip of his beer. "I can live with the break-up with Melissa. But to find out that the little girl you brought up as your daughter for her entire life isn't your kid and you've got *zero* rights to her, its like...I can't even describe it." He sadly shook his head. "I was there when she was born. I've been there for everything and now, I got nothing."

"I can't believe Melissa did this shit to you." Jimmy was suddenly furious. "No wonder I never trust women, it's 'cause you *can't* trust them. They're always out for number one and don't care who they fuck over along the way."

"No, Jimmy it's not like that." Patrick countered. He took a deep breath. "Not every woman is like that. Melissa was a kid, she lied, and then she had to spend every day of her life trying to hide that lie. I'm not taking her side of things, but believe me when I say she's paying for it now. Her family has practically disowned her. They all felt awful for me. Melissa almost had a breakdown after all the shit hit the fan. It was a huge mess. In the end, I can still visit Hope, but I kind of think it might be better to just move on. That's why I'm here tonight. I wanted to tell you what was going on and that I'm moving to British Columbia with my brother."

"Are you sure you want to do that?" Jimmy asked skeptically. "Maybe you should wait for the dust to settle a little more."

"Nah man, I think it's best for me to move on," Patrick insisted.

"I still can't believe that Melissa lied." Jimmy shook his head in disgust. "Look at what's she's done to your life."

"It isn't all bad. It made me grow up. Something I probably wouldn't have done otherwise." Patrick faked a smile; his eyes were full of misery. "But yeah, I'd rather it wasn't this way. Hope *was* my daughter, regardless of what the tests tell me."

Jimmy tried to think of the right words to say as he studied his best friend's grieving face. Feeling his own rage subside, he felt overwhelmed with sympathy. Everybody lost in this situation. There were no winners.

"Maybe you should stay here and still spend time with her," Jimmy suggested. He couldn't believe they were having this conversation. "It will upset Hope if you're suddenly out of her life all together."

"No, that would just confuse her now that her real father is being introduced," Patrick explained. "And you know what, when you love someone you sometimes have to do what's right for them even though it kind of makes you miserable in the process."

Jimmy nodded. Now *that* was something he understood.

The two talked a little longer until Patrick announced that he had to leave and start packing. He was planning to fly to BC five days later. They said their good-byes and Patrick left. Jimmy sat for a few minutes and digested his friend's words. All around him, small groups of people happily sat together talking and laughing.

When he eventually left the bar, he was surprised to find a winter storm had developed outside. The flurries of earlier that night had accumulated into drifts, and a chill ran up his spine as he made his way through the swirling, freezing gusts. Feeling depressed after his conversation with Patrick, he was lost in his own little world. Suddenly a huge orange poster in the window of a music store he often visited grabbed his attention. It was advertising *Jar of Flies*, a CD by Alice in Chains. On impulse, Jimmy went inside and bought it.

Sliding the bright orange case into the inside of his leather jacket, he chatted with the guy working the store for a few minutes before leaving. As soon as Jimmy walked back out the door, he was hit by a huge gust of wind. Wet snow covered his face and he wanted nothing more than to just go home. But he wasn't in the mood to deal with Michael so instead; he turned and went in the other direction. He knew that William wanted to hear the new Alice in Chains CD. Jimmy decided to push his feelings for Tarah aside, suck it up, and drop by to see them. If Patrick could face the cards he'd been dealt with, then so could he.

Arriving at the building where the couple lived, Jimmy recognized which apartment belonged to them. Although he had only been there once for a band meeting, he still remembered the view from the huge windows in the couple's living room; the same windows he could now see a glimmer of light shining through. Before he had second thoughts, Jimmy walked up to the door and rang their buzzer.

"It's me, Jim." he quickly responded to Tarah's voice. "Can I come up?"

She buzzed him in.

Chapter forty-two

"Hi," Tarah was friendly and welcoming when she answered the door, if a little surprised. Jimmy detected a light feminine floral scent when he walked in the door. He wasn't sure what it was, but it automatically made him think of sex. It was probably because he associated the scent with some of his past experiences with women. He never was sure what it was, but it made him inspect Tarah more closely. She was wearing the kind of clothes his sister wore for working out. The comfortable, loose fabric that still managed to show off Tarah's ass perfectly.

After explaining why he had stopped by, Jimmy barely had the *Jar of Flies* CD out of his jacket pocket when Tarah excitedly ripped it out of his hand. That's when she announced that William wasn't home, but *she* wanted to listen to it. Rushing into the living room, Tarah left Jimmy standing dumbfounded in the kitchen. *William isn't home! Fuck! I got to get out of here now.*

But it didn't look like Tarah was going to give him an easy out. She already had the CD playing in the next room. He slowly walked toward the entrance and leaned against the doorframe, thinking of how he was going to find an excuse to leave. It wasn't that he *didn't* want to be there alone with Tarah. It was the fact that he wanted to be alone with her a little *too* much.

Tarah interrupted his thoughts when she began to talk about how much she loved the CD. Then glancing in Jimmy's direction, she coaxed him to go into the living room and join her on the couch. He reluctantly did so as she rambled on about how William would also love the CD.

"Where is he?" Jimmy asked guardedly, wondering if her boyfriend was expected to return soon.

"Oh, his aunt died. He went to Springdale for the funeral," she responded, referring to William's hometown.

After Tarah revealed this information, Jimmy did recall Eddie mentioning that a relative of Michael's had passed away, but he hadn't really been paying attention at the time. Glancing at the blistering storm outside it was clear that the brothers wouldn't be returning to Thorton before the next morning. That left him alone with Tarah, which should have delighted him, but knowing that there was no chance that she would ever want him like he wanted her, Jimmy simply felt depressed. It was a torturous opportunity.

"So, where were you tonight?" Tarah's innocent blue eyes searched his as she faced him on the couch. Jimmy told her about meeting a friend for drinks, but didn't elaborate on the details.

"Hmm…I haven't had a drink in ages," Tarah commented showing only a hint of a smile. Jimmy quickly looked away and thought about how William had her wrapped around his finger. He had made her exactly into the person he wanted - the girl next door- while meanwhile he was making out with bar skanks after their shows. Well, at least *one* bar skank. Jimmy bit his tongue.

As their conversation moved forward, he was surprised to learn that Tarah used to smoke pot. Stunned by this news, Jimmy turned to make eye contact with her once again. Staring back at him innocently, Tarah revealed that it had once been a big part of her past and it was something she greatly missed. With a burst of laughter, he made an impromptu move and pulled a bag out of his jacket pocket, revealing two joints. He had planned to share them with Patrick - but that obviously hadn't worked out. He was surprised to see Tarah's eyes light up.

"Can we smoke one?"

Jimmy hesitantly agreed – somehow, he felt as if he were doing something wrong, like smoking up with a kid, or something else that the world would frown upon. He was still looking for an excuse to leave, but as much as he wanted to go, his body refused to budge from the couch where he sat beside the one person he wanted to be with more than anything.

Five minutes later, after she arranged an eclectic collection of candles in front of them, he used one of them to light up the first of two joints they would share that night. And that's when the *real* Tarah emerged; the one he remembered from a year earlier, before William. They talked about irrelevant stuff and laughed. Jimmy relaxed, no longer hearing the voice that had encouraged him to leave. Removing his jacket, he teased her and listened to a story about how she had caught a former boyfriend getting sucked off in a bar bathroom. He really hoped that Tarah wasn't headed for the same disappointment with William, but decided not to reveal a thing. It wasn't his place to say anything. Overall, he was having a lot of fun.

Somehow they started to talk about Jimmy's personal life. If he hadn't been so high, this would have been an extremely uncomfortable topic for him. He had always assumed that Tarah thought he was a dog and was disgusted with his lifestyle. However, he could detect no judgment in her voice as she commented that he was just out having fun. That was a surprise. But when she asked if he was having too much fun to settle down, Jimmy made it very clear that that wasn't the case. He confessed that witnessing happy couples together made him feel like he was on the outside looking in.

Jimmy turned to see sadness in Tarah's eyes and automatically regretted not being more guarded about his feelings. She suggested that he 'find someone' that he really liked. That's when he made a slip. Jimmy confessed that he *had* found someone he really liked, but she was taken. Suddenly something changed in the room. Everything felt still.

He became mellow. His entire body was relaxed and after putting the last of their second joint in the ashtray, Jimmy sat back and turned to look into her eyes. To his surprise, she didn't look away. He eased closer to her until their faces were only inches apart. His heart was racing as he leaned in, carefully touching his lips to hers. He hesitated for a moment, until Tarah kissed him back. That was his sign; all he needed to encourage him.

The kiss that started gently became very intense in a matter of seconds. Her fingers were exploring his face and he felt himself quickly becoming hard. His hands ran over her back, urging Tarah closer to him. He heard her gasping and slipped one of his hands underneath her sweater, touching her warm, soft skin. He didn't care if she had a boyfriend. He didn't care that she was in his band. Jimmy didn't care about anything else in that moment, other than the fact that he wanted to spend the night with Tarah. He didn't care about consequences or what happened the next day. But apparently, she did because Tarah suddenly stopped him.

"What?" Jimmy breathed, as his fingertips continued touching the soft skin on her back. "What's wrong?"

But he already knew the answer. Tarah had a boyfriend. She felt guilty and was starting to cry.

"I've never cheated on anyone before," she sobbed. "I can't believe I just did that."

"We just kissed," Jimmy insisted desperately, but he knew he was making light of the situation.

"Isn't that enough?" Tarah wiped away a tear and he felt guilt for upsetting her.

Jimmy moved away from her, momentarily closing his eyes. He wanted to tell her about William's deception, but didn't; instead, he bit the bullet and revealed how he felt about her.

"Tarah, I didn't plan for this to happen tonight." His voice was a low, gentle murmur as he looked into her face and leaned in close to her. She didn't stop him. "But I'm not going to lie to you. When I was talking earlier about finding someone I really liked, someone who already had a boyfriend?" He saw her slowly nod. "I was talking about you." He ignored the pity in her eyes. "Tarah, I've never felt this way about anyone before. Ever."

But it didn't matter. He said the words that were difficult to say and she still gave him the expected speech. She was in love with William and they had a commitment. Jimmy could only listen to so much before he grabbed his jacket and got up to leave. She followed him to the door, trying to explain, but he wouldn't listen.

The next thing he knew, Jimmy was back at the same bar he had been at earlier that night. Now he was doing tequila shots. The bartender was an older lady named Liz who recognized him as a regular, but also as a local musician who had previously played there. Her eyes were full of concern every time he ordered more alcohol, and she finally asked Jimmy if he was okay.

"No," he answered honestly. "Thanks for asking."

"If you want to talk," she gestured around the almost empty bar, "I've got lots of time."

"Not really," Jimmy shook his head. "Thanks, Liz."

However before the night was over, Jimmy started to bare his soul to the compassionate woman. He told her about Tarah, that night, everything. She listened attentively, leaning on the counter. The look in her eyes suggested that Liz had heard this kind of story before, but took it all in before commenting.

"You took quite a risk by telling her how you felt, so this girl obviously means a lot to you," Liz said thoughtfully. Although she had cut Jimmy off from anything other than water, he was still drunk out of his mind. The entire room was spinning, but he didn't care. He just wanted to disappear. Wake up on another planet, away from people and feelings - away from love. "That takes a lot of courage and I admire you for that."

"Stupid!" Jimmy slurred his words almost to the point that she didn't understand him. "Can't believe, so stupid."

"No, it wasn't stupid," Liz insisted. "I think that in the end you'll see that you made the right decision."

Jimmy shrugged sadly. "Don't matta, she's with William."

"Yes, but you have to remember something important," Liz straightened up to watch the remaining customer leave. "She kissed you back."

Her words didn't really make Jimmy feel better. Not that he could think straight at that point.

Jimmy could see the bar was closing and stood up to leave, but staggered and almost fell over. Liz insisted that she give him a drive home. Although it wasn't something she normally did for her customers, she felt pity for the kid and told him to just make sure not to puke in her car.

"I won't," Jimmy promised on their way out of the bar.

He threw up in the parking lot while she cleaned the snow off her car.

"You're going to feel like shit tomorrow." Liz grinned when he stopped and she helped him into the car, mentioning casually that he had some vomit on his shirt.

When they arrived at his house, she helped him up the front step and made sure he got inside okay. He thanked her as she left.

"Hey?" Eddie met him at the door. "Are you okay?"

"Greaaaaaaaaaaat!" Jimmy said in a voice mimicking Tony the Tiger, and then began to laugh at his own joke. Wandering into the kitchen he grabbed a bottle of rum that was sitting on the counter and began to drink it straight. "Never fucking betta." He then proceeded to pelt the bottle against a wall, smashing it into pieces. "Wonderful."

Stumbled toward the phone, he picked up the receiver and ordered a pizza. Eddie appeared stunned.

"Are you sure you're okay?" Eddie looked at him nervously. "You're not acting like yourself at all. Did something happen tonight?"

"Yeah well, shit happened tonight, Eddie," he slurred. "Stuff and shit stuff."

Jimmy knew he wasn't making sense and began to laugh. "You sound like Liz asking me how I am, funny."

"Who's Liz?"

"The bar girl, bartender?" he replied, somewhat confused "You know the girl who runs the bar thingy. She drove me..ummm..here. And I know whattcha thinking, I didn't fuck her."

"Aha."

"Nah, a girl, the girl I wanna fuck tonight said no 'cause of her boyfriend and William stuff."

"William?"

"Ha?" Jimmy shrugged. "Oh nothing."

"Did you see Tarah tonight or something?" Eddie seemed to be putting the pieces together.

"Yeah, oh shit." Jimmy was now leaning up against a wall. "Left my CD there."

Jimmy wandered into the living room and turned on the television. He flipped channels continually until the pizza arrived. After having only two bites of his first slice, he threw up all over the kitchen floor. He insisted on cleaning it up but Eddie ushered him into the living room. The next thing Jimmy knew, he was in his bed and someone was knocking at the door.

"Oh fuck me!" He muttered and rolled over to see the sun peaking from around his blinds. Then he realized it was the next day and Tarah's voice was outside his bedroom door. Memories from the previous night flooded back. At least some of them, mostly the ones he would have preferred to have forgotten. Glancing around, Jimmy felt his head spinning. Why was Tarah at this house? He slowly got out of bed and headed for the door.

Chapter forty-three

S he stood on the other side of the door. Her hair pulled back in a ponytail and barely any makeup on at all and yet Jimmy thought she looked perfect. Tarah appeared nervous as she stared into his face and Jimmy felt genuine embarrassment. Not only had he humiliated himself the previous night after confessing his feelings for her, he now had to stand before her smelling like vomit and alcohol. Unfortunately, that odor combination was making him more nauseous.

"What? What are you doing here?" Jimmy's words were barely audible, and his throat hurt when he spoke. Pain was shooting through his head, his eyes were burning, and his stomach was still queasy.

"We have to talk," Tarah announced, looking over his shoulder. Jimmy assumed that she was sizing up the complete upheaval of his bedroom. Since moving into his new home, he hadn't taken the same care looking after his room as he had at either his sister or parents' house. Her eyes met with his once again and she asked if it was a bad time. As much as Jimmy wanted to crawl back into bed and die, he was curious as to what she had to say, so he moved aside to let her enter. The two of them sat on the bed.

Before he could hear why Tarah had dropped by, Jimmy felt his stomach turning. He was going to be sick. After quickly excusing himself and asking her to wait, he rushed to the bathroom. He hoped that the shower he turned on covered the sound of vomiting, but after a few minutes of his non-stop puking, there was a gentle tap on the door as Tarah asked if he was okay. He felt so weak and miserable that the sincere concern in her voice made her rejection sting even more than it already had. He insisted that he was fine, and after a brief hesitation heard her footsteps walking away. He continued to throw up. He wanted to die. Laying his head on the side of the toilet seat, a small tear crept from his eye and slid down his face. His body was weak when Jimmy finally stood up and flushed the toilet and he feared passing out. Removing his clothes, he slowly got into the lukewarm shower and began to wash his hair.

Ten minutes later he turned off the water and brushed his teeth, then grabbed a towel and wrapped it around his midsection. Taking a deep breath, he headed back to his room. He was surprised to see that Tarah was still there. A chill ran through his body and Jimmy realized that she must have opened his bedroom window; probably because his room stunk like a motherfucker, he decided. He couldn't blame her. Still he was freezing and strode across the room to close it. He noticed Tarah giving him a once over as he passed her, but then quickly looked away.

She started to back paddle right away. Before Jimmy had a chance to say anything, Tarah was standing up and glancing for her escape route. She tried to make it sound as if her motivation for visiting was to drop off the Alice in Chains CD he had left at her apartment the previous night. When he glanced at the orange case on his nightstand, all the words and feelings from the night before came rushing back at him.

Still standing in his towel and a little nervous it might fall off, Jimmy gently told her to wait while he got dressed. Grabbing some fresh clothes, he returned to the bathroom and pulled them on. He caught sight of himself in the mirror. There was no denying that he looked like fucking shit.

Returning to his room, Jimmy shut the door and sat beside her on the bed. Their conversation started light and he inquired if William was home yet. Tarah said no and jumped ahead. "Look, Jimmy, we have to talk."

He hated those words. They were never followed by anything positive. And this case was no exception.

Tarah said that she didn't want things to be weird between them. Didn't she realize that it was a little too late for that? Then again, maybe it was his fault that this situation was such a mess. Maybe he was wrong to follow his instincts. But he *knew* she had wanted him to kiss her. Why did chicks do this shit all the time? Say one thing then do another.

Jimmy was pissed. He felt like Tarah wasn't *just* rejecting him, but now she was rubbing his face in it. He told her to go back to William and he'd continue screwing every girl in sight. Things were probably easier that way. Even though she seemed upset, he had to make one last point to her before she left - and it was an important one. Jimmy felt the need to let Tarah know that she was a completely different person when William wasn't around. There was no way she would've smoked a joint and mellowed out like she had the night before, if William had been there. His next question made her cry.

"How can you be in love with someone who you aren't even yourself around?"

Even though he could see the tears about to fall down Tarah's face, Jimmy didn't stop. He asked her why she had kissed him back, if she was in love with William. She had been an enthusiastic participant at the time, he pointed out. Then he felt guilty for making her cry and apologized.

As the two of them talked, Tarah continued to sob quietly. Jimmy wanted to comfort her, but held himself back.

However any compassion he felt for Tarah quickly disappeared when she suggested that he just *thought* he had feelings for her. Jimmy suddenly was seventeen again and being rejected by his first girlfriend. Hadn't she said the same words? That he just *thought* he was in love with her? Anger rose, and words flew out of his mouth.

"Tarah, please! Please don't tell me how I feel," he snapped, and this time, Jimmy didn't care if she cried. What the fuck? Did she seriously think he was someone who followed girls around like a lovesick moron? How long had he wanted to be with her? How long had he wanted *her*? And now Tarah was dismissing his feelings, or maybe she was dismissing *him*. Her attempt at challenging his beliefs only made him determined to prove her wrong.

So he told her everything. Jimmy once again put himself on the line and expressed how he felt, explaining that he hadn't been looking for this to happen. He admitted to always looking forward to seeing her and thinking about her when she wasn't around. It didn't matter if they were surrounded by strangers or a hundred women, Jimmy always was aware of exactly where to find her because to him, she was the only face in the room. The words all sounded so stupid when he said them out loud, like some kind of corny bullshit that you hear on television, the kind of stuff that you assume isn't real until *you* actually feel it. He felt vulnerable and stupid. But if Tarah was going to reject him, she wasn't doing so without him having his last say. At least then he could move on and never regret not telling her the truth.

But something had changed. When Jimmy now looked in her eyes, there was a silent tranquility suggesting that his words had caught her attention.

"No one has ever said anything like that to me before," she admitted, wonderingly. Jimmy gave a small smile, feeling even more frustrated with the whole situation. William hadn't said anything as meaningful to her, yet *he* was her boyfriend? Maybe that was just a girl thing. It seemed that women always were quick to lower their standards when it came to men. No wonder so many guys were idiots to women - they let them.

Recognizing that her walls were slowly crumbling, Jimmy added that she was brilliant on stage. That *she* was the band. "You light up the entire room."

He knew that his words probably sounded like bullshit but it was how he really felt. She was amazing. Even if she left that afternoon and went back to William, married him and had babies, at least Jimmy knew he tried.

Nah, that was bullshit - he'd be fucking pissed.

Suddenly, the room was silent, and Jimmy wasn't sure what else to tell her. His words were settling all around them both like debris after an explosion. She turned toward him as if to say something and Jimmy knew he had to kiss her one more time. Just to see how she'd react. Just to see if she pulled away. Just to see.

Jimmy put his hands on each side of her face and stared into her eyes, holding her gaze to his. She *knew* he was going to kiss her. There was no way she couldn't have known. But she didn't back away. Tarah followed his lead and their lips fiercely met. As his heart raced, he felt an intense desire building up inside him. He pulled her into his arms, caressing her thighs over her jeans. He felt her hands running through his wet hair; she was clearly as caught up in the moment as he was. Slowly his hand roamed up her thigh, and by the time he had reached between her legs she was gasping.

Suddenly he didn't care what happened. The entire house could fall down around them at that moment and Jimmy wouldn't have let go of Tarah for anything. Instead, he sheltered her body with his as they both fell back on the bed. He had never wanted anyone so intensely as he wanted her in that moment. When he felt her fingers lightly on his dick through his jeans he momentarily let go of her mouth as his head fell back. Breathing heavily, his lips quickly moved to her ear, where his tongue laved her lobe, and his hand moved into the back of her pants and over her ass.

As Tarah attempted to suppress her breathing, she started to quickly unbutton his jeans. Suddenly, she stopped. It took a moment for Jimmy to understand why the abrupt end to their make out session. But then he heard William and Michael downstairs. Had they just walked in the house? Did they see Tarah's car outside?

Jimmy swallowed his frustration as Tarah started to pull back. Her face was flushed and if William were to catch her right then, he'd *know* something had just happened between them, even if they were on opposite ends of the room. Jimmy gently pointed that out to her.

"Oh my God!" Tarah covered her face with one hand then rolled off his body. "I can't believe William's *here.*"

"Don't worry," Jimmy calmly assured her. *Figures that Will would have such bad timing.* "Just say I dropped by last night and I was really depressed or something. And you came over to see if I was okay. I don't care, tell him whatever you want." He closed his eyes for a second and tried to ignore how incredibly horny he was in that moment.

She sat up on the bed.

"Tell him the moon is made out of ice cream for all I care," Jimmy impatiently pushed his hair back. He focused intently on her face. "Just be honest with me. That's all I ask."

She nodded in understanding, before straightening her clothes and walking toward the door. "I'll talk to you later."

Chapter forty-four

Everyone noticed a change in Jimmy. He was quieter, he was relaxed, but most of all, he wasn't picking up random girls.

"What the fuck's up with you?" Michael finally asked Jimmy. It was two weeks after his make-out session with Tarah and the jury was still out on his future. However, he knew that something he had said to her that day had made a difference. The brief conversations he had with Tarah since indicated that she was feeling very torn. "Where's the usual parade of skanks that we used to see here all the time?"

"Why? You miss 'em?" Jimmy avoided the question. The last thing he needed was for William's brother to be suspicious. Michael had already made a few comments about Tarah spending time alone in Jimmy's room. Although William seemed to accept that she was merely there trying to talk the band's guitarist out of jumping off a bridge, his brother did not seem convinced. As much as Jimmy wanted Tarah, he didn't want everything to blow up in their faces.

"Do I miss you waking the entire house up while you fuck some dirty assed whore? No, not really," Michael curtly replied. "I just find it strange is all. Did you get some kinda disease and scare them all off? Herpes or something?"

Jimmy laughed. "Right, like an STD would keep girls off my dick? It's not like I'm *you*, asshole." He then left the room, purposely ending the conversation.

Michael wasn't the only person who was suspicious. Coworkers were questioning his dwindling social life. One of the most disturbing discoveries that Jimmy made was that when he wasn't sleeping around, he wasn't very popular. Once he stopped flirting with women and stepped back from his former playboy image, he started to realize that his life was actually quite empty. Not that he hadn't recognized this before but this time it was brought into much sharper focus, especially when he wanted to talk to someone about what was on his mind regarding Tarah. He had no one. Patrick had moved and he really didn't have any friends outside of the band. Obviously he couldn't talk to them.

But the month moved forward and the dreaded Valentine's Day came and went. It fell on a Sunday, and the band was together that night for a practice. Jimmy noted definite tension between William and Tarah, indicating that they probably weren't celebrating the day of love. Even Michael later commented on how the couple should just break up since they clearly weren't happy. Jimmy exchanged looks with Eddie but neither said a thing.

Fire was looking forward to a big show that was scheduled at the end of the month at Ginger's Ale House. It promised to be a huge success because fans bought one ticket that covered Friday, Saturday and Sunday night and gave them access to a variety of local talent. Fire was scheduled to play during the latter part of the Saturday night and wanted to make sure the show was no less than perfect since it was also expected to grab a great deal of media attention. It was going to be awesome.

On the night of the show, Jimmy arrived at the bar early. He knew Tarah was supposed to meet her brother for drinks before Fire played, and Jimmy was hoping to get a moment alone with her before William arrived. He needed to find out if she wanted to stay with her boyfriend or explore her obvious attraction to him.

Before he had a chance to ask her, she dropped a bombshell. She was thinking of leaving the band.

"No." Jimmy was adamant. Regardless of her choice between him and William, he reasoned, it was no reason to leave Fire. But Tarah felt guilty about everything and hated herself for fooling around behind William's back, especially since she believed that her boyfriend was loyal to her. At that point Jimmy felt anger rise inside of him. He thought back to the night when William was outside a bar, sharing a very passionate kiss with some other girl. Even though Jimmy felt tempted to share the entire story with Tarah, he held back. Instead, he merely indicated that the same woman who had so boldly grabbed William at the bar had later told Jimmy that William had encouraged her. It was just a smidgen of information, enough to pull Tarah off the path of shame.

She took the news in stride. He wasn't sure if it was because it didn't surprise her or if Tarah simply didn't believe that Jimmy was telling the truth. It appeared that she was staying with William out of guilt, and Jimmy felt it was time that she knew the reality of the situation. Not that they had much time to discuss it - Tarah's brother arrived shortly into their conversation.

The show that night went off without a hitch. Fire definitely stood out against the other bands that played earlier on the same stage. Fans were cheering, and while standing on stage during the show, Jimmy felt secure about the band's future. They had the right formula and maybe things might just fall into place. Things felt promising. Jimmy felt confident and strong about his future. The lights seemed brighter, and the fans were more enthusiastic than ever before. Regardless of what the future brought, Jimmy knew he was in exactly the right place at the right time.

Tarah practically flew off the stage at the conclusion of their performance to meet with her brother, so Jimmy was surprised when she approached the rest of the band a few minutes later, just as they were about to finish packing up their equipment. With her, was some older guy wearing a Metallica t-shirt. Jimmy assumed that it was either a friend or family member and didn't really pay attention until he heard her say something about 'Peter Sampson of FUTA Records'. Then the entire band stopped what they were doing and gave Tarah and the stranger their full attention. Future United Together Artists was a division of a major label and this stranger was representing them. Jimmy thought his heart stopped beating.

"If I could just have a few minutes of your time tonight, I'd love to talk about your future goals," Peter said with an enthusiastic smile. His open and friendly manner made him seem very likeable. He encouraged the band to meet him outside of the bar to discuss things farther.

All the blood drained from Jimmy's face as he made eye contact with Tarah, who also appeared to be in the state of shock. He broke out in a cold sweat, while excitement spread like wildfire through his veins. It could be their big break! Jimmy felt like he was frozen in time. This couldn't seriously be happening. But it was. This could be *it*.

Peter Sampson arranged to meet the band later that night in a dumpy café. The six of them gathered in a booth. Feeling as though the sky was the limit, Jimmy made sure to sit next to Tarah. She looked petrified so he occasionally gave her leg a squeeze under the table; it wasn't like anyone would notice with everyone's eyes on Peter and maybe it would help her relax. Looking around the table, Jimmy realized that he was the only one of the five members of Fire who was actually calming down and taking everything in stride.

Peter seemed like a nice guy; pretty down to earth, but not someone Jimmy would necessarily give his trust to in business matters. He was smooth. Apparently he had been keeping track of Fire for the past year and felt that they were consistent, dedicated and talented. All in all, what Peter was saying was that he wanted to sign them to his label. Jimmy felt his heart race. This *was* it. His dream was going to come true. In that moment, he thought of Sean Ryan. He would be proud.

After a brief conversation with the band, Peter said he'd like to meet with them all again early the following week. Everyone was quiet when he left.

Eddie looked like he was either going to faint or cry. William was excited but skeptical. Michael was distrusting. And Tarah was simply shocked. It was the predictable reactions from everyone, in Jimmy's opinion. However when Michael started to rant about how the deal they were being offered could be crap, Jimmy lost his tempter.

"Who gives a fuck, man?" Jimmy snapped at him. He was so *sick* of Michael's shitty attitude. He countered that no one had anything to lose by looking into it and chances were, they'd also have nothing to lose by signing a contract. With the exception of William, who was a mechanic, most of the band worked dead-end jobs. Predictably, William defended his brother and that's when Jimmy jumped up and announced he was leaving. Since he'd expected to drink that night, he didn't have his car and bluntly asked Tarah to drive him home. Everyone at the table looked surprised by his bold request, but no one commented. Tarah quietly agreed but after they were outside, admitted being shocked by his boldness. Not that he cared.

As she drove him home that night, Jimmy felt light and happy. The more he thought about Peter Sampson and his proposition, the more he smiled. At one point Jimmy looked at Tarah and told her that the only way that night could be better, was if she spent it with him. He would've done anything to have that happen. Although he knew that Tarah would go home to William yet again, something told him that those nights were numbered. He could tell that she had feelings for him. He could see it in her eyes. When they finally arrived in his driveway a few minutes later, their third make-out session all but sealed the deal.

She had reluctantly agreed to go in the house with him.

"Come on, you gotta walk me to my door," Jimmy teased as they pulled into his driveway. Putting the car in park, she turned it off and stepped out.

"Just for a minute."

"Yeah, yeah," Jimmy capitulated as he walked slightly ahead of her, only stopping to reach back for her hand. "But you gotta walk me to the door to make sure I get in safely." He watched her smile perfectly before rolling her eyes. "Plus," he added, "What if there were some burglars inside?"

"Like I'd be a big protector?" Tarah giggled referring to her tiny frame, then she walked in the house with him. All the lights were out. The only sound that could be heard was the furnace running. Jimmy closed the door behind them and without saying a word, began to kiss her. Unlike the previous time, he carefully pulled her close and his fingers gently ran down her body. Then he stopped and stared into her eyes. Through the darkness, he could see that his feelings for Tarah were mutual. He could feel it. He was positive.

"I'm not gonna keep going," he whispered, running his fingers over her face. Tarah's skin was soft and perfect. "But I know I'll be disappointed when you leave. And I know you have to leave. But I also know that you'll be back someday. And I think you know it too."

She just smiled.

Chapter forty-five

The following week flew by. There were meetings. FUTA was trying to convince Fire to sign with them, but at the same time letting them know that there would be a lot of work involved in making their careers a success. The label certainly wasn't about to give them a free ride. However, they *were* giving them an opportunity and that was much more than most people in their shoes would ever get. In Jimmy's opinion, they had to grab on to it and give it everything plus 110% more. This separated the winners from the losers; and Jimmy just hoped that no one in the band would drag them down.

Peter Sampson knew what he was talking about. Jimmy found his perspective interesting; although he *did* question his theory that grunge was on its way out. He was a man who clearly knew the industry. Peter was insistent that Fire continue with their style rather than feel pressured to adopt a similar sound as the latest popular artists. It made sense. People wanted something new and different.

Jimmy felt optimistic about his future by the end of that week. He would soon have a music contract and if all went well, maybe Tarah too. Life was good. Life was improving. When he thought back to his dismal days of non-stop drinking and not caring about anything, Jimmy realized how easily he could've given up everything. It was surprising how much life could really turn around, sometimes when you least expected it.

On Saturday afternoon Jimmy was home alone when there was a knock at his door. He answered it to find William. At first, there was no indication that anything was wrong. He neither appeared to be in a good nor bad mood. He just looked very serious. Assuming that William dropped by either about band issues or to talk to Michael, Jimmy didn't hesitate to move aside and allow him in the door.

"So, what's up man?" Jimmy spoke casually as he sipped on his cup of coffee. "If you're looking for Mike, him and Eddie went out."

"Actually, no Jimmy. I was looking for you," William replied. He almost seemed apprehensive but at the same time, his eyes were challenging Jimmy's. "I got to talk to you about something."

"K." Jimmy closed the door behind William and followed him into the kitchen. "Want a coffee?"

"No," William said as he leaned with his back up against the counter. Appearing frustrated, he rubbed his eyes. Taking a deep breath, he looked back at Jimmy who continued to casually drink his coffee even though he could sense that something was very wrong.

"So, I don't even know how to say this but," William said before hesitating for a moment, "Is there something going on between you and Tarah?"

"What?" Jimmy asked, remaining calm while his brain ran full-speed ahead. Sensing that William wasn't confident in his accusation, Jimmy decided to deny it. Jimmy thought he'd believe him. But he was wrong.

"Are you sleeping with Tarah?" William quietly asked.

"No!" Jimmy denied and heard his own relief as he answered the question. At least he wasn't lying. "God, who told you that I was?"

"It's not that anyone told me that you were," William confirmed. "I just know you aren't exactly the relationship kind of guy. So if something were going on between the two of you, I would assume it was just sex."

Jimmy felt his earlier relief fading. It shouldn't have mattered what William thought about his ability to commit, but for some reason his words stung. It was kind of suggesting that he would actually sink so low as to screw Tarah and toss her aside, even *though* she was both in his band and a relationship with a friend. It made him sound like some kind of dirt bag who had absolutely no standards. Then again, Jimmy decided that perhaps he deserved that comment.

"No," Jimmy replied as he finished his coffee and set the mug on a nearby table. He faced William and tried to remain casual and relaxed.

"Jimmy, I don't want to say who told me what, but I've had more than one reason to believe that something is going on between you and Tarah," William said, watching Jimmy's face closely. "Some people have seen and overheard things that add up to the same thing. And Tarah is acting different around me lately. I can tell something is wrong."

"Look Will, I don't know *who* saw whatever but there's nothing going on," Jimmy spoke with confidence. "I'm assuming your source is Mike, which isn't saying much since he can't stand either me *or* Tarah. Just let it go, forget about it." However his attempt to brush things under the rug didn't work. It only seemed to increase the tension in the room.

"Jimmy, please don't do this," William pleaded, shaking his head. "I've seen things too. And anything that I was told by my brother or anyone else, only confirmed what I already knew."

Jimmy remained silent.

"I know you were touching her leg under the table the night we met with Peter Sampson," William confirmed. "And I know you two spent some time alone together while I was in Springdale for my aunt's funeral. Anything else I was told only made things make more sense to me."

"When you were away, I just dropped in to see *both* of you but you weren't there. I had no idea." Jimmy spoke honestly but had a feeling that William wouldn't believe him. "I brought a CD that I thought you might like to hear. You weren't there, so Tarah and I listened to it. That's it. Tarah was concerned about me and dropped by the house the next of day, end of story."

"Something happened that night. I *know* something happened that night." William said while crossing his arms.

Jimmy didn't know what to say. It was clear he couldn't convince William that it was all a lie and hope he moved on.

"Jimmy, I like to think we're friends. I *thought* we were friends," William spoke gently while uncrossing his arms. "So please just tell me the truth. Have enough respect for me as a friend, as someone you work with and just tell me the real deal here. I need to know."

After a slight hesitation, Jimmy nodded. "K, well the truth is that I have a thing for Tarah and I wanted her to know, but she made it clear that she was in a relationship with you and that was that." He realized he was once again floating through half-truth land. If nothing else, he might be able to take some heat off Tarah.

"So, you hit on her and she didn't respond?" William asked skeptically. "She didn't react?"

"No, she didn't."

"So, why Tarah? I mean there are tons of women out there that are all over you after the shows. Why did you chase after *my* girlfriend?" William asked him bluntly. "Do you really think that was a smart thing to do? Did you really need her added to your list of girls you hooked up with?"

"I didn't do it because I wanted to just hook up with her," Jimmy decided to at least try to save face. "I really like Tarah. I've always liked Tarah. I just never did anything about it before because you two were together. I had a couple of drinks that night and then smoked so I guess I just wasn't thinking straight. It just happened. It's not her fault."

"I realize that you're trying to cover her ass but the truth is that Tarah should have told me all this herself," William said. He showed no change in composure as he spoke. "I don't like the fact that she hid it from me. I've asked her a million times in the last few weeks what was wrong and she wouldn't tell me."

"Well obviously, she didn't want to create friction." Jimmy stated the obvious. "I don't think she was *hiding* it from you."

"But she knows I'm not the kind of person who flies off the handle. She could have been honest with me," William insisted. "No, I think she hasn't said anything because she *wanted* that attention from you. I think she has some kind of thing for you."

"I don't know-

"And if she has a thing for you, then clearly our relationship isn't very strong." William continued. "I can tell. I can tell by how she's acting and everything just fits together. It makes sense now."

Jimmy didn't know what to say. Regardless of how much he tried to fix the situation, it just seemed to continually get worse. Jimmy didn't want William to start an argument with Tarah because of something *he* said, but it appeared that he had already made up his mind.

And just like that, their conversation was over. William was heading toward the door, leaving a stunned Jimmy behind.

"Will, please don't blame her for what I did," Jimmy begged, following him to the door. "I wasn't trying to start shit."

William turned to face him and with sincerity in his voice replied, "Thanks Jimmy for being straight with me about everything." Then he was gone.

Jimmy panicked. William was going to talk to Tarah. His first instinct was to call and warn her, but he knew that the couple had caller ID, so it would look even more suspicious if William returned to see that Jimmy had called a few minutes earlier. His brain raced frantically. He wondered who had told William what. He wasn't even sure *what* he knew. Finally, Jimmy decided to wait a few minutes before driving by the couple's apartment. If Tarah's car wasn't there, maybe he could check her work. But hadn't she already finished her last shift at Rothman's? Where else would she be?

Grabbing his car keys, Jimmy headed out the door and toward the couple's apartment. Her car wasn't there. William's was though. Jimmy returned back to his place and stood helplessly just inside the door. Suddenly it hit him, if William and Tarah had a big fight, she might need a place to stay that night. Chances were good she'd avoid the house that Michael was living at, but just in case, Jimmy wanted to clean up his room. If she needed a place to crash, he would let her stay there and he'd sleep on the couch. It wasn't that he didn't want to share the room *with* her, but it wouldn't be right.

Walking into his bedroom, Jimmy felt frustrated. Looking around at the clothing tossed all over the place, magazines and God – the porn! He'd have to do a lot of work to get his room looking half decent and in a rush. Quickly he started with the clothes, most of which went in the laundry basket. He then started to pick up bottles and dishes to take downstairs. Eventually he got to the porn that had recently become his new best friend, and stashed it in the back of a drawer. Opening a window, he made his bed and organized books and magazines.

Finally feeling it looked half decent, he grabbed his car keys again and started for the door. Then he stopped. Maybe it would look too obvious if his car was sitting in the couple's parking lot. He considered parking it farther down the street, but then decided against it. He'd use foot power. It was a mild March day after all.

Heading out the door, he briskly walked in the direction of their apartment. Thoughts raced through his head. While he was excited that things seemed to be finally ending for the couple, he was scared that everything might backfire in his face. He knew that Tarah might need an extra boost to get out of a declining relationship; it was clear that she was too guilt-ridden to just walk away.

Arriving at their building, Jimmy noticed her car right away. She was upstairs. He didn't know what to do so he decided to wait outside. Not wanting to look like an idiot hanging around the building, he sat on the back step. If she left, she'd have to go out the back door to get to her car. He'd wait for a bit and if Tarah didn't come out, he'd go home.

Jimmy was barely there five minutes when he heard the sound of feet on the steps leading out to the door. Even before the door opened, he instantly knew it was Tarah. Did he know her so well that he even recognized how she walked? Maybe it was just wishful thinking on his part. As it turns out, it wasn't.

The door slowly opened. Tarah didn't see Jimmy sitting on the step when she first walked outside. He had just enough time to notice that she was as white as a ghost. Tears were streaming down her face and her hair was disheveled. Tarah had a suitcase in one hand, and car keys in the other. He could see the keys shaking.

Jimmy immediately jumped up from the stairs, startling her. Once she saw his face, her whole body relaxed and she dropped her suitcase. As he moved closer, she began to cry harder. She appeared to be in a state of shock, and he quickly gathered her in his arms.

"I'm sorry, Tarah. He somehow knew and I tried to tell him it was all me, that you didn't do anything wrong," Jimmy attempted to reassure Tarah as her body shook in his arms. She managed to gasp a quick, 'I know!' between her tears and he continued to hug her tightly. He didn't know what William had said to her – but clearly, it caused a lot of damage.

He suddenly had a bad feeling that she was this upset because she didn't actually want to break up with William.

Chapter forty-six

The drive to his house was bittersweet. While Tarah sat on the passenger side of her own car because she was too upset to drive, Jimmy was lost in his own world of thoughts. He quickly began to regret everything. What if he had never kissed Tarah? Never started any of this mess? Would she still be with William now? And just because she had broken up with her boyfriend didn't mean she was going to run into Jimmy's arms. In fact, there was always a strong chance that the couple would rekindle their relationship before the weekend was over. There were just too many 'what ifs' that pushed back any chance of happiness for Jimmy. He probably should've known better than to get his hopes up.

But at the same time, it didn't make him any less compassionate. He still cared about Tarah. He didn't want to see her hurt. He didn't want to see her cry. Jimmy wondered what William had said to her. It was clearly quite vicious if she was *this* upset. Then again, Tarah was an emotional person and seemed to have a lot of guilt over the entire situation.

Arriving at his house, Jimmy parked Tarah's car beside his own and turned the ignition off. He turned to her as they silently made eye contact. Tarah cleared her throat and asked if Michael was home.

"I'm sorry Tarah, I don't know," Jimmy admitted. He really hoped not. The last thing either of them wanted to hear was William's brother make snide remarks about the situation. Tarah was upset enough without Michael's cold and hurtful comments. Jimmy could see the concern on her face and offered to go check before Tarah went inside, but she said it was fine. He nodded and they both got out of the car. Grabbing her bag from the backseat, Jimmy glanced at Tarah and noted her mournful expression. Did she regret going to his house? Maybe she'd prefer to stay with a family member? He kept his thoughts to himself.

She looked relieved when they entered Jimmy's house to silence. Clearly, no one else was home. He shut the door behind them and continued to search her face, unsure of what to say or do.

"Can I have a glass of water?" she asked with a scratchy voice.

"Sure," Jimmy replied, relieved that he actually had a productive way to help her feel better. He rushed to the kitchen and quickly poured her water. She gave him a small smile when he returned and handed it to her.

Jimmy then invited her to his room. It wasn't until he heard the words that he realized how completely inappropriate it sounded. He hadn't meant it in a sexual way. He quickly explained that she could use his room and he would sleep on the couch. Seeing a small grin form on her lips when he struggled to explain himself, he added playfully, "Take advantage, it may be the only time I ever ask you to my room and don't try to fuck you."

She began to laugh and Jimmy felt like he had managed one minor triumph. He wasn't very good at comforting women and had no idea how to act in this situation. He didn't want to come across all fake and stupid like the pretty boys that were in movies, but at the same time he wanted her to see that he cared.

Although Tarah insisted that she didn't want to steal Jimmy's bed, he told her it was no big deal. She was a guest, after all. The two walked up the stairs and while Tarah stopped at the bathroom to wash her tear-streaked face, Jimmy took her suitcase into his bedroom. She joined him a few minutes later, looking slightly refreshed. They sat on the bed and began to talk about the break-up. Jimmy was reluctant to hear her words but knew that it was necessary to get everything out in the air.

Jimmy told her all about his conversation with William earlier that day. "I tried to tell him that nothing was going on," he explained, adding how it appeared that William already had his mind made up before dropping by to talk to Jimmy. Tarah nodded and agreed that she had the same feeling.

"He was just so quick and to the point," Tarah shook her head sadly.

"I didn't even have a chance to explain anything. Will said his thing and that was it. Done."

Jimmy thought maybe that was why Tarah appeared so shocked when she first walked out the door of her building. No wonder. She barely had time to digest the news and was essentially kicked out of her home. Tarah certainly had the rug pulled from beneath her. Jimmy never would've thought that William would be so cold. Then again, if he really believed that Tarah was cheating, it probably wasn't such a stretch. It wasn't so unusual for someone to turn into a completely different person when they were angry.

Tarah's next words stunned Jimmy. She had apparently been discussing the entire 'love triangle' issue with a friend earlier that day and had come to an epiphany. "…He pointed out that it was clear that I wanted to be with you, otherwise I would've avoided you like the plague." Tarah then added that she had planned to discuss her feelings with William that night, but unfortunately he had beaten her to the punch.

"Really?" Jimmy asked. His heart felt light at the realization that Tarah was there with him because she *wanted* to be, not because she had nowhere else to go. Yet a small part of him didn't want to completely dive into the land of happiness and love. What if she changed her mind? What if he was simply her 'plan b' if things hadn't worked out with William? When he looked into her eyes, Jimmy didn't think that was the case, but he knew that life didn't deal him too many winning hands. Jimmy also knew that he wasn't the easiest person in the world to love. He didn't have to look much farther than his own family to figure that much out.

They continued to discuss William and their mutual guilt for developing feelings for one another behind his back. Neither of them wanted to hurt or create bad tension with William, but neither could deny the spark that was developing between them. Jimmy had attempted to deny and avoid it since he met Tarah, but it hadn't gone away. And she had seen her relationship with William slowly crumble. Her reluctance to end things sooner was because of the fact that William was just a good guy. It wasn't like he was horrible to her, but their constant arguments about Michael's disrespectful attitude, accompanied by the stream of women who seemed to seek and receive his attention was just too much.

He didn't have to cheat on her in order to make Tarah feel insecure in their relationship.

Jimmy decided that it had been a long day and he could see that Tarah was exhausted. He leaned in to give her a quick kiss on the cheek before leaving her alone. When Tarah's lips met with his, it was apparent that she wanted to spend the night with him. Jimmy wanted her so bad that he almost gave in to her advances but he quickly moved away. Seeing the disappointment in her eyes, he shook his head. "Not like this, Tarah."

Regardless of how much he wanted her at that moment, Jimmy knew that she wanted him for all the wrong reasons. At least right then, she did. The break-up with William was much too fresh and he didn't want her having sex with him only as a way to escape her own misery. Plus, who was to say that Tarah wouldn't wake up the next morning and decide she wanted to go back to William? It was just too soon and he cared about her too much to do the wrong thing. He'd spent most of his life making the wrong decisions and it was time to start making some right ones.

Tarah did manage to convince Jimmy to stay with her platonically that night. It was one of the first times in his life that he slept in the same bed as a woman that he hadn't just had sex with. He rarely spent an entire night with a woman, under *any* circumstances. Although he was concerned that the physical contact would be too tempting, he fell asleep almost immediately. The next morning, he awoke to the sound of voices downstairs. William and Michael were in the house.

Jimmy slowly rose from the bed. He didn't want to wake up Tarah, but she was sound asleep. He crept to the door, slowly turning the knob before quietly exiting and closing the door behind him. Turning around, he saw William glaring at him from the bottom of the stairs, as Michael was rolling his eyes.

"Figures man, not even a day and he's got her in the sack," Michael remarked to a disgusted William, while Eddie stood helplessly nearby. William had dark circles under his eyes, and he had a day's worth of stubble. He studied Jimmy's face.

"It's not like that," Jimmy insisted as he started down the stairs. "She just crashed in my room because she didn't want to be alone."

"Sure," Michael grunted.

"Mike, please. I'm not in the mood." William curtly remarked.

"She was just really upset," Jimmy ignored Michael and spoke directly to William. "I swear, nothing happened."

"Why not?" Michael asked. "It probably already has *anyway*, so why stop now?"

"Mike, would you please shut up?" William snapped at his brother. "If Jimmy said nothing happened, I believe him." Returning his attention to Jimmy, he added, "I don't think he'd lie to me."

"No man, I swear," Jimmy vowed, raising his hand in a gesture of surrender. "She's fully clothed and sleeping right now. Nothing happened. Nothing."

William looked frustrated as he calmly began to speak. "Okay, we're here to get some of Mike's stuff. He's going to move in the spare room at the apartment. I have a bunch of Tarah's stuff here in the van too. I figured if she was here I'd drop it off, if not I'd take it to where ever she was staying." He seemed to be lost in thought for a moment. "... Umm, yeah, so if you want to help me while Mike goes and gets his shit together?"

"Sure," Jimmy nodded. "I'll just grab a jacket."

The two worked together to move a majority of Tarah's stuff upstairs and into the hallway, while Michael quickly gathered his junk and threw it in garbage bags and boxes. The only thing that was left when they finished filling up William's van, was his bed, a couple of guitars and a dresser.

"We'll come back in a little bit to get the rest of it. I have some more of Tarah's stuff to bring, but most of it's here already. Fortunately both her and Mike travel light." The two stood alone outside while Michael grabbed a few more things upstairs.

"Yeah," Jimmy nodded uncomfortably. Now that he was face to face with William and had no Michael to divert their attention, he wasn't sure what to say. Should he be apologizing? He didn't want there to be tension between him and William.

"Look man, I really didn't mean to cause all this," Jimmy pointed at Michael's belongings in the van. "I don't even know what to say."

"Jimmy, you were honest with me and I don't hold a grudge against you," William assured him. "I'm not ecstatic that you were fooling around with my girlfriend..ah, my former girlfriend, behind my back, but at the same time I'm not too happy with her for hiding it from me. I wish she had been direct with me. Like I told you yesterday, I gave her lots of opportunities to tell me the truth and she didn't. I gave you one and you did. I think that says something about the entire situation."

"Still," Jimmy shook his head. "We all got to work together. This sucks."

"I know and for that reason, we'll have to figure out a way to get along," William spoke logically. "But the bottom line is that she clearly has a thing for you. If she didn't then Tarah would've told me everything right away and drew a line in the sand with you. And I don't think she was exactly pushing you away."

"But it wasn't just her," Jimmy shook his head. "Please don't shit on her."

"Yeah, but there's a big difference," William reminded him. "You were single, she *wasn't*. I'm not shitting on her; I just don't respect how she dealt with this situation. She owed me more than that."

Jimmy nodded slowly. He understood where William was coming from. But he also saw Tarah's side of things, and he didn't think it was his place to get involved any farther.

Michael came out the front door, and Jimmy silently stood back and watched as they drove off.

Chapter forty-seven

Jimmy spent the remainder of the weekend trying to make Tarah laugh. It didn't matter if he had to make himself look stupid in the process; it was a small price to pay to see a smile on her face. The situation was difficult enough and anything to lighten the mood was welcome. Especially since the band would be getting together in Toronto to meet with Peter Sampson of FUTA on Monday morning.

Fortunately when Monday rolled around, things went much smoother than he expected. Although there was definite tension in the FUTA boardroom that morning, it wasn't too bad considering the circumstances. Everyone was civil toward one another. Everyone was professional. Probably because the entire band was much too focused on making it in the industry to allow their personal feelings about one another get in the way. It was a mature attitude and Jimmy was relieved that things went so well.

A lawyer named Bob Jameson met with the band and Peter to discuss the details of the contract. Nothing in it really surprised Jimmy. It was all about give and take. Sure the label was going to help them out to a point, but for the most part Fire would have to reimburse FUTA for various expenses. It made sense. The label was insistent that they push their music and get it 'out there' as much as possible. It wasn't a free ride. It wasn't a handout. It was an opportunity for Fire to prove that they were capable of holding up against bands that were already established in the industry. And Jimmy was confident that they would.

Peter Sampson was encouraging the band to get in and out of the studio in record time. Although Jimmy thought that it was possible since they had already written songs, it just depended on how on the ball everyone was during the recording process. If anyone had a day full of fuck ups, it could affect the entire band. Although he was insanely crazy about her, Jimmy was concerned that Tarah might be the person to hold them back while recording their CD. Not because she wasn't talented but because of the stress of the situation with William. What if she became anxious and started to fuck up? Would her voice hold up if she had to make repeated attempts at their songs? But overall he felt that the band was very strong and could make a CD that reflected their talent.

And that was the meeting in a nutshell. Jimmy was surprised that the label hadn't suggested that Fire get their own lawyer when they signed the contract. No one else seemed concerned so he didn't bother to bring it up. It was a contract and he felt that they didn't have a lot of choice but to take the terms offered to them.

It was obvious that Tarah was relieved after leaving the meeting. She chatted more freely on the way home from Toronto and her mood seemed to lighter. However when they got back to the house and found a message from her father on their machine, Tarah's mood immediately changed. She became very quiet and quickly erased it without returning the call.

"What's that about?" Jimmy asked without skipping a beat. He wanted to know everything about this girl and wasn't going to let anything slide under the radar. Judging by the stunned look on her face, she hadn't expected his reaction. She rarely discussed her family. "Come on Tarah, I've never seen your dad at any of our shows and now you're ignoring his message. What's the deal?"

"My dad and I don't really have a relationship," Tarah answered honestly as Jimmy passed her a cup of coffee from the pot that he had just brewed. Her eyes dropped to the hot drink she was holding; although she was uncomfortable discussing the topic, he wasn't hesitant to push for answers.

"Come on little girl, tell me a story" he cajoled, guiding her into the living room with his free hand on the small of her back, while drinking his coffee with the other. They sat on the couch, and he turned to face her as they traded smiles. "What's the deal with that? Why aren't you calling him back? Please don't tell me you got *daddy* issues."

"Not exactly," Tarah smiled, recognizing that he was obviously teasing her. She glanced down at her legs and he thought about how tiny Tarah was; he couldn't help but think of her as delicate, even though she had proven to be strong many times over. "I have *parent* issues. My mom's completely nuts and my dad is, well…we aren't close."

" 'Cause?"

" 'Cause my parents broke up when I was a teenager and dad drifted out of our lives," Tarah appeared to be speaking more toward her cup of coffee than Jimmy. He could tell this was a touchy issue. She finally looked back into his eyes. "My parents used to fight a lot and dad left my mom one night. *Literally* in the middle of the night, and my mom fell apart. She couldn't work or even function, or at least *thought* she couldn't, and I was left to pick up the slack. Like look after my brother, clean the house, grocery shop, everything."

Jimmy listened attentively while sipping on his hot coffee. Tarah clearly had to grow up fast, which was something he understood. "How long did this last?"

"Long enough," Tarah was quick to answer, nodding. "I guess I kind of resent dad for leaving us in such a mess. A part of me resents both of them. The divorce seemed to mess up everyone in the family."

"Yeah, but if he wasn't happy with your mom, he had to do what was right for *him* in the end," Jimmy reasoned, trying to be fair. "And your mom's reaction isn't his fault. The message he just left sounded sincere. Maybe you should give the guy a chance."

"Yeah but we hardly talk anymore. That message was just a fluke thing," Tarah replied, shaking her head. "He probably felt obligated to call. Trust me, he couldn't be any more out of touch with my life."

Jimmy decided to leave well enough alone. He was certainly not someone to be dishing out advice on dealing with parents, especially when he hadn't even told his own about the contract yet. He didn't really think they'd care. They continued to be a distant part of his life. He thought it was unlikely that they'd ever understand him.

Jimmy and Tarah decided to go get some food and returned home to stay. Climbing the stairs hand in hand, they went to his room. Jimmy turned on the lamp beside the bed and closed the door. Hitting a button on his CD player, 'Something in the Way' by Nirvana filled the room. Adjusting the volume so that it was at a soothing level, he invited Tarah to join him on the bed. She automatically sat next to the headboard and

Jimmy did the same. The two faced one another and the mood was very mellow. There was no where else in the world that Jimmy wanted to be in that moment, but right there with her.

They quietly discussed how it was one of the most important days of their lives, yet it seemed much like any other day. It really was hard to believe that they had signed a contract that morning. And yet, life moved forward as normal. The sun still rose and set. Time continued to move forward. Nothing else really changed. It was quite surreal. It was amazing how quickly life can take a turn, Jimmy mused. After all, how many times had he practiced guitar, went from band to band and listened to lectures from his family, fearing all his work would be for nothing? And then suddenly, everything happened at once. He got the music contract and the girl, all within the same week.

Their eyes were locked as they discussed all the changes that had recently taken place in Tarah's life. At one point, she leaned in and kissed Jimmy and he automatically wanted her. Before he had a chance to make his move, she threw him off guard with the one question that he *didn't* want to answer. Tarah asked him how many women he had been with. Not something he wanted to discuss, considering he was well into the triple digits.

"Baby, you don't want to know," Jimmy began to laugh uncomfortably and shyly looked away from her eyes. Suddenly all the girls from his past and their encounters seemed to run through his head like a train that was about to crash. In retrospect, he was kind of ashamed. He insisted that it didn't matter. Jimmy even tried to play it down, saying that it was *just* a number. After a few minutes of insistence that this was not a topic she wanted to unravel, Tarah dropped it. She seemed relatively composed about the whole issue, leading him to believe that it probably wasn't going to be an issue between them. After all, the girls in his past didn't matter to him. She did.

Jimmy told her about Sally and losing his virginity, and how hurt he was when they broke up. He was brutally honest about how his dog reputation began and continued over the years. He wanted to be truthful with her and expected the same from Tarah. And there was no doubt that she was on the same page.

Jimmy explained that he had a hard time respecting women. He saw the compassion in her eyes as he told her about being a fat kid that girls used to pick on. He even told her the Suzanne Bordon story. And Jimmy didn't leave out the fact that as a teenager, he had sex with her and then promptly dumped her after the act. Although Tarah seemed slightly shocked by his story, she didn't seem to hold any negative judgments toward him. She appeared to accept him for who he was, which was without a doubt something that Jimmy truly needed. Having Tarah accept him was one of the many things that made him feel that he was falling for her. And fast.

"My first was a guy that I met during high school," Tarah slowly began her story. They were holding hands now and although Jimmy knew it wasn't the right time, he was *really* horny and wanted to do more than just talk. However, he also wanted to do things right. Jimmy had almost no experience with relationships so he took each step carefully and hoped for the best. He hoped to not fuck up. He prayed she accepted him and his many flaws. It was frightening to reveal his true self; it was a vulnerable place to be.

"Were you together long?"

"Not really," she replied and made a face. "He was – well, he was really into me until we had sex, then he was gone," Tarah reluctantly admitted. Jimmy felt bad for her. Even he had never been *that* much of an asshole, something he quickly pointed out to Tarah. If nothing else, he had always been direct about his feelings, or in most cases, lack there of. At the same time, he did sort of get where those kinds of guys were coming from; a fact that he didn't share with her.

"I guess that's not so abnormal," Tarah continued, gently squeezing his hand. "Unfortunately, it started a bad pattern of guys. William was the first guy who ever treated me good. I guess that was why it was so difficult to admit when things were over. He was never bad to me in any way, unlike all the others in the past, and I felt guilty for ending things." She cleared her throat and glanced down at their conjoined hands. "But in the end, I guess it would have been a lot less hurtful if I had been direct with him right away. By trying to not hurt him, I actually made things worse."

"You didn't know. It wasn't your intention," his words were soothing and careful. "Someday, I promise you he'll understand."

"I hope you are right." She looked into his eyes and smiled.

Chapter forty-eight

As it turned out, the band decided that they should hire a lawyer. Unfortunately this wasn't until after signing their contract. That's when they found Colin Whitfield. But it was too little, too late.

Not that Jimmy really cared. But as the members of Fire sat in the arrogant lawyer's office a week later, it was clear that the majority of the band was ready to shit a brick. Essentially Colin nicely told them that they were stupid to not hire a lawyer *before* signing their contract, but that they were lucky because it didn't look too bad. Then Colin dropped a bomb that created even more tension between the members of the band – Tarah was apparently considered the 'key' person in the band. In other words, FUTA felt so strongly about keeping her in Fire that they put it in the contract that she had to stay with the band for three years.

Jimmy automatically turned to see Tarah's face turn red – she was clearly very uncomfortable with her newfound status. It appeared that she would have been happy to be swallowed up by the floor. Eddie and William looked surprised, maybe even a little nervous with this news while Michael was wearing his usual pissed off expression. Jimmy thought she deserved the recognition and was excited for her. However in the car after the meeting, Tarah was anything but happy.

"Everybody in the band already hates me, and now *this!*" Tarah said dramatically while covering her eyes for a moment. "I can't even believe that I'm that important."

"Babe, you're the shit and it's about time that the entire band recognized where you fit into the big picture." Jimmy attempted to encourage her but she didn't look happy.

Later that day they had a meeting with the band's newly hired manager, Maggie Eriksson. Jimmy's first impression was that she was young, hot and was very cold. She reminded him of one of the girls who used to go to his bar and act like a bitch all night, then tried to get him to fuck her when closing time rolled around. Sure, she was encouraging and positive but Jimmy wasn't completely convinced that Maggie was out for the band's best interest. Then again, he wasn't sure if *anyone* was concerned with what was in the band's best interest.

The ink was barely dry on their contract and already everyone was talking about touring, videos, the CD and photo shoots. It was a bit overwhelming but Jimmy decided to just go with the flow. Wherever the fuck they wanted him on whatever day, he'd show and do what he had to do. Case closed. That was his job.

The day was exhausting. When they arrived home that night, all Jimmy wanted to do was get high and relax. But as he sat alone on the back step of his house inhaling the remainder of his joint, Jimmy felt weighed down by the tremendous responsibility of having to successfully fulfill their contract. He felt excited about the prospects of the future and nervous about the possibility of failure. He felt like he was living in a wonderful dream and was frightened that at any moment he would wake up.

And he was horny. Really fucking horny. Jimmy wasn't sure if it was the effects of weed or simply going too long without sex, but he really wanted to get laid.

He thought about Tarah. He had strong feelings for her and he didn't want to fuck up everything. Was it too soon after her break-up with William to initiate sex? Sometimes he feared that maybe she wanted her ex back. After all Tarah seemed very preoccupied with what he thought about her since the break-up. Although she insisted that it was because she didn't want William to hate her, Jimmy feared that maybe she was having second thoughts about ending their relationship.

But whenever they were alone together, he could see her face relax and a sense of tranquility take over. Her voice would become very soft, almost like that of a little girl; so innocent and sweet. Tarah would gently hold his hand and her thumb would lightly run over his knuckles. He knew she had strong feelings for him. He could feel it.

At night he would lie in bed alone and think about how she was in the next room, wearing her little nightdress. And every night he would struggle to not make any noise as his hand drifted into the front of his underwear and gripped his erection. He somehow managed to control any sounds that indicated that he was jerking off, in what seemed to be the quietest house in history.

It wasn't just a sex thing. Jimmy wanted Tarah beside him in bed every night and morning. There was just something comforting about waking up in the middle of the night and knowing that the person you cared for was lying beside you. In his days of whoring around, it would have been a nightmare to live that scenario. Now he wanted that connection. It was something he needed in his life. But was it time?

After sitting in silence for a few more minutes, Jimmy finally went inside. He felt vulnerable as he glanced toward Tarah, who was on the phone in the living room. She sat on the couch's edge, leaning forward so that her blonde hair spilled over her face, almost completely hiding it. She spoke quietly, apparently involved in a serious discussion, and didn't look up as he passed the doorway and ran upstairs.

Once in his room, Jimmy removed his jacket and sat on the edge of the bed. He grabbed his guitar and began to play around with 'Swim on my Beach', one of the songs William and Tarah wrote together. He needed to preoccupy himself and change his thought process. But moments later, he recognized the sound of Tarah's footsteps as she ran upstairs. Feeling very calm and relaxed, Jimmy looked up in time to see her walk by his room. She stopped and lingered in the doorway, as if apprehensive to join him. Jimmy momentarily wondered if she was feeling the sexual tension between them. He started a conversation to see her reaction and much to his relief, she walked into the room.

Tarah was apparently still stressing out about what the band thought of the section of the contract suggesting she was a key person in Fire. Jimmy quickly reassured her that it was something she should be proud of rather than worried over. He stood up and approached her. She didn't move. His heart raced. Trying to comfort her, Jimmy leaned forward and gently kissed Tarah's lips before hesitating. They were so soft and smooth. Warm and inviting. Standing very close, Jimmy was suddenly very conscious of every breath he took, fearful that she would hear how it had become labored. He wanted her. Badly.

He leaned forward and kissed her again. As if sensing his desire for her, Tarah's arms quickly wrapped around his neck and Jimmy automatically put his hand on her back, pulling her close. Knowing he couldn't hold back anymore, his mouth eagerly enclosed hers as she released a soft moan from the back of her throat. He finally stopped and leaned forward to stare into her face, trying to decide whether this was the right time. Her long eyelashes fluttered while she seemed to be attempting to control her own breathing. That's when Jimmy knew. It *was* time.

Leaning forward, he softly pushed his bedroom door closed, watching her reaction. She looked nervous but inviting. He silently began to remove his clothing, leaving on only a pair of boxers. She stood frozen to the ground and quietly watched him. Jimmy couldn't help but grin and he shyly teased her that the process would work better if she took off her clothes too.

Not that she had to, because Jimmy was already starting to unbutton her sweater revealing a soft pink bra underneath. Tarah shrugged out of the piece of clothing and it fell to the floor. She was so tiny and beautiful. His fingers traveled down her flat stomach to unclasp the button of her jeans and soon they joined her sweater on the floor. She wore a pair of girly thongs that were pink with hearts all over them. Her hips were small but curved perfectly. She removed her socks and stepped away from the clothing. Jimmy automatically wrapped his hands around her waist then slid them down to rest on her hips, pulling her close as his mouth roughly clamped down on hers.

Jimmy felt Tarah's grip around his neck tighten while she hungrily kissed him back. His hands grasped her hips and pulled Tarah's body firmly against the bulge in his boxers. His fingers drifted below her hips and explored the hot, moist region underneath her thong. Tarah moaned again, but this time it wasn't as subtle as the previous time. This time he knew she was as horny as him.

Slowly moving toward the bed, Jimmy guided Tarah's body down on top of the sheets. Tarah pulled her body back farther on the mattress, and Jimmy leaned over her and focused on removing her bra. They were kissing again, and Jimmy moved his lips over to her ear as she gasped and wrapped her legs around him. He was no longer hiding the fact that his breathing was erratic. He was panting as his tongue trailed down her body, pausing momentarily to lick both of her hard nipples, wringing another loud moan from her. Knowing that he was on the edge, he continued to move down her body. And for the first time since him and Tarah started to develop a relationship, Jimmy was thankful for all his past sexual experience. Because if there was one thing he knew his way around, it was a clit. He quickly removed her thong and within moments of both his tongue and fingers working together, Tarah was squirming underneath him and really starting to make some noise. Jimmy knew it was time.

Moving back up her body, Jimmy quickly discarded his boxers and his mouth roughly met with Tarah's as he spread her legs. Kneeling over her, Jimmy grabbed a pillow and put it under her hips. As he lowered his body on top of Tarah's, he heard her whisper that she wanted him. Just when he was about to enter her, he grabbed both of Tarah's ankles and swung them over his shoulders. And then he did what he had been dreaming of for months – Jimmy was *finally* having sex with Tarah Kiersey. Both were equally caught up in the moment – panting and moaning loudly, making Jimmy thankful that they were home alone. The bed squeaked beneath them and as it became louder and faster, Jimmy could feel Tarah trembling beneath him, finally until releasing a loud, animal-like noise while clamping onto his body. Knowing that he couldn't possibly hold out any longer, Jimmy pushed deeper inside of her until he felt himself completely let go.

His face was burning, while sweat was gathering along his hairline. Jimmy felt his heart race at such an incredible pace that he thought it was ready to jump out of his chest wall. Falling against Tarah, who had dropped her legs to each side of him, he felt their bodies stick together while her arms tightened around his body.

"That was absolutely perfect." She whispered, her hot breath flowing into his ear as Jimmy encircled her with his arms, squeezing her body against his own.

He looked into her eyes and whispered, "*You're* absolutely perfect."

Chapter forty-nine

Jimmy felt no incentive to call his parents and tell them about the contract. He doubted that the same people who had encouraged him to go to college and get a *real* job would be enthused. Even if they were happy for him now, it was too little, too late. Their love was conditional. And if there was one thing that being with Tarah had taught him, it was that love should never be conditional. It was about acceptance and understanding – two things neither of his parents had displayed to him when he really needed them.

Two days before Fire was set to get in the studio, Jimmy finally decided to attempt calling them. It wasn't going to be a huge love fest conversation, just a brief catch-up session to tell them about the contract with FUTA. But when he was not able to reach his parents, he finally called his sister to see why they were never around. Certainly, they wouldn't just stop talking to him all together? Sure they hadn't communicated with him much since he moved, but Jimmy didn't think that he was completely cut out of their lives.

"They're on a cruise, remember?" Jillian revealed in a suspicious voice. "Why? What are you looking for mom and dad for? Please don't tell me you need a place to live?"

"Hell no."

"You're not in jail?" she asked with laughter in her voice. "Please don't tell me you got some girl pregnant?"

"Too funny!" Jimmy teased her. "You're going to feel like a real bitch when I tell you what my news is."

"What?" she giggled.

Jimmy told her about the contract and Tarah. He wasn't sure which piece of information shocked her the most.

"Oh my God! Jimmy, that's *amazing*!" Jillian replied with a slightly shaky voice. He wasn't sure if she was crying or laughing. Finally, Jimmy realized that he heard pride in her voice." I'm so happy for you, Jim! You deserve this, you really do."

Jillian then went on to ask a million questions about the contract and Tarah.

"Everything just changed so fast," Jimmy admitted while playing with the phone cord. "I've never had anything ever go right for me and suddenly *everything* is just amazing. It's perfect."

"That's wonderful, hon." She spoke quietly into the phone. "I'm very happy for you."

Before they hung up, Jillian said that she wouldn't tell their parents the news. She insisted that Jimmy do it instead. She also warned him to not move too quickly with Tarah. "Take things slow. There's no need to rush things along," she cautioned. He didn't tell her it was too late for that advice; his relationship with Tarah was advancing very quickly.

Their first sexual encounter together had sparked an incredible physical relationship that saw no limits. The chemistry between them was intense and was nothing like anything Jimmy had previously experienced. He might have had a lot of sex with many women, but doing it with Tarah was a completely different level of ecstasy. He often thought about the factors that made the sex so powerful between them. Was it because he had wanted Tarah for so long? Was it because he had abstained for weeks leading up to their first encounter? Finally Jimmy admitted that there was only one difference in his relationship with Tarah as opposed to other women – this time he was in love.

Not that he was ready to say the words. The topic hadn't come up and Jimmy simply wasn't ready to tell her how he felt.

For the next week, the band worked like dogs. Producer Rick McClure had Fire in the studio for 15-hour days in order to fulfill FUTA's wishes to have the CD done in a week. Not that it happened. It ended up taking a couple of extra days. Just as Jimmy had feared, Tarah started losing her voice by the end of the first week. Fortunately, she regained it late Sunday night and was ready to record again Monday morning. Recording the CD went better than expected. Considering all the tension that could've followed Fire right into the studio, it was amazing that they were able to record together at all. However there was a clear distance between Tarah and William. Neither really spoke to one another unless necessary. So when Jimmy saw the two having a conversation one afternoon, he felt jealousy creeping into his heart.

Although he certainly never expected the two to not talk again, they appeared to be having a serious conversation that could've meant anything. What if they were rekindling their relationship? Jimmy decided to interrupt them. He didn't hear what was being said, but Tarah's face was red and William had a cold expression on his, while his eyes avoided Tarah all together.

Jimmy later asked about the conversation. Apparently she had apologized for hurting him and William admitted that their relationship probably had already passed its due date. He also commented on how he would've preferred it if she had been with another guy, someone William didn't know. That made sense. Jimmy could appreciate his feelings on the matter. But he continued to have an uneasy feeling about the former couple. Then he realized that perhaps that's why Jillian warned him to not jump into things too fast. Jimmy hoped he hadn't.

The band finally finished the CD and everyone was happy. Rick McClure liked it. FUTA loved it. Maggie gave it her seal of approval. But most of all, the band thought it was a perfect reflection of their talent. It was time to begin promoting it.

But as Jimmy floated along in his world of happiness, something was about to knock the wind out of his sails.

On April 8, 1994 the world would learn that Kurt Cobain was found dead. Jimmy was devastated to learn that yet another one of his idols was gone; Nirvana's lead singer had committed suicide. How many times had Jimmy thought about ending his own life while listening to the very music that had actually soothed him while depressed? It was unsettling and difficult to understand. Although he would never admit it to anyone, Jimmy was relieved that his own life had taken a turn before this horrible tragedy. At one time, the suicide of his idol would've only encouraged him to consider the same path. It wasn't right to feel that way, but he would have.

Tarah had done her best to comfort him on the day that the news broke, but Jimmy just wanted to be alone. He didn't want to talk about how it brought back a lot of feelings of misery from his own past. He didn't even want to think about it. He just wanted to go to sleep and not face reality. The next morning he awoke early and silently watched Tarah. Fast asleep, she was curled up next to him with her blonde hair cascading over the pillow, a peaceful expression on her face. He was lucky. Regardless of where this crazy ride in the music business went, at least Jimmy had one stable force in his life. He had someone in his life that made him want to do better. To live better, rather than follow a path of self-destruction. He had already come close to the edge. He didn't want to go back.

Later that day, the phone rang and Jimmy was surprised to hear Patrick's voice. The two hadn't spoken since his childhood friend moved to British Columbia earlier that year. Patrick revealed that he had thought about Jimmy after hearing about Cobain's death.

"When I heard about his yesterday, I was thinking about how you were always such a huge Nirvana fan," Patrick admitted in his usual upbeat voice, much different from the last time the two had spoken. "And I thought, what the fuck, wonder what Jim's doing these days? Thought I should call to make sure you hadn't caught AIDS yet."

"Well thanks for your support, asshole," Jimmy replied with laughter in his voice. He truly missed his friend. "But I'll have you know that I've been tested and I'm negative."

"I would've gone to your funeral," Patrick continued to joke. "You fucking whorebag. It's just a matter of time before you fuck some dirty assed skank and catch *something*."

"Nah, I have a girlfriend now." Jimmy admitted, thinking how weird it felt actually saying those words. *I have a girlfriend now.*

"No *fucking* way!" Patrick sounded astonished. "*You?* Wow, did hell fucking freeze over?"

"Nah, she's cool," Jimmy insisted, glancing toward Tarah in the kitchen. She was talking to Eddie and laughing. "She's the girl who sings for my band."

"Wow man, she's hot!" Patrick congratulated him. "Cool shit! How is your band doing, by the way?"

"Well, actually-" A smile grew on Jimmy's face as he told Patrick about the band being signed. He felt light as he recapped the details. "It's just crazy."

"Hey, I'd say I'm surprised but I'd be lying," Patrick responded. "I always told you that you were fucking talented. Look at all the pretty boy pussies that are out there putting out CDs, who couldn't play guitar to save their lives and then there's you, an ugly fucker that can play like crazy. I guess you kind of balance things out, Jim."

Jimmy cheeks almost hurt from grinning. He missed having Patrick around. "Yeah, well I do what I can to keep things in balance."

"I'm impressed. Not surprised, but impressed," Patrick continued. "I can actually say that one of my friends is a rock star. Maybe I can work for you and fuck all the girls that you can't touch now since you have a *girlfriend* now. Fuck man, does she know about your past? I mean, seriously does she know how many girls you screwed?"

"Nah, I won't tell her." Jimmy quietly confessed with his back to the kitchen. "But I think she's got an idea."

"And she still puts up with you?"

"Yup."

"Marry her," Patrick laughed, "Cause she's a saint."

"Yes, she is."

"I still can't believe you never got AIDS," Patrick ribbed him. "Seriously, I've seen some of the girls you left with back in the day. You must've got something? Herpes? Something?"

"Nope." Jimmy answered truthfully. He had himself tested for everything once again before getting involved with Tarah, just to make sure he had a clear conscience. "Thank the good people at Trojan."

"Yeah, the *good* people at Trojan had me convinced that I was a father for about four years," Patrick replied and continued to be in good humor even though it was a touchy subject. "Thanks for nothing."

Jimmy reluctantly asked if he ever spoke to his ex or Hope since moving. He said no.

"It's just easier to make a clean break," Patrick admitted. "I'm not always sure if I did the right thing. But the real father is in the picture now, so I don't want to confuse the kid anymore than she has to be. But it's not easy."

Jimmy recognized the sadness in his friend's voice.

Patrick went on to say that he had a job in his field and was dating a girl he met at work. There were clearly some reservations on his part about getting too serious too fast, but it was still nice to know that Patrick was doing okay, especially after the hand he had been dealt.

"Well asshole, I have to go and get some sleep. We're not all rock stars that can sleep in every morning," Patrick complained. "Good night."

"Good night," Jimmy repeated, "And Pat?"

"Yeah?"

"Keep in touch, man."

"Will do, Jim. Good luck with the girl and the band thing. You deserve it."

It wasn't his parents wishing him well, but it meant more to Jimmy to hear from an old friend.

Chapter fifty

*L*ife could be overwhelming. Jimmy had learned that the hard way at age ten when he walked into his family home to discover his sister being raped. Nothing in the world would ever make him forget that moment. It was brutal and shocking. It was vile and frightening. It was the worst day of his life. And he often wondered what kind of person he would've been if that day had been removed. Would Jimmy Groome's life have been less of a struggle? Would he be a better person?

The ironic part was that all his misery eventually led to the happiest period of his life. If he hadn't walked in on his sister being raped, Jimmy might never have fallen into a depression. If he hadn't fallen into a depression, he might never have gone to a counselor who encouraged him to get into music. If he hadn't felt so disliked by other kids, he probably wouldn't have spent so much time alone and therefore encouraged to practice guitar. If he hadn't practiced guitar, he wouldn't have been good enough to have people take notice, or for William Stacy to ask him to be in the band. And it was Fire, which paved the road for a career and to Tarah Kiersey.

It was strange to think that such misery would lead up to something so wonderful. For the first time ever, Jimmy didn't feel like he was on the outside looking in. He *was* in.

The band was on the road to success. Jimmy could feel it every time they played. Everything just flowed. It felt so natural and beautiful. It wasn't something he'd ever be able to describe in words. It was the feeling a writer had after creating characters that were so real that they almost jumped off the page. It was the feeling a photographer had when they took a picture that captured a moment in time. It was the feeling a musician had when on stage and the entire room felt connected on an unexplainable level. It felt like love. And maybe that's why Jimmy had always craved being on stage. Maybe he needed admiration. And when he looked around at everyone else in his band, weren't they all broken in some way? Maybe they all needed to fulfill an empty feeling in themselves.

If Jimmy's parents had their way, he'd be in college, learning some profession that required him to sit in an office for the rest of his life and slowly die – or wishing he would die. Too many people lived that existence already. There was this strange belief that there was safety in college and following someone else's dream. Life was too short. Jimmy found it ironic that people such as his parents that went to church every week, made so many attempts to kill his soul. Religion was the hypocrisy of modern society.

Jimmy no longer needed his parent's approval. All he really needed was his music and Tarah. There was no doubt in Jimmy's mind that he was in love with his girlfriend. It was something he never expected to feel about anyone. And yet as often as he thought it when they were together, he couldn't say it. He couldn't tell her. It was too frightening. What if she was still in love with William? What if she didn't feel the same way about him? Things were going too well to screw them up with three simple words. At the same time, he *wanted* her to know. So he attempted to show his feelings both in and out of the bedroom. He was willing to bet that William wouldn't have any problems expressing his emotions, so why was it so difficult for him?

A week after the CD was finished, Jimmy felt exhausted.Deciding that it was the strain of recording along with all the recent changes in his life, he decided to just relax for a day. He lay in bed and watched television while Tarah fluttered around the house doing whatever it was that girls did on a rainy, dreary afternoon. When she finally came upstairs around dinnertime to tell him about a phone call from Maggie, he tried to coax her into bed. He couldn't think of a better way to spend the rest of the evening than to be in bed with Tarah. Just as a smile lit up her face and she appeared to agree, the doorbell rang.

Jimmy grinned and Tarah looked irritated as she ran downstairs. He closed his eyes, but it was Tarah saying the words ' hi mom', that made him suddenly jump out of bed and get dressed. She made her mother sound like a tyrant so he wanted to be downstairs in case Tarah needed him. He knew that their relationship was quite strained, especially since her break-up with William – not that she knew about *their* relationship. It appeared that her mother also wasn't happy that Tarah was living in a house with two guys. Or that she was in a band. In fact, Tarah's mom didn't seem too impressed with *any* aspect of her daughter's life. Jimmy certainly could relate to having a disapproving mother.

After pulling on some clothes, he rushed downstairs and quickly glanced in the living room. Tarah appeared relieved to see him. He said 'hi' to her mom and noted her look of disapproval as she returned the gesture. Jimmy didn't let this bother him though. Instead he went into the kitchen. Noting that Eddie was cooking food, Jimmy loudly joked with him. "Where's my fucking dinner, Eddie?" The band's drummer grinned and glanced toward the living room. Jimmy rolled his eyes and shrugged. It was the first time Tarah's mom had been by the house. Chances were good that it would also be the last.

The sound of footsteps on the stairs indicated that Tarah's mom wanted to check out the rest of the house. Jimmy didn't care. Let her fucking look.

"Her mom seems like a real bitch," Eddie bluntly commented as he carefully turned off the burner where his steak was cooking. "I think she was giving Tarah a hard time."

"Really?" Jimmy wrinkled his forehead. "What do you mean?"

"She was like, ragging her out cause the line was busy earlier when she tried to call Tarah." Eddie shrugged. "Her mom has something important to talk to her about. She is being pushy about seeing the house. It just seemed weird."

Jimmy sighed. "I probably should go up to see what's going on. See if I can prevent a murder scene from taking place in our house." He watched a grin cover Eddie's face before leaving the room and heading back upstairs.

Tarah's mom was talking loudly but he only managed to catch a few words, something about people being dressed in the house. Arriving at the top of the stairs, Jimmy was not happy to find Tarah's mom in his room. As soon as she spotted him, she made up some lame excuse about accidentally going into the wrong room and left. Jimmy wasn't buying it. He glanced at Tarah who looked genuinely nervous. It was clear that her mother didn't have to know about their relationship.

Feeling as though he had to protect his room, Jimmy went back inside and sat on the bed. After making a few attempts to make Tarah laugh while her mother wandered, he grabbed one of his guitars and began to inspect a scratch on it. Suddenly, he could sense that someone was standing in front of the doorway. It was Tarah's mom and she looked very displeased.

"Tarah, are you *sharing* this room with him?" Her mother seemed to be throwing out an accusation rather than a question. Jimmy felt his mouth fall open and his eyes automatically looked toward Tarah, who appeared nervous. That's when shit hit the fan. Suddenly Tarah's mom launched an attack on her daughter. Jimmy was stunned. His own mother's disinterest in her son's life was starting to look pretty good in comparison.

Trying to keep out of it, Jimmy was shocked to hear Tarah's mom harshly attack her daughter. After seeing all Tarah's possessions in 'his' room, she clearly caught on to the fact that Tarah had left William for Jimmy and reprimanded her for doing so. Tarah attempted to explain herself but to no avail.

"You sound just like your father when he left me for another woman." It was clearly a low blow. But it was about to get worse; during their heated argument, her mother revealed some painful news - Tarah's dad had cancer.

Jimmy felt his heart sink. Tarah looked as if someone had slapped her in the face. She began to shake and tears quickly began to run down her face. Her mother continued to attack Tarah for not keeping in close enough contact with her family. "Otherwise, you'd know these things! I'm your mother, and I didn't even know that you were shacked up with this guy!" she snapped.

"His name is Jimmy," Tarah loudly sobbed, and went on to explain how she had been very busy with the CD and everything involved with the contract. Jimmy felt his throat become dry as he watched Tarah continue to cry. Her body was shaking and yet her mother showed her no mercy, no compassion. Jimmy couldn't believe that this woman could be so cold. Tarah was gasping slightly, and he remembered how she spoke of having panic attacks; in fact, she had started to have one on the night she and William broke up.

Jimmy felt anger erupt inside him as he watched and listened. What was wrong with this woman? How could she rip her daughter apart? Even his own mother wouldn't have attacked him like this and yet, he probably deserved it more than Tarah. One of the last times he had seen someone he cared about in this much anguish, was the day his sister was raped. He hadn't been able to protect Jillian from the vicious bully that raped her, but he *was* going to help Tarah. He didn't give a fuck if it was her mother.

Jumping up from his bed, he flew into the hallway. He felt blood rush to his face and a part of him wanted to tell off Tarah's mom, but he wouldn't. That's what she wanted. Instead he gently touched his girlfriend's arm, coldly glared into her mom's eyes, and calmly told her, "Look, you may not like me and that's fine. But you know what? Don't do this. Don't attack her."

Just like any bully that had been stood up to, she shrank back and immediately rushed away. Jimmy put his arm around a sobbing Tarah and led her into their room. After the main entrance door had closed behind her mom, Tarah quietly talked about her father having cancer. Jimmy felt helpless.

Jimmy was stunned by everything that had taken place in the last few minutes. It all happened so quickly and Tarah clearly felt guilty over all her mother's accusations, including the fact that her father was very ill. Jimmy suggested that she could still get in touch with him. He reminded Tarah that her mother was way out of line to talk to her in that manner. It wasn't acceptable.

Jimmy looked into Tarah's face. She was crushed and defeated, slouched over beside him with her head tilted down. With his arm still around her, Jimmy continued to squeeze and caress her arm and kiss the side of her face. But she looked frozen. Nothing was getting through to her. It made Jimmy hate her mother for what she said. It was uncalled for to give such horrible news in what appeared to be a purposely-hurtful manner. He just wanted to make things better. He silently stared at Tarah and decided that one of the things you did when you loved someone was to put their needs ahead of your own. Jimmy needed to hide his feelings and in that moment, Tarah needed to hear them.

Feeling his own heart racing and fear running through his body, Jimmy thought about what he was going to say. He pointed out that loving someone meant that you tried not to hurt them as Tarah's mother had just done to her. He then rambled on about how *he* would never hurt her.

She stared into his eyes and Jimmy could see that Tarah was slowly processing the words, but they weren't necessarily helping her at all. He was scared to say what he knew she had to hear. It was the most frightening thing Jimmy had ever done in his life. As his heart continued to pound furiously he bit his lip then said it. "I love you, Tarah."

Tarah's eyes widened and her lips slowly moved apart. A peaceful smile crept over her face and her eyes lit up. Everything in the room stopped. Even the clock no longer seemed to tick. "I love you, too Jimmy."

And that's when Jimmy Groome knew he had grown up.

Want to read more about Jimmy and Tarah? Check out *Fire* – the sequel of *A Spark before the Fire.* For more information, go to www.mimaonfire.com